SHANGHAI
SPARROW

First published 2014 by Solaris
an imprint of Rebellion Publishing Ltd,
Riverside House, Osney Mead,
Oxford, OX2 0ES, UK

www.solarisbooks.com

ISBN: 978 1 78108 185 3

A CIP catalogue record for this book is available
from the British Library.

Designed & typeset by Rebellion Publishing

Printed in the US

GAIE SEBOLD
SHANGHAI SPARROW

SOLARIS

To all the women whose contributions to the sciences never made it into the books, and to those who will come after them:

"Never doubt that you can change history.
You already have."
Marge Piercy

London

EVELINE DUCHEN SIPPED her tea, ladylike as all get-out, and smiled at the cook.

Ma Pether would've killed her if she knew Evvie was actually in the house. "Scope the place out," she said. "Look over the grounds if you can see 'em, see who's about, how many servants. Check where the back doors and windows are, and whether there's cover. You know what to look for." What she hadn't said was, "Wait till a maid comes to shake the rugs out and go up to her bold as brass pretending to be looking for work, get invited in for a cup of tea and sit gossiping for an hour."

But this way was so much better! Heart fizzing in her chest with excitement and satisfaction, Eveline accepted another slice of cake. "Ooh, this is lovely. I don't s'pose you could give me the recipe, my Ma'd love to make this." Eveline was used, by now, to ignoring the brief stab she felt at the thought of her mother. She told herself she didn't even notice any more.

"You can read?"

"Yes ma'am, my papa taught me. He was a clergyman." He had actually been a schoolmaster, and she barely remembered his face.

The cook nodded solemnly, adjusting the black mourning band on her arm that Evvie had spotted as soon as she came in. "I lost my George just a few months back."

"I'm ever so sorry to hear that."

"Your papa taught you manners too, I see," the cook said. "Most of 'em around here – cheek! And *young men,*" she said, looking meaningfully at the skinny maid, who blushed and hid her face behind the candlesticks she was polishing. "Not like where I'm from. She's a good girl, if she'd only keep her mind on her business."

The maid went even pinker and polished furiously.

"Where's it you're from, ma'am?" Evvie said.

"Dorset."

Eveline nodded, carefully stowing the cook's soft burr in her mind for later reference.

"Lovely down there," the cook said, looking blindly out the soot-grimed window at the passing legs and feet, seeing other sights long gone, "but we had to come to London for the work. Still used to see a lot of the Folk, back home, too... well, them that's left. I don't know, you hear things, but I always liked seeing 'em about, and they never did me no harm."

Eveline kept her face carefully neutral. She had her own opinion about the Folk.

"Ooh, I don't know about that," the maid said. "Bogles and nixies and what-all. And they play dreadful tricks, I heard."

"'On slovens and fools and them that breaks rules,' we used to say," the cook said. "And speaking of rules, if that's your young man coming down the steps, miss, I'll thank you to tell him we don't allow *followers*. At the very door! What the mistress would say..."

Evvie glanced up to see a set of dark blue trousered legs coming down the area steps and, atop them, a brass-buttoned dark blue coat. A policeman, a bloody peeler! If he saw her face... oh, Ma'd have the hide off her. She leaned forward and whispered to the cook, "Can I use your... you know?"

"Out the other door, on the left. Mind the latch, it sticks."

Quick as a ferret, Evvie was out the back door. She turned around and pressed her ear to the kitchen door, heard the cook's gruff tones. *See him off,* Evvie thought; *go on, cook! This is a respectable house!*

But the cook laughed. Obviously the peeler had some charm about him. Now what? Evvie glanced around her: to her left, the privy, and what looked like the door to a coal cellar. Steps down to an overgrown garden – good cover, Ma'd be pleased – but there was a great bank of shrubs and nettles before the wall at the end of the garden. She wore the neat, inconspicuous clothes of a respectable maid-of-all-work, part of Ma's stock (Ma had more costumes than a travelling theatre). They were well enough for moving about without drawing attention, but if she tore them getting over the wall, there'd be hell to pay – and no telling who might be walking past on the other side, ready to raise hue-and-cry after her.

Besides, if she disappeared the minute the peeler turned up, there was every chance it might put the wind up them. She could imagine the conversation now: "Oh, where's that nice lass who was here looking for a job... funny she disappeared just as you arrived," "That's odd, sounds like suspicious behaviour, that does, let's have a description of her..." and then she'd be in enough hot water to drown a coach-and-four.

She slipped into the privy and pulled the door shut – she could blame the sticking latch if they thought she'd been in here too long. Her brain ticking away like clockwork, she bit her lower lip and stared at a spider-web, where a fly buzzed furiously as it tried to escape its fate.

EVVIE PEERED THROUGH the kitchen door; the peeler was a youngish fellow with ginger side-whiskers, his uniform jacket somewhat strained about the middle and his wide leather belt on its last notch. Evvie hovered until he was looking at the giggling maid, and the cook was looking towards the door.

She stepped as though to come in, glanced at the peeler, and threw the cook a wide-eyed gaze like a trapped rabbit. Then she ducked her head, and crept up to the cook, still keeping her eyes on the ground. "Thanks very much for the cake, ma'am. I gotta go, I promised myself I'd try another dozen streets today," she said, in a rapid half-whisper, still shooting glances at the peeler.

"I'm sorry we couldn't get you a place. At least let me put you up some of that cake to take away, we'll never get through it all, not with the family out in the country till next month," the cook said, giving her a curious look.

"Oh, no, really..."

The cook took her wrist in the firm grip of someone who spent hours of her life kneading dough. "It won't take a moment," she said sternly, and led Evvie through into the scullery.

She leaned back against the countertop and folded her arms. "Now, miss," she said. "Perhaps you'll tell me what all that was about?"

"All what, ma'am?" Evvie said, flicking glances towards the door.

"You look like you seen Satan and all his devils in that kitchen. You in trouble?"

"Oh, no, ma'am."

"Because you were looking at that bobby like I don't know what. I've a good mind to go back in there and..."

"It's just I know him," Evvie said. "From a place I used to work. He came round after one of the maids there, and she... well, she ended up turned out." Evvie glanced significantly down at her own flat stomach. "I heard them outside one night, she was crying, begging him to do right by her, and he just called her a bad name, hit her and walked right off. And him a policeman!"

"Oh, ho," the cook said. "Like that, is it?"

"Only I'm afraid he'll recognise me," Eveline said. "He's the sort to make trouble, just to shut me up about what he done."

"Don't you worry about that." The cook swiftly wrapped the remaining cake in a bit of clean muslin and thrust it into Evvie's hand, then pointed. "See that door there? You go through that, and along a bit of hallway with a black-and-white floor, and let yourself out the front. That piece of worthlessness that calls himself a butler won't trouble you, he's fast asleep in his pantry with the paper over his face and some of the master's best beer in his belly, I've no doubt. And I'll deal with young Mister Brass-Buttons, I've seen off tougher than him."

"I hope your girl is all right."

"She's due off for Whitsun, like the rest of us – I'll take her home along of me, keep an eye on her."

"You're ever so kind," Eveline said. She stood on tiptoe and kissed the cook's cheek.

"Get along with you," the cook said, smiling. "Right." She took a deep breath, pumping up her considerable bosom until her starch-stiffened apron creaked, and headed back towards the kitchen.

Eveline slipped out of the house, grinning to herself as she heard raised voices coming from the kitchen behind her. She moved swiftly away, and the voices were soon drowned out by the clatter of hooves and the rumble of wheels, and the *chuff-chuff-chuff* of a steam hansom. Briefly louder than everything else, above it all, a zeppelin throbbed slowly overhead on its way to the Beddington aerodrome, dignified as an elderly duchess looking for her seat at the opera.

Never mind that she'd disobeyed – Ma'd be pleased as punch after this. Eveline could give her the layout, she'd made sure a nosey copper was given short shrift that would have him far less interested in hanging about, *and* she knew when the staff would be away. Always better if the staff were out of the way; Ma wasn't a one for violence, but it didn't mean someone wouldn't do something stupid and maybe get hurt.

Eveline wasn't bothered about respectability – the respectable world had spat her family out and left them to rot, and cutting a coin or two from its coat-tails bothered her not at all. But she didn't like violence, and she wouldn't be party to murder, not if she could help it.

After this, she might get some extra food, or even a word or two of the praise Ma doled out as parsimoniously as she did everything else. But whether she did or not, Evvie knew she'd made a fine job of it. She began to hum the tune to a filthy music-hall song, and dawdled towards home as a smeared red sun struggled to burn its way through the ever-present smog.

Shanghai

"There! Now that beastly horse had better win, that was my best glove." The woman – the wife of one of Shanghai's many prominent businessmen – took her friend's arm. "I do think betting actual money would be far more exciting."

"Oh, no, too vulgar. People might take one for any sort of person," said her friend, adjusting one of the several thick diamond bracelets that adorned her wrists; a present from her husband, and, unknown to her, only slightly more valuable than those he had recently bestowed on his latest mistress, a sixteen-year-old Eurasian girl.

"Who *is* that young man?" the glove-gambler whispered behind her fan, watching a slim, upright figure moving through the racetrack crowd.

"He's attached to the Consulate, I believe. Hopeforth, I think. Something like that."

"He's rather dashing, isn't he?"

"Oh, really, Elizabeth."

"Well, he is."

"Yes, dear, but that doesn't mean one must *notice* him."

The roar as the horses were released for the last race covered the rest of their conversation. Thaddeus Holmforth, whose preternaturally sharp hearing was no great advantage in such circumstances, straightened his already-rigid shoulders. Betting, in public, in a place like this – and they were British! They should know better. One couldn't expect much from the French or the Germans or, certainly, the Americans.

The personal insult was nothing. But they represented the Empire, and should, like Caesar's wife, be above both suspicion and vulgarity.

Holmforth himself did not bet, nor was he greatly interested in horses; he came to the races only in order to maintain an agreeable appearance. The Chinese, of course, bet like maniacs... but then, they were a degenerate race, in Holmforth's view. If only his countrymen – and women – would set a better example!

Of course, these were *riches* of the most *nouveaux*. Shanghai was a regrettable example of what happened when business was allowed to take over and good government was sidelined. He had had hopes, at the beginning of his posting, that he might play some small part in things here... but China would have to be left to other men. He had a greater prize in mind, though China would be instrumental in grasping it.

And his contact would be arriving at his apartment shortly. Holmforth did not bother summoning a rickshaw – he could travel more quickly on his own feet.

He moved swiftly along the Bund, where the great banks and manufactories swelled and gleamed, fat with money from steel and tea, opium and porcelain. Shanghai roared and stank, chattering with a dozen languages and two dozen dialects. He had learned to ignore most of the noise, though he clenched his fists unconsciously as he walked.

His looks were European enough that the locals gave him a respectfully wide berth. A velocipede growled past him, the driver clearing the way with his whip. An addled scarecrow in rags barely escaped its wheels, crawled to the mouth of a nearby alleyway and collapsed. *The poor are always with us, but few of them are much use.* They needed a firm hand, to be of any worth. But here, they scrambled like dogs on a dunghill, working for scraps until they dropped, opium-riddled, to death.

Of course, they might be lucky enough to obtain a position with one of the great houses, helping their masters create the glittering social events with which Shanghai abounded. To some, Holmforth would be invited; a ball, perhaps, but not dinner. A charity concert – his money was, after all, the same colour as everyone else's. Where concerts were concerned, he almost always found a reason to stay away. He hated music. If it was bad it hurt his ears, if it was good... it was unbearable.

Holmforth's rooms were adequate; he did not care much for such things. His houseboy was reasonably efficient and apparently discreet, which was all that mattered. As the boy – a man of fifty with a manner so self-effacing he was nearly invisible – made him tea, Holmforth paced, checking his watch every few moments, and stared out of the window into the pullulating mass below.

He need not have hurried. He should have remembered these damn Orientals had no sense of time.

Eventually, a rickshaw pulled up outside the building, its ragged and skeletal driver slumping in the shafts. A shiver of anticipation rippled through him.

The figure that emerged from the rickshaw was small, wearing an immense coolie hat that gave him something of the appearance of an animated mushroom. He paid off the driver, and a few moments later Holmforth heard the creaking of the stairs.

Holmforth opened the door carefully, cane in his hand. The man who entered bowed, taking no notice of the cane. Beneath the coolie hat he had a calm face with a slight, permanent smile.

"Well?" Holmforth said. He spoke Cantonese well, having a knack for languages. He avoided pidgin, finding it uncomfortably clownish.

The man bowed again, and extracted from his sleeve a roll of rice-paper.

Holmforth took it, pushing the teapot out of the way, checked that the table was dry, and unrolled it.

Mechanisms curled across the page, carefully drawn in deep blue ink. Holmforth read the notations with growing excitement. There was something here, he knew it. He concealed, with ease, the surge of triumph that rose in him; he had learned young not to show his feelings, and if this smiling devil knew Holmforth was pleased, his price would go up.

"Have you seen Wu Jisheng operating the machine? Does he do it himself?"

"Yes, I have seen him getting into it. But it is not complete. If you will forgive..." He bent over the page. "This, here, is done. But these, this – none of this exists. He is trying to obtain the materials he needs. But since the recent troubles, he is having difficulty."

Holmforth tapped the page with one finger. This alone would not be sufficient to convince his masters. He needed to have a working device, not these hints, suggestions. He needed his own operator, too. He already had someone in mind.

And it would have to be done here, in Shanghai. He had neither the resources nor the influence to simply appropriate the device, though once he had proved its worth, that should not prove difficult.

The opium wars had broken open China like a child's piggy bank, but much of the coin had been scooped up by the fat fingers òf merchants, instead of going into the Empire's coffers where it belonged. This... this was a real prize. *If* it could be proved to work. But not yet. Not until Holmforth had all the pieces in place.

He had to ensure that Wu Jisheng did not get any farther, for the moment. And he must not draw the attention of the Imperial court.

"Should it seem that he may start to obtain what he needs," Holmforth said, "I would like things diverted. Delayed. Can you arrange that? Nothing to draw attention – simply ensure that any supplies he orders for the work are diverted. *That* should not create difficulties." He was well aware of the healthy trade in 'lost' goods that somehow ended up in the households of local mandarins.

The man bowed, and waited.

Holmforth gave him silver, a substantial portion. Not Her Majesty's money, but his own. "Twice as much again, if I am pleased with the results. Return in ten days." That should be time enough.

With one final bow, the man was gone.

Holmforth seldom smiled, but he did so now. He stared out of the window, no longer seeing the surging crowd. First, he would book passage home. He would take a zeppelin, though it probably meant a refuelling stopover in Africa, which he loathed; but hang the expense. There was no time to waste. His fingers prickled with impatience.

Before his posting to the Shanghai Consulate, Holmforth had spent the last few years toiling in a Government post whose major purpose, he realised after the first month, was largely obstruction. Yet it was that post which had brought James Lathrop before him, and without Lathrop, the potential of Wu Jisheng's creation would have passed him by.

Working in a tiny draughty office in an obscure corner of Whitehall, Holmforth had become accustomed to the parade of the deluded, the desperate, and the merely fraudulent who were shunted off onto him – the ones, at least, who, like Holmforth himself, had *connections*, and could not be completely ignored for fear they might prove an embarrassment.

Thaddeus Holmforth treated every single one of them with a precise and unwavering seriousness. He took notes. He recorded their ramblings, pleadings and blatant deceptions. Because it was his job, and if he did it well enough, his worth – one day, despite everything – would be recognised.

Paunchy, sweating, and overdressed, Lathrop had seated himself, without being invited, in the creaking chair in Holmforth's office; wiped his face with an embroidered linen handkerchief, and looked him over. "Oh, there must be some mistake. I was told I would be speaking to the person in charge of scientific advances."

"Well, there is no-one with precisely that title," Holmforth said. "I am, as it were, the first port of call."

"Really? Well I must say... this is important stuff, you know. And I have responsibilities, serious responsibilities, at home, I can't be dashing up to town every five minutes just to speak to someone who isn't in a position to –"

"I assure you that I am the person you need to speak to, Mr Lathrop. My function is to assess the information and pass it on to the proper person."

"Well, if you're sure."

"Unless, of course, you feel you would rather seek private interest?"

"Oh, well..." Lathrop slumped back in his chair, his lower lip protruding. "I suppose it will do."

At that point it became obvious to Holmforth that Lathrop had already attempted to raise private funding for his venture, whatever it was, and had failed.

"Now, if you would be so kind as to explain?" Holmforth said.

"Etheric Science," Lathrop said. "The use of sound to, among other things, affect mood and behaviour. My... I have designed a number of instruments, which used correctly have an astonishing ability to tranquilise and pacify." He began to lay out charts and schematics on the desk, all written in a surprisingly neat, small hand.

Holmforth, against his will, found himself intrigued. Lathrop did not exactly sell it well: he frequently backtracked, muddled his references and at times barely seemed to understand his own discoveries. But there was a persuasive elegance in what he described that was far more appealing than the man himself.

To tranquilise and pacify. If it worked, it was something Holmforth had every reason to believe might hold interest for his superiors.

"And what is this notation here?" he said.

"Oh, that was something to do with... I mean, I made some experimentation with the Folk." Lathrop gave him a sidelong glance. "They seemed intrigued by the sounds. But I found no profit in taking it further. Should it be of interest, of course, given sufficient investment, I could make further experiments."

"I see. Well, thank you for bringing this to me," Holmforth said. "I feel this might well be of interest. I shall contact you as soon as I have a response."

It took, as expected, another hour to persuade the man out of his office, after which Holmforth wrestled open every window in order to rid the place of the pervasive reek of sweat, over-scented pomade, and self-importance.

Then he took the matter to the head of his department, Rupert Forbes-Cresswell.

"Etheric science?" Forbes-Cresswell said. Sun poured through the high window of his much larger office, haloing his thick blond hair. "My dear fellow, it's nothing but one of those fads, like the health-giving properties of electricity."

"I thought there were some interesting points in his work. He appeared to have some evidence for its effectiveness."

"Oh, it's obvious people are affected by sounds. Especially weaker minds: women, children, the lower orders. One only has to attend the music hall to see it in action."

"I haven't done so."

"It provides an interesting evening's study of the vulgar, though I did end up having to throw away a perfectly good coat afterwards. If you want to know more, there's always old Frobisher. He became interested, briefly. But I can tell you what he'll say; he gave me quite the treatise on the subject. Sound manipulation of this sort is an ability, not a science. It tends to manifest in certain people, usually women – rather the way some simpletons can calm horses. Possibly because their voices are different, you know. Frobisher thought it might be why lullabies are effective! It could be this Lathrop is some sort of hermaphrodite, and that is why he has the ability? Or he could be simply deluded. Oh, the Higher Folk, of course, have some ability to use sound to manipulate the senses, singing, and so on..." He let the sentence hang, but Holmforth said nothing. "There may be a connection there. Do you have any reason to believe Lathrop may be, ah..."

"I don't believe so," Holmforth said. "He had apparently made some experiments and found they were intrigued by the sounds, but didn't see worth in taking it further."

"I'm afraid I don't either," Forbes-Cresswell said. "He may have stumbled upon something that imitates a natural effect by accident, but all these instruments..." He swept a hand over the paper Holmforth had put on his desk. "Rubbish, really, I'm afraid. An attempt to gild a not very impressive lily."

"Well, in that case, I'm sorry to have taken up your time."

"Not at all, not at all. Do give my regards to your father, next time you rusticate."

Holmforth bowed himself out of the office, his face utterly calm. He had a great deal of practice in hiding his humiliation. And until he had been posted to Shanghai, and first encountered a rumour about what Wu Jisheng was up to, in among all the other fragments, half-truths, blatant lies and wild exaggerations, he thought he had forgotten the incident.

But now, he had the evidence in his hands. Etheric science existed, and could be used in ways that no-one had imagined. There had been that single notation in the margins of Lathrop's work, of course – but the man had had no idea what he had found.

And Wu Jisheng's ability seemed to militate against the idea that it was a female trait. Perhaps it had to do with his being Oriental.

In any case there was little doubt, in what few works he had managed to find that actually took Etherics seriously, that innate ability was a factor. Lathrop would have to be brought here. His vanity would no doubt be flattered.

Holmforth would show his superiors what Etheric mechanisms could do, in the right hands. *His* hands. And they would see that he had been right, that the borders of the British Empire should not stop with India, or Russia. The borders of Empire should extend beyond this world, to encompass and bring under its wing not just the primitive and barbaric peoples of the Earth, but the Folk as well. Others might believe they were no longer relevant, the last fragment of a dying race, but Holmforth knew better. They had wealth that could be put to good use. Besides, their arrogance was an insult to the Empire, and their immorality a bad example. It was beyond time they were brought to heel.

The Crepuscular

"O MOST EXALTED, Highly Honoured, and Elegant Mistress; I humble myself at your feet, which allows me to appreciate your exquisite slippers. As always, you outdo all others in taste."

The fox, his tail quivering and his eyes brilliant, tilted his head at an angle precisely calculated to charm.

The lady at whose feet he sat smiled. Her slippers were indeed exquisite, embroidered all over with mermaid scales whose constantly shifting sea-shades echoed those of her eyes. The eyes themselves, at this moment, danced merrily, sunlight upon gentle waves. She was fond, in her way, of the fox, and found him a source of amusement.

"Well, little fox, what do you want?"

"Lady, I bring news."

"I know you would not be so foolish as to come here without *something* to entertain me. What news?"

"Pearl divers off an island under the sway of Oro have found a great treasure. A pearl of exceptional beauty and size, dark as my lady's hair, and nearly as lustrous. Already it is on its way to the temple, where it will be placed in a statue of laughable ugliness but great value in the eyes of the priests. And it will become an offering, and a Gift."

"I see. And why should this concern me?"

"Because it is a Gift of some... merit, Lady. In my unworthy and no doubt mistaken opinion."

"Some merit. How *much* merit?"

"A thousand hours of work by three separate craftsmen, one of whom lost his sight on the endeavour, the eldest of them dying as he set his chisel, having prayed and fasted overmuch in order that he might be inspired, and the youngest, possibly the best craftsman the island has ever produced, having cut his thumb, an injury that will eventually cripple him and prevent his ever creating so fine a piece again."

"Ah." In her eyes, a thin cloud veiled the sun, the sparkle faded from the sea.

"Forgive my presumption, but I thought your Ladyship would wish to know."

"You are correct, little fox. And what, in your *opinion*, do you deserve in return for this information?"

"What could I ask more than your Ladyship's pleasure?"

"Oh, you could ask many things. Some of them I might even grant."

"Your Ladyship's generosity is outweighed only by your Ladyship's beauty. I ask merely the freedom to suggest something that might, if your Ladyship should deign to consider it, outweigh this Gift in value."

"And what has my clever fox found, to overbear so weighty a Gift?"

"A pebble."

The fox kept his eyes on her slippers, but from their darkening colours he could see that in her eyes, now, there would be the suggestion of reefs, of depths where no diver would ever find the wreckage. He was something of a gambler by nature, and rather enjoyed the shiver of risk.

"A pebble."

"Yes, your Ladyship."

"Explain."

"A child has spent hundreds of hours searching for this pebble. She has collected and discarded stone after stone, to find the perfect one. She knows it must be perfect. She has built a cairn upon the grave of her little cat; this stone is to mark the apex. She has ignored calls to supper, she has searched in the rain and as darkness fell, and despite scoldings and beatings. Only if she found the perfect stone could she finish the shrine, and release her grief." He paused, and added, "She is seven years old."

"Hmm." The scales on her slippers became still, the colours those of a lake beneath an empty sky. He kept his eyes lowered.

"Seven," she said.

"Yes."

"A significant number, even to them."

"So I believe," the fox said, and silently cursed himself. A misstep.

"You do not believe; *you* know." But her tone was musing, not yet dismissive.

"Yes, lady."

"At such an age, constancy of that nature is a rarity among them."

"Indeed."

"A pity to waste it upon a cat." She disliked cats; those with the knack passed between the mortal and magical worlds without shame, they refused to grovel, and they could go where she could not.

"Alas." The fox himself admired cats; they tended to be, like himself, survivors.

"Now, little fox." She bent down and put one long, pale finger beneath his chin, tilting his head up so that he must look into her eyes. "You know that if you were wrong, on a matter of such delicacy, I would be... displeased?"

Enough to skin me alive and hang me writhing by my own pelt from the arm of your throne, to provide amusement to your guests for a hundred mortal years? He let a little of his genuine terror show, but only a little. Though, of course, she would use fear, she did not bask in it. She far preferred adoration. He narrowed his eyes as she scratched his chin, and let a small moan of pleasure escape his throat.

"Good. Then fetch it for me." She sat up. "And when I have it, you may receive a gift of your own."

"Ma'am."

The fox bowed and danced his way out of the Presence, careful to display nothing but delight. Smugness was something the Court preferred to keep entirely to themselves.

The child would know something had changed, of course, when she next visited her little shrine. The heart, the soul, the intention would be gone. What was left would be just a stone. She would probably believe the change was in her, the first dulling of the gemlike passions of childhood.

With the cat, who might choose to be irritated, he would have to make other accommodation. Find something it wanted, or could be persuaded it wanted, and obtain it – or provide a means of getting it. That was what the fox did, and he was exceptionally good at it.

Shanghai

HOLMFORTH RETURNED FROM booking his flight at the aerodrome to find a letter lying on the table. His houseboy was packing, flipping crisply folded shirts into a clean but battered leather case reinforced with polished wooden struts.

Holmforth opened the letter.

> *Dear Sir,*
> *Further to your enquiry of the 18th December, we regret to inform you...*

As he read on, his fingers tensed on the discarded envelope, crushing it.

No.

"Massa wanchee tea?" the houseboy said.

"No. Leave that. Get out. *Out*, I said!"

The man bowed, and scurried away.

Holmforth flung the crumpled envelope into a corner, and scanned the letter again with eyes that felt hot and dry.

Lathrop was dead. Dead! And just as he might have been useful!

He would not be thwarted. But who else could he find to operate the thing? Wu Jisheng was no possibility – he was fanatically loyal to his hopeless, crumbling mess of an Empire. That, presumably, was why he had risked the wrath of the influential Iron Hats, with their loathing of Occidental technology and innovation and everything else. Holmforth could have brought them down on Wu Jisheng's head easily enough, but that would have risked the device being destroyed, and he could not have that.

Lathrop must have had other family, close relatives... *someone* must have the ability, and he *would* find them.

He would have to be careful. There could be no missteps. He would keep his thoughts and the possibilities to himself for now, and use his own resources, rather than those of the Department. He had the Empire's best interests at heart, after all. Why should he risk someone else taking the credit? It had happened more than once, in the course of his career. He was determined it should not happen again.

London

BIRDS WERE SINGING and the deep red wallflowers in the little private park smelled like warm cake. Eveline hung over the railing for a moment, sniffing, and caught something out of the corner of her eye.

It was him. The cove in the grey coat. She was sure of it. Carefully, keeping her head still as though admiring a flowering tree just ahead of her, she peered from the corner of her eye until her sockets ached.

There he was. Watching her. He hadn't been around while she was scoping the house, she was sure of it... but he was there now.

If she hadn't seen him before, she wouldn't have made much of it. But she had, a day or so back. A good-looking cove with neat small features and unusual, pale gold skin; a few shades paler than the Indian man with the splendid embroidered coats, who sometimes came to see Ma and always smelled so deliciously of spices Evvie was near tempted to take a bite out of him. There was something faintly reminiscent about his colouring, too, but she couldn't put her finger on it.

It was definitely him, the same man she'd seen last time she was down on the docks. She called up every swear-word she knew – an impressive number – under her breath.

A peeler? If he was, why hadn't he arrested her already? Though what for, she didn't know, she hadn't so much as dipped a pocket all morning. Maybe he was one of those detective sorts, like that Whicher, that everyone spoke of under their breath as though they were wizards or ghosts, hovering there waiting for her to make a step wrong?

Could he be someone Ma Pether had sent, to keep an eye on her, see she was doing as she was told? In that case she'd be in for it, if he'd seen her come out of the house. Did Ma still trust her that little? She felt a jab of irritation. All right, so she'd gone against Ma's instructions, but she'd got to know far more than she would have otherwise! She even knew which cupboard the silver was kept in and where the key was, which would save a deal of time and noise!

Well, either way there was one thing for it, she'd have to give him the slip, and she could decide what to do once she was back at Ma's.

HOLMFORTH WATCHED THE girl. Nothing but a skinny urchin. A shuffle to her step and a lack of proportion between feet and legs suggested her shoes were too big. The only thing about her that was even slightly remarkable was the unmistakable sharpness with which she scanned her surroundings, wary as a bird in a garden full of cats. A plain, nervy little Cockney sparrow.

He felt a moment's black, swamping doubt. What if he was wrong? What if the talent had died with Lathrop? None of his enquiries about the younger sister had been in the least successful; it had to be presumed that she, too, was dead.

As her glance moved his way, Holmforth withdrew behind the wall. He was sure, now, that it was her: he had obtained an old portrait from Lathrop's former household, and the girl was growing into a likeness of the mother. Finding her had taken months; months in which he had spent an inordinate amount of silver, both in London and in Shanghai, trying to move things forward in the one and hold them back in the other.

He had visited Lathrop's home, and there he had had his first stroke of luck. The former servants were still in place, awaiting the confirmation of a male heir. The housekeeper had remained chilly and disinclined to be charmed, but one of the maids, sufficiently bribed, had managed to procure him a picture of the family: the mother, father, daughter and a wrapped bundle of lace that was presumably the younger child. It was faded, but the features were sufficiently clear. They had run away, and London was the nearest place they might have reached, other than small villages in which they would immediately have been spotted.

Acquiring the machines had been comparatively simple. The things were not regarded as of particular value. Money in the right hands, a suggestion that Her Majesty's Government would be grateful for cooperation in the matter, and the mechanisms were his. The rest of the estate would no doubt be tied up in probate for months or years while the search for a relative – any relative – went on.

Then it had been a matter of time, money and persistence. He had a sufficiency of the first two, and an exceptional amount of the last. Honour among thieves there might be, but Holmforth found that the right combination of money and threat could make it evaporate like morning dew.

The girl's background had been respectable. If she had not fallen too far into degeneracy, she might still be useful to the Empire. But if she had no Etheric talent, she would be of no use to *him*. His hands clenched.

EVVIE DAWDLED AWAY from the park, walking as though she'd not a care in the world, until a steam hansom came chuffing and rumbling along behind her. A quick glance told her it had cut her off from the sight of Grey-Coat – she grabbed the wheel-arch and lifted her feet, holding on grimly. Her hands were the strongest part of her. Luckily for her, the driver was sloppy with keeping his vehicle up – the arch had been a while between polishings, and the grime helped her grip. The driver, humming to himself, didn't notice her; and the cab was empty of any passengers who might have raised a fuss. She briefly considered trying to slide inside, but though the driver might not notice her clinging like a monkey to the outside of his cab, he'd be pretty sure to notice the door opening. Instead she waited until they passed an alleyway and dropped to the ground, landing at a run, ducking into the smelly, narrow space and pelting like a hare for the other end. She made swift, not entirely random jigs and turns, nipped into a pub and out the back, through another four or five turns, keeping up the pace until she felt safe enough to glance behind her.

No sign of Grey-Coat. She wiped her hands on the rag she'd lifted from the pub kitchen, smoothed her hair, raised her chin, and sashayed, grinning, along the back alleys towards Limehouse, Ma Pether's, and home.

* * *

"*Nihao*, Evvie!" A young man in the green and gold uniform of the Brighart Steam Transport Company waved at Eveline as he balanced easily on top of a pile of crates. "How are you today?" Behind him one of the ships gave a great blaring whoop and a blurt of steam. Chains and crates clashed and creaked and groaned.

"*Nihao*, Liu!" Eveline dropped a brief curtsey. Liu had been hanging around for the last month, as his ship underwent apparently endless repairs. The first time he had called out to her, she had ignored him. The third, she had sighed and made a rude gesture. The fifth time he had not called out at all, but had dropped a little parcel in front of her, of bamboo wrapped in a green silk ribbon. She had picked it up suspiciously. It turned out to contain a small figurine of a grinning fox carved in pale green stone, nestled in silk padding.

She had turned around and glared at him. "I'm not in that game," she said. "So you can take this back." She thrust the figurine at him, not without regret. It was a very pretty thing. Automatically, she wondered what its value was; she had seen something like it in a fancy shop off Regent Street, but didn't know if it was of the same stuff.

He had looked so miserable, she almost laughed. "What, you can't get it somewhere else?"

He bowed. "I am not seeking anything but the pleasure of your company." She looked him over, properly this time. She had dismissed him before as just another of the Chinee sailors, with their chattering singsong voices and funny eyes. Now she saw him properly, he was slender and neat, in his smart uniform, a matching green and gold cap perched on sleek black hair tied in a pigtail. His eyes were strange, but it was only a matter of the way they were set in the skin – for that, he looked pretty much like anyone, and a deal more like her than half the Folk did, especially the lesser Folk, like the bogles.

"Why?" she said. "And how come you speak so fancy?"

"You wanchee pidgin talk my?" he said.

"I dunno what you just said, but if it was something rude..."

"It was not. I would like to know you because you are very clever, and I speak good English because *I* am very clever." He bowed again, grinning at her.

"How do you know I'm clever?"

He leaned towards her, put a finger on his lips, and then held up, before her eyes, a linen handkerchief embroidered with the initials *JK* in pink silk. "*Very* clever," he said.

Evvie's heart speeded up. She'd lifted that handkerchief just this morning, and had never felt it being lifted off *her*. "You... cheeky *sod*."

"I think *that* was rude, yes?"

"Bloody right. What're you doing with my billy?" She should be furious, but somehow the way he was looking at her, with his head a little to one side, like a dog that had just fetched a stick, kept bringing a smile to her lips.

"*Your*... billy?" He gave it to her, with a flourish, like a fine gentleman bowing to a fine lady.

She snatched it from his fingers, and made it disappear before he had straightened up. "What billy?" she said.

He laughed.

Since then, an odd, intriguing, half-wary friendship had developed. Evvie didn't let herself get too fond of him – after all, his ship would eventually be mended, loaded, and back on its way.

People disappeared out of your life easy as handkerchiefs. It happened all the time.

Liu dropped lithely to the ground in front of her, and scrutinised her face. "What have you been doing, Evvie? I can see mischievous spirits in your eyes." He grinned.

"Get away with you; you can't." She grinned back.

She hadn't told Ma Pether about Liu, though if she didn't know already she'd probably find out soon enough. She might even be pleased, though not about Evvie speaking with a young man – outside picking their pockets or otherwise making off with their goods, she didn't encourage her girls to have any dealings with men. But Ma would be pleased about the words he was teaching her, because Ma believed in knowledge. She believed in it like some believed in the Life Everlasting. "The more you know, my birdlets, the stronger you are. Be you little as a kitten, if you've got a brain and the means to fill it, you can outwit the Queen and all her ministers."

But Liu was a friend, not business. She'd keep him secret from Ma as long as she could. "I gotta go."

"Meet me later and I will teach you how to ask for a cup of tea."

"It's late. Tomorrow, if I can get away. By the pie shop on Matlock Street, about three."

He sighed. "Their pies are made of bits the pigs did not want even when they were alive. I will not eat one."

"No one asked you to," she sang over her shoulder as she hurried away. "I'll have two of 'em."

Where she'd been earlier, the city's ever-present stinks – of sewage and soot, hot metal and humanity – had been overlaid with expensive perfumes, laundered linen, and well-tended gardens. Limehouse, on the other hand, *reeked*. The presence of human wastes was not a hint, but a bold declaration in letters fifty feet high. Other smells – filthy bodies, rotting food, damp, vermin, sickness – could hardly compete, though they tried. The only occasional relief, a banner of clean air, came when the wind blew up from the harbour. Even that was as likely to smell of fish as of the open ocean. Eveline noticed the stench, because she was a noticing girl, but it hardly bothered her. She had spent her last seven years here. It was home.

Only when she passed the transport moored near the bridge did she put her handkerchief in front of her face, and hurry past. The ship, restrained by a great black dripping chain, loomed above her like some terrible ancient half-dead thing, dragged up from the depths, its sails hanging like dying seaweed rotting on the rocks. A miserable ragged line of convicts shuffled up the gangplank, their chains clinking. As the wind shifted, she could hear the roaring and moaning of those already below decks and, clear as gunshot, the cracking of whips.

The streets churned with people. Some were decently covered, others ragged to near nakedness; almost all were dirty, thin, and tired. Sailors, dockworkers, men and women and children from the mills and the tanneries.

Docky Sal was sitting on the steps of the Duke of Windsor, taking advantage of the last of the sunlight. Sal smiled at Evvie, shifting her latest baby from one breast to the other. She had a dramatic bruise around one eye and bundle of crumpled linen draped over her lap.

"Awrite, Sparrow?"

"What's that, Sal?"

"Fancy shirt. See?" Sal held it up. A needle marked the end of a row of fine, tiny stitches. "Lucky we got the sun today. I'll get it done by tomorrow, then that's me off me back for a few days. *If* that cheapskate in the shop pays me what I'm owed."

Eveline leaned down and stroked the baby's fluff of bright red hair. "Look at him, proper little copper-top."

"Ah. Reckon it was that Irish stoker fella. Lovely head of hair he had. Ha'n't seen him for a long time. Shame, really, he was all right. Not like the last one." She made a face.

"He give you the shiner?"

"Some of 'em are more for hitting than wapping, love. You're better off with Ma."

"Don't I know it. Here." She tossed a guinea in Sal's lap. "Buy him something, eh?"

"Oh, Evvie."

"Shut it. Just don't tell Ma, all right? You know what she's like." She'd want to know where Evvie'd got the guinea for starters, and why she'd given it to Docky Sal instead of Ma herself for seconds. "You take care, Sal."

"You too."

Evvie continued through the weary wandering crowd. Those who had no room for the night were already starting the evening's desperate search for somewhere to sleep for a few hours. The soot-blackened scraggle of buildings often held three or four families to a room, and even when there was space to spare, it cost. If you had no money, you'd like as not end up sleeping on the docks or under a bridge, until the peelers came and moved you on. She'd spent plenty of nights that way herself, before Ma took her in. There were already dozens of children settling on the roofs or jamming themselves into tiny crannies. She'd done that, too – if you found a place too small for an adult you were less likely to get hauled out of it by someone bigger and stronger.

They called it a *rookery*, but the people, especially the children, always reminded Eveline more of sparrows. Small and scruffy and dirt-brown and noisy, ignored by almost everyone. Like her.

She jumped over the swollen, gut-burst corpse of a dog, raising a roar of flies. Clean, small, and respectably dressed, she could have been a less colourful version of Little-Red-Riding-Hood, striding innocently through the forest.

And here came a would-be-wolf, perhaps fourteen or fifteen, nearly as small as Eveline herself, and skinnier, his thin legs so bandy he looked as though he had an invisible gas-balloon between his knees.

When he reached for her pocket Eveline spun around, grabbed both his arms and held his hands up. "That," she said, "that was a right munge. What were you trying to do, pat me on the arse? Saw you coming halfway down the street." The nice young country girl the cook had fed with cake was gone like the hallucination she was; now Eveline was a city rat, all lash and grimy bite.

The boy swore and tried to kick her shins.

"Need some help, love?"

Eveline glanced at the grinning, broad-shouldered man standing behind the boy, an ancient stained bowler tilted over one eye.

Her captive hunched and tried to twist out of her grip. "*He* needs help more'n I do," she said. "Bugger off, then. Juggins." She let go. The boy gave her a final look of fierce dislike, spat at her feet and darted off into the crowd.

"Not a local, is he?" said the smiling man. "Or he'd know better." He eyed her maid's getup. "You going into service, turning respectable? That'd be a waste, that would."

"No," she said. "I gotta go, Bartie, Ma's waiting."

"Tell her I said hello." He waved jauntily and set his hat to an even more aggressive tilt before striding off. Eveline watched him go with slightly narrowed eyes. Bartholomew Simms thought well of himself, but she didn't like him. He gave her the cold grue. He ran a string of girls, and she heard things. Well, he wasn't getting *her* into that line of work. Like Sal said, she was better off with Ma.

"WELL, HOW WAS it?" Ma Pether was seated at the vast littered table, a chewed and weary cheroot in the corner of her mouth, poking a screwdriver at something that looked like a dismantled pistol with a bulbous barrel and a fancy chased-silver stock. Evvie moved around to one side of the table, so the barrel wasn't pointing at her. She knew Ma and her mechanisms.

There was a *pop* and a spurt of vapour; something pinged off into a corner of the room, and Ma swore.

"Did I hear you cheeking Bartholomew, Sparrow-Girl?"

"No, Ma."

Ma raised her head. She had a jeweller's glass screwed into one eye; the other was grey, sharp, ready to be amused or to glower. Her strong coppery-blonde hair was streaked with white, pulled back in a rough bun under a net. She wore a coarse cotton shirt, a hide weskit and battered canvas trousers.

"Better not. I know you ain't never going to be best of

friends, and let's be honest, he ain't none of mine either, but he's too useful to go making an enemy of. Enemies are bad seeds you sowed yerself, remember."

"Yes, Ma."

"So, the house. Anyone scope you?" Eveline had given her answer some thought on her way home. She'd been pleased with how her morning's business had gone, but the more she'd thought about it, the more Grey-Coat had wormed his way into her head.

If he was a copper and she didn't tell Ma about him and there were consequences, she'd be up to her neck in shit. And if Ma had sent him herself, the fact that Evvie had spotted him would show Ma how good Evvie was.

"The house went well," she said. "I know where everything is, and it'll be empty on Whitsun. But there was someone hanging about. Not while I was checking the place, but after, a good street away. Smelled like a bluebottle, though he wasn't in uniform. Darkish, not so tall, in a grey coat. Neat-looking." She eyed Ma for some sign of recognition, but Ma's frown looked genuine. "Seemed like he was watching me. Well, he wasn't actually watching me, I just got that feeling that he'd been looking, and looked away, just as I caught him. I'd not have made anything of it, only I think I seen him before. Anyway, I lost him."

"I hope you weren't staring, Evvie. You *know* what I taught you."

"'Staring's foolish, staring stinks, staring gets you thrown in clink.' Yes, Ma, I *remember*."

"You'd better. You seen him before. When and where?"

"Down the docks, about three days back. I dunno what made me take notice, only he didn't seem quite *right*. Then seeing him again – it seemed odd."

Ma blinked the glass out of her eye and dropped it among the other debris. "Sounds like a copper, all right. That's it, then, that house is blown. I'm not risking it. Hell and the devil, what a waste. I thought that might be the one. You never know what you're going to find in a place like that. Enough to retire on, maybe." She looked Evvie over and sniffed, shaking her head. "Dunno how he spotted you. You look all soap and Sunday in that getup. And with your talents – you do something stupid?"

"Not as I can think, Ma." She picked up the pistol. "Where'd this come from?"

"Never you mind, and put it down." Ma eyed her, and Eveline, feeling it, looked up enquiringly. "You sure you didn't make a botch of it?" Ma said, taking out her cheroot and pointing it at Eveline. "I worry about you, Evvie Duchen. You're getting too full of yourself. And that's…"

"'The fastest way to a fall.' Yes, Ma. I know."

"Don't you roll your eyes at me, missy. You get caught, I can't help you. You want to get transported, die of the flux halfway to hellangone and be thrown over the side for fishes' dinners, hmm?"

"No, Ma." Eveline said, her voice small. The thought of transportation was one of the few things that really frightened her, and Ma knew it.

"Well, then. You're to stay indoors for a week. You can do some mending and such, and make yourself useful. And see if you can get some letters into Saffie's head. Now get out of the maid's rig, 'fore it gets all over muck. And brush that mud off and put it on Lazy Lou."

"Yes, Ma."

"I'll check."

"Yes, Ma."

"Then come down and tell me the rest."

Evvie slouched upstairs, scowling. What was the point in talking about the house she'd been checking over, since now they'd not be robbing the place? But Ma always wanted to know everything. Or maybe it was Grey-Coat she wanted to know about, but there was so little to tell.

"I dunno, Lou, what's she want?" Evvie said, getting out of her dress and apron and fitting it over Lazy Lou, the brass and copper mannequin who stood in Ma's room, staring blind-eyed out of the filthy, rag-curtained window. Lou chimed faintly, as she always did when dressed or undressed. She was a clever creation. She had jointed limbs that all folded inside each other so you could pack her into a box no bigger than a travelling-bag, and was supposed to be able to move about, but as long as Evvie had been working for Ma, Lou had been no more than a clotheshorse. Ma was forever picking up mechanical bits and pieces and fadgetting with them, trying to make them work, then she'd get bored before they complied. The cellar was piled with the things.

Eveline's mother had liked mechanisms too. But hers were stranger. They had sung and whispered and shivered the air, and she had never seen anything like them anywhere else.

She shook off the memory. Mama was gone, like Papa, like Charlotte. The cossetted happy little girl she'd been was gone too. Eveline looked back on her former self with something like exasperation. She wouldn't have lasted a minute on the streets – the only thing Uncle James and Aiden between them had done for her was start the process of turning that trusting, stupid child into someone who could duck and thieve and manipulate... and survive. Sparrow-Girl, that was what Ma called her – and that was what sparrows did, survive around the edges of things.

Eveline brushed the mud off the skirt, doing a thorough job despite her sulk. After all, she might be the next one to wear it – although not for at least a week. Mending! She scowled. She could stitch all right, but sewing bored her silly. Vengefully, she spent a few moments poking about Ma's room, careful to put everything back where she found it. The fascinating clutter was a right old jumble, but Ma could spot anything missing in the blink of an eye.

Pictures of men and women and children, horses and houses and trains; some in fancy frames, others jammed into the surround of the big dusty mirror. Most of the people in them were strangers, the pictures acquired in a variety of robberies: sometimes Ma just took a fancy to them. Only one, of a boy of about ten, stood by itself atop the dressing table, in a heavy elaborate frame with a miserable-looking angel draped over the top. Unlike everything else in the room, it was dusted and cared for. That was Paulie, Ma's son, who had died in one of the fevers that swept through every few months on hot dusty wings, leaving corpses in their wake. The boy's face stared solemnly out, pale and dark-eyed, a sailor hat perched on his head. Eveline stuck her tongue out at him. He might look like a little angel in the photograph, but she remembered him as a proper little imp, forever pinching and whining and telling tales.

There were heaps of costume jewellery and a tottering pile of fancy hats. A few books, with gilded pages and bright illustrations. Ma couldn't read, but she liked books, especially picture books. Eveline had had some schooling, back before everything went to the bad – though if Ma thought she'd be able to teach Saffie to read, she was dreaming. Saffie was a sweet little thing, but had no more brains than a poodle.

Eveline picked up a necklace of amber beads and tried them on, posing in front of the mirror, grabbing a vast gilded fan with two broken sticks. "My dear sir, I can't possibly allow you the next dance, my card is quite full," she said, fluttering the fan below her eyes.

Not much of the day's brightness got into this room. The dust on the mirror made a ghost of her; nothing but a pale smudge of face between a grubby shift and black hair, which wouldn't curl despite Ma's occasional efforts with the tongs. "Hair like a heathen Chinee," Ma always said. Eveline smiled, thinking of Liu, then saw a figure in the doorway reflected in the glass. "Ginny."

"Ooh, look at Miss Fancy-Drawers." Ginny grinned, showing several missing teeth. She had been a factory child, thrown out when a machine chewed her arm up. Ma had spotted her neatly dipping pockets with the arm that still worked, down in Whitechapel, and brought her home – much as she'd done with Eveline. Ginny's wasted arm might not be much use as a limb, but as a distraction and a source of pity it made them some money.

There were fifteen of them at the moment, ranging from Saffie, who was six, to Margot, who was seventeen. There were no boys. Ma didn't want any of her girls pregnant or poxed, and discouraged mucking about with a heavy hand. She could spot a swelling belly in a blink. She'd get you dosed up, and if it didn't work, out you went, to fend for yourself and the result of your folly. That troubled Eveline not at all; if she sometimes felt a pang at the sight of a young couple walking hand in hand, she only had to look at Docky Sal.

There'd been a boy, a long time ago. They'd been too young for sweethearts, but he'd been something more than a friend – or so she'd thought. He'd not stood by her, though, when she needed him, and she'd never seen him since.

MA PETHER AND her girls all lived crammed in the narrow old crumbling house, and made their way by whatever form of trickery, stealing, and general illegality came to hand. They did well enough; everyone ate at least once a day, there was a roof to sleep under, and if you'd no shoes you could borrow some. All the girls knew what it was like to have none of those things and, sleeping out, to be fending off men who'd offer a few pence for a grind – and like as not wouldn't pay, or would just take what they wanted whether you would or no. Eveline had learned early that you couldn't always trust a smile or an offer of food. She got good at running, and if she couldn't run, she would fight with whatever she could and then run. She hadn't always got away.

Eveline sneezed, glared at the fan, and put it back. More reluctantly, she took off the amber beads and let them slide back into the glimmering heap on the dressing table.

"Any good, that Stepney place?" Ginny said.

"No. But she wants to hear it anyway. Don't you tell her I said where I was going, you know what she's like."

"'Sif I'd blab," Ginny said.

"*I* know that. *She* doesn't. You seen that thing she's got now? What is it?"

"I don't know and I don't care, 'slong as she don't aim it at me."

"Ain't you even *interested*?" Evvie said.

"Why? If Ma wants me to know, she'll tell me. You're too curious, Evvie. You always got to pick and poke and try to find out stuff that en't nothing to do with you. Get you in trouble, that will."

"Ma says 'A long nose's kept many a thief out of clink,'" Eveline said.

"Unless it's her business you're poking it in. Besides, since when do *you* give ha'pence what Ma says?"

"Ginny?"

"What?"

"If Ma thought someone'd made one of us, what do you think she'd do?"

The girls looked at each other for a moment, Ginny cradling her useless arm in her other hand. "You been made?" she said.

"I think so. Maybe."

"You told her?"

"Yes."

"Why?"

"Don't be daft, Ginny. If I hadn't and he'd followed me here, or the peelers turned up..."

Ginny was silent for a moment, chewing her lip. "I dunno," she said eventually. "She likes you, Evvie, she thinks you're smart, but if you're a risk..."

"Yeah, that's what I thought."

"She wants out. At least, she says she does."

"Yeah she said about retiring. Again. Talks about it a lot, these days."

"What d'you suppose will happen to us?"

"We'll be setting up on our own, I guess. Anyways, I'm

going to be stuck here for days. Once she lets me out, though, you want to go see a mentalist? Cumberland's on at the Egyptian Hall next month."

Eveline never passed up the chance to watch a stage magician, even sometimes going so far as to buy a ticket.

"Oh, no, them people give me the creeps." Ginny gave a not entirely exaggerated shudder. "'S unnatural, is what it is."

"He can't *really* read your mind, you beef-wit."

"Why go, then?"

"Because he works things out about people. It's clever."

Eveline had not the slightest interest in Spiritualism (to be fair to Cumberland, neither did he – except to debunk it). But stage magic, the deceptions of eye and hand and mind, those she found very interesting indeed.

EVELINE, HAVING JUST spent a frustrating hour trying to get Saffie to understand her ABCs, or her As, or what a book was for, other than pulling about, had given up and was sitting with some mending crumpled in her lap by the upstairs window that gave the best light. Mending bored her, but she was neat-fingered, and had managed, the last time she was in a theatre where a magic show was on, to sneak backstage and obtain a magician's stage-coat. She was now attempting to adapt its internal construction to a jacket of her own. Secret pockets, capacious but inconspicuous, she thought were an excellent idea – though she had no plans to stuff a live pigeon in one. Not unless she found a use for it.

"Hello, Lady Sparrow."

Liu was perched on the windowsill, grinning at her.

"Bugger it, Liu, you made me stab meself. Look!" She held up a bleeding finger.

"I am desolated."

"You'll be worse if Ma catches you up here. Are you off your chump?"

"You missed our appointment. I thought perhaps you had found more congenial company. But instead you are locked away. I have brought you one of those disgusting pies you like."

"Ooh, I could just do with that. Thank you."

He passed her a pie, wrapped in a handkerchief. She shook it out, and the little green jade fox tumbled onto her lap. "What's this?"

"A gift."

"Liu..."

"He spoke to me and said that he was very bored of my company, and would rather be with you. He thinks you might have troubles. Perhaps you could tell him about them, when there is no one else to listen."

The little fox had its head on one side in a quizzical way. It did look friendly. "I can't..."

"I ask nothing in return except, if you are in great trouble or distress, you tell him."

"You *are* off your chump, you know that? But... thank you. He's bone."

"He is jade," Liu said. "I should be very interested to see something with bones like that."

"*Bone* like 'nice,' silly."

"Oh. Well, I am glad you like him."

"I'm out in four days."

She could have got out before, had she wanted – there were ways – but she didn't want to risk getting on Ma's bad side. Ma had ears like a hound and eyes like a hawk and seemed to sleep with one of each open.

"You do not wish to leave now?"

"Nah, I'm here to be safe. There's been some cove sniffing about after me. Ma thought it'd be best to keep me out of view a while."

"Has there, indeed? Would he be a certain fellow in a grey coat, with a silver-headed cane?"

"Why?" Eveline gave him a hard look.

"You think I would betray your whereabouts?" He looked at the little fox and shook his head sadly. "See how little she trusts me."

"I got to be careful, Liu. You know that."

"I do, yes. And I must be careful too, and leave, or your Ma Pether will be hounding me."

"Yes, you'd better. But thank you. I'll see you later... If your ship's still here?"

"Oh, well, if they decide they must leave, then perhaps they will do so without me." He waved, and disappeared – upwards, onto the roof. She ran to the window and caught a glimpse of his foot and some sort of fluffy scarf trailing behind him – she hadn't noticed that before – and he was gone.

She sewed the little fox into a pocket in her shift, where it would be safe. The little cold lump warmed quickly, and though she had no intention of gabbing to it like a sapskull, it was nice to know it was there.

Three nights later Ma Pether took her aside.

"Well, seems like no-one's seen that cove of yours. So you can get back to it. But I'm going to be straight with you, Eveline." She was sitting in an ancient chair with the stuffing crawling out. She had a glass of brandy in one hand, a pipe in the other and her boots off, but her eyes were sharp and hard. "You get picked up, you don't say one word about me, or the house, or the other girls, no matter what they ask you or what they offer."

"Of course not, Ma."

"You're a bright girl, Eveline. Stick by me and I'll see you right. But you draw the law down on us and you'll be sorry for it."

"Yes, Ma."

"You got a home here, but only so long's you follow the rules."

"I understand, Ma."

"Good. See you do. And bring me back a pouch of tobacco tomorrow, I'm running out."

"Ah, Holmforth." Rupert Forbes-Cresswell looked up with his usual small, slightly pained smile. "Do take a seat, dear fellow. I shan't be a moment."

Holmforth strove to place himself in the deep, comfortable chair with the casual elegance that the Forbes-Cresswells of the world managed with such unconscious ease, knowing, all the time, that he could not relax too much or he would have to struggle to his feet, and Forbes-Cresswell would look at him with that smile again.

The dark-panelled walls, the leather-topped desk with its green-shaded lamp, the crisp rustle of documents and subdued murmur of well-educated English voices surrounded Holmforth. Home. But a home in which he did not quite belong.

He had been delighted, at first, with his own office, though it was small, and cold, and ill-appointed. The desk wobbled, the chair sneaked out intrusive splinters at every opportunity, the lamp had an ancient, stained parchment shade and the panelling had been gouged by the removal of better furniture. But it was an office, *his* office, in the Ministry. An office of one's own, at his level, was exceptional. A sign, he'd believed, of great favour; of acceptance, and good things to come.

But turning back for his umbrella one wet November evening he had overheard two of his colleagues, to whom he had just bid goodnight, gossiping in the corridor.

"Bit much, giving him Faldwell's old office."

"My dear fellow, they could hardly do anything else. I mean, would *you* want to sit in the same room? Share one's pens, and so forth? Next thing one would have to invite the fellow to dinner!"

"Ah. See what you mean. Really, the whole thing's a disgrace, if you ask me."

"Under the circumstances, there wasn't a deal of choice. Besides, better here than the Treasury, old boy; come in one morning and discover the entire budget's been calculated in leaves, or some such?"

Laughter, burning like acid.

He had left, without his umbrella, the rain running cold down his neck.

"There," Forbes-Cresswell said, pushing aside the document he'd been working on. "Now, what can I do for you?"

"I wanted to speak to you about the Britannia School."

"Dunfield's pet project! Not your area of interest, surely?"

"Hardly. It's just that I have a candidate. I think she may be of use, but at the moment her situation is unsuitable. I want her somewhere secure, and the training could be helpful."

Forbes-Cresswell's right eyebrow inched a fraction northwards. "A candidate."

"Yes."

On the journey Holmforth had stared unseeingly at the ever-changing cloudscape, wondering how to handle this moment. He didn't want to reveal too much too soon. He knew there was every chance that should the slightest hint leak out of what he was really about, either his efforts would be dismissed as nonsense or credit for his work would somehow, mysteriously, attach to someone else. But without a good reason, why would they provide the girl with a place at the Britannia? He had planned to use a little of the truth – he had seen her at work. She was a thief, a trickster of unmistakable talent, but she was also an orphan of the streets and – should she be troublesome or simply unsuccessful – could be disposed of easily enough.

"She is..." Holmforth stalled. In the face of that raised eyebrow, his efforts seemed foolish, his story ridiculous. A thief and trickster at Her Majesty's service? Before he could go on, Forbes-Cresswell's mouth curled with a faint but unmistakable hint of prurient amusement.

"My dear chap, I'm sure something can be done."

Holmforth, wrong-footed, opened his mouth and hastily closed it again.

"There's no need for details," Forbes-Creswell said. "Not quite what Dunfield intended, as if such a ridiculous idea could ever bear fruit, but there's no doubt that the school is proving useful. You'd be surprised if you knew who she'll be mixing with!" He looked about himself theatrically, like a prank-planning schoolboy scanning the corridor for prefects. "At the *very highest level*, I assure you, there are sometimes unfortunate reminders of indiscretion to be... tactfully dealt with. In any case, I'm sure I can arrange something."

"Thank you," Holmforth said, with a smile that felt painted on. "I would be most grateful."

Perhaps he had been naïve. Dunfield's plan for a school for spies – female ones, at that – had struck more than a few as a folly of the highest order, but it had, nonetheless, been passed, and funded. Perhaps even then it had been seen as a potential dumping-ground for the unwanted female offspring of Ministry men. An operation funded by the government, intended to provide useful servants of the Empire – and instead it was providing for ministers' bastards, freeing up both the ministers' consciences and their pockets.

Holmforth was no candidate for such an arrangement. Once he was properly established, he would make a respectable marriage to an appropriate woman of character. There would be no mistresses, no improper liaisons. In the meantime he, at least, was perfectly capable of exerting self-control.

The misuse of a government facility offended him, on a number of levels. But for the moment, it made this easier.

"I assume they do actually *have* lessons?" he said.

"Oh, indeed, Dunfield's original timetable is very much in operation. I'm almost tempted to go along some time and watch the poor dears wrestle with navigational charts and poke at each other with hatpins!"

"I wish to arrange specialised tuition for her. Would that be possible?"

"Of course, of course, just as you wish – so long as it doesn't cost enough to make the Treasury blink. I will give you a letter of introduction to the headmistress. I warn you, she's a veritable dragon. Just what one needs, of course, in that situation, otherwise one dreads to think what they might get up to. The first pupils are due to 'graduate' in a few months. I don't know what's to be done with them. It will have to be handled with great discretion, or it might cause embarrassment."

"They may prove useful after all," Holmforth said.

"You really think so?" Forbes-Cresswell laughed, but his eyes were suddenly hard-focused on Holmforth. "You have plans for your little... protégée?"

"Yes."

"Fascinating."

FENCHURCH STREET STATION, a morning heavy with rain.

Men with stovepipe hats shedding glistening drops, clutching high collars about their throats with one hand and leather cases with the other, bustling to make their trains. Beggars everywhere; a beached sailor, one hand resting on the wall for fear of his peg-leg slipping on the rain-slick floor, the other hand holding out a shapeless, greasy cap. A woman collapsed against the wall, a small pallid child cupped in the lap of her ragged black dress, her face emptied out with exhaustion and hunger. A peeler, high helmet, blue coat and brass buttons, making his way through the crowd towards the pair with *move-along* in his eyes.

The clanging roar and reek and hiss; great clouds of steam exploding along the platforms, the smooth tug-and-pull of the great shining rods heaving around the wheels, slow then faster, *chuh-chug, chuh-chug*. The high imperious shriek of the whistles, sending pigeons in a great fluttering rush up into the rain-streaked iron-framed dome of the roof. The great engines of Empire, proud in their glossy paint and noble names, the *Flying* this and the *Royal* that, hustling their human cargo to its many destinations. And far above, like a fat, expensive cigar, the prime airship *Gloriana* humming her way over them all, carrying pricey necessities, like diplomats and brandy, far over the sea.

Eveline glanced up as the *Gloriana*'s shadow flowed over the station. The *Gloriana*. What a prize she would be! Stuffed to the gills with rich travellers and fancy cargo.

Sometimes she amused herself with schemes to rob the *Gloriana,* but she always got stuck at getting the stuff away. Unless you could fly the whole ship somewhere, without interference from passengers or crew, and whisk away the loot once it had landed, she couldn't see how to pull it off. It would need too many people, and someone who could fly the blasted thing, and all in all it was far too complicated.

She preferred schemes she could manage all by herself, without relying on other people – at least, no-one other than the marks.

The station was crowded and noisy, and everyone was flustered and in a hurry, which gave plenty of opportunities for a quick profit. But she was finding it hard to pick a target. Frankly, she was bored. She liked something more challenging than pockets. Something that required a bit of planning. She looked around. Plenty of people who would yield, at most, a handkerchief or a handful of coppers; hardly worth it. Small stuff. She had bigger plans, like Ma. Ma was forever talking about one final big scheme, something that would set her up for life, so she could retire, but somehow it never happened. And even if Ma happened on such a thing, Evvie didn't think she'd tell her – though she should. Ma was clever, yes. But Eveline knew that when it came to a proper scam, though she had less practice, she was better at seeing how things went together, and where they might fall apart. Maybe it was all the reading that had done it. Who knew?

Finally she spotted a prosperous-looking clergyman, his black coat straining at its buttons, his whiskers a-bristle with self-satisfaction, bustling through the crowd, fussing at his pockets. His hair shone with pomade, and his side-whiskers were so gleamingly black that they appeared to cast a faint shadow on his skin. Eveline knew that shadow for what it was – dye. *Oh, ho,* she thought. She felt in her purse. Yes, she had it. Now, she needed to think. Again she was dressed like a maidservant, neat and unobtrusive.

She pulled her mouth down, put a handkerchief to her eyes and worked her way towards the clergyman until she bumped into him. "Oh, I'm so dreadfully sorry!"

"Quite my fault," the clergyman said. "Are you all right, my dear?" He laid a thick white hand on her arm.

Eveline looked up at him and gave a quivering smile. "Yes, only... my mistress is going to be so *dreadfully* angry!" Rounded vowels and a faint burr on the consonants, a country lass not long in town.

"What, because you bumped into someone? Surely she couldn't be so unkind."

"No, it's... oh, I shouldn't trouble a gentleman with this. You're of the clergy, sir, ain't you? Be so good as to offer a prayer for a poor girl, for if I get turned out, I shan't know what to do, and can only hope the angels are watching me!" She gave a small gasp as though she were fighting tears. She didn't let herself actually cry

– some girls could do it and look pretty, but it turned Evvie into a gargoyle of swollen eyes and snot.

"Hush, hush," the clergyman said. "I'm sure it's not so bad as all that. Why don't you sit down with me and tell me all about it?" He put a heavy arm around her shoulders and guided her to a nearby bench. He smelled of Macassar oil and snuff.

"The thing of it is, sir," she said, between sobs, "my mistress sent me to... oh, I shouldn't say it... but she's not had an easy time, sir. And she gave me her dead husband's stick-pin to take to the dolly-shop, to get some money, saying we should get it back when her investments come good. Only they told me it's worth nothing, being only brass and glass, and they wouldn't advance me but a few pence for it. And he was *smiling* so."

"Well, well, that's hard, but surely your mistress won't blame you?"

"I think she will, sir. And as I was leaving, he said, 'Come back when you're less proud,' and I'm not proud, sir, only afraid I shall be turned out."

"He sounds like less than a gentleman. I think your mistress should better have sent someone else to deal with him."

"There was no-one else to send, sir, apart from the boot-boy, and he's a good boy, but simple. But why would my mistress' husband have had a cheap pin? He was always a well-dressed gentleman, like yourself. And a gentleman like you is sure to know. Do *you* think this is nothing but a gimcrack?" Eveline took out of her purse the stick-pin she had been carrying for just such an occasion. It was a very fine stick-pin, in gold, with a gleaming diamond set in its head; she had lifted it from the cravat of a swell cove in the Strand only days before.

"Well, it certainly *looks* fine enough," he said, judiciously, feeling its weight in his hand, then holding it up to the light. "And you know, I think I see a hallmark. Yes, look, see that mark there?"

Eveline widened her eyes. "Yes, sir. What does it mean?"

"That means it's made of gold, you see? So it's most probably genuine. I think the pawnbroker, seeing an innocent young girl... you're not long up from the country, are you?" He put his hand on her shoulder this time.

"Why, that's right, sir. However did you guess?"

The clergyman gave her back the pin, tapped his nose, and gave a smug smile. "I think this villain tried to get this from you for less than it was worth, that's what I think."

"Oh, sir, how dreadful! Whatever shall I do? I daren't go to another, what if they are all such cheating wretches?"

"I tell you what, I'm about to go visit my dear mother at Tunbridge Wells. Why don't you accompany me? The train leaves shortly. And then perhaps we can..."

"Oh, dear," said a voice. "Eveline, what are you about now?"

It was him, the grey-coat man, turning up right there, quiet as a cat, smiling patiently. *He knows my name!* She jumped up, but before she could run, his hand was on her arm, clamped like a steel cuff. "Don't be foolish, child."

Fear rose jittering in her brain, all ratsqueal and clawscratch. Her hands went cold. But part of her pulled back, like it always did, watching. She knew that trick, speaking the target's name; she'd heard of Whicher doing that. It was meant to make a person feel hopeless, as though he knew so much they might as well give up. But cons did the same, getting under a mark's skin by seeming to know things about them.

He wasn't acting like a copper. He hadn't arrested her. "My dear sir, I hope she hasn't been troublesome. I'll take her now."

Eveline realised she was gaping like an eel on a slab and closed her jaw.

The clergyman looked almost as confused as she felt. "Are you... who *are* you?"

"The person who just prevented you from being robbed."

"Let go my arm!" Damn, in her panic she'd let the accent slip. "I don't know what you want, but I don't know you!" She tried to shift her arm and his grip clamped down harder, grinding flesh against bone. Eveline turned to the clergyman. "Please, sir, don't listen to him, I've never seen him before!" She widened her eyes and looked helpless. The clergyman was going red with discomfort.

Grey-Coat leaned down and muttered in her ear, "Stop it, Eveline, or you'll be on a transport to Australia within the week. Be *still*."

Transport? So he *was* a copper. How long had he been following her? *What did he want?* He had her arm behind her back now, pulling her tight against him so the clergyman wouldn't be able to see. If she tried to run, she'd tear her own arm out of its socket.

"She seemed to be in distress," the clergyman said. "She told me some story about her mistress, and a diamond stick-pin..."

"A diamond stick-pin? If she has such a thing, sir, I assure you, she did not come by it honestly. It seems I intervened just in time. The pin?" He held his hand out with a patient expression. Evvie thought about jamming the pin through it, but he gave the smallest possible shake of his head, as though he'd heard her think it. "I don't advise any foolishness, either." He raised the hand holding her arm, so she was almost on tiptoe. It hurt. If she jabbed him, he'd dislocate her, that seemed clear enough.

She dropped the pin in his palm. *There. Now you're handling stolen goods. Maybe I should call a copper.* The grey-coated man raised his eyebrows, and put it in his pocket. "I can assure you she stole it," he said.

"Well, sir," the clergyman said, glaring at Eveline, "I shan't waste any more of my time. I might have missed my train!"

Eveline felt an uprush of fury. She knew what he'd intended for her, she was certain. A little 'now don't you worry,' a hand on your arm, and the next thing you knew they thought you owed them whatever they wanted to take. And of course he'd believed every word Grey-Coat said, just because he was a man, and posh with it.

She bit down on her anger. Fury'd get her nothing but trouble – Grey-Coat had, at the moment, all the cards.

He smelled of clean linens and soap. He might be slightly-built, but he was strong, and had looked as though he could run – she already knew he could move swiftly and unobtrusively. He was a nice-looking cove, if you went for that sort of thing, with that pale gold skin and those grey eyes. Oh, and he looked familiar... no, that was wrong. Not familiar like she knew him, but familiar in some undefinable way.

Fear swelled into her throat; she swallowed it back and tried to think. Grey-Coat was smart, and wanted her for something badly enough to grab her in broad daylight, in front of a witness, but without arresting her. Why?

You're too curious, Evvie.

Maybe, Ginny. But I want to know why he's so all-fired interested in me.

She relaxed her stance a little. He didn't let go.

The clergyman disappeared in the direction of the Tunbridge Wells train, casting a suspicious glance over his shoulder. "So much for the church," Eveline said. "Abandoning a girl that way. Shameful, I call it. You could be the devil himself for all he knows. All *I* know, too. What do you want, mister?"

"I have a proposal for you."

"That's very flattering of you, sir, but I don't think we should suit," she said.

"I suggest you stop attempting to display your cleverness, Miss Duchen, and listen." He leaned closer, and whispered in her ear. "That is, if you wish to have a future that does not involve the steerage section of a dying hulk. It *is* possible you might survive the journey; a number of convicts do, though I believe about one in three die. Even should the ship prove seaworthy, the chances of disease are high. As, indeed, are the chances of rape. Should you survive, the fate of young women in the colonies is seldom a pleasant one. I know you are no Drury Lane vestal – it is to your credit that you have, at least, avoided that profession – but women being very scarce in the colonies, it is unlikely you would have a choice in the matter."

Eveline knew plenty of whores; Sal was only one of them, and Sal only did it when she couldn't make enough with her stitching. There'd been poor Millie

Stephens, younger than Eveline, already rotting and crazed with the pox. She'd tried to drown herself in the river, and been hauled out, only to end up in Cross Bones graveyard a bare few weeks later. The thought of that, *and* in a country so far from anything she'd ever known, with no chance of ever coming home... "What do you want with me, then?"

"Come with me," he said, beginning to walk, shifting his grip so it was less painful but no less firm.

"Where?"

"To my carriage, to begin with."

"I don't think I should be getting into carriages with men. That sort of thing can stain one's reputation."

The look he gave her was utterly without humour. "You are a very lucky young woman, Miss Duchen. I am about to offer you the chance at a better life. Strive to appreciate that."

She wondered, briefly, if he was after a mistress – then dismissed the thought immediately. A fancy cove like him could afford a lot fancier than Evvie Duchen. And he didn't strike her as the type, unlike the clergyman. He looked at her and handled her as though she were a parcel – or an untrained dog.

But he wanted something from her. And that was a good place to have a mark – if they didn't want something, you'd no lever. If this was a long game, he'd have to get up early in the morning to play Eveline Duchen. "All right then, guv'nor," she said, now all East-End-and-a-lump-of-coal. "Lead the way, why don'tcha?"

HE LED HER to a horse-drawn carriage, plain as homespun, even a little shabby, though the horse looked glossy and well-fed. She was glad it was not a steam-hansom; with their hard-latching doors and disconcerting speed, they were a lot harder to get out of in a hurry. The driver was huddled in a greatcoat with a battered hat pulled down over his brows – apart from a brief glance at them, he neither moved nor spoke.

Her captor handed Eveline in as though she were a lady, though without letting go of her arm until they settled, opposite each other, into the creaking leather seats. He leaned back and regarded her with a cold, unreadable eye. "Well," he said. "You are in some ways a rather foolish young woman, are you not?"

Eveline looked back at him, warily, and said nothing.

"I would have thought your pride in your abilities would force a disclaimer from you, but perhaps I was mistaken," he went on.

"You can't expect a common girl like me to understand all that fancy talk," she said.

"Now you see, I rather *do*. Because you have already demonstrated your cleverness. Really rather unwise, in your profession. My name is Holmforth. I work for Her Majesty's Government. You may be able to be of service to the Empire – if you are capable of being educated, of taking orders, and of operating with discretion. It is that last part, the matter of discretion, which troubles me. It troubles me, Miss Duchen."

"If you find me so troublesome, Mr Holmforth, then why don't I just go on my way, and we'll say no more about it?" Eveline reached for the door of the carriage.

Holmforth's cane whicked through the air; the bronze ferrule slammed into the door an inch from her fingers. "Don't be more foolish than you can help," he said. "Besides, you must be a little curious, surely?"

She shrugged. "All right. Don't see why Her Majesty's Government would be interested in the likes of me. Never have been before, that I know about."

"You may have skills that will be of use to us." He leaned back, placing his cane carefully at his side, steepled his fingers in front of his mouth, and regarded her with those icy blues.

"What sort of skills?"

"That, you will discover."

"You don't know whether I'm any good at what you want, but you want me anyway? What happens if I'm no good at whatever it is?"

"I am sure you will do your best, will you not? It is a chance at a better life. What is there to keep you from it? You have no family, only a gaggle of thieves. They will hardly notice your absence."

Wrong twice, Eveline thought. She did have family. Uncle James, who had so kindly offered them a place under his roof. And if she disappeared, Ma Pether'd do her damnedest to find out what had happened, if only out of caution.

Much good that'd do her if she was face down in the Thames.

"You are unconvinced," Holmforth said. "You know James Lathrop is dead."

Two emotions jabbed through Eveline so fast they were hard to distinguish from each other. One was shock – not only did he know *her*, he knew about Uncle James, which meant he knew more than anyone else, including Ma Pether. In fact, he knew more than Eveline herself.

The other emotion was a furious joy. *Dead, is he? Good! I hope he suffered!*

Holmforth was watching her closely. She tried to school her face to a look of calm disinterest. "Do you wish to tell me why, having been offered a comfortable home on the death of your parents, you chose, instead, the life of the streets?" He leaned forward. "Or perhaps you would like to tell me what happened to Charlotte?"

Eveline's breath caught, before she could help herself; she knew he'd noticed, too, but refused to give him the satisfaction. "Don't know what you mean," she said.

"Charlotte. Your baby sister. I'm sure you remember, since you both disappeared at the same time. Perhaps she was stolen away by gypsies?"

Eveline said nothing.

"The remaining servants said that Lathrop had had two wards briefly living under his roof, that their mother had died, and that the older had run away, apparently taking the younger, who was barely more than a babe-in-arms. He placed a notice in the papers, stating that you were not of sound mind, and he feared for you and your sister."

"Did he."

"Lathrop was a local councillor. Much respected. Did he discover he had taken under his roof someone who was not worthy of his generosity? Someone whose behaviour, perhaps, did not reward his kindness and care? Who was, in fact, even at that tender age, a corrupt and unregenerate criminal?"

Eveline stared at the curtain over the window. *He came looking for me. He already knew who I was. What are you up to, Mr Holmforth? You want something from me, but you're not all flattery and pretty words, are you?*

"Hmm," Holmforth said. "It seems that you are capable of discretion after all. Well?"

"Well what?"

"Are you prepared to enter the Empire's service?"

"I still don't know what you want me to do."

"You will work for Her Majesty's Government, completing the tasks you would be set to the best of your ability, with absolute loyalty, absolute discretion, and absolute obedience. To this end, you will receive housing, clothing, food, and an education."

"Why me?"

"Because you, Miss Duchen, may have the skills I need."

I, she thought. *Not* we, *not Her Majesty's Government*. She stored it away.

"And if I don't?"

"You may still be of use to the Empire."

He was doing his best to make her feel she'd no choice in the matter, but that was a trick she'd seen played on more than one mark. She'd done it herself. What he had, and she didn't, was information. *Knowledge*, Ma Pether's voice whispered in her ear. *If you've got a brain and the means to fill it, you can outwit the Queen and all her ministers.*

She knew what her skills were: deception, trickery, lifting... any way of getting by on the wrong side of the law that she'd been able to find out about, she was good at, bar murder. Did the Empire need thieves and tricksters? Her brain raced. How much did he already know about what she could do? She wasn't going to sit here listing every trick she'd pulled; for all she knew this could be some elaborate ploy to draw her in. To get not just her, but Ma and all the girls.

His face gave nothing away. He might as well have been a stone angel in a churchyard, for all his expression betrayed. His eyes remained fixed on hers throughout, but she could read nothing in them except, perhaps, a cold curiosity.

"For all I know they might want me to walk a high wire like in the circus, twirling a parasol."

"Under what circumstances do you imagine Her Majesty's Government would require you to do such a thing?"

"I dunno. P'raps Her Majesty might be bored and fancy a laugh?"

"I hope you are not in the habit of referring to our Queen with disrespect."

"I ain't disrespecting no-one. So you'd train me like a circus girl, would you?"

"That is hardly likely to be necessary. You will receive a somewhat wider education than is normally available to girls, even of the highest class. Does the idea appeal?"

She shrugged. "Depends if it's useful. I can read and I know me numbers. I get by."

"You disappoint me. I thought the idea of knowledge might appeal to you. I understand you read for pleasure, as well as when it might be useful to... Ma Pether, you call her. Her real name is Fulshott, by the way."

Was that true? If it was, he knew far more than he should – far more than Eveline, and more, perhaps, than Ma.

"How'd you find me?"

"I made enquiries. It took time."

"Who peached?"

"Is it relevant?"

"It is to me."

"An intimate of the Pether household. He was most helpful, for the right sum."

An intimate... Bloody Bartholomew Simms. It had to

be. There were no other men who hung about the place enough to be called an 'intimate.'

That tiny bit of knowledge fought against Eveline's increasing chill. If Holmforth thought that hadn't been enough of a clue, then he didn't know quite as much as he thought. Besides, fear would do her no good at all, nor would thinking about what would happen to the others if Ma got taken up. Saffie, pretty little curly-haired Saffie who wiggled like a puppy at the slightest kindness, out on the street with no-one to watch her... she'd not last a day.

She kept her voice calm. "You said housing, clothing, food?"

"You will be housed in a dormitory with other young women, and of course, fed. On completion of your training, you would be provided with accommodation. Clothing as necessary and, once you are trained, a personal allowance." He looked down at her feet, which were clad in a pair of broken-down black boots that were too big and stuffed with paper at the toes to keep them on. "Shoes. New ones. That fit. And a pension, do you know what that is?"

"No." Although she had heard the word. She remembered hearing it in those dreadful days after Papa had died, when everything had started to go so wrong. There had been supposed to be one, but there wasn't.

"A sum of money, regularly paid, once you are too old or otherwise unfit to work."

Food. A roof. A personal allowance. Shoes she didn't have to share. And money when she was too old to work.

She had a vision, then. A room, her own room. An armchair. A little footstool, a roaring fire, a plate of sausages. A door that locked. Even when she was old and too crippled with the rheumatiz to lift a handkerchief.

She wasn't scared of work; she worked hard for Ma. And a *pension* sounded like a very good deal indeed. The thought of it was like a big soft blanket. As for an education... Ma wasn't the only one who believed in knowledge. Knowing her letters and numbers gave Evvie an edge others didn't have – not to mention that reading helped you forget cold feet and an empty belly in a way nothing else did. An education meant books, of which she'd never had enough, and chances, of which she could do with as many as she could grab.

A good-sounding deal, right enough. But she knew about good deals. She'd offered them herself. They tended to have a great big fishhook stuck somewhere in the middle.

"And if I don't 'complete my training' in whatever it is you want me to do, fall off me tightrope too many times, maybe?"

"A return to the streets, without even the fragile protection of Ma Pether. You may be lucky enough to find employment in the factories." He leaned forward. "Clever as a monkey you might be, Miss Duchen, but you are young, poor and female. You have been lucky so far. Luck runs out."

He was right, she knew. And she also knew, in the depths of her gut, that he was lying, or at least, not telling her something. *What?*

Clever as a monkey.

That wasn't such a compliment, when you thought about it. Monkeys got caught and put in a fancy jacket and a little red hat and chained to a barrel organ, holding out a tin cup in a shivering paw.

I'm nobody's monkey, mister, Eveline thought. *Not yours, not Her Majesty's Government's, not even Ma Pether's. I'll go along. And I'll see what's to be seen.*

And we'll find out who's the clever one, Mister Holmforth.

The Britannia School

THE CARRIAGE MOVED steadily out of the centre of town, up through St James's, into the park and out the other side, uphill, always uphill. The shuffling foot-traffic, the clatter of iron wheels and clopping of hooves, the chuff and rattle of steam-cars all dropped away. As the last of the daylight faded, leaving only a sullen red glow in the west, they were out in the country, with no light but the carriage's own swaying lamps to show the road ahead and no sound but the brisk clopping of a single set of hooves, the rumble of just four wheels, the creak of springs and leather. As the roar and stink of town and its endless smoke faded into the scents of a spring night, dewy green and sweet, these small, familiar sounds seemed to make the surrounding silence bigger; as though all around the carriage, something, some living, breathing thing, listened.

The shadows of great trees loomed beside the road. Eveline shivered, but could not stop looking, gulping in the cleanest air she'd smelled in years. She had been born and bred a country girl. Until that last terrible journey with Charlotte, the woods had held few fears for her. In the spring she'd lain for hours among the bluebells, half-drunk with their scent, watching the tiny flickering figures that hummed and dived among them, teasing the bees and stealing their pollen and sometimes, if she stayed very still, landing on her skirts, or tugging at her ribbons with minute, mouselike hands. They had huge insectile eyes in pale pointed faces, and wings like coloured glass.

In the winter Eveline had run among the wet black trunks, catching her stockings on the hooked thorns of the bare red-stemmed brambles, leaving a tribute of stolen cake or bright ribbon in the fork of a tree; glimpsing a spike-headed bogle like a teazle with legs, and once a nixie with green-ripple skin and webbed fingers and a crown of ice, brooding at the edge of her frozen pool. Eveline had brought her a flowering snowdrop bulb stolen from her mother's garden, and the nixie had smiled at her.

Her father declared the Folk a still-living but less relevant version of the fossils that fascinated him and filled every spare shelf of the house – a fading mystery, soon to be relegated to academic lectures and browned-ink footnotes. Her mother had, like her daughter, been fascinated by the Folk. She had sought them out, sometimes with the instruments she made.

A great tree stood by itself in the middle of a field, barely more than an outline in the gathering dark. Eveline had a sudden, painfully clear memory of her mother, cross-legged under just such a huge spreading oak, her hair falling out of its bun, a humming box in her lap, surrounded by curious Folk, many Lesser like bogles, and even one or two of the Higher, who looked like people, only prettier. They had laughed, when a change of note sent the little ones spiralling madly up into the branches.

Eveline took every opportunity to escape from chores and lessons into the woods to seek out the Folk. They seemed to her, even then, such carefree creatures, unburdened by rules and *Don't*s and *Mustn't*s. And eventually, there had been Aiden.

She didn't want to think about Aiden. That was a long time ago, like her last trip through the woods. Then a wall of dark brick, blood-coloured in the swaying carriage light and at least eight feet high, imposed itself between Eveline and the view. She glanced at Holmforth; he had closed his eyes, but she knew he was not asleep.

The coach slowed and turned left, and stopped. Eveline heard the driver speak – she assumed it was the driver, though she had yet to see his face. She peered out of the window, and could see only a brick column surmounted by a gas lamp, which threw yellow-green light on a strange object in brass, a little like the mouth of a trumpet, set into the column at the height of the coach-driver's head.

There was a clunk, a hissing creak, and the coach moved forward, the wheels clattering on gravel. The bars of a high iron gate, straight and unadorned, passed by the window, and Eveline could see the edge of a well-kept lawn fading into darkness beyond the reach of the carriage lamps.

It occurred to her that there had been nothing on the gate or the column to mark what sort of place this was. She felt a cold churning in her stomach and glanced sidelong at Holmforth. Had she been gulled? Was this some sort of bawdy-house after all, or something worse?

Holmforth opened his eyes. "There's no need to look so anxious. I would hardly bring you all this way if I intended murder."

The coach crunched to a halt in a spatter of gravel. "One thing," Holmforth said. "I wouldn't advise trying to run. There are dogs that patrol the grounds, and they are exceptionally temperamental."

He opened the door for her and handed her out, courteous again. She noticed a faint tracery of scar-tissue on both palms, a row of pallid overlapping crescents like the bite marks of some furious ghost.

Eveline drew in a great gulp of spring-scented air. Her heart tugged in her chest, and despite herself she could not help looking out over the grass to where the shapes of trees clustered against the last faint light of the sky. They were properly out in the country, all right. She pulled her gaze away and stood blinking at the vast building in front of her.

It bulked against the night sky, its roofline bristling with chimneys. A dozen faint slivers of light indicated the presence of firmly curtained windows; black bars crossed them, as though trying to prevent even that much light from escaping. A door big enough for a church, bound and riveted with iron, stood like a muscular sentry in a stone porch, faintly illuminated by a gas lamp in a wrought-iron cage.

It didn't look much like the village school Eveline remembered; one room, a thatched roof, and a privy out the back. Not that she'd gone herself, of course. Only the boys got schooled. She'd sneaked up to peer in the windows and listen, but the endless lists of Kings and Queens and the chanting of times tables had bored her. Her mother had been teaching her to read and write and reckon, in the cluttered, chiming, whirring room that served her as a study. Her father had occasionally, absentmindedly passed on such scraps of history or biology as he himself found entertaining.

The building bore down on her, with its walls and

bars and frowning ironwork, trying to make her small and helpless and afraid. She lifted her chin and glared at it. After what she'd been through, no mere heap of bricks was going to make Eveline Duchen feel like that.

The door opened and a figure stood outlined against light. Tall, straight, female, hair drawn close to the skull; that was all that could be made of it.

"Mr Holmforth," it said.

"Miss Cairngrim." Keeping his hand firmly on her shoulder, Holmforth steered Eveline towards the door. "This is Eveline."

Close to, Eveline could see that Miss Cairngrim had a high-browed, handsome face, darkly drawn brows, greying hair, and an expression of chilly reserve, which changed not at all as she looked Eveline up and down. She had a strange, harsh, throat-catching scent that added to Eveline's unease, making her feel suddenly weak and tearful.

You're hungry and tired, Eveline Duchen. Perk up and keep lively or you'll get in trouble.

More trouble.

"I see," Miss Cairngrim said. "You had better come in."

Eveline marched up the steps and through the door, holding her chin high.

The hall was high-ceilinged and chilly, the floor laid with a complex pattern of black and white marble. A large, plain lamp hung from the ceiling. A small dark table with a mirror in a gilded frame, spindly gilded legs and a single shallow drawer stood against one wall, bearing a brass plate on which a lone letter sat forlorn. Eveline gave the table a professional once-over; the drawer might be worth a look, the brass plate would fetch a few bob, but the table itself was cheap, the gilding already flaking from the legs. That aside, the hall contained nothing but closed, white-painted panelled doors and a faint scent of cabbage and gravy.

Miss Cairngrim's dress was grey wool, with a narrow skirt and a small bustle that hardly seemed to move as she walked. Eveline followed the bustle down the hall.

Miss Cairngrim opened a door to reveal a small parlour. It was just as chilly as the hall – the fire lay unlit in the grate. Three green-upholstered chairs stood at bay around a circular table shrouded in yellowed lace, and a faded red sofa huddled in one corner. A lamp with a yellow silk shade missing two tassels stood on a battered escritoire. The mantel bore chipped figurines of a shepherd and shepherdess, in the sort of flounced, beribboned costumes that always made Eveline give a silent snort. Anyone who thought you went herding sheep guyed up like that had never hauled one of the stupid beasts out of a bramble patch – or helped with a lambing.

Neither figurine had been worth a lot, even before whatever rough handling had robbed the shepherd of some of his fingers and the shepherdess of her elegantly pointing toe. Between them, leering, was a Toby jug of immense and grinning ugliness, stuck full of pens and slate pencils. Eveline took to him immediately – he was worth even less money than the chipped shepherd and shepherdess, but was by far the most cheerful thing in the room.

"So, Mr Holmforth, what have you brought me?" Miss Cairngrim said, turning up the lamp and examining Eveline as though she were a dusty mantelpiece.

"Eveline Duchen. A thief," Mr Holmforth said. "A child of the streets, of little education, uncertain temperament, deceptive nature, and excessive pride."

Eveline, who had been called worse, though seldom

in such fancy language, simply sighed. She was weary, hungry, and despite her resolution on the doorstep, more than a little unnerved. It was all very strange. And where was everyone? Going from the lights she had seen, and the sheer size of the place, there must be other people in it, but she couldn't hear a sound. It was all reminding her rather too much of arriving at Uncle James's. *Shoes,* she told herself. *Shoes and clothes and a pension.*

"I see," said Miss Cairngrim, apparently unmoved by Holmforth's litany. "And this is the girl you believe is suitable for training?"

"Whether she is or not, I require it," Holmforth said, his voice cold as a knife blade. Eveline saw the muscle in Miss Cairngrim's jaw twitch. "Her education is to concentrate on those areas in which I instructed you. Otherwise, she is to receive the same as the other girls. She has received the basics and not much more, but she appears reasonably intelligent. She may have a facility for languages; I have heard her speaking French."

He *must* have been the man she saw on the docks – or perhaps he had overheard her chatting with her friend Bon-Bon.

"I believe she can read," Holmforth went on.

"Come here, child." Miss Cairngrim beckoned her forward.

Eveline obeyed. She tried to hold her chin up, although her stomach was churning and her knees felt as though they had been replaced with some sort of shuddering liquid.

Miss Cairngrim walked around her, looking her up and down. She came back to the front, and took Eveline's chin in her hand. "Hmm. Open your mouth." She peeled Eveline's lips back from her teeth, exactly as though she had been a horse, then let go and stood back, the elbow of her right arm propped in her left palm, tapping at her own lip with a forefinger. "Lift up your skirt."

"I don't think so," Eveline said.

The slap landed before Eveline knew it was coming. "Shit!" She put a hand to her stinging cheek, and eyed the door; she didn't quite manage to duck the next slap. The calm, considering expression on Miss Cairngrim's face never changed.

"Understand this, Eveline Duchen. If you are to stay here, you will not use such disgusting language. You will obey instantly whenever I or any of your instructors ask something of you, whether it is to lift your skirt, do a headstand, or wash your mouth out with lye. If you do not, you will be punished. Every time you transgress, the punishment will be more severe. Do you understand?"

Eveline glanced towards Holmforth, who was watching calmly, as though this were all in a day's work. Which it probably was.

She bit her lip. Even if she could make it out of here, she was a long way from home, and there were the dogs. She'd been far from home in unsafe places before, and survived it, but it wasn't an experience she had any desire to repeat without more information and some food in her belly.

The door was locked – she'd heard the click. The windows were barred. Tomorrow, she would be less tired, and with luck they'd feed her.

And if they thought she was beaten, and obedient, then all the better.

"All right," she said. "I'm sorry for the language, miss." She dropped a little curtsey. "Only it was a shock. I can learn better."

Miss Cairngrim's expression did not change. "Skirt."

Eveline lifted the hem of her skirt to her knees, glancing at Miss Cairngrim.

"Higher... Enough. Good, you're not bandy. You may lower your skirt." She turned to Holmforth. "Unusually modest, for a street child. Normally one has to persuade them to keep their skirts *down*."

"I would hardly have thought that was a problem here," Holmforth said.

"You would be surprised, Mr Holmforth. How old are you, Eveline?"

"I'm not sure. About fifteen or thereabouts."

"Mr Holmforth seems to think you have had some schooling. Add six and five."

"Eleven."

"Multiply three by seven."

"Twenty-one."

"Divide thirty by four."

"Umm... seven and a bit."

Miss Cairngrim took a slate from the mantelpiece and a piece of chalk from the Toby jug. "Write your name on this slate."

Eveline did so, glad Ma had needed the occasional letter sent.

"Now form your letters."

Painstakingly, she traced out *A, B, C*....

Miss Cairngrim took the slate, glanced at it, and wiped it clean.

"Miss Cairngrim?"

"What is it?"

"I need..." It had been a long coach ride, and she was getting desperate, but Eveline didn't want to get slapped again for being vulgar.

"You need what?" Miss Cairngrim gave her a high-nosed glare.

Eveline shuffled backwards a step and reached for the most respectable expression she knew. "I need to make water."

This time she avoided the slap. Seeing the sudden blank fury on the woman's face, she thought, *Stupid, Eveline. She'll make you pay for that.* Next time, she wouldn't duck.

"You do not mention such things," Miss Cairngrim said, "*especially* in the presence of a gentleman. There is a time and a place and you will be informed of these when it is appropriate. Learn to control yourself, Duchen. It is obviously something of which you are sadly in need. Now, Mr Holmforth appears to think you can speak some French. Show me."

Eveline gritted her teeth, clenched her muscles, and held on.

French was bad, as most of the words she knew either came from Bon-Bon, a dancer and occasional whore, or had been picked up around the docks, and were pretty sure to provoke another slap. Even trying to avoid the bad ones, she got slapped again. She had only known the word was French, and thought it was something to do with food. She vowed privately to find out its real meaning as soon as possible.

Holmforth hadn't mentioned Cantonese. Did that mean he didn't know about Liu, or that he wanted her to think he didn't? At the thought of Liu, waving in the sunlight, she felt suddenly very low. Would she ever see him again, or Ginny, or Saffie? She even missed Ma, who might give you the odd slap herself, but would also give a word of praise and even ruffle your hair if she felt inclined. Eveline suspected that wasn't likely with this chilly, dangerous bitch. She tried to blink the brief blur of tears away before they could be spotted.

"I think that's enough," Mr Holmforth said. "The child's near collapsing with fatigue, and I must return to London tonight."

Eveline glanced at him. Had he noticed her trying not to blub? It was hard to tell, he was looking at his watch, not at her. A fine piece it was, too.

"The language teacher I arranged for her, has he arrived yet?"

"Yes."

"Good. And she is to have at least two hours a day working with the materials I have brought with me. There is no teacher for this subject, so she will have to do the best she can."

Eveline felt that chill again. He had been preparing for this, maybe for months. What was the subject he wanted her to learn? What was going on?

"Without supervision, she will play about and waste time. She will have to work in the barn, under Mr Jackson," Miss Cairngrim said. "I still do not think it is suitable, however."

"Whether or not it is suitable is not your concern, Miss Cairngrim."

"I do not encourage favouritism, or singling out, Mr Holmforth. These girls need discipline, and to be reminded of their place and what they owe to the Empire. Also, the rest are not street children. Making an exception in this way, especially of a girl like this, will give entirely the wrong impression."

"Miss Cairngrim." Holmforth looked, not at Miss Cairngrim, but at the head of his cane, silver, with a coat of arms. (Eveline had already priced it for what it would fetch from Davey Slype, Ma's favourite fence). "Your work here is valued, of course. But do not presume upon your position."

Miss Cairngrim pressed the bell-push set into the wall.

A moment later the door opened, to reveal a tall, skinny girl with a prominent nose and big hands, dressed in brown with a brown apron. "Yes, Miss Cairngrim?"

"A probationer, Miss Smythe. Put her in the usual room." Miss Cairngrim unhooked a key from the bunch at her belt and gave it to the girl.

"Yes, Miss Cairngrim."

"Go with her," the woman said, with a flick of her hand towards Eveline.

"Study hard," Holmforth said. "I will see you soon, and I expect progress."

Eveline, tired as she was, dropped a curtsey and gave him a smile; sweet and open as a daisy in the sun. "Yes, Mr Holmforth."

He did not smile, but only nodded.

Miss Cairngrim said nothing.

Eveline followed the tall girl out of the room. They turned the corner into another corridor. The sound of the front door closing echoed after them. Eveline said, "I'm busting for a piss. We got to go far?"

"No. There's a pot in the room."

"What's this place like, then?"

"You'll find out, if you stay," the girl said. She had a low, soft voice, and didn't look Eveline in the eye.

"Oh, go on, give us a help, love. I've no more idea what's going on than a new-born babe, and I don't want to put me foot in it before I've even started."

"Miss Cairngrim doesn't encourage chatter."

"At least tell us your name."

"It's Smythe. Didn't you hear her?" She stopped by a small, white-painted door and unlocked it.

Inside was a room with a bed made up with coarse sheets and a grey blanket, a basin and ewer in plain white chipped enamel, a candle in a battered enamel candlestick, a small, dead fireplace, and nothing else. Not even a window. But it was a room to herself, something she'd never in her life had before. Eveline knelt down and there under the bed, praise be, was a large, ugly, enamelled chamber pot.

"Any chance of some food?" Eveline said, tugging out the pot. "I'm starved."

"I'll see. First, you have to take off your shawl and turn out your pockets."

"My pockets? Why?"

"You just have to." The girl looked weary. "I can make you. I'd rather not. Please just turn them out, put whatever there is on the bed."

Eveline rolled her eyes. "What do they think I've got in there? All right, here." She unwrapped the plain black shawl and shook it out, showed the girl both sides of it with a flourish, like a magician. Then she turned the pocket of her apron inside out, dislodging two handkerchiefs, one very grimy and one clean and unused, and a comb with two teeth missing.

"All right, you can put them back." She was out of the door, locking it behind her, without another word.

Eveline used the pot with a groan of relief, then sat on the bed. The room felt chilly. She tucked her hands into her sleeves and waited.

Eventually there was a noise at the door. The girl opened it a bare few inches and thrust a thick, slightly burnt pasty through the gap. "Here. Please don't leave any crumbs."

"Don't worry," Eveline said, "I never left food uneaten in me life." She grinned at the girl, who looked away, shut the door, and locked it.

"Seems like you're my only friend," Eveline said to the pasty. "Cheers." She tucked in. It was dry, and there was more potato than meat, but it was food. She sucked the last blackened crumb from her fingers, and coughed. And coughed. And began to gag and wheeze as the crumb lodged in her windpipe. She was locked in this room, on her own, choking. She grabbed the ewer. An inch of cold, dusty water lay in the bottom. She tilted the jug and gulped at it, and finally, the crumb dislodged. She collapsed back on the bed, her mouth full of the taste of dust.

No-one had come, no-one was knocking on the door. She could have died and no-one would know.

The walls seemed to press in on her. She'd never had a room to herself in her life. This wasn't a bedroom, this was a prison. No; even in prison there were other people. This was a coffin.

Without taking off anything except her boots, Eveline huddled into bed, blew out the candle, and tucked her cold hands under her arms. Bloody hell, it was quiet. She couldn't hear so much as a mouse in the wall. Maybe they were scared of Miss Cairngrim.

In the rookeries of Limehouse there were always people coming and going, yelling and singing and fighting and having at each other in a thousand ways; the roar of the factories and the clamour of the docks; the great deep howling whoops of the big ships' horns and the little piping cries of the smaller ships' whistles; the rattle of wheels and clatter of hooves, the pulsing hum of the zeppelins passing overhead. Even as a child the country nights she'd known had been full of the sound of small life and wandering breezes and sometimes the songs of the Folk, faint and far.

The silence pressed on her ears, making her too aware of her own heartbeat. Well, that she could do something about. Grinning to herself in the dark, she extracted Mr Holmforth's watch from one of her hidden pockets and tucked it under her ear. It ticked happily to itself, soothing her down into sleep.

London

Holmforth kept a small, chilly set of lodgings near the Athenaeum. As he prepared for bed, his mind returned to the Duchen girl. He had rushed things, but if she had got on the train with the clergyman, he might have lost her, and tracking her down, confirming her identity, had taken so long. Fortunately the clergyman had not been inclined to make a nuisance of himself.

She might be worthless, of course. But she was oddly intriguing. He had found himself almost trying to *persuade* her, instead of simply telling her what was going to happen, as though she were a wild animal he was trying to coax to his hand.

He spent several minutes looking for his watch before he realised what must have happened to it, and shook his head, exasperated. Obviously she could not resist the temptation to steal, even from someone who was offering her so much more than a mere watch! But she did not seem stupid. It must, surely, be mere ingrained habit. Given discipline and training, she might be able to overcome her years on the streets. She came, after all, of respectable stock.

But he must not lose sight of the purpose of all this. Wu Jisheng's mechanism, and its possibilities... that was all that really mattered.

He only hoped the girl could be brought up to scratch.

The Britannia School

EVELINE WOKE EARLY and sat on the bed, waiting for the door to be unlocked. She had neatened up as best she could. She bounced one of her hairpins thoughtfully in her hand, looking at the door. But though she might manage this lock, the one on the outer door had looked a deal heavier, and besides, she'd rather find out more about this place before she took such a risk. Last night, when she'd been choking, she'd been far too panicked even to think of picking the lock. She put the hairpin back in one of her secret pockets. Then she sat, and she waited. There was still no sound to be heard until footsteps approached her door.

It was Smythe, with her arms full of clothes. "You're to put these on and come to breakfast," she said. "Have you washed?"

"No water," Eveline said. "Not enough to wash in, anyroad."

"Oh!" For the first time, the girl looked at her. "I'm sorry," she said.

Eveline shrugged. "I've gone without washing before. More'n once."

"It's important here. Miss Cairngrim... she likes things a certain way." There was a carefulness around the way she said *Miss Cairngrim,* as though the woman might be listening. "Get dressed."

Eveline pulled on the school clothes over her shift and put on the pair of sturdy boots. Proper boots! And they fitted! She wiggled her toes gleefully. "How'd you get the size right?"

"Practice. Come with me now."

Silently they hurried down chilly, echoing corridors until Smythe pushed open a pair of double doors.

They were met with the smell of food, the low murmur of conversation and the subdued *clink* of forks, faltering to a stop.

Two long tables ran down the room. They were lined with young women in identical, dark brown dresses with paler brown aprons on top. At the head of one was a thin, elderly man; at the other a small woman with tight black curls.

Some of the girls were looking at Eveline. The old man rapped on the table with the handle of his knife, twice, sharply, and they looked back at their plates.

Staring's foolish, staring stinks, staring gets you thrown in clink... Eveline thought, halfway between amusement and apprehension. She wondered what staring got you here.

The room was tall and long and chilly. The walls were painted a pallid streaky green, their tops bordered with once-fancy mouldings of winged Folk holding up strings of flowers, now chipped and blurring. From one of the two elaborate plaster roses on the ceiling hung a chandelier with half its crystals missing, and from the other a cheap, ugly iron lamp.

A vast black marble fireplace occupied much of one wall. Eveline could have stood in it, with room to spare. Huge curling pillars held up a mantelpiece on which she and several friends could have sat. It was the sort of fireplace that should have roaring flames, a boar turning on a spit, and its mantel covered with photographs in heavy silver frames and mementoes of the Grand Tour.

A mean basket-grate holding two small, dusty logs stood in the echoing space, and on the mantel were three dented brass candlesticks, none of which matched.

"Over here," Smythe said, pointing to a table by itself, in the corner.

"They afraid I've got lice?" Evvie said. "Because I been doused with Persian Flower powder, regular." Ma Pether had a horror of lice.

"You're to sit here. Don't speak to anyone except the staff, and only if they speak to you."

She scurried off.

Eveline looked over the other girls. The oldest was maybe twenty, the youngest about her own age.

The uniform clothes made them look like workhouse girls. An older girl with soft brown hair tied back in a net and a warm, pleasant face gave her an encouraging smile, then quickly looked back down at her plate. Another, fair as a primrose with blonde ringlets, pursed her pink mouth and rolled her eyes as though Eveline were something unfortunate that had just landed on the floor.

No-one else looked at her, not even the staff.

A harassed looking girl appeared with a tray. Without speaking, she slapped a bowl of porridge, a spoon, a slice of bread, and a mug in front of Eveline. When Eveline opened her mouth to say thank you, the girl caught her eye and gave a tiny headshake.

Eveline had been in enough situations where silence was essential that she didn't have to be told twice. She mouthed *thank you* instead.

The girl gave her a nod and rushed off. Eveline watched her go.

She was dressed like the others, except her apron was white instead of brown. She was slight, and her skin had the tan of a country girl. Her movements were neat and quick. She had attempted to confine her curly, light brown hair in a bun, but it escaped in clock spring coils about her temples and against her neck.

Eveline couldn't quite work out if she was a maid or one of the pupils. Dismissing the question for the moment, she examined the mug.

Tea! Proper, hot tea. There was even a little milk in it, the way she liked it (Liu would have wrinkled his nose). Eveline wrapped her chilled hands around the thick, chipped china mug and inhaled fragrant steam. This place wasn't so bad, if they got tea with breakfast.

She sipped it gratefully, then applied herself to her porridge.

It was hot, and filling. Had she been used to a more elaborate diet, Eveline might have been bothered by the fact that the thinnest of skimmed milk had been used in its making and neither sugar nor salt had been anywhere near it, but to her it was as good as breakfast got unless there was sausage to be had. The bread was coarse and stale, but it was bread and she'd had worse.

She ate fast, but neatly. Street child she might be, but her mama had taught her manners and she could use 'em when she had to. As soon as she had finished, she looked about to see if any more food were forthcoming, but it seemed not. The clock struck eight, the elderly man rapped his knife on the table again, and everyone stood up. Eveline, thinking it wise, did the same. The girl who had served her darted out of the door that presumably led to the kitchens, surreptitiously wiping her mouth and trying to tuck a wayward curl behind her ear.

Smythe beckoned her over. "Assembly," she said.

"What's..."

"Shhh. Just follow me and do what everyone else does."

The two staff left the room, and the girls followed, still silent.

They walked along yet another corridor, this one with windows on the left. Eveline glanced out as they passed. A square of lawn, sparkling with dew in the sunlight; a couple of stone benches. Outbuildings, stables, someone leading a horse. In the distance, trees.

Then they were turning away from the bright morning into another cold room.

Light fell through a leaded window, showing a constipated-looking saint in a white robe, with a yellow halo propped behind his head, holding up his hand over a square-lamb standing in a field of pallid green. Sunlight falling through the scene patched rows of pews with pale colour. At one end was a pulpit.

Church? Eveline had vague memories of church. Cold and boring, for the most part. This must have been the family chapel of whoever once lived here. It smelled faintly of mice and more powerfully of damp.

She shuffled into a pew next to the tall girl.

The door opened with a groan to reveal Miss Cairngrim, looking no more at ease for a night's sleep.

"Good morning, girls."

"Good morning, Miss Cairngrim."

Miss Cairngrim held a thick notebook in one hand, with a coarse dark-blue cover. In the other she held a fountain pen. As she swept past the end of Eveline's pew, Eveline caught a whiff of that strange harsh scent again, and with it, unbidden, the memory of the scullery at her parents' house popped into her head – her mother, in the midst of instructing the new maid, pausing with her hands full of pillowcases and the faraway look in her eye with which Eveline was already well familiar.

Her mother's laundry soap. That was what Miss Cairngrim smelled of. The great yellow bars of the stuff that had stood by the sink, ready to scrub everything as clean as it could be.

Miss Cairngrim climbed into the pulpit, propped the notebook on the stand where in a church a Bible would go, and swept her chilly stare over the assembled girls. She focused briefly on Eveline, who felt herself pinned. She was tempted to stare back, but dropped her gaze, trying to look humble and compliant.

"You are here," Miss Cairngrim said, her voice echoing into the roof, "as servants of the Empire. That is your function. To drive forward the vision of Britannia, to bring light to darkness and order to chaos.

"Your worth, your *only* worth, is in what you can do for the Empire. Without it, you are nothing; no better than those heathens who still crawl in their own filth in the places in which our Empire has yet to shine its glorious light.

"Never forget this. Whatever your past, whoever your family, however talented or special you may believe yourselves to be, you are now tools to serve the Empire, without whose generosity you would be disgraced, impoverished, or dead."

Or if I was lucky, getting sausage and small-beer for breakfast and horsing about with the others, Eveline thought. What a lot of jaw! Empire this, Empire that. All she knew of Empire was that lots of people a long way away, without many clothes, thought the Queen was some sort of god. She'd never seen the Queen herself, except on coins. She looked stuffy.

"Now, the notes for this morning. The Bartitsu class has been moved to the Small Hall. Miss Clevely is unwell; those taking Russian classes will use the time for mending of personal linens and other practical tasks." She drilled them with a gimlet stare. "This is not an excuse for slacking or gossiping in corners.

"Beth Hastings is on kitchen duty for three more days for disobedience, inattention and tardiness. Smythe, bring the new one to my study after assembly. That completes this morning's notes. Dismissed. "

EVELINE KNOCKED.

"Enter."

A square of bright sunlight splashing through the parlour window succeeded only in making the parlour look scruffier than it had the night before. The green upholstery on the three chairs was faded, and torn in places. The sofa was not so much red as a dusty sort of remembrance of the colour. The china shepherd and shepherdess, with their rosily painted cheeks, looked hectic and tubercular, and every chip and crack was highly visible, as though the sun had come out for the sole purpose of pointing out each one.

The sunlight was no more kind to Miss Cairngrim. It dug deeper lines beside her mouth, and emphasised the shadows around her eyes and the papery, stretched look of her skin. Eveline realised she was very thin, her gown dragging from her shoulder bones. Only the Toby jug took on the sun and gave it back with a glow of colour; he had the grin of a man who had spent a good night with good company.

Eveline put her hands behind her back and stood waiting. She wondered if Ma had started worrying about her yet. She'd have some of the girls out looking in a day or so, just to make sure she hadn't been taken up by the law.

Had she, or not? She still wasn't sure. Was Her Majesty's Government the same as the law? Either way she was caught; partly, she had to admit, through her own curiosity. The best thing she could do now was keep her eyes and ears open and stay out of trouble until she had a better idea what was what.

"Mr Holmforth takes an especial interest in you," Miss Cairngrim said. Her nostrils flared, as though she had caught an unpleasant smell. "However, you need not expect any favours, petting or laxness as a result. Whether you can be dragged from the muck of the streets and turned from the despicable creature I see before me into a worthwhile tool of Empire is yet to be seen. Firm discipline, strict morality and unstinting application will be required. I shall be informing the rest of the staff that particular attention needs to be paid to these matters and that you are not to be trusted until we can be assured that every last scrap of vileness has been scrubbed from you. Do you understand?"

"Yes, Miss Cairngrim."

"A uniform will be issued to you. Then you will have your first lesson, studying the history of our empire with Mr Clancy, followed by Bartitsu with Miss Laperne, then Map-Reading and Navigation with Miss

Prayne. Lunch is at one. This is followed by languages. Mr Holmforth tells me he wishes you to be instructed in Cantonese. You will be instructed by Mr Wen Hsu. You will take French with Mr Duvalier, and Retention with Miss Fairfield. I don't suppose you have ever ridden a horse?"

"Not, so to speak, an actual horse. There was a pony, once." She hadn't thought of the pony in years. It belonged to a neighbour child, a nasty, pinching, sneaking sort of girl. Eveline had got on it when no-one was about, mainly to prove she could.

She had fallen off, and been bitten on the way down.

It hadn't stopped her trying again, bribing the pony with stolen apples and surreptitious soothings and pettings. Since she treated it rather better than its own mistress, it had learned to tolerate her, and she had finally succeeded in staying on and even persuaded it over some small jumps.

Doing so in full view of the neighbouring girl and her parents had been a mistake, of course.

"A pony?" Miss Cairngrim's gaze sharpened. "Your people had horses?"

"No, miss, it wasn't mine." And she'd been properly scolded, too. Had her parents had anything to do with it, she'd not have ended up a thief; but then, had they still been alive... Eveline gave herself a mental shake and tried to look attentive and eager.

"Hah." Miss Cairngrim nodded with a sort of grim satisfaction. "I didn't think so. Then we will have to start you at the most basic level. I suppose if you can stay on, it is as much as can be hoped for. You will also receive instruction in disguise and studying the special subject Mr Holmforth has arranged for you."

Eveline struggled to hide her excitement at the thought of disguise. She could do a little with Ma's collection of costumes and wigs, but to actually learn it... now *there* was something properly useful. As for whatever Holmforth was up to... "Miss Cairngrim? What is the special subject?"

"Some sort of mechanical studies. I think it ridiculous to encourage such nonsense, but of course, it is not my place to say so."

"Mechanical studies?" What the hell had made Holmforth think she had an 'aptitude' for mechanisms? She might be interested in the stuff Ma Pether was always messing with, but Eveline had no more idea how they worked than she did of how a bird flew. Had he seen all the stuff Ma kept and somehow thought it was hers?

Her brain raced to deal with this. It meant Holmforth didn't know everything, which was good – but it also meant his only reason for interest in her, and for keeping her out of irons, didn't exist.

So she'd better develop some aptitude, and fast, if she planned to stay here.

The old man's pointer hit the map with a *thwack*. Eveline no longer jumped; she just kept an eye on where the pointer was aimed, since it was as likely to be employed on the nearest pupil as it was on the map.

Mr Clancy turned out to be the man she had seen at breakfast, glaring everyone into cowed silence. The instant dislike she had taken to him proved completely inadequate.

"Thoroughgood! What is the current position of Baluchistan?"

Thwack.

"Lovett! When did Bombay become a Presidency and what does that mean for good government?"

Thwack.

"New girl!" *Thwack,* the pointer hit her desk, sending chalk-dust and splinters into the air. *Thwack,* it hit the map. "What is this country here?"

Eveline stared, desperately trying to dredge up her memories of lessons. "France?" she said.

"Spain." *Thwack,* the pointer smacked against her upper arm. "Take this..." He hauled a vast leather-covered book from a shelf and dropped it in front of her with a *bang.* Dust puffed up, making her cough.

Thwack, on the back of her hand, leaving a burning sting. "Cover your mouth, you disgusting creature. This is an atlas. Have you heard of an atlas?"

"Yes."

Thwack, on the upper arm this time since she had dropped her hands to her lap, cradling the hurt one in the other. "You will address me as *sir*," he said. He opened the book and slapped the pointer onto the page, which showed a version of the same map that adorned the wall. "By your next lesson, in two days' time, you will have learned basic manners and the names of all the countries marked in pink, their position, and their most important contributions to the Empire. If, that is, you can read. Can you read?"

"Yes. Sir."

"That is a relief. Now concentrate and do not disturb the other pupils."

"Yes, sir," Eveline said, meekly, mentally calling him every filthy name she could come up with and some she had just invented. If this was education, she thought, glaring at the many, many countries coloured pink and the tiny print that swarmed over the pages like frantic ants, she could do without it.

But it was a *book*. And she'd seen so few proper books in the last few years. Although she'd rather have one with stories in it than this, with its stupid countries she'd never heard of and the world squashed out flat in big circles, as though it was all stamped on a pair of giant coins.

There was England, a funny-shaped little squiggle a little like a dog sitting up to beg. Somehow it was much smaller than she had thought – on this map, she couldn't even see London, never mind Limehouse. How much of England did London cover? She moved her finger across the map. *Madeira* – Madeira was a place? She thought it was a drink. She wondered if there were places called Gin and Beer... how odd. She tried to find China, where Liu came from. But though she could find the China Sea it lay between somewhere called Hainan, the Philippine Islands and North Borneo, none of which she had ever heard of. Then she pieced together the black letters marching boldly across the map. *CHINESE EMPIRE*, they said. She stretched her eyes, then looked back at England. The Chinese Empire was *huge*. And arching over a vast portion of the map, the Russian Empire was even bigger.

The British Empire wasn't even marked. But if all the countries in pink were the British Empire... that was strange, too. Why was the British Empire all about the place, when the Chinese and Russian ones were one big chunk each? She glanced up at the teacher. He was holding his pointer as though he couldn't wait to smack someone with it. She'd rather find out on her own. *Can you read,* indeed. She'd show him.

She studied the map until her eyes ached. So many strange names, so many countries in pink. The Cameroons sounded like something to eat. She was starting to get hungry again. But she'd spent most of her last few years hungry; she ignored it.

By the time the Bartitsu lesson started she had a head full of names, and felt as though they were all pushing at the sides of her skull, trying to get out.

Miss Laperne was the small woman with tight curls who had also been at breakfast. "Get into your gear and pair up. You, new girl, these are yours."

The 'gear' Eveline received proved to be a sort of high-necked, stiffened bodice with long padded sleeves and a pair of... "What are these things?" she said, holding them up.

"Pantaloons," one of the girls whispered. "Take your things off and put those on over your underwear."

"But they *are* underwear! What sort of lesson needs underwear?" Eveline backed into a corner, staring, holding the absurd garment up in front of her. "If we're getting taught whoring, I ain't doing it."

Someone yelped with laughter and several girls stopped in the middle of changing and looked at her, wide-eyed, one leg in and one leg out, or an arm halfway down a sleeve.

"Well!" the blonde girl said, shaking her curls out of the collar of the bodice. "*Somebody* was brought up in a pigsty."

"Didn't think *respectable* girls knew what such a word meant," Eveline said.

The blonde girl flushed and fixed Eveline with a glare that should have pinned her like a butterfly.

"I'm afraid I'm going to have to inform Miss

Cairngrim," the blonde girl said. "She doesn't permit *language*."

Eveline opened her mouth to say something about how funny it was that the blonde girl was able to talk, then, and thought better of it. She was going to be in for a slapping as it was.

The other girls returned to dressing, buttoning the pantaloons and stepping into flat boots that laced up the front. Reluctantly, Eveline put on the pantaloons and pulled on the boots.

They fitted. *Two* pairs of footwear – the button boots she'd been issued with her gown and apron, and these. And both fitted. She'd not owned a pair of shoes that fitted for as long as she could remember, never mind *two* pairs. Everything else forgotten for the moment, she vowed that whatever happened, she was keeping them.

The bodice, even laced as tight as she could get it, was too loose on her. She wondered if it had been made for someone else. She shuffled into the room after the other girls. At least they all looked as absurd as each other.

"You, new girl, what is your name?" Miss Laperne said.

"Eveline Duchen, miss."

"Have you heard of Bartitsu?"

"No, miss."

"Good," she said. "Then you will have no misconceptions. There are those who consider it inappropriate, or unpleasant, that young women should be taught to fight. You, however, are to be trained servants of the Empire and as such, you will be valuable assets, not to be thrown away because you lacked even the most basic ability to defend yourselves. If you have any objection to being taught to fight, endeavour to rid yourself of it."

"I got no objection, miss." Fighting was fine. Fighting she'd done plenty of, one way and another.

"Have you ever been in a situation where you had to defend yourself?"

"Yes, miss."

The blonde girl gave a quiet snort of derision, which Miss Laperne did not appear to hear.

"Tell me what happened," Miss Laperne said.

"There was quite a lot of times, miss."

"Excellent. Describe one."

Feeling inclined to take the blonde girl down a peg, Eveline described a fight with a man who had made a grab for her outside a pub in Clerkenwell. "I kneed him in the... the trousers, miss. Went down like a felled tree."

"Can you show me how he approached you?"

"He just reached out and grabbed me, miss." Eveline held her arms out.

"From in front?"

"Yes, miss."

"Stand there." The woman moved behind her.

The hairs on the back of Eveline's neck shivered, and she almost got away, but the next thing she knew she was flat on her face on the floor, with Miss Laperne's knee in her back.

"Unfortunately," Miss Laperne said, her voice absolutely calm, "one's opponent does not always approach in so convenient a fashion. Nor will they always be vulnerable at the groin, especially if they have the least idea of what they are doing." The blonde girl giggled; again, Miss Laperne appeared not to notice. She got up. Eveline breathed floor-dust. She wasn't hurt, but she was humiliated and startled.

"You may stand up, Duchen. Now, I will show you some basic methods for dealing with someone approaching from behind. The rest of you, practise your grapples, as I showed you last week. Oh, and Treadwell?"

"Yes, miss?" said the blonde girl.

"The equipment cupboard is a disgrace. Restore it to order, if you please."

Treadwell gave Eveline a glare as she passed, keeping it carefully out of Miss Laperne's sightline. Eveline pretended not to see, and wiped dust from her face.

BY THE END of the lesson Eveline was panting, sore, and filthy. Miss Laperne looked her over, and gave a single, brisk nod. "You are small, and like many of the class, must rely on quickness where others can use weight. However. Girls? Your attention, please."

They lined up. Eveline was pleased to see that they all looked as dirty and sweat-streaked as she felt. Miss Laperne said, "Duchen here has learned a lesson that I endeavour to teach you over and over again and which some of you still have not embraced. What is the first thing you should do in any fight?"

A few hands were raised.

"Yes, Calendar?"

"Disable your opponent, miss?"

"No. Hastings?"

Hastings proved to be the girl with the curly brown hair who had served Eveline's breakfast. On closer expression she had a determined nose, grey eyes and a slightly distracted air; she jumped when addressed as though she had forgotten why her hand was up.

"Oh! Try not to be there, miss."

"Correct." Miss Laperne looked around at her class. "I do not know, nor have I any interest in, your individual histories. But it is obvious that Miss Duchen's life has taught her something of value. You would do well to follow her example in this. The most important thing in a fight is to try and prevent it from happening in the first place, or at least, prevent it from happening to *you*. Fight only if you cannot run.

"Tomorrow we will be covering the use of the parasol. And why will we be using parasols?"

Another girl put her hand up. "Because they won't let us have guns, miss?"

"No. Anyone else? No? Parasols are something that ladies may carry, indeed are *expected* to carry. Less useful than a cane or swordstick, but still of worth. Remember this, girls – always adapt, always be alert. There will almost always be something in your immediate vicinity that you can use as a weapon if you have to.

"Those of you who wish to practise with the parasol may take one from the cupboard, but work outside, please. A sufficient number of innocent lampshades have already been sacrificed."

There were a few subdued giggles.

"Now go wash before your next lesson. Dismissed."

Eveline splashed her dusty face with almost equally dusty water – as the new girl she had last go at the basin. Damn, she hurt; skinny as she was, she bruised easy. She'd be as colourful as a rag-rug by tomorrow.

It had been so busy she had hardly thought of leaving. When would Holmforth come back? And what would he say when he did? His watch lay safely tucked in one of the secret pockets in her drawers. At least she'd been allowed to keep her own underwear – though given needle, thread and a couple of handkerchiefs, she could make near-undetectable pockets in almost anything. Not to mention false arms that could lie innocently folded in the lap while hands delved about elsewhere. She wondered what Miss Cairngrim would think of 'mending time' being used for such purposes.

MISS PRAYNE, WHO taught Map-Reading and Navigation, had the look of something left too long in the sun. Her eyes, hair, skin and gown all appeared to be fading towards the same dull snuff-colour. She delivered her lesson in a drifting monotone, and when her pupils' attention inevitably wandered, employed not the cane that lay on her desk but a put-upon sigh which made Eveline feel both guilty and intensely irritated.

Eveline already had a headful of maps and country names and looked at the work in front of her with a sense of mounting dread. Why did she need to know all this? Would they expect her to go somewhere? On a ship? She only knew one thing about ships. They sank.

And as for Navigation... the words *latitude*, *longitude*, *celestial*, and *sextant* flew past her ears. "Hand in your work from last week." What work? She hadn't been here last week. She stared at maps and charts in a state of increasing, furious frustration. She was used to being *good* at things. Ever since she'd joined up with Ma, she'd been Ma's star pupil. Now she was faced with descriptions of things she'd never heard of, and as for stars, she'd barely seen them since she came to London. The constant smog made the sky one roiling smear that even the sun struggled to pierce. Luckily the daft bitch seldom asked questions – she simply pointed at things and told them, in her die-away voice, what page to look at. In fact, Miss Prayne seemed entirely unaware that she had acquired an extra pupil, although someone had provided Eveline's battered, splintery desk with a slate and chalk.

Not that she had anything to write on it. Feeling as though her head were coming to the boil, Eveline sat back, trying to get some air, or space.

It was quiet, except for the squeaking of chalk on slates and the occasional cough or sigh. She looked around at the collection of bent heads. Some of the girls had made some effort with their hair, others had done the bare minimum, but all were neat with the exception of Hastings, who was muttering and pushing her fingers through her hair so that her curls fell out of their bun and around her face. Then, to Eveline's amusement, she became exasperated, twisted them up out of the way and stuck a pencil in to hold them in place. *Bet Miss Grim won't like that.* She had a strong feeling pencils in the hair were not something Miss Cairngrim would find acceptable.

She looked around for another source of entertainment, or information, or anything at all. The maps on the wall were all at least five years old; the books too were old, stained here and there with tea and other, unknown substances.

The windows were sash ones – one or two open a few inches at the bottom, and easy enough to get out of, if they hadn't been barred on the outside. Air in, no-one out.

Miss Prayne's monotone seemed to coat her eyelids, weighing them down. Her head drooped.

A sudden scuffling all around her and the squeak of chair legs on the floor roused her to the realisation that the class was over. She closed her book with a thud, feeling no better off than when she'd started.

She followed the rest of the girls back towards the room where they'd had breakfast. She had a good idea of the layout by now, at least of the ground floor. There wasn't a window she'd seen that didn't have bars.

This time it seemed she was to be permitted to eat with the rest of them. Miss Prayne sat at the head of one table; at the other was a slight man with a head that seemed too large for the sparse amount of oiled black hair scraped across it.

An unoccupied chair stood near him. Treadwell sat opposite. The blonde girl seemed subdued, her gaze fixed on the table.

Eveline sat herself down. The teacher gave her a nod, and a small smile. He was the first of the staff to smile at her. She gave him a cautious half-smile back, in case Miss Cairngrim had a thing about excessive smiling.

Lunch was watery stew whose main ingredient seemed to be cabbage, with elderly bread to sop it up. So far as Eveline was concerned, it was a feast. Ravenous as always, she had eaten more than half before she became aware that there was something going on across from her.

Treadwell was pushing her fork through the food, but so far as Eveline could tell not a morsel of it had left the plate. She was sitting oddly hunched, and the hands holding her cutlery were gripping it white-knuckled. She stared down at her plate as though she expected to find something in the mush of greyish gravy and pallid green leaves and stray fibres of mud-coloured meat.

The teacher turned to Eveline. "You are the new girl," he said. "I am Monsieur Duvalier. I will be teaching you French. Your name is?"

He didn't *sound* like a Frenchy to Eveline, just posh English, but for all she knew posh French people and posh English people sounded the same when they spoke English. The only Frenchies *she* knew were sailors, the onion-man and Bon-Bon.

"Eveline Duchen," she said.

"You should address me as *monsieur*, but you are new, and have probably not heard the word before. It means the same as *sir*, you understand?"

"Yes, monsieur," she said, doing her best to say it the way he did.

"Duchen? That sounds as though it might have been a French name. Did you know that names change over the years? Your great-grandfather, perhaps, was Du Chien."

"Oh," Eveline said. "How... interesting. Monsieur."

"Shall I tell you what that means? Or perhaps Mademoiselle Treadwell can tell you? Mademoiselle?"

Treadwell shot Eveline a glance she couldn't read. "It means something to do with dogs," she said. "*Chien* is dog."

"Indeed. Du Chien is of, or pertaining to, the dog. It is possible your ancestors were the lord's kennellers, or some such thing – the men who trained his lordship's dogs for the hunt." He gave Treadwell a reproving glance. "Dogs are useful and necessary beasts, you know."

"Yes, monsieur," Treadwell muttered.

Eveline wondered if Duvalier actually thought he was being helpful. She glanced at her plate, where the remains of her stew was cooling, hoping he would shut up jawing long enough for her to finish it before Hastings whisked it away, as she was already doing with empty plates at the other table.

Duvalier lifted a forkful of stew, and sighed. "Ah, English cuisine. Well, it is only to be expected. If you are very good in class, and work hard, Mademoiselle Duchen, there may be bon-bons for you, to take away the taste."

"Yes, monsieur," Eveline said, briefly imagining a line of Bon-Bons, dancing away, grinning gap-toothed grins and swigging gin. Hiding her smile, she hastily scooped up the rest of her stew.

AFTER LUNCH, THE French lesson proved somewhat easier than Navigation. Her time around the docks had given her a smattering of half-a-dozen languages, and not all the words she'd learned were rude, though a good many of them were. For the first time she realised how a word that meant almost the same thing in another language could help you pick up the sense of a phrase.

Duvalier was pleased with her and did, indeed, give her a bon-bon – which proved to be a piece of pink marzipan, from a box tied up with green satin ribbon. When she took it, she caught Treadwell giving her that look again – an odd mix of resentment and a sort of sly satisfaction.

Marzipan and pleasure at her own cleverness aside, Eveline didn't particularly enjoy the lesson. Duvalier would *pet* her so, smoothing her hair as though she really were a dog, or squeezing her arm, whenever she pleased him. She was still bruised from Bartitsu and Mr Clancy's stick, and it hurt. And she just didn't *like* it.

By the time it came to the last lesson, Retention, Eveline was tired in a way that was completely unfamiliar, wide awake but distracted, her brain pulsing and buzzing with information. She didn't think she'd be able to fit a single other thing in there.

Which proved to be the entire point of Retention. Miss Fairfield was a large, brisk woman with black hair so very thick and shiny and tightly wedged in its bun it looked as though it was all of a piece, like a hat. Eveline wondered whether she took it off at night. "Memory!" she snapped. "Memory, girls, is your greatest treasure, and your most useful ally. Nothing you learn here, not one word or chart or position of a star, not the name of an ally nor the location of an army, is of the slightest use unless you can *retain* it. Who can recite the Four Principles of Retention for our new girl?"

This time a number of hands shot up.

"It should be all of you, come on! Recitation..."

"Recitation, Repetition, Association, Imagination!" the class shouted.

"Good!"

And away they went into memorizing lists of names and objects on a tray and a number of other things for which Eveline struggled to imagine the slightest use.

She just about managed to keep her eyes open during a supper of cold fat bacon and bread and dripping. Afterwards the girls gathered in another echoing, high-ceilinged room with peeling paint, a battered assortment of uncomfortable chairs, and an inadequate fire muttering to itself in the grate. Here, they did mending or schoolwork under the half-hearted supervision of Miss Prayne, who was absently tatting some lace, in the same faded snuff-colour as everything else about her, in between bouts of staring out of the window at the darkening evening, and sighing.

Eveline got the woman's attention long enough to supply herself with needle, thread, and scraps of cloth. She tucked them away in her apron pocket; she wasn't going to go putting secret pockets in her uniform with the others watching. Instead she opened the great atlas she'd been lugging about since this morning's lesson, and stared at maps.

She only realised she'd fallen asleep when someone nudged her foot. She jerked awake to see that Hastings had taken the chair next to her. She smelled faintly of bacon and still had a pencil in her hair. She nodded at Eveline and opened a large book with a blue cloth cover, full of drawings, and a small battered notebook.

Eveline stared, fascinated, at the drawings. Wheels and levers and cogs and things she had no name for. Tiny precise labels saying *fig 1* and *ratchet assembly*. They reminded her of her mother's workbooks.

Hastings dug around in her apron pocket and looked exasperated. She leaned close and whispered, "Do you have a pencil spare?"

"You've got one," Eveline whispered back. "It's on yer head."

Hastings' hands flew to her hair and she whipped out the pencil, sending her curls tumbling. "Thank you."

"*Some* people are trying to *work*, miss," Treadwell said loudly. "And *other* people are *chattering*."

"Quiet down, girls," Miss Prayne said.

Hastings rolled her eyes at Eveline, who grimaced back.

A few moments later, she felt something nudge her hand and realised Hastings had turned her notebook towards her. Written there in tiny, precise letters she saw, *My name's Beth Hastings. I saw you looking at my notes. Do you like machines? I like machines.*

Glancing around to make sure no-one was watching, Eveline scrawled, *Eveline Duchen. I like* – she hesitated – *games. Card tricks and such. My mama liked machines, but hers weren't like the ones in your book. How did you get here?*

She realised Treadwell was eyeing them and gave her a cool stare, then looked back at her atlas as though it occupied all her attention. When she could see, out the corner of her eye, that Treadwell was no longer watching, she slid the notebook back to Hastings.

Some time later it reappeared. *You're to learn about mechanism. I'll see you in lessons.*

That night Eveline lay in a bed in a long room lined with beds, listening to the shuffles and sighs of the other girls. Tired as she was, her brain was still whirling too fast to let her sleep.

Her life had changed again, big and sudden. Did everyone have lives like this, suddenly swinging from one thing to another like a conker on a string?

Margate

FIRST THERE HAD been the place she still, in weak moments, thought of as home: the cosy little redbrick house in Margate, with the sea before and the woods behind and Mama and Papa and Eveline and, later, Charlotte, safe as rabbits in a burrow. Mama with her instruments and Papa with his books and fossils and Eveline with her family and the Folk, and especially Aiden. Aiden who was her best friend, who had first appeared when she wandered away from Mama and found a pretty, plump boy the same age as herself, laughing and surrounded by little Folk. He had smiled at her and taken her hand and the little brightly coloured flying Folk had spun and danced about their heads. When Mama had come looking for her, he had disappeared; but after that, she saw him often.

He would appear sitting on a branch above her head, swinging his legs, and drop down beside her light as a leaf, making not a sound. He was light and swift as a squirrel in the trees, and liked to tease the naiads, pulling leaves from their branches while they scolded in their silvery whispering voices. He would coax her away from the house with promises of secrets, and he always kept them. Aiden was one of the Higher Folk, a son of the Court.

He showed her the houses of the goblins down among the moss, and the den where the fox laid up with her cubs, bringing them out to play at dusk. He made her crowns of leaves and berries and put them on her head and hung necklaces of dew and cobwebs around her neck. She had no gifts to give him in return but a crust of fresh bread stolen from the kitchen, which he liked; when she brought him some he would tear into it eager as a puppy.

Between her sixth and seventh year they spent hours together in the woods and fields and along the shore, though Mama would come and search for her if she was out too long, calling her in to eat or do her lessons.

She asked him to take her to see his house, but he always shook his head. "Maybe later," he said. "And you can't go without me, you can't cross into the Crepuscular without permission."

"Why not?"

"You just can't. If you try, something will happen to you."

"Like what?"

But he had gone. He often disappeared when she talked about something he didn't like, and most of the time she had no idea what she had said wrong. It was better, in the end, to let him do most of the talking.

One day Aiden took her down to the shore at dusk and made her sit on a rock while he called a strange sweet cry across the water, and there was a glittering stir in the waves and out of them rose the heads and shoulders of three of the merfolk. Eveline had caught glimpses of them, but never so close. Their hair was green-gold and their eyes were silver and they had strange long ears, not pointed like Aidan's but ribbed like a parasol. He called to them again and they laughed, and began to sing.

Eveline listened in a wild dream of wind and water and shifting blue light, until the tide came up and wet her boots. She woke to cold feet and a wet bum and the splash of the merfolk disappearing. Aiden had gone and the sun was dipping below the waves.

She wandered home still half in the dream. Papa came striding out and took her arm roughly. "Eveline, we thought you'd got lost! You know to be home before this. And look at the state you're in. Your good boots, all soaked! You're a careless girl, and this is no time for your mother to be upset."

"I'm sorry, Papa, but Aiden..."

"Yes, well, I think we need a little talk about Aiden."

Mama was cross, and tugged her boots off roughly, and Eveline cried because Mama was upset.

"Oh, my poppet, I didn't mean to make you cry. Come, come, don't fret, there. Mama was only cross because she worries about you."

She took Eveline on her lap – with a little difficulty, as her belly was getting big with the coming baby – and glanced at Papa, and said, "I want you to spend more time with people, darling, and less with the Folk."

"Do you mean Aiden? I like Aiden, he's my friend."

"I know you think so, but the Folk aren't like us, my pet, especially the Higher. They see the world differently. I'm not saying he's bad, or anything like that, you understand? But if the tide had come in, and you'd not woken from the dream the merfolk sang you, well, Aiden might not have realised you were in danger. He's not like you, you see. Things that can hurt you can't hurt him. Besides... oh, you're very young, I know, and not thinking of such things, but... Folk are Folk and people are people. I don't want your heart broken. And if he ever asks you to go home with him, you're not to."

"Aiden wouldn't hurt me, Mama."

"He might not mean to, sweetheart. But he might not be able to help it."

"Emma Povey didn't know any Folk, and her mama said she had her heart broken."

Papa coughed into his hand and he and Mama exchanged glances.

"Oh, my dear, people can break your heart too." Mama hugged her so hard Eveline was barely able to breathe. "I wish I could save you from everything bad, my dove. I do. But I can't. All I can do is give you advice."

Eveline tried to be good, and come home early and do her lessons and help the maid as Mama got slower and heavier.

And Aiden was about less and less.

Days would go by, then weeks, when she never saw him. Autumn, with all its fruit and colour and sweetness, ripened. The local landowner obtained a steam tractor which was a wonder and amazement, though very loud, but Aiden did not come to see and she wondered if he had forgotten her. Some days she wandered the woods and fields and shoreline, occasionally calling his name, but he did not come. She wondered if he'd heard Mama and Papa and was cross that they thought so badly of him, or if she herself had done something to offend him.

But Papa said that the Folk were retreating, withdrawing from their old ways. And Mama thought that perhaps it was the new farm machinery that they did not like, with its clatter. "Remember how they used to come to hear my instruments?" she said. "I never see them now."

Then one frost-crisped day as sweet as an apple, as Eveline clambered among the rocks along the tideline, Aiden appeared, so suddenly she slipped and almost fell in a pool and he caught her hand, laughing. "How clumsy you are!" he said.

"Aiden! I've been looking for you."

"Have you?"

"I thought you'd gone away."

"I had. Come with me, I've found the nixie's new pool where she takes her baby to wash him. You'll like him, he's very funny and makes such faces."

"Why did you go away for so long?"

"It wasn't long."

"It was to me."

"Silly Eveline." He took her hand and tugged her down from the rocks and into the forest. The nixie wasn't there, but he showed her a fallen tree-trunk that someone had hollowed out into tiny rooms and passages, and a dormouse tucked into a curl in a nest of grass, so thoroughly asleep that even when Aiden put him in her hand, he didn't wake. She held the tiny thing, feeling its warmth and the strange sleeping life in it, then tucked it back into its nest. "Aiden?"

"Yes?"

"Mama says..."

Aiden was playing with something in his hands, tossing it from one to the other. It glittered. "What?"

"It doesn't matter. Would you like to see the new tractor? I know where they keep it."

"Not at all. Why must you make such noisy things?"

"I don't know," Eveline said.

"You're sad I went away. Don't be sad, Eveline. Hold out your hand." He dropped the glittering thing onto her palm, hard and cold after the soft breathing warmth of the dormouse. It was a crystal, a milky ghost-coloured thing, hung on a thin silver chain. "This is for you." He stroked her hair. "I'll always come if you really want me, you know."

"It's so pretty."

"So are you," he said. "My pretty Eveline. Put it on." She did, and he nodded. "Don't fret if I'm gone awhile." And in that moment he was gone, only a swirl of red and gold leaves to show he had ever been there. Eveline smiled and walked towards home, still smiling.

"Don't you know respectable ladies don't go into the forest?" said a voice.

Eveline turned around. Peering at her over a neat hedge were a pair of wide blue eyes: Theodora Veal, the vicar's daughter. "The Folk are wicked," she said. "And don't know about Morality. Do you want to come to tea? I'll show you my dolls. Some of them are very expensive, they come from London."

"All right," Eveline said.

Theodora marched ahead of her into a hall overcrowded with small wobbly tables and umbrella stands (one brass and one, at which Eveline gazed with horrified fascination, which appeared to have toenails), and tugged the long velvet bell rope. A maid appeared, panting, through the green baize door at the end of the hall. "We want some tea," Theodora said. "Bring it to the nursery."

"Yes, miss," the maid said, and disappeared.

"What's that?" Eveline said.

"It's an elephant's foot. Don't you know anything?"

Eveline wanted to ask what an elephant was, but didn't want to admit to another thing she didn't know, so she followed Theodora's lacy skirts upstairs to the nursery.

It was the size of the main room in her parents' cottage, and full of fragile furniture and dolls with eyes as wide and blue and skirts as lacy as Theodora's own. The maid brought tea and they drank from tiny rose-painted cups, only big enough for a mouthful, but very pretty, and added milk from a matching jug, which Eveline wanted more than she had ever wanted anything, because it was so pretty and perfect and small.

"That's Marie and that's Lucy and that's Angeline – she's from France, she was extra specially expensive – and this is Miss Biddy, she's my favourite. Unless she does something naughty." Miss Biddy had pale curls and blue ribbons in them and a tiny pursed pink mouth not unlike Theodora's own. "You can touch her if you like."

"Her hair feels real!" Eveline said.

"Of *course* it's real. Proper dolls have real hair. Poor girls cut it off and sell it. My papa says it's a good thing, it prevents Vanity."

Eveline envied the dolls at first, but after a while she found them rather unpleasant. They stared so. Their flat blue eyes had lids that clicked when they opened or shut, and beneath the fine velvet and lace their bodies were oddly pulpy.

Theodora, too, seemed slightly ill-at-ease – she fussed with the dolls and teased their hair but except for Miss Biddy she didn't caress them or cuddle them the way Eveline did with her own battered doll. "At night they go in the trunk," she said, "except for Miss Biddy."

"Why?"

Theodora shrugged one shoulder pettishly. "They shouldn't be out. My mama said bad 'fluences will come in the window and make them misbehave if they're left about at night. I have to tell the maid ever so many times to put them away."

Eveline felt a moment of wonder at a maid who had time to put dolls away. Theirs only ever had time to do laundry and help Mama with the heaviest work.

Once all the dolls had been named and their dresses admired, there didn't seem to be much else to do. Theodora had lots of books but didn't like reading, because her mama said it promoted forehead wrinkles. She didn't seem to want Eveline to read them either, however. So they sat in silence drinking cooling tea until Theodora said it was time for her tea and Eveline, not ungratefully, went home.

"Did you make a friend, dear?" Mama said.

"I had tea with Theodora Veal."

Mama and Papa exchanged one of their looks, but Papa said, "Well, at least she's human. Probably." And Mama giggled, and the baby went *Bah!*

That was the last good day.

She was never sure what happened, except that Papa was walking to his work, and a herd of cows being driven to market panicked, and Papa couldn't get out of the way in time.

Eveline was looking out of her window when she heard the gate creak and saw the neighbours bringing Papa home on a trestle, his smart coat all torn and covered with mud and his face slack and grey. Mama had come to the door wiping oily hands on a rag, and had fallen to her knees in the mud by the step.

After that were days of confusion and weeping and kissing Papa's cold grey face before they put him in a box and took him away. They had to go to church and

Mama sat there pale and still as a wax candle that had gone out. They went home and Papa was not there.

There was the vicar who droned at them and his wife and a gaggle of women from the village. Eveline didn't like them. They took Charlotte out of her arms just when she had settled, and said they were "poor mites" and pinched her cheeks and called her pasty, and nodded at each other and said "no wonder" in meaningful tones when Mama was out of the room.

"There's a brother, isn't there? Perhaps he'll take her in hand," said a woman in a purple bonnet. "Those poor dear children!"

Eveline bristled. "We're not poor. My papa earned good money and Mama's work will, too. Papa said."

"You shouldn't interrupt your elders, child." The vicar stared down at her from under heavy brows. "Poor manners," he said, turning back to the women. "Of course, it was only to be expected, in such an *irregular* household. It seems the brother was unable to attend the funeral, but perhaps I should write to him and suggest that his sister would benefit from some... moral guidance. A firm hand."

"Come here, child," said Purple-Bonnet. "You have a smudge on your face." She caught Eveline in a firm grip and applied a heavily-scented handkerchief to her cheek. "Now, tell me" – she looked over her shoulder, then whispered – "is it true your mother sometimes worked at her mechanisms all night, and never made you supper or mended your clothes, and your papa did it all?"

Eveline pulled away. "Go away. I don't want you. I want my papa!"

"Well, really!" Purple-Bonnet humphed and shook

her finger at Eveline. "Your papa has gone with the angels, who are respectful to their elders and *never* naughty, and answer questions when people ask them. You would do well to follow their example!" She turned back to the vicar. "Quite the little fury. You had better write to the brother straight away, Reverend!"

"Your bonnet is crooked," Eveline shouted, and stormed out into the woods.

She sat yanking up handfuls of wet brittle grass, miserable and furious, mud soaking through her skirts.

"Hello, Eveline. What are you doing?"

"Hello Aiden." She had waited so long to see him, but now she didn't care. One thought filled her whole world. "My papa's dead."

"Oh."

"They say the angels took him. I don't want the rotten angels to have him! They can't have him! He's my papa, *I* want him!"

Aiden reached out and took her cold muddy hand, and stroked it. "I expect you do."

"Do you know angels? Will you tell them to give him back?"

He looked away from her. Later, she would realise it was the only time she ever saw him look... *embarrassed* was too strong a word. Thrown, perhaps; the self-confidence that ran through the Higher Folk like a vein of quartz through rock, for once disturbed. "Would you like to come and see...?"

"I don't want to see anything, Aiden, thank you."

"I can make you a vision of your papa," he said. "If you like."

"No!"

He looked at her, startled.

"No," she said, more quietly. "He's gone. It wouldn't be real."

"You're not wearing your crystal," he said.

She tugged up more grass between her fingers, and when she looked up, Aiden was gone.

GRADUALLY, THERE HAD been less food, and fewer fires, and then the maid had gone away.

Mama, trying to cheer them both, took Eveline to May Day at the village green. Eveline's dress was too small and faded around the seams where Mama had let it out, and her shoes pinched badly, but the sun was shining and the sound of laughter reached them on the path through the woods.

Lots of other children were there, and at the centre of an admiring crowd was Theodora Veal, tossing her glossy brown ringlets and laughing. Eveline ran towards the group, smiling. Theodora caught sight of her and said, "You can't be with us. My mama says I'm not to play with you."

Eveline stopped in her tracks, humiliation burning her cheeks.

"My mama says *your* mama is mad and should be put away. She says that's why you look like a gypsy child."

Eveline felt the bile rise in her throat, but no words would come. Theodora smugly stroked the pallid blonde curls of her favourite doll as she watched Eveline, her head slightly tilted, a smile on her pretty pink lips, like someone looking at a curious animal in the zoo. Her court gathered around her, tittering and staring.

A strange, fizzing sensation rose into Eveline's head,

not a plan, exactly, but the ghost of one, expanding outwards, driving words out of her mouth. "I'm not a gypsy child," Eveline said, "but there were some came through last month and they did a curse."

"They did no such thing."

"Oh, they did. But you wouldn't want to know about it. I expect *your* dolls are all right."

She turned and walked away, hatred and excitement burning together in her.

The vicarage was a huge rambling old house and often open for the dispensation of charity by the vicar's wife, who had brought her own money to an already substantial living, and enjoyed the chance to lecture the villagers on frugality and thrift from beneath a succession of fetching and expensive bonnets.

Eveline, a shawl about her head, sneaked past the dispirited queue to which the vicar's wife was dispensing pennies and homilies, her heart jumping in her throat like a trapped frog.

Theodora's room stood silent. Eveline crept to the toy box and opened the lid; the dolls lay like pretty corpses in their linen and lace.

EVELINE WAS SITTING on the back step of the house, dandling her own ancient doll on her knee, when Theodora came scurrying down the lane, red-eyed and white-faced.

"You have to tell my mother about those gypsies!"

"What gypsies?"

"The ones who put a curse on dolls! I told her that it was the gypsies and she doesn't believe me!"

"What happened?"

"They moved around! And they made a mess! And I don't like them any more!"

"Oh, dear," Eveline said. "I remember the gypsies said they made one of the dolls the leader. If that one was given away it couldn't tell the others what to do and then the curse would stop working. That's what they *said*. I have to go in now."

"But which one?"

"*I* don't know, *I'm* not a gypsy child," Eveline said. "But I 'spect it was the biggest and fanciest, don't you?"

She skipped up the steps, grinning to herself. And the next day she had a new doll, and Mrs Veal was going around the village saying how her daughter had given the poor Duchen girl her favourite doll out of pity, and didn't it do your heart good to see such charity in one so young.

But once she had the doll, Eveline didn't play with it much. Getting it had been more than fun enough.

Mama worked very hard, with her instruments, writing dozens of letters and sometimes leaving Eveline with one of the village women while she travelled to London or Bristol. Sometimes she cried.

"Mama?" Eveline said, watching one of the ball-bearings run down its track, *rhoum, rhoum*.

"Yes, sweetheart?"

"When you get paid, may I have some new shoes?"

"Oh, dear, are yours pinching already?"

"A bit."

"I'll have to see..." She sighed, and ran a hand over the rosewood casing of the mechanism. "I may have to sell some of these."

"Oh."

"No-one will listen to me, Eveline. I *know* that Etherics can work to help people. Like poor Miss Fremantle, remember her?"

"She drowned in the pond."

"That's right. Poor lady. Her mind was very troubled. I *know* she improved after I tried some of the new sounds on her, but her family thought it was witchcraft. I didn't dare carry on; I was afraid..." She looked at Charlotte sleeping in her cot. "Oh, never mind, dear, this isn't for you to worry about. We'll manage somehow."

A man took away some of the instruments, and Eveline had new shoes, but it was getting cold and there was no firewood. And Mama wrote another letter.

When the answer came Mama stared at it for a long time, then took Eveline onto her lap and told her they were going to live in Watford with Uncle James.

"Who's Uncle James?"

"He's my brother, Eveline. He's going to take us in. I..." She looked down at Charlotte snoozing on her lap, nothing visible but a small bump of nose among layers of wool, and sighed. "Never mind. Things will be different there. Uncle James isn't used to children, so you must be very quiet and good, and do as you're told. Will you do that for me?"

"Yes, Mama."

And they had left the little cottage that was home, and had gone to the town where Uncle James lived.

Watford

IT SEEMED TO Eveline almost unbearably noisy and crowded, an endless, shouting, roaring muddle of people and carriages and factories, roars and rattles and bangs. Trees stood at regimented intervals along the pavement – sad, bumpy, amputated things – and the houses were shoulder-to-shoulder like toy soldiers crammed in a box.

Uncle James's house was large and broad with great imposing windows that seemed to frown down on the passers-by. Its bricks were a shade between mustard and dried blood. Two grey stone lions sat bolt upright and snarling on the gateposts, each with one front paw resting on the upper rim of a blank shield. Dark laurel, with its hard, shiny leaves and bitter dusty bark, grew along the drive.

"I don't like it," Eveline declared, matching the house glare for glare.

"Be good, Eveline," Mama said. "We must be grateful to Uncle James for taking us in."

"I want to go home."

"This *is* home now, my poppet."

A SERVANT LET them in, and they stood in the high chilly entrance hall, which smelled of what Eveline later realised was Uncle James: his pomade, his expensive coats that were always a little too tight so that he sweated even more, his reeking, fussing, overpowering self.

He eventually emerged to greet them. His big red face, with its blobby nose, made him look rather like a giant baby. He moved with something of a baby's awkwardness, and creaked when he bent. "Well, well," he boomed. "Here we all are." He made no move to embrace his sister, nor she him. "Jacobs will show you to your rooms," he said. "I've arranged for dinner to be brought up to you."

"Thank you, James," Eveline's mother said. Her voice was flat and weary.

They were tucked away into a small gloomy chamber near the top of the house. Mama had looked at it when they moved in, and sighed, and then simply started to put their things away as best she could. Many of them went into a bare-floored dusty room which seemed to be used mainly for storing broken chairs. "He'd have put us in servants' rooms, if not for fear people would talk," she said, one day, in that absent way she did when she forgot Eveline was there. It happened more often now, and later she would scoop Eveline into a hug and tell her she was her precious girl and that Mama was sorry, sorry to be such a dreadful neglectful mother, and that she would do better.

Mama seemed to have got smaller since Papa died, and smaller still since they had moved to this big strange house. She was reduced and sad and frightened.

Eveline didn't know what Mama was frightened of. Perhaps the angels. Sometimes Eveline woke up in the night and stared fiercely into the darkness, daring the angels to come and try and take Mama or Charlotte.

She planned traps for them in her head, and even built one out of boxes and broom handles, but they never came. She wasn't afraid they would take *her*, she knew she was too naughty for angels to come for her. They only came for good people. The village women with their bonnets and sharp noses had told her so.

She didn't think they would come for Uncle James either, because Uncle James was horrid. He was big and loud and always in the middle of things, usually talking about something in a loud voice, about Important things he had done and Important people he had met and Important things he had said to them. He did something to do with the Town, which was very Important, but other people did not seem to realise how Important he was.

Conversation at meals, and before them, and after them, was dominated by Uncle James talking about how he had told people things and they had not listened, and how they would, mark his words, regret it. And how he had been passed over.

Eveline imagined that *passed over* meant Uncle James being handed like a big sack from one person to another, like pass-the-parcel, and thought perhaps that was his job. She even tried to explain it to Charlotte, how Uncle James got passed from someone to someone else, and that if they held onto him long enough to listen to what he was saying, then they won. She thought the other people in the Town offices must have very strong arms.

Charlotte only stared and gurgled. Mama, on the other hand, hovering in the doorway, had gulped, and her face had wrestled with itself, until she lost and laughed as Eveline had not heard her laugh since Papa died. She had told Eveline, as sternly as she could while laughing, that she must never talk about Uncle James that way. Eveline had disobeyed, but she had only talked about Uncle James and his job as the Parcel when Mama could hear. Making Mama laugh had become Eveline's job.

A few streets away were the mills. Hundreds of workers passed every day, going to and from their shifts. The first time Eveline heard them she woke in the night, thinking that the river had burst its banks and was rushing past their doors, and had peered out of the window to see, instead, a river of people shuffling along in the predawn darkness, like ghosts that had lost their way.

Eveline was not allowed outside alone as she had been at home, so instead, she explored the house. She ventured into the other rooms, which felt very tall and chilly after the cottage, and were full of heavily carved furniture upholstered in dark red velvet. All the tables had the oddest feet, like the claws of birds clutching a ball, and everywhere were photographs of solemn heavy-chinned people in elaborate frames and candelabras of brass or glass with hanging crystals and maps and paintings of piles of dead birds or overdressed men on fat horses or soppy-looking girls making sheep's-eyes at skinny men in armour. It was a great deal bigger than the cottage, but despite the height and the cold it felt stuffy, as though all those things somehow tangled up the air and stopped it moving about.

Eveline missed home, with its chairs still dented by her father's weight, and the space by the fireplace which was just big enough for her and a book, and her mother's workroom, and her father's fossils, and the shaggy garden with its snuffling hedgehogs and its secret treasures of raspberries and currants and sweet apples. Uncle James's garden was a gravel path and a statue of a rather silly-looking young man standing in what looked to Eveline like a thoroughly uncomfortable position, and two stiff rows of rosebushes, with flowers no-one was allowed to pick.

She missed the woods most of all.

She became extremely good at getting into rooms she was not supposed to be in, and hiding from the servants in the smallest and most unlikely of spaces once she got there. The guest-rooms were dull, once she had bounced on the beds and explored the drawers, finding nothing but spare unused linens tucked away with lavender bags. The servants' rooms held only the few clothes they owned that weren't uniforms, a few photographs in cheap frames, spare shoes, and here and there a sprig of St John's Wort to keep off the Folk. Eveline thought it must be working, since she'd seen not a sign of them since she arrived. She missed the little mischievous fairies and the funny rude goblins and the strange beautiful nixies. She missed Aiden too. She still had the crystal, but she seldom wore it. It lived in her box of precious things, and sometimes she stroked it and wondered, when life was especially dull or miserable, whether to call on Aiden for help, but it never seemed that things were quite bad enough.

Uncle James's dressing room was smelly, but oddly fascinating. He had a great many pots and bottles of things with pictures of smiling gentlemen on them which proclaimed themselves to be Tonics or Elixirs or Revitalising Lotions. Some of them smelled very nice indeed, and Eveline would dip a finger into them and rub them on her skin and pretend she had been invited to a party.

One day the manservant came in while she was there, and Eveline scooted under the chaise that stood against one wall. Here, she discovered a mysterious box which proved, rather disappointingly, to contain a couple of corsets, like Mama's, only a great deal bigger and without any lace on them. She asked Mama why Uncle James had corsets, and was told that it was to keep his stomach in. "Like the old Prince Regent," Mama said, smiling. "Now you mustn't mention them, my dear. He thinks no-one knows, for all he creaks like a ship at sea. Always vain, my brother. If he'd only use his legs instead of his carriage, and eat a little less, there'd be no need for them... but there."

Though the kitchen smelled inviting, Eveline rarely ventured there after the first time. The cook had a large nose and big hands and a skinny face with flaring patches of red on his cheekbones, as though he had been slapped.

A girl barely older than Eveline was hastily peeling carrots. There were potatoes piled next to her and apples beyond them. Amidst all that food, she looked hungry.

The cook turned from the roast he was preparing, saw Eveline and snapped, "This is no place for you! Girl, take her back to her mama."

The girl flinched and the knife slid off the carrot and into her finger, blood welling dark.

"Clumsy chit!" The cook aimed a slap at her head, then grabbed the girl's shoulder and propelled her towards Eveline. "*Take her out of my kitchen.* And no hanging about and gossiping above stairs."

The girl ducked past Eveline, clutching her wounded finger to her chest. Eveline turned to the cook. "You're horrid. You're a horrid man. The angels won't come for *you*."

He turned back to the stove, muttering about paupers and hangers-on. Eveline wondered what a hanger-on was. It sounded like somebody trying not to fall off something, holding on as best they could.

Perhaps he meant her mother. Eveline understood in some dim way that that was what Mama was doing, just hanging on, as best she could.

She wanted Mama happy again. She knew what had made Mama happy before, but Mama was not working; the sounds were all silent, wrapped up in cloth and dust. So one day Eveline had gone rummaging about among their things from the cottage, unwrapping baby clothes that Charlotte had grown out of and her own old toys, shoving them aside impatiently, until a dial beamed up at her from among its wrappings like a friendly face made of numbers.

She had always been told that the mechanisms were very delicate, and must be handled with the greatest respect. She was afraid to get them out in case she broke something. She sat on the dusty floor – the maids never bothered with this part – and thought.

There was a flicker of movement at the corner of her vision, and there, sitting up, looking at her, as though it was waiting to be noticed, was a mouse.

Eveline looked at the mouse. Then she tore bits of the wrapping away in a nibbled-looking way, and made a hole in some of Charlotte's old baby clothes with her teeth, and went and told Mama that mice were getting into their things.

And Mama had gone and looked and had seen the dial and had pulled out the mechanism from its wrappings.

It was a small rosewood box with tiny brass levers, and on its top a little thing like a rabbit's ear made of wire which when the box was wound moved from side to side. Eveline remembered the sound it made, a sweet high note that swooped and rose, swooped and rose, and always made her smile.

Mama had turned the box in her hands for a long time, then she had gone to the room next to where they slept and cleared some of the folded clothes from the long table that stood at one end.

It was a battered, stained table, but Mama didn't care. "Look, Evvie. Solid as a rock," she said, shoving it with her hand. She set the little ormolu clock Papa had given her on the table, and began to unpack the rest.

Eveline sat happily surrounded by familiar things, drawing traps for angels on a sketchpad, as the dim room filled with the sounds she remembered, soft and subtle and magical sounds, intermingled with the scratching of Mama's pen as she made notes and occasional soft exclamations of pleasure or frustration.

The clock chimed the hour. "Now, Eveline, that will do," Mama said. "It is time I took you both out."

And so it went on for a few months. Mama would work for an hour, then she would take the girls out or teach Eveline some history or nature, or read them both a story. Eveline grew out of her clothes, and Mama, frowning and muttering, lengthened them and let them out.

One day Eveline found her with one of her own dresses, a pretty primrose-coloured silk, laid out on her lap, squinting as she unpicked the seams. "Do you need your dress let out, Mama?"

"No, my love, I'm going to alter this for you."

"Oh. But what will you do?"

"I've other dresses, Eveline. And who is to care what I wear nowadays?" For a moment she looked lost and grey. "Not even me," she said, quietly, to the crumpled silk in her lap.

Eveline, not understanding but knowing only that Mama was sad, put her arms around her.

Mama was no dressmaker, and the dress bagged in places and was too tight in others, but Eveline primped and danced in it for Mama and managed to make her smile, though it was a trembling smile and when Mama hugged her she whispered fiercely in her ear, "I *will* do right by you, Eveline. I will, I promise."

Mama kept the sounds of her work very quiet, and most of the time they were drowned out anywhere but her own room by the constant roar and pounding of the nearby factories. But of course, eventually the rest of the house noticed.

Uncle James hauled his bulk up to their rooms to see what Mama was doing. He poked at her papers and asked her questions.

Mama, pleased and excited, alive again, had shown him everything.

And for a while Uncle James had gone quiet and thoughtful and had smiled at Mama and Eveline and even Charlotte, whose existence he normally completely ignored.

SCRAPS OF CONVERSATIONS, arguments. "James, of course I am grateful for your assistance, but..."

"Madeleine, you do realise that if anyone should happen to think that you have been concentrating on these things and been *neglectful*..."

That word, that word which always made Mama fearful and quiet. "I would *never* neglect my girls, James. Never."

Sometimes Uncle James's friends came to the house. Eveline peeked through the bannisters at the men in black and white, like magpies, and the ladies in their huge-skirted dresses, floating like great water-lilies. Good smells drifted up the stairs along with their voices. At first Eveline liked these parties, even though she was not allowed to attend; it was good to hear the house fill up with the sounds of other people, and interesting to watch them all. There was the thin stooped man with the long sad face who she thought of as the Crow, because he walked along just that way, with his hands behind his back, his head dipping with every step. The Sugar Lady, always dressed in pale sweet colours, always smiling and tilting her head so her soft brown ringlets danced and fluttering her pale hands. The Dog Man, who had a bristly moustache that made her think of terriers, who snapped out his words, *yapyapyap*, making people laugh, and the Sugar Lady would rap his wrist with her fan.

The second time she saw Dog Man he looked up, right to where she was hiding behind the bannisters. She drew back, but she knew he had seen her.

But there was no punishment, no summons to Uncle James's study. So the next time there was a party she risked it again, and this time, Dog Man looked for her on purpose, and winked.

It became a little game of smiles and expressions. She began to look forward to his visits. Apart from Mama, there were no grown-ups to take her the least bit seriously, or treat her as anything other than a nuisance or extra work. Dog Man seemed to like seeing her there.

Mama, on the other hand, hated these parties.

"James, please. I am happy to eat in my rooms."

"Madeleine, they will say I am keeping you locked in the attic. Don't be foolish. Come down. And do try to make yourself presentable."

"But the girls..."

"Surely you don't expect me to allow children at the table? And besides, I am sure Eveline can watch her sister for a few hours. Can't you, Eveline?"

Eveline looked from one to the other. If she said yes, Mama would have to go to the party. If she said no, Uncle James would talk again about how she was ill-disciplined and should be sent away to school. She had a deep terror of being sent away from Mama and Charlotte. The angels might come for them while she wasn't there to watch. Or other bad things, things she did not know the names of, things that hung like ghosts in the shadows of the house, might happen to them.

"I can watch her, Mama. Go to the party. You can tell us all about it afterwards."

Mama's face twitched, and then she smiled. "Very well."

"Tell me what Do – the man with the moustache says to make everyone laugh so."

"Oh, that's Everard Poole. I think his jokes are too sophisticated for young ladies!" James said, pleased and expansive now he had got his way. "Well, well, must go and check on things, lots to do!"

What he had to do Eveline didn't know, since it was the maids who cleaned and the cook who cooked and his man who sent out the invitations (she had sneaked into his study and seen the cards, written out in the manservant's neat, careful, rather square hand, instead of Uncle James's blotchy sprawl).

"*Make myself presentable*," Mama said, scowling at the mirror. "I believe your Uncle is hoping to marry me off, Eveline. Let us disabuse him of that notion, shall we?" She put on one of the black mourning dresses she had stopped wearing a month ago, which was now too big and had never suited her to begin with, and twisted her hair up into a rigid bun. She pinned a large, ugly mourning brooch Purple-Bonnet had given her to the front of her dress. "There. Do I look sufficiently discouraging?"

Eveline giggled. "You look like a witch, Mama."

"Perfect. Be good, darling, and remember Charlotte's posset."

Charlotte had a weak chest, and as the weather got colder, had to be given hot possets and flannels, to stop her coughing. Eveline had got tired of asking the beastly cook to do it, since he always made a great fuss as though it was a huge trouble for him. She watched him make it until she worked out how to do it herself, and did so, now, when he was out of the way.

Eveline struggled to stay awake until Mama came upstairs, but ended up asleep on the floor next to Charlotte's cot, when she felt herself picked up, and tucked into bed.

Mama stroked her cheek, and got into bed herself.

"Mama? Was it a nice party?"

"Not very, Eveline. But it's over. Go to sleep now."

She had hoped to hear about Dog Man, but before she could ask, she fell asleep again.

EVELINE WAS STRUGGLING with some figures Mama had set her to do. She tried not to interrupt when Mama was working, but Uncle James had no such qualms. Eveline could hear them arguing again, through the wall.

"If you present it yourself, even if your name is on it, Madeleine, you can imagine the reaction."

"But it's my work, James."

"Of course it is, my dear, but it might cause... well, questions. Not only the fault, but even the appearance of the fault should be avoided. Caesar's wife, you know... or sister, in this case, must be above suspicion."

Uncle James had left the house in a temper, to go to one of his meetings.

"Mama, who's Caesar?"

"Darling, have you been listening at doors? You know that's not proper."

"I wasn't *listening*, I just *heard*. Who's Caesar?"

"A very important man in olden times."

"Oh. Important like Uncle James?"

"Uncle James certainly thinks so. Darling, are you happy here?"

"I'd rather be at home."

"Oh, my dear, so would I, but there's no money, you see. But you don't mind Mama doing some work, do you?"

"I like it when you work. I like the sounds. They make me happy. And Charlotte hardly ever cries when you're working, especially when you have that thing on, with the rabbit-ear on top, and the other one, the pretty box with the brass handle that goes *whoom*."

"It's true, isn't it? She doesn't." Mama paused, holding a pencil in the air, and staring at Charlotte. Then she nodded vigorously and made notes in one of her books. "Thank you, darling, that's very helpful."

Over the next few weeks she worked harder than ever, waking with the maids and going back to her workroom after she'd put the girls to bed. One night she came in while Eveline was still awake, and was humming to herself under her breath, something she hadn't done for a very long time.

"Mama?" she whispered.

"Oh, did I wake you, my pet?"

"No, Mama. Has something happened?"

"Yes, poppet. Something has. Your mama has made a breakthrough. It's the *combination* of sounds, that's what does it. The right combination. Oh, my pet, we're finally getting somewhere."

And for a little while, Mama had a lighter step and a brighter eye. But Uncle James's voice came through the wall more often, loud and bullying.

Then one day Eveline saw some of Mama's devices being loaded into Uncle James's carriage. "Mama, why is Uncle James taking your things? Don't let him!"

"Now, Eveline, it's all right. I've given my work to Uncle James for him to get people to look at, important people who might give some money for more equipment and things I need. Do you understand?"

"Then they'll know how clever you are, and give you money, and we can go home and not live with Uncle James any more?"

"Well, no. They'll think Uncle James is clever. He's not giving them my name."

Eveline had frowned, so hard she felt the tension in her forehead. "Why?"

Mama's head drooped and she rubbed her eyes as though she were very tired. "Because it's the way of the world, my darling. Now, never mind, let's go for a walk. We could all do with some air."

The only place that was nice to walk was all the way out of town, where the houses petered out among fields and woods. Charlotte could hardly toddle more than a few steps, so they took her in the baby carriage, and she squinted at the sunlight and tried to grab butterflies out of the air, and Mama smiled at her, but – for almost the whole walk – said nothing at all. It was only when they were rattling along the pavement back towards the tall stony house that she said, "Eveline, you mustn't mention this to anyone, you understand? About my work, and Uncle James. If you do, you might get Mama in trouble. And if Mama gets into trouble, they might take you away from me, you and Charlotte. So you must be good, and never speak of this, not to Uncle James or anyone."

"Yes, Mama."

SOMETIMES EVELINE TOOK out the crystal that Aiden had given her, and dangled it from her fingers. He had said he would come if she really wanted him.

"What's that?" Mama said.

"Aiden gave it to me. Remember?"

"Oh, yes. Yes, I'd forgotten. There aren't any Folk here, are there? I think they dislike the factories. Certainly the noise, maybe the smells too. Do you miss him, Eveline?"

"Sometimes," Eveline said. But that made Mama look sad, so she put the crystal away and didn't mention it again.

It wasn't the volume of the next argument that sent Eveline creeping out of their room and pressing her ear to the door of the workroom; it was the tone. She had never heard Mama sound quite so angry.

"James. What is happening to my work? What are you planning?"

"Don't be silly, my dear, I'm doing exactly what we discussed."

"I saw the notes. This is not what I intended and you know it! It was never meant for such a use!"

"Only because you did not have the imagination, the... *drive* to see it as I see it. You may have contributed to the research..."

"Contributed? James, *it is my research.*"

"But it is the application that will gain recognition. All these factory disputes, workers demanding this, that and the other thing – it's a disgrace, and bad for the country. Something that could encourage good, productive behaviour, though... well, it's just what the doctor ordered!"

Eveline heard her mother use a voice that she had never before heard, a voice so cold, and so full of something terrible, that it barely sounded like Mama at all.

"James, that would be an utter perversion of everything I have worked for. I will write to the Royal Society myself. I will not permit this."

"Madeleine, that would be very foolish."

"Please leave my room, James."

"I remind you that it is not your room. You – and your daughters – are living in *my* house, on *my* generosity."

"And in return, you plan to steal my work and turn it into this... this abomination! I will not have it, James. If I have to leave and take the girls with me, I will do so. We will make our way. Now please *leave.*"

Charlotte woke and started to whimper. Eveline crept out of bed and went to Charlotte's cot, where she was sitting up, her eyes huge in her chubby face, her breath hitching on the verge of sobs. "Hush, now," Eveline said. With some effort, she lifted Charlotte out of the cot. "Hush. Mama... Mama is just playing a game. A special one for night-time. Let's play our own. Pat-a-cake!"

She held Charlotte on her lap, warm and solid, and played pat-a-cake with her, one ear cocked for any more sounds from the other room.

But there was silence. Mama would be coming to bed soon – Eveline didn't know what time it was, but it felt late – and would be upset if they were still awake.

Charlotte's head was already drooping again. Eveline hauled her into the cot and got back into the bed she shared with Mama. She shut her eyes so Mama would think she was asleep. She heard the door open and close, but no-one came in, and eventually pretended sleep became real.

The next morning Mama was not in her bed. Eveline left the room quietly, so as not to wake Charlotte, and crept along in her nightgown to the workroom. Mama was seated at the table, writing.

"Mama?"

Mama jolted, the pen in her hand spattering ink. "Oh, Evvie!"

"Are you writing a letter, Mama?"

"Yes. Yes, I am. To the Royal Society, though I don't know it will do much good." Mama's hair was coming down from its pins, and she looked terribly tired. "Once I'm done I shall take a walk and post it. Would you like to come with me?"

"It's raining."

"Yes, it is, isn't it? Never mind, I shall go on my own; I don't want you or Charlotte to catch cold."

"You've dropped some of your papers, Mama." Eveline could see a triangle of paper poking out from under the table.

"Have I?" Mama glanced down. "Oh, that was stupid." She pushed her chair back and stood up. "Eveline, come here." She knelt down on the floor. When Eveline got closer she could see that the scrap of paper was not lying on the floor, but poking out between two floorboards. Mama took her letter-knife and levered the board up. Underneath was a biscuit tin, sporting a picture of a boy holding a dog on the lid. The boy wore blue breeches and a blue jacket with a lace collar. His cheeks were so round and rosy they made her want to bite into them like apples. The dog was black and white with floppy ears. The dog looked nicer than the boy. Mama opened it, and shoved the scrap of paper into it. "This is Mama's hiding place. You mustn't tell anyone, Evvie, do you understand?" She slid the box back into hiding, and put the board down – there, it was all concealed again. Now you couldn't tell the board from all the others, except for a slight splintered place along one edge where the letter-knife had gone in.

"Why are you hiding papers, Mama?"

"Because I don't want Uncle James to find them." Mama looked distracted, turning the letter-knife over in her hands. "What he's taken already shouldn't be sufficient... I made sure the essentials weren't there, but it looks plausible enough if one doesn't know the underlying principles..."

"Mama?"

"Never mind, Evvie. Just remember that these are Mama's notes and Uncle James mustn't know of them, nor anyone. Not even Charlotte."

"Yes, Mama."

"Now come here and give Mama a kiss. Is Charlotte awake? I think it's time for some breakfast, don't you?"

AFTER THAT THINGS were quieter for a while. Mama even smiled one day, telling Eveline that Uncle James had invited a man to the house to speak with her. "I do believe he's attempting matchmaking, Evvie, imagine! How foolish. As though I could ever find a man as understanding as your dear papa. And what a curious fellow he was – so many questions! I was polite, of course, but answered him very shortly, and left him in no doubt I was a thoroughly dull bluestocking! I think I have poured sufficient cold water to dampen any romantic thoughts. He came out of Uncle James's study as I was coming upstairs, looking very grim."

"Why would he talk to Uncle James?"

"Because, darling, Uncle James is my only male relative, and if anyone wished to marry me it would be considered proper for them to ask his permission."

"What if I wanted to marry someone?"

"Then they would have to ask me. Why, is there someone you want to marry?" Mama smiled.

"No, not at all. I don't know any boys."

"You don't know many people at all, do you, my poor pet?" Mama looked worried again, and Eveline felt she had said something wrong, but wasn't sure what it had been.

A week later Uncle James had invited another man. Eveline, who felt a personal interest in potential stepfathers, hoped this one might be someone Mama could like. Anything, surely, would be better than this horrible unfriendly house and wretched Uncle James who made her so unhappy.

She decided to eavesdrop. Mama said she was a noticing girl, and often asked her opinion; perhaps she would ask Evvie about her beau.

Eveline managed to conceal herself under the ottoman in the drawing-room, but it was not a very good hiding place: all she could see of the gentleman was a pair of highly polished shoes and the tip of an equally polished cane.

After the usual pleasantries, this man, too, started asking questions.

"Councillor Lathrop tells me you have been somewhat troubled."

"James is overly concerned, Dr Bower. He thinks I have a weak constitution. I assure you I am quite robust."

"But I understand you have a hobby involving mechanisms, on which you spend a great deal of time. Do you not find that leaves you fatigued?"

"Surely, if something is only a hobby, it is a source of amusement and relaxation, not fatigue?"

"Mechanisms are an unusual pastime for a lady."

"Yes."

"You have two children, I understand."

"Daughters."

"And have they, too, shown such an inclination?"

"The youngest is barely two, she is a little young to be showing an inclination towards anything."

"And the older?"

"Oh, Eveline is a bright girl, she manages to keep herself occupied. She can figure well enough, but she shows no signs of following in my footsteps."

"I see. It must be a great strain on you, bringing up two daughters alone."

"Living here, surrounded by servants and under my brother's constant supervision, I would hardly say I am alone."

"You feel surrounded?"

"Only occasionally. More tea?"

The conversation was dull. Eveline dozed off in her hiding place, only waking to the scrape of chairs. "Well, this has been a most enlightening conversation, Mrs Duchen," the man said. "I am sure we will have the pleasure of meeting again."

"Good afternoon, Dr Bower."

Eveline waited until it was safe, and crept out, dusting down her pinafore. On her way back to her room, she heard Dr Bower's voice coming from Uncle James's study, but she couldn't hear the words. Was he asking Uncle James for permission to pay court to Mama? Eveline hoped not. She hadn't taken to him, despite the shininess of his shoes.

EVELINE WOKE THINKING Charlotte had cried out, but the little girl was sleeping quietly. A moment later she heard the shift-change whistle at the mill. It was later than they usually rose. Mama's bed was empty. Maybe she had worked all night. Sometimes she did, but she always came in to rouse the girls for breakfast.

The door of her workroom was locked. "Mama?" Eveline knocked. "Mama, are you there? Do you want breakfast?" But there was no answer.

Eveline went downstairs.

But neither Mama nor Uncle James was anywhere to

be found. She saw the servants pausing to watch her as she passed. Creeping dread started to churn in her stomach and weaken her legs. One of the maids was brushing the carpet in the dining-room. Eveline planted herself in front of her. "Have you seen my mama?"

"Oh, dear..." The maid looked over her shoulder as though afraid of someone, and said, "No, well, a carriage left this morning..."

"Girl! Are you *gossiping with your betters?*" Uncle James's manservant had appeared in the doorway, and was looking down his thin nose at them both. "Get back to your work at once," he said.

The maid scrambled to her feet, clutching the dustpan to her apron, and scurried out of the room.

"Miss Eveline, your uncle wishes to see you," the manservant said.

"I don't want to see him, I want to see Mama."

"Well this is your uncle's house and you are obliged to do as he says. Will you go, or shall I carry you?"

"If you try to pick me up, I shall bite you," Eveline said. "Where is my mama?"

"If you want to find out, you'll go see your uncle. He's in his study."

Eveline lifted her chin and walked past him. As she did so he bent down and said, "I would advise you to mind your manners, young lady – unless you want to end up in the poorhouse."

The walk to Uncle James's study seemed very long. And there were servants everywhere – the hall and stairs need extra special cleaning this morning, it seemed. Even the cook had emerged from ruling over the kitchens to stare. He and the manservant nodded meaningfully at each other. "Well *I* wasn't at all surprised," the cook said, hardly bothering to lower his voice. "The child's a positive savage. The apple doesn't fall far from the tree."

And then she was in Uncle James' study, and Uncle James was sitting behind his desk.

"Ah, Eveline."

"Where's Mama?"

Uncle James sighed, looking down at his hands, as they took a pen out of the inkwell, put it back, turned over a piece of paper... as though his hands were nothing to do with him, acting entirely on their own. "Uncle James?"

He frowned at her. "This is very difficult for me, Eveline. This whole thing is extremely distressing."

"Uncle James?"

"Your mama has been behaving in an increasingly erratic manner, Eveline. Making wild accusations. She was even talking about leaving, attempting to set up some sort of business in the town – one can easily imagine how that would have ended, and my reputation would be ruined."

"Where is she?"

"Madeleine has had to go away." Uncle James heaved himself out of his chair and stood with his back to Eveline, staring out of the window. "Really, it is all dreadfully awkward."

"But where is she?"

"In a place where her eccentricities can be dealt with."

"But when is she coming back?"

"She will come home if her behaviour can be controlled, if she can stop making these ridiculous claims."

"I don't understand. Who has she gone to see?"

Uncle James reached for the bell-pull and yanked viciously. "No-one. She is being treated."

"Is she sick?"

"Yes. She is mentally unwell. Suffering from hysteria, and delusions."

Eveline did not know what either of those words meant, but they sounded worse than the croup or even the scarlet fever, that Mama had been so afraid either of them might catch. She must be dreadfully ill. What if no-one was looking after her properly? "I want to go see her!"

"Certainly not. Children are not permitted in such places."

"Why not?"

"It isn't suitable. Where is that wretched maid? Flirting and gossiping no doubt, I really will have to speak to..."

"But what about Charlotte?"

"If you cannot deal with Charlotte, I suppose I will have to find some woman to take care of her. Which will be a great trouble and expense. Or perhaps she will have to be sent away where she can be suitably attended to."

First Mama, and now Charlotte? "You can't send Charlotte away!"

"Then you must look after her." Uncle James turned around, and glared at her.

"But Mama..." Eveline's breath began to hitch. Everything had happened so quickly, Mama was ill, and gone, and all in a night.

"Don't blether, child. I can't bear hysteria and blethering."

Hysteria was what Mama had. If Eveline had it, too, she would be sent away, and then what would happen to Charlotte?

Eveline grabbed onto herself with everything she had, clamped down on the tears, and blew her nose. "Yes, Uncle James."

And even when the maid appeared and ushered her upstairs, she did not cry, and she did not cry in front of Charlotte because what if hysteria was catching? And all through the next horrible weeks she straightened her mouth and blinked fiercely if the tears threatened, and fed Charlotte and read stories to her and every now and then would ask Uncle James if there was any news.

However quietly and calmly she asked, he always got angry, glaring and blustering and snapping that there was no change before ordering her out of his study. So Eveline started to sneak into the library when he wasn't there, and look in his books for anything about hysteria. Perhaps she could find out something that would help Mama.

All she found was that hysteria was something only women had, and that it was to do with wombs. Eveline wasn't sure what a womb was, so she asked Violet, who was the nicer of the two maids, but Violet didn't know, except that it was something to do with babies. Eveline wondered if Mama was going to have another baby, and if that was making her ill, but the book used too many words she didn't know and there was no-one else she trusted to ask.

Eveline and Charlotte were in a strange position in the house; not Important like Uncle James, but not quite servants either. With no-one to talk to, Eveline began to eavesdrop whenever she could, in case someone should happen to be talking about Mama. She never heard anything about Mama, but she heard about other things.

Violet the under maid was an orphan, and so didn't get a day off to see her family like the other maid, Harriet, who was older and crosser. Harriet's mother was 'off her legs' and couldn't earn, and Harriet sneaked food from the pantry to take home to her. Both the maids were terrified of being turned off.

One day Harriet came up and told her she must come down for dinner. Eveline thought they were to come down and eat with the servants; it would be a relief to have some company. She pulled Charlotte to her feet.

"Just you," Harriet said. "You're to put on something appropriate, and wash, and come down and eat with your Uncle and his guests."

"But what about Charlotte? Who'll give her her supper?"

"I'll do that." Harriet kept her face still, but she was clearly resentful at the extra work. Eveline thought fast. Charlotte had been fussy and unsettled since Mama left, and Eveline often had to sneak down to the kitchen when the beastly cook was out of sight to find treats to tempt her appetite. Harriet wouldn't do that, unless she was given a reason – she would probably be impatient and rough, and Charlotte would eat nothing.

"I've terrible trouble feeding her," she said. "Uncle James said she'd have to be sent away, if she wouldn't eat. And me, too, for not looking after her well enough. I think he'd like that. He was saying how expensive everything was getting. If we both get sent away, he said he wouldn't need nearly so many servants to keep things up."

Harriet's jaw tightened. "Don't you worry, miss," she said. "I'll fatten her up nice." She picked the little girl up, and her weary, rigid face softened. "You're a pretty one, aren't you?"

"Yes, she is. Much prettier than me. She's got hair like yours."

"Oh, and how would you know under this cap?" Harriet said.

"I saw that day it blew off when you were hanging the washing. It's all yellow curls." She'd actually first seen Harriet brushing it when, lonely and bored of being with Charlotte who couldn't have a proper conversation, she had sneaked up to listen outside the servants' rooms.

"Much good it does me. And you're not so bad, miss; you just need some weight on you and a pretty dress or two."

Now Eveline felt bad for what she'd said – Uncle James complained about money a great deal, but he'd said nothing about turning off any servants – but she hardened her heart. Charlotte was more important than anybody.

She had no pretty dresses, but went down to dinner in the yellow dress Mama had altered for her. It fitted even worse than before, since she'd grown, but it was a little like having Mama with her.

She could hear their voices coming from the drawing-room and stood for a moment outside, listening to them. Fragments of conversation about India and China, about tea and Sepoys and clippers, whatever they were. Someone mentioned the Folk, and Eveline edged the tall door open and peered in.

"It seems they're dying out," Crow Man said. "Fewer and fewer sightings, especially in the cities."

"But how sad!" the Sugar Lady said, pouting and shaking her curls. "Can nothing be done?"

"Oh, well, my dear, sentiment is all very well," Crow Man said, patting her hand, "but they are the last remnant of a fading world, you know. They couldn't move forward, so must be left behind."

"I don't believe you," Eveline said.

"Why, who is this?" Sugar Lady said. She looked Eveline over and hid her face behind her fan, but her eyes crinkled up with amusement.

"Don't believe what, my dear?" Dog Man came over and bowed to Eveline. "You must be Eveline. How charming. Is that your mama's dress?"

"Yes. What did you mean about the Folk?" She turned to Crow Man. "They're not dying, don't say that!"

"Ah, you ladies, so sentimental!" Crow Man said. "You mustn't be sad, my dear. It's not as though they're like us, after all – why, they probably don't even know what's happening."

Eveline felt her chin start to shake. The thought of all the Folk, dead like Papa, dead like her pet rabbit that had simply fallen over one day, its bright eyes gone dull and its warm fur chill under her hand... and Aiden. Aiden couldn't be dead. Even though she hadn't seen him for so long, he was part of the old days, back when everything was better.

"Now, now, Peter, you've upset the poor child," Dog Man said. "Come, my dear, I'm sure that it's not true – the Folk are very cunning, you know. I expect they're well able to take care of themselves. Why don't you have one of these delicious almonds, and you shall sit next to me at dinner and tell me all about yourself and your little sister, hmm?" His moustache quivered at her and it made her smile. He gave her his handkerchief, which was so very clean and crisp that she was hesitant to blow her nose on it, but he smiled and nodded and she knew it was all right.

He did indeed make her sit next to him at dinner, though Uncle James sniffed and glared, but soon they were all talking of other things, except for Eveline and Dog Man, who turned out to be called Everard. "Everard and Eveline!" he said. "Why, it sounds like an old romance, does it not? We were clearly fated to be the best of friends."

He paid a great deal of attention to her throughout dinner, even giving her a little wine from his own glass, well mixed with water. Sugar Lady, whose real name Eveline never bothered to learn, said, "Really, Everard, do you think it's quite the thing? She can't be more than six."

"I'm eight," Eveline said sharply. She didn't like the taste of the watered wine very much, but drank it anyway, to prove that Everard the Dog Man had been right to give it to her, and he patted her hand and said she was quite the sophisticated young lady.

She began to look forward to his visits. No-one else ever paid the slightest attention to her except for Charlotte. She had read all her books several times over and he brought her more, and a new dress, with blue silk ribbons. She put it on for the next dinner party, and he told her how pretty it was, and stroked her hair, and said it was silkier than the ribbons.

He wasn't Mama, but he was her only grown-up friend. Her only friend at all, apart from Charlotte, who hardly counted.

ONE DAY EVERARD the Dog Man had come up to see Charlotte, and had petted her cheek, and said she was going to be as pretty as her sister.

And he had put his hand on the back of Eveline's neck, and run his fingers under the collar of her dress, and her nape had shivered. The feel of his fingers was wrong, like a spider running over her neck. "Pretty dears," he said. "My pretty little dears."

Then Harriet had come in, and he had snatched his hand away so fast a stitch in Eveline's collar had ripped.

He started to come around at odd times, after that, bringing some apples from his garden or a clipping from the paper he thought Uncle James might like. And he always brought something for Eveline and Charlotte, like ribbons, or marzipan.

Harriet seemed often to find something to do in their room when he was there, and Eveline wondered if she liked him too. But she didn't act like Sugar Lady, fluttering and laughing. She hunched her shoulders and kept quiet as she stitched or folded.

"Harriet?" Eveline asked one day when Everard had gone, pulling a strand of bright pink satin ribbon through her fingers to watch it shine.

"Yes, miss."

"Do you like Everard?"

"You should call him Mr Poole."

"He asked me to call him Everard."

"Did he indeed," said Harriet, and her mouth went tight at the sides.

"You don't like him, do you?"

"One of these days, young miss, you're going to have to learn not to let the first thing in your head fly right out of your mouth."

"Did I say something wrong?"

"You just can't go about commenting on everything people do or don't do, or how they look. It's not polite. And it'll get you in trouble. Watch all you like, but you don't have to speak. As it happens, no, I don't like Mr Poole."

"Why?"

Harriet's mouth went tight again. "I know his type, and he shouldn't be around young girls giving them ribbons. You watch out for him, Eveline. Someone gives you ribbons, they want something."

"But we haven't got anything."

"That's as maybe." And that was all she would say on the subject.

What she had said about watching people was interesting, though, and Eveline, having little to do except watch Charlotte, made a game of it. She watched the maids as they worked and the cook as he cooked, and Uncle James and the boot-boy and the coal man who came to the door. She began to learn the little tics and twitches of face and body and hands, the things that gave away a stomach ache or a worry or a hope. The way the youngest maid looked when she thought the boot-boy wasn't looking; the way the cook's face sagged in relief when he sat down.

She became adept at walking quietly and concealing herself where she could watch and listen. She learned how faces and words sometimes didn't match; how a clenched hand could say one thing while a polite tongue said another.

And she watched Everard. She saw how he looked at her and Charlotte the way Uncle James looked at a roast goose or a candied almond. The way every time he gave them something he asked for a hug or a kiss or to put the ribbon in their hair for them.

Charlotte had begun to recognise him and hold up her arms when he came into the room, and he would pick her up and dandle her on his knee and wind satin ribbons around her dimpled wrists. She was a quiet child, but would babble happily at him and tug at his moustache and he would laugh.

And Eveline realised that Harriet was right, that he did want something, that he wanted kisses and hugs and sittings upon his lap, a little more every time. She understood that it was some sort of game, but it was a bad, uncomfortable game. And she began to make excuses when he came to visit. She said she and Charlotte were sick with the grippe, which worked twice; then Uncle James called the doctor to dose them both with foul medicine and whined about the cost and what he had done to be left with two useless sickly females on his hands.

Eveline was very sick after the medicine, and so was Charlotte, who cried for a long time until she was choking and wheezing with every breath. Harriet brought up a soothing posset which put her to sleep as though with a spell.

"How did you do that?" Eveline said.

"I put a drop of laudanum in it, miss."

"What's laudanum?"

"Something people use to make them sleep." She looked at Eveline. Eveline's face was stiff with tears, and her throat and chest ached. "I'll make you up one, if you should fancy it."

"No, thank you, Harriet." Eveline didn't want to go to sleep. She wanted to think.

Mama's workroom was kept locked, but Eveline had the spare key, which everyone seemed to have forgotten about. Uncle James wheezed and groaned his way up the stairs every few days to mess about with Mama's mechanisms. He couldn't make them sing like Mama did, and he would get angry, after an hour or two, and stomp away muttering.

When she unlocked it, the room was all a mess. Not a mess the way Mama kept it, but a different kind of mess altogether. It smelled of Uncle James instead of Mama.

Eveline ran her fingers over a few of her favourite instruments, but she couldn't make them sing like Mama did, and even if she could, she wouldn't dare in the quiet of the house, with everyone sleeping. Outside, the factories thudded and groaned, making the sky flare red and yellow, as though they were trying to make their own sun to replace the one that their smoke covered over during the day, but inside, the house was terribly quiet. Eveline sat down among the remains of her mother's work, and cried for a long time.

Some days later Uncle James summoned her to his study. "You're a very lucky young woman," he said. "Everard has asked for your hand. As your guardian, I have accepted. Of course, the marriage can't take place until you are twelve, but he has very kindly offered to assume responsibility for you and your sister. You are to go and live with him."

Every hair on the back of Eveline's neck was shivering, as though Everard-Dog-Man's hand were still there, brushing her skin with his fingers.

"But I don't want to go and live with him."

"Contrary child! After he's been so kind! Why he should even consider you a suitable bride I am at a loss to understand! You will do as you are told."

Looking at his face, she realised that even if she told him why – a *why* she herself barely understood – he would not listen, because he never listened. That this was something he wanted, something convenient that would get her and Charlotte out of the house, and so he would ignore anything she said.

Except, perhaps, one thing.

"But what about Mama? He's supposed to ask Mama." Men were supposed to ask a girl's father, but when a girl didn't have one, surely, he had to ask her mother instead? "I shall ask him to take me to see Mama so he can ask her properly." She knew Mama would not let her marry someone she didn't want to, however sick she were.

Uncle James huffed, and his eyes narrowed. She had a moment of satisfaction, knowing he hadn't expected that. "Eveline... you can't."

"The man is supposed to ask the papa. I don't have one, so he must ask Mama."

She saw Uncle James' face redden and swell, the way it always did when he couldn't have something he wanted, just like Charlotte's. "Go to your room!" he snapped, and he yanked on the bell-cord.

She went to her room. She wanted to put on the yellow dress, to feel close to Mama, but it fit even worse now and she couldn't get it over her arms. Instead she picked up Charlotte, who was getting too big to carry for more than a few steps, and sat down with her on her lap, her arms tight round her, her face pressed into the mite's thick soft curls. Charlotte didn't even fuss, but stared at Eveline with wide dark eyes and her finger in her mouth, as though she understood that something was wrong, until she fell asleep with her cheek against Eveline's chest.

Eveline wondered when Everard would come visit. He must be waiting for Uncle James to tell him what Eveline had said, so it would be soon. She would explain about him asking Mama's permission, they would go see Mama, and Mama would not give it. She began to feel better, and excited about seeing Mama at last. What would it be like, where she was? She had been sick for months, why hadn't they made her better yet? Perhaps it wasn't a very good hospital, perhaps they could find a better one. She wondered if they could take Charlotte – no, better not, Charlotte still had a weak chest, and the doctor said she shouldn't be around people who were sick. She would make a drawing of Charlotte to show Mama how much she had grown. She would like to take Mama some flowers, but it was winter now and the flowers were all gone. She would make a drawing of some instead. Thinking of flowers, she fell asleep herself.

She woke to darkness. Charlotte was grizzling and fussing, hungry, as Eveline was herself. She put the baby down and went to the door, only to find it wouldn't open.

She banged on it, banged louder and louder until she heard a voice on the other side saying, "What a fuss! I've your supper here, and Charlotte's. If you're going to be a bad child I shall take it away."

Eveline backed away from the door, and heard the click of the lock.

Jacobs, Uncle James's manservant, came in with a tray covered with a cloth.

"Why was the door locked?"

"Because you've been a bad girl and defied your uncle."

"But I haven't! I just said I don't want to marry the Dog Man without talking to Mama!"

"Now don't talk such nonsense. Marry a dog man indeed! You've been reading too many fairy tales and given yourself nightmares. You're lucky you're getting supper at all, lots of bad children go without!" And before Eveline could protest any more, he had gone, locking the door behind him.

Eveline waited for him to come back for the tray, but he never did. The next person to unlock the door, the following morning, was Uncle James. Jacobs followed behind him and scooped up the empty tray. Charlotte sat on the floor, banging on the boards with a spoon.

"Eveline. I have some grave news, child." Uncle James looked at the window, the walls, the floor, anywhere but at her. "Can you make that child be quiet?"

Perhaps he had told Everard-Dog-Man what she had said and he had decided he didn't want to marry her after all. That would be good, except then she would have no reason to go visit Mama. She would have to think of another one. She took the spoon gently out of Charlotte's hand, and gave her an ancient doll with one arm missing. Charlotte banged the unfortunate doll on the boards instead.

"Are you listening?"

"Yes, Uncle James."

"I'm afraid it's your mother," he said, looking out of the window. "You must be brave."

The words fell into Eveline's mind like small, cold stones. "Mama?" She felt the earth shudder and tilt.

"She was very sick, Eveline. And now she's gone."

Jacobs fumbled the tray as he was taking it out of the door, and paused, righting the tilting bowls.

"But *where's* she gone?"

"Sir... should I perhaps fetch the cook? One of the maids?" Jacobs said.

"Leave this to me, Jacobs." Uncle James bent down, enveloping her in a fat, thick cloud of scented pomade and sweat. "She's with the angels now."

"Like Papa?"

"Yes, child, exactly like Papa. You must be a good brave girl."

And Uncle James straightened up and turned to Jacobs, and the world went to shards and swirled away like broken china tipped down a well.

SHE WOKE UP to see Harriet by the side of her bed. "Look at you, you poor little thing. Here, eat some of this."

Eveline looked at the spoon, with its burden of soup. It didn't seem to have anything to do with her. "Mama."

"Yes, child, I'm afraid your mama is gone. Your Uncle told us. I'm very sorry. She's with the angels now."

"Like Papa." Eveline had stopped being angry at the angels some time ago. She'd decided they weren't real in the way the Folk were real. She didn't have anything to be angry with, anyway. Everything was cold and empty, inside and out.

"Eat your soup."

"I'm not hungry."

"Well, I'll leave it here. I've fed your sister, don't you worry."

"Thank you."

Harriet looked at her for a moment, shook her head, sighed, and went out.

Eveline hugged her knees and stared at the wall. Mama was gone. Mama wasn't ever coming back.

She looked at Charlotte, who was babbling to the one-armed doll. Charlotte didn't understand. Charlotte didn't realise they were all alone now.

It was several days before Eveline could think properly again, and realise that this meant Everard-Dog-Man didn't have to ask permission of anyone.

No-one in the house would help them. They were all scared of Uncle James, or on his side.

She only had one person left to turn to, and that was Aiden. But to find Aiden they would have to leave, and go into the woods.

SHE WAITED UNTIL the house was silent, or as silent as it ever got. The thud and boom of the machines never ceased. The clouds, thick and rolling, underlit by the gouts of flame that roared from the factory chimneys, loured close over the blackened rooftops. A few cold stars blinked in the gaps, pinned against the sky.

Eveline crept into Uncle James's study, her bare feet wincing from the cold tiles of the hall. His desk was locked, but his coin-purse was in the pocket of the jacket he had left hanging over the chair, and she knew where he kept a roll of notes in the tankard on the mantel. She paused before taking the notes; it felt, somehow, more like stealing than the coins. But she knew that without money she and Charlotte wouldn't get far. Everyone needed money. If Papa's money hadn't disappeared, they wouldn't have had to come live with Uncle James and none of this would have happened.

She tucked the notes into the pocket of her apron, but the bulge they made was obvious. If she was caught, she'd be in a great deal of trouble. She'd be in trouble anyway, but more if they found the notes.

She lifted her skirt and tucked the notes inside her underwear, where the fall of her skirt covered them.

Back in their rooms, she put on all her own warmest clothes and Mama's winter coat, which was too big for her. She rolled up the sleeves and wrapped a belt around her waist, pulling the excess material up over it so the coat didn't drag about her feet. The coat still smelled of Mama. She pulled the collar close around her face and breathed deeply, taking a little comfort and courage from the faint, sweet memory of perfume. Last of all, she took the crystal Aiden had given her and hung it around her neck.

She roused Charlotte, hushing her sleepy protests. She didn't protest loudly or for long. Once so lively and mischievous, she had become too thin, too quiet, since Mama had gone. Eveline dressed her in all the warm clothes she could find, until the little girl could hardly toddle.

She left her boots off and carried Charlotte, whose head was already drooping heavily against her shoulder. She turned the handle of the great iron-heavy front door, and pulled.

The door didn't move.

She'd forgotten the bolts.

The bottom one came loose, eventually – though she winced at every scrape it made against its brackets. The top one she couldn't reach.

There was nothing in the hall except a fragile little pot stand, barely able to support the ugly sharp-leaved plant in its massive, acid-green pot, writhing with embossed figures that seemed to grin and caper at her as she stood clutching the sleepy child.

Back door. She would have to go out the back door.

She scurried desperately through the sleeping house, her feet whispering on the cold tiles, stopping to take some bread and cheese. The kitchen still held a faint warmth; she wished she could take some with her as she opened the servants' door (the bolts here were easily reached with the help of a kitchen chair) and the cold grabbed her like a big hard hand. She paused to pull her boots on, propping Charlotte next to her, then wrapped her scarf around her head, pulled the door to behind her, and started down the steps.

She hurried through the regimented roses, bare sticks now, rigidly strapped to their supporting posts, and opened the garden gate that led onto the alleyway behind the houses. It was a narrow, muddy track between high fences, stinking and shuffling with rats, piled with discarded rubbish and heaps of rag. A bare filthy foot stuck out of one of the heaps, and Eveline stared, horrified. The foot withdrew into the rags, convulsively, like the leg of a wounded spider. Eveline clutched Charlotte tighter and ran as best she could.

Once out of the alley she looked back at Uncle James's. The house hunched against the sulphurous sky. There were no lights on. No windows flew open, no shouts competed with the boom and thump of the factories. It looked not one whit different from the day they had arrived, as though the three of them had never been there at all.

She had picked a time between shift changes. The streets were almost entirely empty except for a few figures huddled in doorways.

It wasn't long before she had to put Charlotte down. Charlotte whimpered and held her arms up to be carried. "No, Charlotte, you have to walk now. Come on, soon we'll see Aiden! He promised. He'll find us somewhere much nicer than Uncle James's. And nice things to eat and everything. Come on. Look, we're out at night-time. We're having an adventure, aren't we?"

Charlotte did not seem very impressed with the idea

of an adventure, but nonetheless stumped along beside her sister, stiff in her layers of clothes, occasionally rubbing at her eyes with her fists.

It seemed a terribly long way to the edge of town. As the houses went on and on, Eveline began to be afraid that she'd forgotten the way, that they were walking not towards the woods but away from them. It was very cold. She paused several times to wrap Charlotte's scarf more firmly and tug her own down towards her eyes and up towards her nose.

Charlotte began to whimper again. "Foots," she said. "Foots."

"Do your feet hurt?"

"Foots."

There was nowhere to sit, so Eveline lifted Charlotte up. Her little shoes were cracked and leaking; Eveline had put three pairs of stockings on her, but her feet were already wet. Eveline knew wet feet could be lethal, everyone said so, only the other day she had heard Harriet talking about an aunt of hers who had got her feet wet and died of the croup.

She wondered if they should turn back. She would be in terrible trouble.

As she straightened up, she caught a glimpse of something above the roofs at the end of the street, a black bristle against the louring sky. Trees! Not just someone's garden, but a proper thick mass of them.

"Look, Charlotte, the woods! Not far now. Come on!"

She held Charlotte against her shoulder, and walked as quickly as she could. Charlotte grew heavier with every step. The houses grew smaller, more like cottages, further apart. Gradually they fell away, and then they were on the road, in the woods.

The factories still thumped away, but here the sound was reduced to something less brutally present, an angry but impotent ghost thumping its fist on an insubstantial table.

"Aiden!" Eveline called. "Aiden!"

There were no glimmers of light, no sounds of the Folk. Perhaps they weren't far enough in. She kept walking. Eventually she turned off the road; perhaps the Folk didn't like the road. Besides, someone might come along and see them, and make them go back.

Under the trees it felt warmer, but the path was muddy and harder to see. Charlotte began to cry, a low, breathless whimper.

"Aiden! Aiden!" Eveline's throat hurt; her cries faded to croaks.

So dark, and the baby so heavy. She staggered, no longer sure where the path was. Then her shoulder hit something, something else scratched her face. She had walked into a tree, and only just avoided bashing Charlotte into it.

She couldn't see, and she couldn't carry Charlotte any longer. She sat down, and held her sister on her lap. She didn't realise she was crying until the tears chilled on her face.

There was a faint patter of something around her, like snow; she was no longer sure where she was. It had been so cold, but it wasn't any longer. She had been doing something important, but she was so tired.

A young voice. One she knew. "Aiden," she mumbled. Aiden was here. It was all right. Aiden would take care of them.

She woke hours later, stiff and cold. The branches of the trees were black lace against a clear chilly sky.

Charlotte was asleep on her lap, fragile eyelids stained purple like the petals of violets. Eveline looked around, muddled. She'd thought Aiden had found them, but it must have been a dream. They were still in the woods, in the mud, alone.

Eveline sighed. They must not have got far enough into the woods. She patted Charlotte's cheek. She would be hungry when she woke. Eveline hoped she would be able to persuade her to eat some of the bread and cheese, at least.

Charlotte didn't move.

"Charlotte, wake up."

The little girl lay limp and quiet. Eveline patted her cheek, harder, and Charlotte's mouth fell open, her chin drifting a little to the left.

She knew at that moment. Although she shook the baby and tried to stand her up and wailed her name and screamed it over and over to the black wet unmoving trees, she already knew that Charlotte was dead.

Aiden hadn't come, she had only dreamed it, and Charlotte was dead and she had killed her, taking her out in the woods at night with her weak chest, and her feet had got wet and now she was dead.

Eveline clutched the heavy cold little body and rocked, until the sun had risen and she heard the first carriage rattle along the road, not very far away.

She laid Charlotte on the ground and gathered wet brown leaf mould and mounded it over her as best she could, though she couldn't bear to cover the little girl's face with the slimy cold stuff. Instead she took off one of the shawls Charlotte had been wrapped in, and laid that over her. There were things one should say, she knew that. She could not remember what they had said at her father's grave. Had anyone spoken over her mother? She didn't know. They hadn't let her go to her mother's funeral. She hadn't even known the day.

"Goodbye, Charlotte." She wanted to say something else, wanted to say she was sorry, but *sorry* wasn't a big enough word. *Sorry* was a feather drifting on the wind.

She turned away and began to walk, finding herself eventually back at the road, or anyway at some road. She hardly cared if someone found her, but though the occasional carriage passed, no-one stopped. At some point she remembered she had the crystal in her hand. She dropped it indifferently in the mud.

And she walked, and kept walking.

So she had walked, and she had begged and been chased off and slept in ditches and dodged men who were like Everard-Dog-Man but poorer and dirtier, and sometimes she didn't manage to dodge, and she had learned to kick and butt and bite and sometimes just to endure. And finally she had found herself in London, which was louder and filthier and far more full of people than Watford. She had tried to get maid work, but she was too young and dirty and had no references. She soon learned to go to the servants' entrance, but even there she seldom got past the door. She stood supplicant before the servants of those great fine houses, sometimes catching glimpses of warm kitchens stuffed with food, and was told to go away, that she was a thief and a gypsy, that the police had been called, that she was a disgrace.

Sometimes people were kind. Sometimes a cook or a maid or a knife-boy would slip her a bit of food. But no-one would hire her.

She saw girls her own age and younger going with men for money. Having lost the last of her innocence on the road, she knew that that was what she'd run from, that was what Dog Man had wanted, and that was why Charlotte was dead. Sometimes she thought that if she hadn't run, at least they would be warm and fed; but having lost so much, she'd rather starve than do it now.

She was close enough to starving when she tried her first pocket, and failed. At the second, she was nearly caught. At the third she succeeded. Not much, a handkerchief. But you could sell handkerchiefs, if they were good enough, and then you could buy sausage or a bit of bread, and survive another day. She'd found it hard to resist a nice handkerchief ever since, no matter what else the mark might be carrying.

She learned. She learned to be quick and clever and to play the innocent if she was caught. She learned that if you approached someone rightly you could get them to *give* you their handkerchief and think they'd got the better of the bargain. She learned not to encroach on other thieves' territory – or at least, not in ways they'd notice and chase you for.

She fell in with Ma Pether and found, for a little while, something like a home again, and something like a family.

The Britannia School

EVELINE WOKE TO the harsh clanging of a bell, with the memory of dreams fading in her head. Mama and Charlotte and Aiden, all long gone. Now there was only Eveline.

Miss Prayne was standing at the door swinging the bell from side to side. Her movements were vague and flat, and the bell rang without rhythm: *clang-ca-clang bang tang*. "Up, girls," she said. The day had only just started, but she looked worn-out, like a cloth washed so many times it had lost most of its colour.

A double row of iron bedsteads stood on bare boards. Eveline's bed was under a window, where a draught snuck about the frame, and farthest from the door.

There was an unlit fireplace at one side of the room, smaller than the ones downstairs. Either side of it were two unmatched dressers; one had been good, once, but was now so chipped and battered it would fetch no more than a pound at best. The other had been cheap to start with and had got no better. One of its drawers was missing both knobs, and the others stuck at various angles. Each held a jug, a bowl, and a small plate with a knob of pallid soap.

Hastings shuffled over to the dressers, yawning, picked up the jugs and went out.

The girls began to dress, shuffling their nightgowns off and their clothes on under the covers. Eveline followed suit; better to do what they all did for now.

Hastings returned with the jugs full of water.

The girls began to line up. Treadwell was first. Eveline and Hastings were at the back of the queue. Eveline because she was waiting to see what happened next, Hastings because Treadwell had given her a shove and told her to wait her turn.

One by one they washed, put their hair up in front of the tiny rust-spotted mirror, and lined up again by the door. By the time Hastings and Eveline got to the water it was grey and scummy. Eveline scrubbed her face vigorously none the less.

Through it all, Miss Prayne stared at a point somewhere beyond the far wall, as though watching something much more interesting than a gaggle of adolescent girls jostling for position and dropping hairpins.

Breakfast was porridge and bread, Assembly another speech about how lucky they were. Eveline, starting out with a full belly for the second day in a row and spare bread tucked in her pockets, was beginning to agree – though all the jaw about what rubbish they would all be without the Empire got her properly riled.

After Assembly came Disguise, run by the waspish and over-rouged Miss Fortescue.

She looked Eveline over. "New blood," she sniffed.

She lined up pots and bottles, brushes and sponges and dyes. "Gutta-percha, putty, greasepaint, mortician's wax – don't make that face, girl, we don't scrape the stuff off corpses. Wigs. Real hair is best, horsehair will do in a pinch or at a distance. Tools of the trade. But most of the time you'll barely need all this. It's in stance, voice, gait. Old women and young men move differently. Someone hiding a secret makes different gestures from someone declaring their love. Keep your eyes open. Watch. Go to the theatre, get backstage. Actors love to talk, and if you can get them off the subject of themselves, they're a treasure-box. You there, new girl. Go behind that screen and take off your outer things."

Eveline stood in her shift and stockings, shivering. Miss Fortescue joined her, her arms piled with clothes. Pulling Eveline around like a small child with a new doll, she dressed her, did things to her hair, and crammed a cap on her head. Then she pulled her out from behind the screen and sat her at a table by the window, where a mirror reflected back a small, pallid face under an overlarge tweed cap. "Not bad," Miss Fortescue said. "But you still look like a girl. Class, pay attention. For a more masculine appearance, enlarge the nose. Just a bit, no need to make a Mr Punch of yourself." She opened a pot containing a strange pink substance. "This is putty. It's too pink, but it will do for this occasion." She looked at Eveline via her reflection. "You'll learn to make up your own, to match your skin. There's no use using prosthetics the wrong colour, they're far too obvious. You're better off without. A little darkening on the jaw – not too much, just to square it, a brush of stubble. Don't overdo it or you'll look like a chimney sweep. Less is more, girls, less is always more."

By the time she had finished, a slight but definite boy was looking out of the mirror. Eveline grinned at her reflection. She *liked* this class.

Treadwell said something to one of the other girls and an outburst of giggling followed. Miss Fortescue paid it no mind. Eveline noticed, but didn't let it trouble her overmuch.

AFTER DISGUISE, SHE was sent to the Old Barn. Low sun spilled across the front of the school, warming the ugly bricks to a gentler glow, and laying long tree-shadows on the rich green grass. The sound of champing and shuffling came from the stables.

Eveline paused, suddenly overwhelmed with memory. Home. The neighbour's horses in the field, the chuffling of hens, the chatter of goblins in the roof of the barn. Sweet apples dropping on the grass for the wasps to find, if she didn't get to them first.

Aiden, sitting on a branch, swinging his legs, smiling and calling out that she was slow, slow, she should come and see the spider-web all jewelled with dew that he had found for her... he had lifted it entire from its branch and placed it around her neck, flickering and glittering, a dance of tiny rainbows. But when, hours later, she meant to show Mama, it had all melted away.

She turned away from the sun and the woods and the memory and marched into the barn, her back rigid.

The Old Barn was a cavern of drifting dust and subtle gleams and pigeon-droppings. It smelled of oil and metal and the ghosts of long-gone hay. Something clanged, and a great plume of steam hissed out past Eveline, making her jump backwards.

"What is it?" A man appeared out of the steam, pushing back a pair of goggles like those the steam hansom drivers wore. He had a long, sour face and straight, thinning hair, and walked as though his joints had not been properly tightened, all lope and dangling hands. He wore what looked like a butcher's apron, only made of leather, and thick leather gauntlets. "What do you want?"

"I'm here for Mechanics," Eveline said.

"Hah! Well I suppose you'd better come in."

"She's here to study Etheric science, Mr Jackson," came a voice. Hastings, also aproned and goggled.

"Oh, you're *that* girl," Mr Jackson said. "Etheric science. Hah. Hastings, show her the..." He gestured towards the back of the barn and turned away towards some great drum-bodied thing of tubes and dials and ugly dark-red paint like drying blood.

"Yes, Mr Jackson," Hastings said. "Come along, all the stuff's over here. At least, what there is."

"But I don't..." Eveline said. *Etheric science?* That was her mama's work. She hadn't heard the words in so long...

Feeling a strange fluttering in her throat, she followed Hastings.

A long, battered table stood by the wall. And on it... Eveline felt a sudden sharp pain around her heart, as though something had sunk its claws into her chest. She backed away, and sat down abruptly on a pile of old sacks.

Hastings realised she had lost her follower and turned round. "Is something wrong? Are you ill?"

"I'm not ill," Eveline said, once she had her breath back, still staring at the machines. "Where'd those come from?"

Hastings looked at them and shrugged in her turn. "I don't know, they just arrived. They're Etheric machines, or that's what Mr Jackson says."

Eveline struggled to her feet. Hay dust puffed up around her, smelling of lost summers.

She walked over to the machines, carefully, slowly, as though they might turn on her like badly-treated dogs. She reached out her hand and ran it over a dial, stroked a loop of wire, caressed a layer of dust from a gleaming wooden casing.

"What is it?" Hastings said. "What's the matter?"

"These were my mother's."

"Are you sure?"

"Of course I'm sure! See that chip?" Eveline pointed to the corner of a rosewood box with a flat, gleaming silver plate set into its top. "I done that when I was little, playing shuttlecock in her workroom. She'd told me not to..." Her voice broke and stopped. She swallowed down her grief, feeling it battling something else, something rising up the other way. "What are they *doing* here?"

"They were brought here for you, I suppose. What happened to your mama?"

"She died. She got some sort of sickness and she died."

"Oh." Hastings crumpled the edge of her apron in her fingers, staring at her feet. "I'm sorry."

"Where's yours?"

Hastings shook her head. "Birmingham, I think. Do you know how these work?"

Eveline looked at them, still strange and beautiful, gleaming under their dust. "They sing. They used to sing. But I don't know how to make them do it, it was my mama did that. I don't know why Holmforth thinks I can do it. He –"

Holmforth. He must have got these from Uncle James's.

You may have the skills I need...

Her thoughts were whirling like a carousel at the fair. She stared at the machines, through a blur of tears, wiping them away with her hands.

"Hastings! Stop chattering and bring me that hammer." Mr Jackson, head and shoulders inside the red machine, his voice distorted by the drum, gestured vaguely at a rack on the wall hung with tools.

"We'll talk in a little," Hastings said. "He'll forget I'm here soon, he usually does." She touched Eveline's arm. "Sit down, you look awful."

Hastings scurried off, and Eveline picked up the machine with the rabbit-ear on top, the one she remembered most clearly, and sat on one of the ancient rickety chairs, holding it on her lap the way she had held Charlotte, so long ago.

The Crepuscular

Fox felt an impulse in himself to go home... or at least, back. *Home* didn't really apply any more. That was gone, such as it had been, and the land where it had stood was covered now with crammed, ugly buildings that no longer carried the scent of his family. No trees stood now to hush in the wind and shed leaves into spice-scented mounds of quick rustling life. The smell of snow was tainted as soon as it fell, and bore no delicate prints pointing the way to prey. Instead it was mushed almost immediately to a granular yellow-grey slush that held few marks, and stank of disease and bitter chemicals.

But something was happening. Fox knew the wind, he felt its shift, the tiny movements within the greater movements, harbingers of change. It was his necessity and his joy, to dance along the edges of things, seeing the patterns in what those at the centre ignored as insignificant. And something was ruffling his fur, making the fine hairs in his ears shiver. A breeze, thin and tiny as a thread come loose from its reel, which could unspool and set a typhoon spinning. What it was, yet, he didn't know. But there was something. His mother's people, such meddlers as they were, were forever poking into things. He had seen nothing yet to tempt his mistress, but he kept his nose to the winds of change, and this still-tiny breeze smelled of brass and oil – and advantage.

He had spent enough time recently in the Crepuscular, and longed for the crude and brilliant warmth of his other life. It was time to pass back again, to wear the other mask.

Sometimes he wondered what his own face looked like, and even if he still had one. But then everyone wore masks. Everyone switched from upper to lower, man to master, bowing the head here and flicking the whip there. He saw all the hierarchies clearly, and though he might dance within them, he knew that it was all a game of masks.

There was, of course, the girl. She intrigued him. Her cleverness was pleasing, and like him she danced along the edges of things.

Though, perhaps, not for long. She triggered his sensitive nose. She smelt... *significant*. Whatever this shift was, she was bound into it.

Also, he liked her. She wore masks, too, of necessity – but sometimes he glimpsed beyond them.

Only when he was curled up alone, one eye open on the verge of sleep, did the thought ever creep past his defences of how good it would be not to wear a mask, to rest from the endless dance of hierarchy and favour, and be simply himself. But he was no longer sure he had a self to be.

The Britannia School

EVELINE TOUCHED THE machines, running her finger over a lever, or the groove where a ball bearing should run. So hard to remember those voices her mother had drawn from them like fine gold wires. So hard to remember how it had been near the end, when she had started making them all sing together. She could remember it was like being in a wonderful cave all made of music, but she couldn't remember what it sounded like, or how to make it happen again.

Her mother's hands had moved on them so surely. Her own hands were neat and quick at their work, but their work was thieving, not this. Tears kept coming, trickling down her face and soaking her collar. With pounding head and aching throat, she tried to think. Hastings came back.

"Hastings, how'd you know these were Etheric machines?"

"I saw some in a book. I told you, I like machines."

"Do you know how they work?"

Hastings gave her a sideways look. She seemed ill-at-ease. "They make noises, and they're supposed to have some sort of effect on people. That's all I know. Your mama never taught you?"

"I was *eight*."

"I've been interested in machines at least as long as that," Hastings said. "It's why I'm here."

"Well I wasn't interested, not then, all right?" Eveline snapped. "How was I to know she was going to die?"

"Sorry."

"Anyway, what do you mean it's why you're here?"

Hastings fidgeted with a coil of wire that lay on the bench. "I was forever messing with things, taking them apart to see how they worked. Mama tried to beat it out of me. She thought I might make a decent marriage – she was daft. I'm a bastard, no-one respectable was going to marry me. Anyway, she wrote to my father and he got me put in here. She told me it was that or Bedlam. This is better."

"She said you'd go to Bedlam?"

"If I didn't do as I was told."

Eveline grimaced. She'd heard about Bedlam, where all the mad people got kept – but she'd never thought you could be put in there just for liking machines. "She *wrote* to your father?"

"Yes. She didn't normally – he'd only pay for my upkeep if she kept out of his way and didn't embarrass him."

"So they're not married."

"I'm a bastard, like I said."

"Well, I'm an orphan."

"Orphan's respectable."

"Not if you're a thief."

Hastings shrugged. "Well, he didn't want me, and in the end nor did she, so it hardly matters, does it? Do you remember how any of these work?"

"Sort of. Maybe. Some of them. But... I know how to get some of them started, but I don't know what the noises are supposed to do. Or how."

"You don't remember that?"

"No. Were there any notebooks, when it was all brought in? Mama had dozens of them."

"I didn't see any, I'm sorry. Why do they want you to study this, anyway?" Hastings said.

"I wish I knew. It's why *I'm* here." Eveline frowned at the instruments, looking so strange in this big clanging dusty space, bits of her childhood yanked from the past and dropped in front of her. What did Holmforth want, with the instruments, and with her?

And if she couldn't make them work, what would happen then?

"Hastings, you ever done any of this?"

"What, Etherics? No. Most people..." She hesitated, glanced over where Mr Jackson was still waist-deep in his machine. "No."

"Most people what? Come on, you've been chewing on something since you said what they were."

Hastings sighed. "Most people think it's nonsense. I'm sorry, Evvie. They either think it's nonsense or that it's something only some people have an ability for – that it's like having red hair, something you're born with. And it's mostly women. So, even people who believe in it don't think it's important."

"Well, if it were something you were born with, I'd know, wouldn't I? Anyway I don't believe it. She worked hard, my mama. Harder'n anyone. Day and night, sometimes. She didn't just *know* what to do from the day she was born."

Hastings looked at the mechanisms, rubbing her nose. "It's never made sense to me," she said. "If people get a chance to learn things they can do things, mostly. Some people are better at some things, yes; but I don't think it's in you when you're born. It's like thinking only men can do engines. I can make an engine work, I learned."

"'Men're good for doing plenty, but women can do that plus twenty,' that's what... someone I know says. She liked mechanisms, too, she just wasn't much good at 'em. I don't think it was anything to do with being female, though. It's not like you gotta hold a spanner in your dick, is it?"

Hastings frowned. "I don't understand."

"You do know what a dick is?" Eveline said. Hastings shook her head. "You know. A chappie's chappie, his...." Seeing Hastings' utter bemusement, she said, "What he pisses outa."

Hastings clapped a hand over her mouth and choked behind it, her cheeks bright red.

"'Sall right," Eveline said. "Jackson ain't listening."

"Yes, well, I was!" Hastings said, her eyes screwed up with laughter. "Oh, don't let Mr Jackson hear!"

"He's got his ears fulla steam."

Eventually Hastings got control of herself.

"So you got no idea how they work?" Eveline said.

"I don't even know *if* they do."

"Oh, they do. My mama could make them work. She was getting somewhere, before she got sick. Mr Jackson know anything?"

"He doesn't believe in it either, so probably not."

"Well that's a fat lot of good, then." Eveline sighed and kicked at the straw. "Now what'm I to do? If I don't work out how they work, I'm like as not out on my ear. Or worse," she said. "That Holmforth, I don't trust him a farthing's worth."

"Who's Holmforth?"

"He's the cove what brought me here. He's the one

thinks I know how to make these work, because... wait a minute, he thinks *Uncle James* could do Etherics. He mentioned him. He never mentioned Mama at all."

"I don't understand," Hastings said.

"Never mind. I do. Bloody Uncle James pretended it was his work. Holmforth must have been one of the people he took it to. Don't know why Holmforth is interested now the miserable old bastard's dead." There was a sudden *clang* and a bout of muffled swearing from the other side of the room.

"What is that thing he's fadgetting with?" Eveline said.

"Jackson's Velocitator."

"Velocitator?"

"That's what he calls it. It's an advanced version of a steam car, much more powerful... or it would be, if... Never mind," she said.

"If what?"

"If he'd let me work on it. I've got lots of ideas. But *he's* one who thinks you should have to hold a spanner in... you know."

But Eveline was barely listening. She could see that cosy little room, the fatly upholstered armchair, the little embroidered footstool in front of the fire. Her feet, in warm stockings, resting on the footstool. The tines of a fork dimpling the grease-shining skin of a sausage. The footstool was embroidered with blue and yellow lilies, like the dusty stolen curtains in Ma Pether's room.

The little room shrank and greyed, fading out of her reach.

If she displeased him... well, she *might* just end up dumped in the country miles from anywhere, with no money. *If* she was lucky. And if she made it back to London... if Holmforth thought Ma wouldn't know she'd been taken up by someone who smelled like law, within minutes of it happening, he was a fool. Not that he needed to care – he wasn't the one that would have to try and persuade her to take Evvie in again, convince her that Evvie hadn't spilled every bean on her plate to Holmforth and whoever he worked for.

Ma Pether'd never trust her again. Never. Which meant half the Newgate birds in London would have no use for this particular sparrow, neither.

She had to make the machines work.

KNOWLEDGE, THAT WAS the key. Without it, she was helpless. She needed to know more about Holmforth and what he wanted, about the instruments and what they did. And until she could speak to Holmforth again, the only person she knew who might know something was Miss Cairngrim.

Of course, there were other ways to get knowledge – cajoling, persuading, getting people to talk about themselves; she knew, and had used, all of them – but sometimes a hairpin in the middle of the night was by far the best way.

The door swung open. Not a scrap of moonlight was allowed into Miss Cairngrim's office; it was as tightly shuttered as the woman herself. Eveline didn't want to risk opening the shutters, in case of noise. She had brought a candle, which would have to do.

She made her way methodically through the drawers of the desk, carefully returning every bit of paper and scrap of pencil where she found it. Miss Cairngrim's tidiness made it all the easier – this would have been a lot harder in Ma Pether's rooms, with everything all of a higgle-piggle. With some people you could trust they wouldn't notice, but not with Ma Pether.

She found a battered book with a blue cloth cover, full of figures. Accounts. Income. The main amount from someone or something called HMG; which, seeing a letterhead with the same initials, she realised was Her Majesty's Government.

The monthly stipend looked substantial, but it got eaten up fast. Clothes, food, teachers' wages, soap... tiny obsessive figures in ever-smaller columns as Miss Cairngrim tried to stretch the money over the bills like thin pastry over too big a pie. *Owed to butcher, 6s 5d. Owed to baker, 2s 9d.* Eveline grinned to herself, wondering if the candlestick maker was in there, too. Then her head shot up as she heard a noise; something scraping the glass of the window, outside the shutters. *Scree, scree.*

A branch shifted by the wind, nothing more; it was only the silence of the house made it seem so loud.

Still, it was a warning she should heed. Well, Miss Cairngrim was short of money, that was interesting; a lever, if Eveline chose to use it and could find the means. But it told her nothing about Holmforth.

Another drawer – more accounts. Another – a diary. Appointments and reminders listed in that same cramped, tiny hand. *Speak to Mr M about books. Carstairs girl's accusations – ridiculous.* Carstairs girl? What Carstairs girl?

Scree, scree, the branch went, scraping on the glass. *Hurry up, Eveline.*

She sighed. Well, at least she knew a few things she hadn't before, but whether any of it was the least use...

Then her eye caught a fine line in the veneer of the desk, no more than a thread of light; if the candle hadn't wavered, in the draft, she'd never have seen it. She'd seen such a thing before, in some of the furniture that had passed through Ma's hands. If she was right, it was a secret drawer. A secret drawer for secret things.

She felt about with careful, clever fingers, gently pulling and pushing, until a little ledge went *click*.

The crack widened, showing darkness.

Carefully, carefully, Eveline slid it open.

Papers. Cuttings from *The Times* and the *Illustrated London News*. Men in top hats. Solemn civic occasions, posh social events. *Lord Tracey meeting the trade delegation... Lord Silverman, Lord Fallwell and friends at the races...*

Who were all these people? Was Miss Cairngrim like one of those old ladies who kept every scrap and clipping about the royal family?

But there seemed to be no connection, except that all the people shown were important persons of one sort or another. And here and there a face was ringed with blue ink.

She held the lantern closer.

There was something familiar about one of those faces. Lord Silverman...

Lord Silverman looked an *awful* lot like Treadwell.

Fascinated, Eveline studied the rest.

She couldn't see it in all of them, but in some, yes; the features of the daughters stamped upon the fathers, clear as day. And there was a Lord Donmar at a hunt ball, with his (presumably legitimate) daughter on his arm, her head adorned with feathers, jewels at her neck; her face a dead ringer for Hastings'.

Well, well, well. So that was where the Britannia school got its pupils, was it? Maybe not all of them, but enough.

It didn't seem that Miss Cairngrim had stooped to blackmail, though. If she had, she wasn't putting the takings into the school. Maybe she just liked to know. Eveline grinned to herself. Well, now *she* knew, too. She slid the drawer back.

It stuck, one corner jutting accusingly.

Eveline swore, jiggled the drawer this way and that, but it wouldn't budge. She dipped her fingers in the hot candle-wax and rubbed it on the visible edges of the drawer, eased and pulled and prayed. *Come on, you wretched, filthy thing!*

Finally, with treacherous suddenness, the drawer slid back into place, taking Evvie by surprise, making the table rock so the candle tilted dangerously. Eveline grabbed it before it could fall, hot wax spilling over her hand.

Footsteps. Footsteps right outside the door.

Eveline's heart jumped into her throat. She pushed the drawer smoothly shut, pinched the candle out with her fingers so it wouldn't betray her with the smell of smoke.

The room was instantly, utterly dark. Eveline crept towards where she remembered the faded sofa standing, knowing she could wriggle behind it and hide, and ran straight into something that drove a brutal corner into her shinbone. She bit down hard on the swearword that sprang up, reached down and rubbed her leg briskly. She couldn't feel any blood, at least.

A light under the door; pale and wavering. A candle. But it didn't stop, and nor did the footsteps. They went on.

Who – or who *else* – was wandering about at this time of night? The water closets were upstairs, it couldn't be that.

Eveline backed away from the vicious table and relit her candle. Quickly, she made sure the drawers she had opened were all tightly locked, that everything looked the same as when she had entered. Then she unlocked the door, snuffed her candle again, and crept out into the corridor.

The other light was wavering, away towards the kitchens. She pulled the door shut, the click of the latch sounding very loud. She had to lock it again, or Miss Cairngrim would guess someone had been in. She took a deep breath, clenched her jaw, and then relaxed it. Impatience never sped a lock yet, that was what Ma Pether had taught her.

Carefully, she relocked it, the snick of the tongue like a breaking glass in the stillness.

The light was out of sight, but a glimmer could still be seen on the walls. Never one to turn down a chance at knowing something someone didn't want her knowing, Eveline followed it.

She got close enough to see that the lamp-carrier was Treadwell, the bright halo of her curls yellow as butter in the lamplight. Well, well, so she wasn't all piety and tale-telling after all. What was she about, at this time of night?

Eveline had learned her way about by now. Treadwell was heading towards the forbidden area where the staff slept. She wasn't hurrying, though; in fact, the closer she got, the slower her footsteps went.

She reached a door, the one all by itself at the end of the corridor, and stopped. For a long moment she only stood there, then slowly, like someone in a bad dream who can't stop whatever is happening to them, she turned the handle, and went in.

The room was Monsieur Duvalier's.

A moment later came the sound of the key being turned in the lock.

Eveline did not need to listen any longer to guess what came next. She made her way carefully and silently back to the dormitory and back to her bed without waking anyone, and lay there with one ear open, slipping in and out of dreams of flapping curtains in broken windows and dead leaves rustling across dusty floors. Eventually, with dragging steps, Treadwell came back. Eveline heard her get into bed.

Then she heard her crying.

Bon-bons, indeed, she thought. *Don't think I want any of your bon-bons, Monsewer Duvalier.*

She was tired, but now she couldn't sleep; her head was full of confused, angry thoughts, like a storm trapped in its clouds. Treadwell stopped crying and fell asleep. Eveline huffed and sighed to herself, angrily shoving the thin pillow about as though battering it might relieve her feelings. Well, now she knew something she hadn't, but she wished she didn't know it. She didn't *like* Treadwell. She didn't want to feel sorry for her.

But she didn't feel sorry for Monsewer Duvalier. Oh, no. Monsewer Duvalier had something coming to him, and if she could, Eveline would take great pleasure in being the one who brought it.

WEEKS PASSED. EVELINE discovered the horrors of French verb construction, the use of the parasol both to shade the complexion and wind an opponent, and the many ways in which a young woman could be made to look like an old one, or a man, or a foreigner. She made good progress in Retention, very slight progress in Cantonese (her fingers were constantly bruised from Wen Hsu's stick), even less in Navigation, and none whatsoever with her mother's mechanisms. Sometimes she managed to raise a wheeze or a dreadful catlike yowling from one of them, sometimes a growl. The only noticeable effect it had was to send Mr Jackson complaining to Miss Cairngrim that he could not work with such a dreadful noise going on. Considering the constant hammering and clanging that he engaged in on his Velocitator, and the way he shouted during his occasional, half-hearted attempts at teaching, Eveline considered this more than a little unfair. She even asked his advice about the Etheric mechanisms, but his only response was to call them superstitious rubbish intended to fool the credulous, and tell her she would be better off paying attention to her stitching.

She lived in dread of Holmforth's next visit.

She attempted to distract herself with gathering all the knowledge she could about the school and its inhabitants, though after dark she kept her explorations to the main building. The dogs that ran loose in the grounds at night were a thoroughly nasty pair of animals controllable only by Thomas, their monosyllabic and odorous keeper. During the day they were chained up in the laundry yard, and hanging the washing was a task all the girls hated, living in dread that one day the chains would break as the vile animals barked and lunged and drooled within feet of them.

It was a rambling place, built for a large family and at least a dozen servants. Twenty girls and half as many staff did little to fill it. Half the rooms on the east side were shut off, and a smell of damp came from them which was only slightly more pervasive than that which filled the rest of the building.

When a carriage pulled up at the house for the third time in as many days and Eveline's heart climbed into her throat for fear it might be Holmforth, she realised there was only one thing for it. She had to get her mother's notes.

If they still existed. If James or whoever came after him hadn't found them.

The house would have gone to strangers now. She just prayed it hadn't been knocked down.

It would be hard to do it alone. Not the robbery, about that she'd no qualms. It wasn't even robbery, strictly speaking; she'd only be taking back what was hers.

Getting out of the school and back in, though, that was a whole other business.

Eveline began to think very hard.

"MR WEN HSU IS UNWELL. We have a replacement." Miss Cairngrim frowned. "He is very *young*. I had hoped for another respectable gentleman of mature years, but I suppose we will have to make do. He does come on personal recommendation. Necessary, of course, in a place such as this. You will be exposed to a great deal of temptation, Duchen, especially when mingling with foreigners. Regard this as an opportunity to practise keeping a proper distance at all times."

"Yes, Miss Cairngrim." Eveline wondered, again, whether she should tell her about Treadwell and Monsewer... but she was pretty certain that if she did so, she wouldn't be believed. She had a feeling she knew what the Carstairs girl's 'ridiculous accusations' had been.

She made her way to the small, chilly room where her Cantonese lessons took place, hoping she wouldn't have to deal with any silliness. Miss Cairngrim couldn't be any more eager for there to be none of that nonsense than she herself was.

She knocked on the door, and pushed it open.

"*Zǎoshàng hǎo*, Lady Sparrow."

Seated on the table, grinning and wearing a robe of dark blue embroidered silk and a small round cap, was Liu.

"What the hell are you doing here?" Eveline said.

"Now, Miss Duchen, that shows no respect at all for your venerable teacher," he said. "I hope you are well?"

"I will be soon's I'm over the shock. Liu, what are you up to?"

"I am here to teach you Cantonese, of course."

"But you work for the Brighart Steam Transport Company!"

"And where is it written that a man must have one job all his life?" Liu dropped neatly to the ground. "What are *you* doing here, Lady Sparrow?"

"Don't tell me you don't know what I'm doing here. I'm learning things. 'Sa school. That's what you do in school, is learn things."

"I will be a far better teacher of Cantonese than my predecessor, who no doubt bruised your fingers and gave you very boring lessons."

"Sure of yourself, aren't you? How'd you get taken on?"

"Now, Lady Sparrow, do you really expect me to reveal all my tricks? We know each other better than that, yes?"

"I don't know you at all. Are you a spy?"

He paused in the act of taking a scroll out of his sleeve, and looked at her with his head tilted a little to the side. "Not really," he said. "Are you loyal to your Empress, Lady Sparrow?"

"Well, she's paying my clothes, board and education, so I s'pose I'd better be."

"Then we are in a very similar situation. However, my Empress and yours are not at odds, so I see no reason why it should concern us in the slightest. Shall we learn some words? I know much more interesting ones than the old man. I can tell you the secret names of *all* of the river dragons."

"I'm not listening to a thing until you tell me what you're doing here."

He propped himself back on the table, swinging his legs. "I was bored," he said. "I wanted to see you. I thought we were friends. Don't you want to be friends, Lady Sparrow?"

"Are you going to get me into trouble?"

"I don't plan to," he said. "In fact, if there is trouble, I may help you avoid it. I'm good at that."

Eveline laughed. "Coming here don't look like avoiding trouble to me. Well if you can get me as good at Cantonese as you are at English, I'll be grateful – but you'd better not tell anyone you know me, or we'll both be for it. I still don't know how the hell you found me."

"I told you before," he said. "I am exceptionally clever."

"Or *why*."

"Because you interest me. I think you are clever, too – maybe even as clever as I am."

He was certainly a better teacher than the old man – in among the joking and teasing, she made more progress in one hour than she had in weeks. Maybe it was just because he explained instead of cracking her on the hand, or maybe it was because he didn't seem to despise her the way her former teacher did. "The one who was here before, he always acted like he thought I smelled bad," she said.

"You do not smell bad."

"*I* didn't think I did. He smelled a bit himself. But he looked at me like I was stuck to his shoe. 'Sfunny: I got used to that, before, but now it proper narks me." She laughed. "I must be turning respectable."

"Oh, I shouldn't let it trouble you. If someone thinks one is nothing, there is more satisfaction in proving them wrong, is there not?"

"If you say so," she said. He was right, of course. There was far more satisfaction in ripping off someone who treated you like dirt. But although he knew her for a thief, she didn't feel inclined to remind him of it.

"In China, women are not much valued, and their education very limited. To have to teach a woman, and a *gweilo* at that..."

"A what?"

"*Gweilo*. It is an insulting word for someone who is not Chinese. He must have needed the work very badly. Or perhaps the people who run things here knew something about him that he could not afford to get out."

"Maybe *he* was a spy," Eveline said.

"Possibly. But what does it matter? He is gone. As to the smell – yes. He was taking opium. It affects the bowels. That teacher of yours, the one who looks as though she were left in the sun too long? She too is taking opium."

"Oh, Miss Prayne! She's a miserable thing, I'd not be surprised if she drinks laudanum like it was tea."

"Does she drink it because she is miserable, or is she miserable because she drinks it? I do not like opium. People go into dreams, and some of them never come out."

"Don't see that it's worse than gin."

"And you have seen what gin can do."

"Oh, I seen that all right."

His mobile, lively face saddened. "I have seen many, many people sicken and lose everything and die from opium. You know your Empire sells a great deal of opium to my country."

"I seen plenty of people lose everything and sicken and die without needing opium, just out of being poor." She shrugged. "And that or gin, it takes 'em out of themselves. If all you got is a clenching belly and grinding hard work when you can get it, you need something to get you through the day."

Her mother had never drunk. Her mother had worked. But even that had been taken from her.

"What is it?" Liu said, searching her face.

"Nothing. You'd better be careful what you say about the Empire, round here, though. This place is all for the Empire, and Her Maj, and all."

"Her Maj?"

"The Queen. The Empress."

"*Her Maj* does not sound very respectful," he said.

"And are you always respectful about your Empress?"

"When there is any chance she might hear of it, yes."

"I see. So are you going to tell on me?"

"How could I possibly do that, when my English is certainly not good enough to know when you are being disrespectful?"

They grinned at each other.

EVELINE CAME OUT of the lesson and paused in the corridor, watching the darkening green sweep of the lawn as the trees laid long shadows over it.

The smile on her face felt strange. She hadn't had so much fun since she'd left Ma Pether's. There was something about Liu that put her dangerously at ease, but she couldn't afford to trust him. She didn't believe he'd come all this way and gone to the bother of getting himself hired just because he felt like it, or because he wanted to see her – it wasn't as though they'd been sweethearts, or anything like that. She liked him well enough. She liked his sharp white grin and his sharper tongue, his long dark eyes, his glossy black hair and quick, neat movements... *You're getting soft, Evvie Duchen. Can't afford to get soft.*

No, she didn't believe it. Since Mama, there'd been no-one in her life who didn't want something from her. He was working for someone: Ma Pether, perhaps, or Holmforth. Spying on her. He had to be. She remembered some of the things she'd said, and shivered suddenly. She was a fool. She'd have to be more careful. If it came back on her she'd say she was suspicious, and testing him out by saying disloyal things.

She didn't like the thought of ratting on him. She kicked at the skirting, scowling. Well, if he ratted on her, she'd do likewise. What'd he have to come here for, anyway? She had troubles enough. She wondered, briefly, if he knew anything about Etheric science, if he was so all-fired clever... but she'd made herself vulnerable enough. She certainly wasn't going to admit to him that she didn't have the first idea how to make Mama's precious mechanisms work.

But she had an idea about that.

"You've been working on something, haven't you?" Eveline said, pushing aside one of the mechanisms with a sigh.

"What do you mean?" Hastings said.

"You should be more careful, you keep sneaking off and then coming in stinking of oil. It don't notice when we've been out here, but it does in lessons. You smell like Lazy Lou."

"Who's Lazy Lou?"

"A mechanical woman someone I knew had."

"An automaton! Oh, I'd give anything to get hold of a good one..."

"Never mind that. You hear what I said?"

"Of course I did!" Hastings looked her up and down, wonderingly, and shook her head. "You're *clever*," she said. "Why are you so awful with Navigation?"

"Because it's boring and stupid and Miss Prayne makes me want to scream and throw eggs."

Hastings giggled. "It's a shame. If she wasn't so *mopey* even you might get interested."

"Can I borrow your notes?"

"Much good they'll do you."

"I know." Eveline sighed. "All them lines and circles don't make the least bit of sense to me. I'm good at *people*, not stupid lines."

"The lines are only a way of talking about real things," Hastings said. "You'll need them if you ever have to travel by yourself. What if you're in a boat and something happens to the person you're with and you have to find your way home?"

"Don't." Eveline hugged her arms around herself.

"Don't you want to travel?" Hastings said.

"Not me. I want a nice warm house and enough to eat, right here in England, thank you."

"You'll have to if they make you."

"I s'pose. But fat lot of use I'll be to the Empire if I get lost."

"I can't wait," Hastings said. "I've never even been on an airship. Oh, can you imagine? Up there, away from everything... you could go anywhere in the world, in an airship." She thought for a moment. "Well, you could with enough fuel, anyway."

"That great noisy thing's bad enough," Eveline said, glowering across the barn.

"That *thing* is a variant of the steam car. Mr Jackson wants to patent the engine. It's revolutionary." Hastings pushed her hair back with a wet hand and said, "At least it *would* be, if he wasn't... he just won't *listen*."

"Well, of course he won't. Never knew a man yet who'd listen when he's got his teeth in something – like terriers, they are. You gotta distract them with something else. How far could you get on that?"

"That? About half a mile before the engine overheats," Hastings said. "Honestly, he keeps trying to push more power through it and he won't compensate properly. I haven't been doing anything to it but what I'm told. What would be the point? If I change anything, he'll only change it back."

"So where is it?"

"Where's what?" Hastings said, her eyes going wide and round like a nervy horse's.

"Come on, I know you been working on something. You been making your own, ain'tcher?"

"You mustn't tell!"

Eveline shook her head. "See? You just give yourself away, saying that. You gotta be more careful. I'd not have known for certain if you hadn't *said*."

Hastings shot a glance at the Velocitator, where Mr Jackson was yet again banging something and muttering, then grabbed Eveline's hand. "Oh, but now you know, and I can show you, I've been wanting so much to show someone, come tonight, please. You're so clever, maybe you can show me how to get some of the things I need...."

"Whoa up, girl!" Eveline tugged her hand away, grinning. "All right. You need stuff, I'll try and help – I need something too, so maybe you can help me."

"Yes, yes, of course, it's just I need more steel, and some India-rubber, and copper wire, and..."

"How close is yours to being ready?"

"Ready to do what?" Hastings said. "It'll run, and it'll stop. I haven't had a chance to test the engine at full stretch – it's a lot quieter than the Velocitator, but if I take it through the grounds the tracks will be so obvious... besides, I haven't been able to get enough copper wire to finish the connections and there's no cover over the differential mass accelerator... why? Are you finally getting interested?"

"Oh, I'm interested, all right."

"Why?"

"If I can get you the materials you need, how d'you fancy taking it for a spin?"

"You mean through more of the grounds? But what about the dogs?"

"Surely it can outrun a couple of dogs."

"Easily, but what's to stop them barking?"

"Oh, you leave that to me," Eveline said, grinning. She had tricks aplenty to stop a dog from barking – geese were a lot worse.

"And the tracks it'll leave?"

"I'll think of something. Once we're on the road, it won't matter."

"The *road*? Duchen, what are you thinking?"

"Fancy a trip to Watford?"

"*Where?*" Hastings shook her head so violently her hair tumbled out of its pins. "No. No, no. Take her outside the school? You're mad. I'd be expelled. I'd go to Bedlam. She'd be stolen, or broken up. No."

"She?"

"She's called the *Sacagawea*," Hastings said.

"What's that when it's at home?"

"A woman who guided Lewis and Clarke on their expedition in America. An explorer."

"I thought explorers *went* somewhere. That's the point of exploring, ain't it?"

"I can't," Hastings said. "Duchen..."

"Oh, call me Eveline, for the love of... ain't no-one else around to hear you bark out my name like I was a soldier."

"All right, Eveline."

"And you're Beth?"

"Yes. But don't let Miss Grim hear you use it. We're supposed to maintain a proper distance. Oh!" She covered her mouth with an oily hand. "Listen to me, you've got me calling her that now," she wailed. "I'll forget and do it to her face and *then* what? And if I try and take *Sacagawea* out... I won't do it. She has to be finished. She isn't finished."

"How long have you been working on it, then?"

"Since just after I got here. About two years, I suppose."

"Can I see it, at least?"

EVELINE LOOKED AT the machine and sighed. "I think maybe I'd just better try and borrow a horse."

"I thought you couldn't ride."

"Well, I stuck on, once. For a bit. I'll have to manage. 'Cos *that* ain't going anywhere, is it?"

It was not a beautiful machine. Its origins in scraps and scavenging were pitifully obvious. Its wheels didn't match, its inner workings were a mass of dull coils and ancient gears, and its seat appeared to have begun life as a church pew, before an unfortunate and extended encounter with a savage woodworm. If she hadn't known better, she might think it was just a pile of old bits and pieces that had somehow fallen together into a vaguely cart-like shape.

"She's not *finished*," Beth Hastings said. "I can't get the materials. But she goes."

"Yeah? How far, before it falls apart or blows up?"

"She won't do either!"

"No. Sorry. I like my skin whole, and I'd rather not be sitting in a pile of scrap covered in burns waiting to see if Miss Grim or the ruddy dogs find me first. Never mind, eh?"

"But she works!"

"But you said yourself, it isn't finished. Anyway, you don't want to risk it, I understand that. What do you plan to do with her when she's finished?"

"I..." Beth's mouth drooped. "I don't know."

"I gotta get to class. I'll see you later. Don't forget and stay back here half the afternoon – they'll come looking for you."

She left Beth standing in the fading light, one hand resting on her machine, both of them looking rather dusty and forlorn.

Am I bad? Eveline stopped, halfway back to the school, and frowned at the trees. Was she? It wasn't a thought she troubled herself with that often.

But she'd said things to Beth that were as calculated as she'd ever laid on a mark. And Beth wasn't a mark. Beth was the only friend she'd made in this place.

She shrugged irritably in the deepening afternoon gloom and headed for Retention, where she performed less well than usual.

Beth avoided speaking to her for days.

Eveline spent every spare minute in the barn. Beth always managed to be busy elsewhere when Jackson left them alone, but Eveline knew better than to push. Instead she poked about at her mother's mechanisms, turning levers, studying dials, placing ball-bearings in the grooves carved for them, without having the slightest idea what she was about. Sometimes she succeeded in getting a noise out of something – a string of faint *ping*s, or a soft wail, or, once, a teeth-jarring shriek that brought Mr Jackson shooting out of the cab of the Velocitator like a jack-in-the-box. He banged his head on the way out and went bright scarlet. Eveline apologised, but felt his glare on her neck for the rest of the afternoon.

Lessons with Liu were a bright spot. Eveline started to feel the language with her teeth and tongue and brain, its singing intonations and sliding scales. The speed she learned at, now, was exhilarating. She was getting better at French, too, but slowly.

Miss Cairngrim tended to fling open the door on her Cantonese lessons. Somehow, so far, they had been lucky – whenever it happened, Eveline was sitting at her desk, following Liu's pronunciation as he read out words he had written on the blackboard. The rest of the time he would be asking her about her life – of which she told him carefully selected portions – or telling her fantastical stories about river-dragons and ghosts and tragic lovers. As the days went on, Eveline realised he was talking more and more in Cantonese, and she was understanding more and more. It happened so smoothly, it was almost like magic.

"You're ever so good at this," she said to Liu one day as she was leaving to go on kitchen duty – which she'd got, again. On purpose, this time, although spilling ink on Treadwell had been a bonus. Eveline was sorry for the girl, but it didn't mean she wasn't still a right royal pain in the backside. "You could teach at a proper school, if you wanted."

"I would not be so successful if I did not have such an amenable pupil."

"You don't half talk fancy."

"You don't believe me?"

"I think you're a flatterer, mister, is what I think."

"No," he said. "You do not need flattery. The Folk, now, their rulers need it. Live upon it. Shall I tell you about the Five Gracious Gifts?"

"Is this another of your stories?"

"Of course. You have done very well and have earned a story."

It was a strange story, of gifts that were not real things, but the shadow of things, the intention of things. It left her feeling strange, disconcerted, and as though her head were no longer quite connected to the rest of her. She sat frowning afterwards.

"You didn't like it?" Liu said.

"It's just... odd. I remember people back home leaving out milk for them."

"Oh, yes. It isn't the milk – they have everything they could ever want to drink – it is the intention. The fear and worship. And if the milk is hard to spare, all the better. Lacking nothing, they crave the knowledge of lack."

Something in Liu's voice made her glance up then, but he was looking away, out of the window, and she could not read his expression.

"How come you know so much about them?"

He turned back, and gave her a smile that was rather thin and sad. "I am very clever, and I study a great deal."

"Liu, where are you from?"

"Is it not obvious?"

"Well, you're Chinese, yes, I can see that – but you speak such good English and you spend half your time here – the Brighart Company's English, too..."

"Spending time in China became... a little difficult for me. I offended someone powerful."

"Ah. Got a bit too clever, did you?"

"Rather say that I was not quite clever enough. I did something that might be seen as giving advantage to a rival of theirs, so, I joined the rival. Who happened to be from... this part of the world."

"So do you ever go back?"

"Now and then. Discreetly." He cocked his head. "The Grim Woman is coming. We should finish the lesson."

"How'd you *know?* You always know!"

"I have most sharp ears."

"THESE ARE THE things I need," Beth said, shoving a piece of paper into Eveline's apron pocket and picking up a dish of greyish mashed potato. Eveline pulled it out, eyes widening at the list of incomprehensible items.

"Wait. You mean you'll do it?"

"Yes, I'll do it. I've even worked something out to cover any tracks."

"But I don't even know what half these things are!"

"You get the money and I'll get the materials. How *are* you going to get the money?"

"I don't know. Yet. I'll think of something."

"You're not going to rob anyone?"

"What, here? No-one's got anything worth robbing, in this place. You could break up the whole building and it'd be worth about thirty bob down the market. If that. Beth..." But she'd gone, balancing dishes.

There wasn't another chance for them to talk until supper was over and they were wearily scraping congealed gravy from the plates. The gas mantle hissed overhead, shedding soft greenish light. The cook had taken her sore feet home. Now the oven had gone out, the kitchen was rapidly getting colder.

"Why'd you say yes?" Eveline said.

"Because I called her *Sacagawea*," Beth said.

"You don't have to, you know," Eveline said, regretting the words the moment they were out of her mouth.

"Well I'm not letting *you* take her."

"Too bloody right – me, drive that thing? I'd blow meself up."

"No, you'd just stall her and make a mess of the engine."

"I *meant,* I can find another way to get there."

"Fast enough and without taking a horse? Besides... I want to." Beth's eyes gleamed. "I want to find out how fast she'll really go."

"Right," Eveline said. "Er... how fast do you *think* she might go?

"Let's see, shall we?"

"Mm, let's," Eveline said. *Eveline Duchen, I suspect you're going to regret this.*

IT WAS AN overheard conversation between two of the staff that gave Eveline her next move. First, she did a little more late night exploring; she made certain enquiries, and took careful note of the social columns of the newspapers that the staff left lying about. Then, she managed to arrange an extra French lesson alone with Mon Sewer. Once she was certain they weren't going to be interrupted, she cut across his explanation of the Future Perfect (she didn't care about Future Perfect, she was more interested in Future Possible).

"I hear you're leaving us to get married, monsewer," she said.

"Monsieur. Mon*sieur*. Really, Duchen, I thought your pronunciation had improved."

"Oh, I dunno, monsewer, I think *sewer's* just about right for you. Or would you prefer..." she switched to a perfect imitation of his own accent, "Monsieur Merde?"

"What?" He spun around on his shiny, black shoes so fast he skidded and almost fell. "How dare you!"

"I dare 'cos I know all about you, monsewer. And I been wondering if maybe there's a few other people should know all about you, too." She slid onto his desk, and sat there, swinging her feet. "About you and Treadwell, maybe."

His face froze. Eveline could see the pulse beating in his temple.

"Because that's the sort of thing a lady who's getting married might want to know about her beloved husband-to-be, don't you think? Especially a nice, *rich* lady."

"What nonsense has the girl been telling you?"

"Treadwell? Oh, she en't told me nothing, monsewer. She don't think anyone knows. But I know. And I know she isn't the only one." That was a risk, she didn't know for certain, but she was pretty sure. She knew the type, and given the chance they were like foxes in a hencoop; they couldn't stop at one. At least a fox didn't pretend it was doing the chickens a favour. "And since you're going to be marrying such a lovely, generous lady, I reckon there'll be some money to spare, don't you? Five hundred, maybe?" Beth hadn't asked for nearly that much, but there was no point being skimpy.

Colour flared along his cheekbones. "You... you... *petit salope!*" He made for her, and Evvie slid off the desk and danced out of the way behind it.

"Oh, and don't think about something happening to Treadwell, or me. There's letters, all over, I left 'em with a bunch of people. I left one with the man who got me in here. Either of us gets sick or has maybe an accident or something like that, them letters is going to get sent. Sent to your pretty fiancée and her parents. Sent to the *Times*. Sent to the House of Commons. Sent to the Reverend at that nice little church you got set for the wedding. St James's, eh? Right posh, that is."

He gripped the edge of the desk. "Who will believe the word of a little street thief?"

"Who says I signed 'em?" she said. "Oh, they may not believe 'em, and even if they did ask, I bet Treadwell won't say a word. But that's how rumours get started, isn't it? Rumours that might make a lady look very carefully at who she's getting married to, and what she might do about keeping her money in trusts, so Dear Husband don't have a lot in his pocket for going on the town and getting up to pursuits unsuitable to a married gentleman."

He lunged around the desk, and the knife she'd concealed up her sleeve shot into her hand, gleaming in the weak afternoon sunlight.

He blinked at it. "Don't be ridiculous."

"Little street thief, you said. Yes, I am. I had to use this more'n once not to get used like you done Treadwell, so don't think I won't. Protecting my honour, I am. They'll believe me about *that*. I found them books and pictures, too. And some of them are still where you hid 'em – but some ain't."

He hadn't even been that careful about hiding the pictures. Maybe the thought of one of the girls finding them and being too shocked and embarrassed to say anything had added to his excitement.

"One more thing, *monsewer*," she said. He looked at her with a dislike so intense it should have burned her skin like etching-acid. She grinned, but it was a fox-grin, sly and full of teeth. "This place, it's turned out to be a proper education and no mistake. I'm getting good at doing what we're taught here. See, I'm like a sparrow, me. I get everywhere. Can't tell me from a thousand others, once I'm in amongst 'em. And those letters, they're staying where they are, even once you're gone from here. But me, I'll be keeping an eye on you. I think you'd best leave Treadwell alone, don't you? And any of the other girls. And any maids, and any daughters you have." He actually managed to look shocked at that, which she ignored. "From now on you'd better be keeping that cock of yours for your wife and her only, and treat her decent, because it seems to me you're getting far better than you deserve."

He writhed like a worm on a fishhook, but in the end, he complied. Two days later she had the money in her hand. She'd made an enemy, she knew; but so long as he believed in the letters, she reckoned she was safe.

So she'd probably better write them. At least her penmanship and grammar had improved enough while she was here that they probably wouldn't read as though they came from a little street thief.

"How DID YOU... no, don't tell me," Beth said, at the same time as Eveline said, "You don't need to know. So, how long before we get the stuff?"

"Some of it not long; the rest, weeks, probably. I have to get a message to the blacksmith's son in the village, and he'll get it for me, and deliver it to the rear gate that no-one uses."

"Weeks? We can't wait that long."

"Well, she'll run as she is, just not as well. And if it rains, we'll get wet."

"I slept out in the rain often enough."

"Oh, you won't be sleeping," Beth said, with a grin. "I'm almost sure of that."

COLLAPSING AGAINST THE corridor wall between classes, Eveline felt a presence and opened her eyes. Treadwell was standing in the corridor, looking at her.

"I gotta go." Eveline pushed herself away from the wall.

"You had a French class." Treadwell had turned away and was looking out of the window.

Eveline looked at her back. She could see the blonde curls trembling slightly. "Yes." Did Treadwell somehow know, what she'd done to Monsewer? *How?*

"He's... he's... you have to be *careful*." Even from behind, the rigidity of Treadwell's posture was obvious. "He's a bad man."

"Oh, listen, 'sall right."

"No, it isn't. You don't *know*."

"Treadwell, I *know*, all right? I dealt with it."

"How?" Treadwell's hands gripped the windowsill.

"I put him off. And I don't think he's going to mess with no-one else while he's here, neither."

"What? What did you do?"

Eveline wasn't going to confess to blackmail. "You know what? If it was up to me, wouldn't just be in here they taught Bartitsu. Most girls I know could do with knowing it. Next time anyone tries it on, maybe a person oughta use some of the moves on them. See if she can give him something to remember her by. 'Specially if maybe she happens to be good at Bartitsu, like you are. I got to go to class."

"Wait."

"I'm late."

THE *SACAGAWEA* PUTTERED gently out of its tumbledown shed, shuddering beneath them. Its makeshift engine hummed as quietly as a purring cat, an odd blue-green light flithering over it like marsh-gas. Eveline wondered what the two of them must look like, muffled in cloaks and goggles, her keeping her eyes open for trouble, Beth muttering over her instruments.

She had created an ingenious device of branches sweeping behind them and a box of fallen leaves to cover their tracks, and Eveline had dealt with the dogs by means of some stolen meat and a raid on the box of patent medicines that Miss Prayne kept in her room. Eveline clung to whatever came to hand and tried not to squeak whenever they ran over a bump. Two carriage lamps hung from hooks at the front, but they wouldn't risk lighting them until they were out of the grounds.

The girls had their nightgowns on under the clothes they wore in the Old Barn. Eveline had insisted.

"Why?" Beth asked.

"If something happens and we're caught in the grounds, you were sleepwalking, I saw you go out and followed you to bring you back."

Beth looked at her with admiration bordering on fear.

They had decided to go out by the rear gate. It had a much simpler lock than the main one. The padlock was horribly stiff, and Eveline broke two hairpins wrestling with it, expecting any minute to hear shouts and see lanterns bobbing among the trees. Then Beth pushed her impatiently aside and dripped something from a nozzle into the lock, after which, with a little more persuasion, it snicked open.

Then there was the path through a thin belt of woodland, and more rattling until Eveline was fairly sure every bone she had was out of its socket. At least it was a good clear night, with a hard frost and a bright moon. Rain would have made everything harder, and slower.

It was slow enough as it was. She knew from the maps that Watford wasn't far, and Beth seemed sure they'd make it there and back with time to spare, but she herself wasn't convinced. They'd had to wait until everyone was well abed, and it was already past eleven before they got away. Now they were going at little more than walking pace.

Finally the road appeared through the trees – a flat grey ribbon like a frozen river. They bumped and rattled their way to the fringe of the wood, and there it was, in the moonlight, clear and silent.

"Well," Eveline said. Suddenly, she had no idea which way to turn. When she had arrived, had they turned left or right into the gate? But that had been a different gate. She swallowed hard and turned to Beth. "Beth..."

"Yes?"

"I don't know which way."

The moonlight gleamed on the lenses of Beth's goggles, turning them white, as she tilted her head up and looked at the stars, bright and sharp as needlepoints pricking through black silk. "It's all right," she said. "I do." She hauled on the wheel – a giant cogwheel from who-knew-what, wrapped in cloth to stop the teeth jabbing into her hands – and sent the *Sacagawea* in a ponderous turn to the right. This surface was definitely smoother, Eveline thought. Maybe they would be able to go a little faster.

Beth lit one of the lanterns, then paused. "There's got to be a more efficient way to do this," she muttered. "I should be able to feed power from the... hmm. Yes."

"Beth?"

Beth gripped the wheel, her shoulders hunched, staring ahead. Something about her posture worried Eveline. She looked as though she might leap out of the makeshift cab and scuttle back to the school.

"Beth?"

"You might want to sit down now," Beth said. "And hold on."

"All right." Eveline sat gingerly on the bench, hoping it wouldn't collapse into sawdust beneath her, and gripped the side of the cab.

The engine's purr deepened. The bluegreen light that fluttered and gleamed among the coils flickered faster.

The *Sacagawea* began to roll, the road unfolding smoothly before her. The trees swept up, and strolled past.

Then they weren't strolling any more. Wind whipped Eveline's hood from her hair and sent her coat billowing out like a sail.

She gripped the side of the cab, feeling rust beneath her fingers. "Beth, what are you doing?"

"Testing the engine!" Beth laughed aloud. "Oh, I knew I was right, I knew it! Come on, my beautiful, come on!"

"Beth! We'll *hit* something! Even trains don't go this fast!" Trees were whisking past her like twigs blown on the wind. The moon raced them above the treetops, smiling serenely down, and Eveline stared at it and wondered how it went so fast. A moth batted her face, some creature's eyes glowed like twin moons in the undergrowth. They shot through a village, rattlebang along the street, the houses in the swinging lantern light like faces shocked from sleep.

Rattle, jangle, twang, clank, ping, swish, *vrrrrrrr*... The *Sacagawea* sang her mad chorus along the moonlit road and Eveline held on with both hands, tried to swallow her stomach back down where it belonged and hoped that Beth knew how to stop this crazed machine.

After an hour of this, Eveline began to believe that the machine wasn't going to blow up or fall apart. She unclenched her teeth a little. The outskirts of the town were on them suddenly, buildings poking up out of the night. Eveline tugged on Beth's shoulder. "Slow down!" she shouted.

"Why?"

"Because this ain't the country any more! Even this time a' night there'll be folk around, so haul back before we come round a corner and find we're nose-to with the London mail coach."

With obvious reluctance, Beth pulled on a lever and the *Sacagawea* slowed, the feathery bluegreen light around the coils dropping back from its feverish coruscation to a soft shimmer.

The chorus of creaks, groans, pings and twangs also died back, though some of the rattling had got more persistent. Eveline's backside felt like dough kneaded by a bad cook.

She took a breath that was laden with hot metal and sewage and coal. A faint, persistent thumping, a labouring heartbeat, undercut the silence.

"Phew," Beth said. "What's that smell? And the noise?"

"I know, stinks, dunnit? I'd forgotten. London's worse, though. The noise is factories."

"Where now?"

"Thought you were the navigator."

"I got us to the town, Eveline. I don't know where the house is."

"It's off the main street. Just go along, slow. I'll recognise it." But the town seemed much bigger than it had been, and the street they had entered by was not the one she remembered. Ghosts of herself and Charlotte trudging along a snowy street haunted her memory – but it hadn't been this street. They passed a blacksmith – there had been no blacksmith, in her time, or if there had she didn't remember it. There should be a draper, Hadforth and Sons, was that the name? But no Hadforth and Sons appeared.

With increasing desperation she looked for a landmark; any landmark. Over to their left she could see the sullen furnace glow of the underlit clouds: the factories. Uncle James's house had been closer to them. She remembered the river of millworkers passing under her window. "Over that way," she said.

They worked their way slowly towards the glow, thud and boom becoming deeper, more solid, until it pounded up through the wheels like a fist. The *Sacagawea* seemed to shake more in protest, and an occasional *ping* added itself to the chorus of noises.

Eveline tried to watch out for anyone taking an untoward interest in the two young women and their odd machine, at the same time as she stared about for something she recognised. A familiar tall-hatted silhouette made her gasp and duck.

"What is it?" Beth said.

"Peeler. Quick, turn down there, maybe he hasn't seen us!"

"I can't turn down there, it's too narrow! Besides, we're not breaking the law!"

"Aren't we?"

"I don't think so."

"Well go slow and smile sweet," Eveline hissed, "like the actress said, and keep yer fingers crossed he's thinking about his nice warm bed and don't want to stop us just on the off-chance."

The policeman raised a curious brow at them, but in the end only touched the brim of his helmet with his fingers as they puttered past, *rattlebang, purr, ping, ping, ping*. Eveline kept her head down. Unlikely a peeler in Watford would know her face, but you never knew.

"What actress?" Beth said.

"What?"

Ping, ping, ping, ping, clank.

"Oh, bother. What actress were you talking about?"

"No-one real, 'sa joke. What's wrong?"

"It's one of the eccentric rods – it's shifted and it's hitting the regulator."

"Is that bad?"

"I'll have to adjust it."

"We can't stop!"

"We'll have to."

"Wait... look! It's there," Eveline said. "It's right there. You can stop."

"We're stopping anyway." They rolled to a halt, a final *ping* sounding forlornly, a single tiny noise against the huge thunder of the factories.

There were the lions with their blank shields, sneering at the empty street; the big ugly house, up to its ankles in the dank gloom of the laurels, its windows frowning down. Eveline felt cold dark swamp her, as though the night itself had clamped around her like a wet, filthy cloth.

They had made it. And she felt nothing but a powerful desire to turn tail and head back, anywhere, anywhere away from this house.

Woking

BETH JUMPED NIMBLY down and started poking at the engine. Eveline didn't move. "Eveline?"

Don't be such a milksop, Eveline Duchen. But still she sat, staring. How could it not have changed? After everything, how could it look so much the same?

"Eveline, are you all right? Is it the right house?"

"Yes. Yes, it's the one. You stay here, I won't be long. Oh, the factory workers come along here, or they used to, so it'll get crowded. You might want to try and get that into a side-street or something."

Beth's eyes went round. "But what should I do?" She backed against the *Sacagawea*, holding up her spanner like a weapon, but without much conviction.

"They ain't lions, Beth, they're just people. Most of 'em'll be half off their legs with hunger and too dog-weary to care about some machine. And that's just the ones going *on* shift. The ones that come off, they're like the dead, most of 'em, they can barely shuffle."

"Why?"

"Because the factories chew people up like dry bread, that's why. Why'd you think I went thieving? I seen what they look like, them as last – and a lot don't. You never seen what happens when that's all the work you can get? You ain't got out much, have you?"

"No," Beth said quietly. "No, I suppose I haven't."

What are you doing, Duchen? She was picking a fight with poor Beth. It wasn't Beth's fault that she'd had a decent life until she got sent away into Miss Grim's clutches. It wasn't her fault that Eveline saw Uncle James's house standing there and felt it ready to stuff her back into its chilly gut to live through all of it again.

I'm Eveline Duchen. I'm the best thief in London, and that makes me ten times the best thief in pissy little Watford. I'm buggered if I'll turn tail and run.

"You going to be all right here?" she said.

"I haven't exactly a choice, have I?" Beth said. "Just be quick, please?"

"Oh, I plan to. And if anyone *does* give you any trouble, you tell 'em... you tell 'em you work for the post office. Everyone trusts the post office. And keep your goggles on and that hat and speak low, they'll think you're a boy."

"All right." She took a deep breath, then said, "Good luck. Please don't get caught."

"En't planning on it." She took the bundle she'd brought from the well of the machine, jumped down, and made for the house, walking open and easy, a girl on an errand, respectable, right out there for any passing peeler to see.

And around the corner was the side-alley that led past the back of the house.

The high fences were still there, but the one that protected what had been Uncle James's garden from prying eyes was new. Most of the rubbish and rag piles had gone.

She couldn't see any bundles that suggested people slept here still; that was good, because it meant there was no-one to raise the alarm, but it put her back hairs up. This was a quiet place, though not very sheltered except for a few overhanging trees. So why was no-one sleeping here?

She couldn't hesitate longer; there was no time. She found the gate. It was the right one, she could see the top of the house, the window that had been Mama's workroom.

The memory of Charlotte hit her, the baby's hair against her cheek, the weight in her arms, the weight she hadn't been able to bear. For a moment Eveline paused, leaning a hand on the nearest fence, as pain clutched at her. But Charlotte was gone, Mama was gone, and there was only Eveline. She looked at the roof of the house hunched against the glowering sky. Once she had Mama's notes, she need never come back here.

She opened the bundle and took out the cunning little folding steps that Beth had made – damn, the girl was clever, Ma Pether would have snapped her up in no time. They snicked open, unfolding like the legs of a crane fly, a jointed stick poking up from the top. She nipped up them and looked over the fence.

There was more drugged meat in the bag, but nothing patrolled the garden, no dogs barked. There were no lights on. She wasn't sure of the time, but she wouldn't have long before the maids were moving about, lighting the morning fires and getting the boiler and the oven going.

The pantry window it was, then.

She swung herself over the fence, picked up the steps with the stick, swung them over, and ran down them, leaving them where they were. Quicker on the way out.

The path was not swept as it used to be, slick with fallen leaves slimy with frost. Some of the roses had died, others were overgrown tangles. Maybe no-one cared for the garden any more.

The pantry window was where she remembered it, but it looked horribly small. Eveline was still skinny – a few weeks of decent grub hadn't made up for years of underfeeding – but when she'd last made it through that window she'd been considerably smaller. Still, she thought, it could be done. There was nothing else for it – even if she could talk her way in as she had at the house in Stepney, she couldn't afford to wait until the servants were astir.

Still, she wasted a precious minute chewing her lip and checking the breadth of her hips. Even once she was certain that she could wiggle through the opening – assuming she could open it – she hesitated.

What's the matter with you, Duchen? Ma Pether's voice jabbed in her head sharp as a glass splinter. *If you can do the job, get on – if you can't, get out!*

That snapped her back to herself. She unlaced the heavy shoes and left them below the window. She carefully extracted an eyedropper – whisked from Miss Prayne's medicine cabinet – and dripped oil on the window's hinges. Next she took a roll of oilcloth from her bag and unwrapped it to reveal a stack of squares of brown paper. The smell of treacle rose into the air, a sweet dark phantom. She'd had to guess at the size. She picked one carefully from the stack, stuck it to the lower left pane. It overlapped all around. Good. Now she had started, everything else went away; memory and grief and fear retreated. Her animal senses scanned the night, alert for trouble. Her mind was all on the paper, the window, the small hammer from the toolbox in the Old Barn. One quick tap and the window broke, almost silently, the glass adhering to the sticky paper. She peeled it away – *careful, don't cut yourself, Evvie* – and levered out the remaining few splinters of glass with a cloth-wrapped hand. Hand through the gap, and there's the latch. Rusted and stiff, but moveable. Now. Ease the window open. Oil's killed the squeak. Smells of cabbage and mice. Watch out for mousetraps. Enough light, just, to see the edge of the stone sink. Bag in first, then easy does it, wriggling like a fish, stronger now after those Bartitsu lessons, more control, hands on the upper frame, pull through. There.

Wait. No lantern yet. One of the maids used to sleep down here in the cupboard-bed next to the pantry door. Listen.

No breathing, no sighing. The door of the cupboard-bed's closed. Creep up close, listen, nothing. Ease the door open.

Empty, the bed not made up. No-one's slept here for some time, by the mouse-droppings and dust. She can hear them, skittering about – things have changed since the old days, cook wouldn't have stood for that.

Find the bag, take out the lantern, all darkened but for a single small gap where the light can shine through. Light the lantern, sweep the little light around the kitchen. There's the green baize door to the main house – not that way. Up the narrow servants' stair, to the passage running behind the walls so the owners won't be disturbed by the coming-and-going of those who bring their food and hot water and morning paper.

It runs all the way to the top of the house, to the rooms that were theirs. If she's lucky and quiet, she can come and go like a breeze, and no-one will even know she's been here.

Of course, if there are servants sleeping up there...
she pauses, caught on the stairs, her hands going cold.
What if there are? There's no-one in the cupboard bed –
maybe the maids sleep in Mama's old workroom now?

What if someone's bed is right above the hiding place?
Won't know until you look, Evvie.

She forces her feet to start moving again.

Hand on the door at the top of the stairs before she
remembers the hinges; drop, drop, not much oil left,
another door to go yet.

Hood the lantern, ease the door open.

The corridor is narrow and cold. The same worn strip
of rug, faded to colourlessness, lies limply on the bare
boards. A draught whistles up between them, making
the rug shudder and stroking her stockinged legs with
chill wispy fingers. Up here, the noise of the factories
is less muffled. There are no thick carpets and plush
furniture to soak it up. *Thu-bump, thu-bump,* an angry
heartbeat.

Three closed, silent doors, and suddenly she cannot
remember which is the one she needs. She's only enough
oil left for one more. *Think.* Mama's workroom was the
biggest – surely that means it's the middle? No, wait,
which way did she used to turn, coming out of their
room? She can't remember.

And she can't stand here. Worst thing you can do on
a job is freeze.

Going to Mama's room that dreadful morning and
finding it locked. *Why can't I remember?* All the doors
look identical, faded paint, round handles. *Move!*

She holds her breath, drops the smallest possible
amount of oil on the middle door's hinges. Checks, it's
not locked. She eases it open.

Two beds. Humped figures. One shifts, the sheets crackling; she shuts the door hastily but quietly, heart bumping in her chest so loud you could hear it over the factories. Along to the end one. Oh, there's hardly any oil in the dropper, she should have brought more, stupid Evvie, remember what Ma Pether said about kit, *think of everything, then think again*. One last drop squeezed out, a thin pitiful thing.

The door's locked. Using her hairpins will give the oil time to soak in a little. This is taking too long – no, Evvie, stop thinking, just do your job.

Click.

Careful, careful, ease the handle round and the door opens. The hinge whines. Stop. Wait. No-one stirs. Open it a little further, the hinge is silent, it's open just enough to see.

There are no curtains. The room is empty, sulphurous light spilling yellow-grey across the dusty floor. She edges through the gap, eases the door shut behind her.

Empty. Even Mama's table is gone. At least a week's worth of dust. All her past, that last bit of her childhood, gone.

But not everything, not quite. The board with the splintered edge is still there.

She drops to her knees, takes the shaped bar from her bag (she's been busy in the Old Barn, has our Eveline, not at work the school would approve, but a girl needs tools to deal with life's difficulties, she does indeed). Eases it into the gap, careful, careful; the nails *scree* as they pull loose from the wood. Wait, listen.

No sound of waking, footsteps, alarm.

And there's the tin. There's the boy in the blue suit, and his ever-loyal dog who doesn't care that he's a spoiled brat, faint through the fog of dust. A tear lands on the lid, and where it lands the boy's suit is still bright blue as a half-remembered summer sky.

Eveline is just carefully levering the floorboard back into place when she hears the sound of movement.

She goes completely still, completely silent, barely breathing, only her eyes moving, flickering over the room. There's nowhere to hide except the great cupboard in the wall, and she *knows* that door will squeal, it isn't hung properly, it squalls against the frame whenever it's opened or shut, she remembers. Mama stopped asking to have it planed after a while. There's the window, but it's three stories down onto the area steps, even if you were lucky enough to miss the black iron railings that jab up like spears.

The space under the floorboards? Not without getting up another board and that'd never go unheard.

The dust isn't thick enough for her footprints to be clear but she takes care to blur them as she rises and drifts quiet as smoke across to the door, to stand just behind it. The narrowest of safety, but all she has. She clutches the tin to her, can't risk putting it in the bag where it may clank and rattle against things.

"Maitland!" A harsh whisper. "What are you doing? You woke me."

"I heard something!"

"You never."

"I *did*. I'm going to fetch Jacobs!"

"Oh, that'll please him, getting him up. You want to be run ragged all day because he's missed his sleep? Well, I don't. Stop messing about and come to bed!"

Ease the clip into the lock, find the point of pressure, wait.

"I tell you it's the ghost! We'll be murdered in our beds!" *Click* while the maid is talking and the door is locked again, should have done it on the way in, stupid Eveline.

"Did you hear something? Like... like *bones?*"

"Will you stop about bones and ghosts, there ain't no ghost but you wandering around in your nightgown like a loon. Come to bed before you get the whole house up!"

"I shan't sleep a wink."

"Can't nobody sleep." Another voice, older, sharper, and strangely familiar. "Not with you two rattling about in the middle of the night."

"Oh, Miss Clarence, it's the ghost!"

"Stuff and nonsense. You had a dream, is all."

"But I heard something, and there was a figure, it came and *looked* at me in my bed!"

"Dreaming."

"I wasn't, Miss Clarence! I swear, there was something there!"

"No such thing as ghosts. Far more likely to be a burglar."

Someone gave a small shriek.

"Be quiet," the older voice – Miss Clarence, why did she know that voice? – snapped. "Let's see, if there *was* a burglar, who went into a perfectly empty room..." – the door handle turned, and Eveline held her breath – "seems he was considerate enough to lock it after him. Now if you fancy going downstairs and checking the sideboard for the silver, maybe he'll have been considerate enough to save you from cleaning it like you should have done last week."

"But what if it wasn't a burglar?"

"Lord save us all from hair-witted bumpkins. There are no ghosts in this house."

"Mr Lathrop died here, though, didn't he? With a terrible expression on his face. And the poor lady..."

"What nonsense have you been listening to? Mr Lathrop died of the gout reaching his heart. Should think that's painful, which would account for any expression he might have had. And there's been no lady died here." *Harriet. Harriet the maid. Housekeeper, now, by the sound. Still here, along with that wretch Jacobs. Hello, Harriet, wonder what you'd think if you knew I was barely a foot from you?*

"His sister died, though, didn't she?" The stupid maid went on. *Shut up, you daft creature, and go back to bed so I can get out of here!* "Maybe it's *her* ghost come back to haunt us all! Oh, oh, what if –"

There was a flat, hard *crack* and the maid squealed. Eveline winced in sympathy.

"Be quiet, you stupid creature," Harriet said. "The poor lady isn't haunting anyone."

"It could be..."

"No it couldn't. Even if there were such a thing as ghosts, she's not dead."

"But that's what..."

"Yes, well, that was the tale that Mr Lathrop had put about, because no-one wants talk about madness in the family. It was his man let it slip. She's in the Bethlem Hospital, poor creature, but she's not dead, so no ghost of hers is walking this house. Now get back to bed, the pair of you. And you're not to gossip about Mrs Duchen! Not a word! I hear that's got out, or I see you in this corridor again outside when you're meant to be, I'll see you both turned off without references. Now get to your beds."

Grumbling and protests faded away down the corridor, as Eveline stood frozen, staring at the closed door.

Still alive?

Still alive and locked away?

Mama?

A bright haze came over her vision, her legs wobbled, and Eveline only just stopped the tin sliding from her grasp to clang and clatter on the boards.

She crumpled to the floor, pressing her hands to the sides of her head as though she could hold onto her thoughts, stop them spinning. It was a trick. It *had* to be a trick. But what if it wasn't? What if her mother really was alive? A sudden flood of warmth rushed up from her feet. It seemed to expand her tightened abdomen, her hunched shoulders, relaxing the stretched muscles around her eyes.

Boom-thud, boom-thud, went the factories. The sound seemed to have got inside her head, and she stared at the tin, at the smeared ghost-face of the blue-clad boy, hearing *boom-thud, boom-thud*, sitting paralysed among the dust.

Ten minutes before, she had been Evvie Duchen, sharp Evvie, Evvie the Sparrow, a spry little fringe-dweller alone in the crowd of them, always scraping for a crumb, always with one eye open for a bigger bird, or a cat, or a cruel boy with a stone. Even under Ma Pether's eye she'd had to duck and scrabble, had known Ma Pether came first and everyone else after.

"My mama's alive," she said, and her voice sounded like a little girl's voice, a little girl in a clean pinafore, her hair lovingly brushed. A little girl who still had a mother and a father, a sister and a home.

A banshee wail roused her from her stupor. Shift-change at the biscuit factory. She should be out by now, should have been out before.

But... *Mama. Alive, and locked away.*

Had Harriet known? Had she known all along?

It hardly mattered now, though there was a growing, roiling fury in Eveline's belly that demanded *someone* pay, for the years of lies and the fear and the belief that they were completely alone. And for Charlotte. Someone owed Charlotte a life. Uncle James should pay, it had been his lie, but Uncle James was dead.

Bedlam. She had to get to Bedlam, and find Mama.

But first she had to get out of this vile house.

No, first she had to think. All the staff – except for two new maids – were still here, which probably meant Uncle James hadn't died long ago. They must be waiting for whoever had inherited. Perhaps whoever it was was already there – not that it meant anything to Eveline. What did, what *might,* were Uncle James's papers. If any of them were still in his office, there might be something there to help Mama, or to confirm or deny what Harriet had said.

She had even less time now, and more to do.

She remembered where Uncle James's office was. Locked, but a hairpin dealt with it – and *his* door had been oiled and properly hung. No squeaks for Uncle James.

There was a desk she didn't recognise – bigger and glossier, with ball-and-claw feet. Fancy, but worth less than it looked like – she knew cheap masquerading as expensive when she saw it, it had been one of Ma Pether's first lessons. *Don't let Fancy take yer eye. Quality's what's there, or ain't. Fancy's just the stuff on top. Dress a rat in a lace collar and it's still a rat.*

Not much in the drawers. Expensive writing paper, ink dried to a scum in its bottle, sealing wax. Nothing she could find relating to Mama.

She paused, one hand on the leather top. Where might he have kept such things? Or would the lawyers have it all? She knew about lawyers. Enough, at least, that she trusted them as much as she would a starving dog.

Nothing. Eveline felt a sudden hard, brutal desire to set the house alight. Burn it all up, every stick and scrap of it. If she couldn't punish James, or Harriet, she'd punish the house.

But that would do no-one any good. And she'd already been here too long.

One more place... if it hadn't been cleared out already.

The dressing room still smelled like Uncle James: pomade and sweat and Gentleman's Hair Tonic. The chaise still stood in the corner. She dropped to her knees.

Yes. The case was still there. The case where Uncle James kept the things he didn't want anyone to know about.

The corsets lay there, thick pink cotton ribbed with bone, like the corpses of some strange animals desiccated by the wind. Wrinkling her nose with distaste, Eveline reached underneath them.

There. A flat leather case, bound about with red lawyers' ribbon. She opened it just long enough to see her mother's name written on the top page, and shoved it into her bag with the tin.

Eveline unlocked the bedroom door, and peered around it. The corridor stood empty and quiet... except at the far end, where the door to the servants' stairs was just closing on the glow of a candle, a flicker of black skirt showing as it did.

Arse and damnation, she'd left it too long. The servants – or one, at least – had given up on any more sleep and made for the kitchens to get a start on the day. Now what? Follow her down, and try and slip past? Or down the front stairs, banking on no-one coming out that way for another two hours? But then she'd have to get out of the front door, with the risk that anyone coming up to lay a fire would see her clear as day as she fadgetted with the lock. And she'd have to leave Beth's contraption, which would make it clear, along with the broken window, that someone had been in.

Her rapid shallow breathing caught, hooked in her throat. *The window.* If whoever had gone down went into the pantry... no time to wait.

Swift and light, she padded along the almost pitch-black corridor, and through the servants' door. She left it open behind her for what little light there was and headed down the stairs, horribly steep and narrow in the dark. She was going too fast and her foot slipped, she caught herself with one hand on the wall, hearing a faint 'chink' from her bag where something – maybe the metal bar – hit the tin.

She stood in the dark, crouched, heart pounding. No sound but her own breathing. Moving more carefully, she went on, a faint flush of light beginning to show the treads as she moved downwards.

Whoever it was had left the bottom door open a crack. Lantern-light. The *chug-clonk* of the pump, water splashing into something, the clink of crockery. Setting up the tea things, probably. Which meant the woman would have to go into the pantry for the tea.

The sound of a match, muttered curses. She was

lighting the oven, or trying to. She'd have her back to the door. Humming, some soft romantic tune.

Eveline fled across the kitchen in her stocking feet, clutching her bag to her chest so it wouldn't rattle, not sparing a glance at the hunched shape by the fire. Into the pantry, bag out of the open window, a faint *thud-clank* as it dropped.

The humming stopped.

Eveline boosted herself onto the sink, hands slipping and scrabbling on the enamel, grabbed the frame, flew through like a circus acrobat, landing on her hands, rolling. Scooped up the bag.

There was a red line in the sky.

Down the garden, skidding on wet leaves, she realised she'd left her boots under the window, looked over her shoulder. No light in the pantry, no cries of alarm, and dammit, they were good boots. She scooted back up the path. Where the hell were they? There, over to the left. She grabbed them by their laces.

She was about to rise from her crouch when she heard Harriet exclaim, directly over her head.

Arse.

"Who left this open?" The creak of the hinges as she pulled the window shut. "No wonder it was cold. Oh, and look at that, the pane's gone. Wind must've took it..."

Don't look closer. Don't notice the treacle on the frame, or the way it broke so neat with all the glass outside...

The window-shaped glow of the lantern on the path faded. Without pausing to put her boots on, Eveline fled.

"WHERE HAVE YOU *been*?" Beth said. "Oh, never mind. Get in, do, or we'll never get back in time." She hauled

Eveline into the machine by her arm, and began turning levers. The *Sacagawea* started to purr, as though she were happy to be leaving. "Did you get them?"

Eveline half-fell onto the hard wooden bench. "What?"

"Your mother's *notes!* The thing we *came* for!"

"Oh, yes," Eveline said. "Yes, I..." She started to shove her wet, numb feet into the boots, and that made her think of Charlotte, her poor little soaking feet, and she began to shake, and then to cry, ridiculously, noisily, a great storm of tears as though they had all been saved up from that single dreadful year.

Beth tried to steer with one hand and pat Eveline's shuddering frame with the other. "What is it? What happened?"

But Eveline could only shake her head and cry harder than ever, great brutal sobs like someone breaking stones in her chest.

"Eveline, I don't know what happened, but please, *please* try to calm down," Beth said, keeping her voice calm and staring straight ahead. "Because there are people now and they're looking, and whatever's wrong, it'll be worse if we're caught."

Whitehall

THADDEUS HOLMFORTH WAITED in the corridor, which smelled of pipe smoke and the nervous sweat of supplicants. Thin-legged chairs with creaking seats stood along the wall, but he declined their uncertain support.

The door of Rupert Forbes-Cresswell's office opened and he ushered out a flushed, well-fed looking man accompanied by a cadaverous, sickly one; it was as though during their meeting with him one had fed off the other. Forbes-Cresswell, as usual, looked as glossily healthy as a prime racehorse.

"Ah, Holmforth, dear fellow. Sorry to keep you waiting about."

Holmforth gave a stiff nod, and followed his beckoning hand.

"Sherry?" Forbes-Cresswell said, lifting the gleaming decanter.

"No, thank you."

"A little early? Quite right, too. So, how are things? How is your little protégée?" The shadow of a wink passed across Forbes-Cresswell's face.

"My... oh, the girl. I have not visited the school yet."

"Indeed? Perhaps you are wise. Showing too great an interest..."

234

"Oh, I intend to. I believe she may be useful. That is what I wished to discuss with you."

"Indeed?" Forbes-Cresswell sat down and motioned Holmforth to a chair, which he took, sinking into a marshy embrace of leather cushions. "Useful how?"

"In Shanghai, I discovered something I believe to be of great importance."

Forbes-Cresswell looked bemused for a moment. "Shanghai? Of course, you're posted there, aren't you? This thing you discovered, you couldn't write to me? It's a dreadfully long journey to take, after all."

"I did not feel confident in committing it to paper, in case it fell into the wrong hands."

"Oh, don't tell me one of our brethren has been caught doing something untoward? Really, can't they sort themselves out? Besides, it is Shanghai. Hardly up to us to drag some businessman out of the mire, they usually seem to manage quite well without troubling us."

"It isn't anything of that nature. It is a weapon."

"A weapon?" Forbes-Cresswell looked startled.

"A hugely powerful weapon that uses Etheric science, and with which, I believe, it will be possible to conquer the Folk."

"Conquer the... I see." Forbes-Cresswell steepled his fingers before his mouth.

"Yes."

"Are you sure you won't take a sherry?"

"Thank you, no."

Forbes-Cresswell sighed, and leaned back in his chair. "You know, Holmforth, I've every confidence in you. However, this business... there's no evidence, old chap, none whatsoever, that 'Etheric science' is anything other than a combination of natural ability, like... oh, singing at perfect pitch, say – quite apt, that – and myth."

"I have reports I consider reliable that the machine is effective."

"Really?"

"Yes." They had made uncomfortable reading, if one was inclined to be upset by that kind of thing. But the subjects were not human, after all. "Here." He passed the papers across the desk.

Forbes-Cresswell flipped through the pages, paused, flipped through again. "You had this from one of the locals?"

"Yes."

"Reliable, you say."

"I have found him so. I pay him extremely well. And other reports he has brought me have proved accurate."

Forbes-Cresswell went back to the report. "Hmmm. Well, I must say, this Chink seems to have something, what? I'd better keep this," he said. "Is there any more?"

"No. Everything is there."

"Good. Well, well." Forbes-Cresswell clasped his hands on the desktop and leaned forward. "I have to say, Thaddeus, I'm impressed."

Holmforth flushed. Forbes-Cresswell had never used his given name before.

"I really think you've found something here. However, this must be handled with the utmost discretion."

"Of course."

"I don't just mean where foreign powers are concerned. I mean within the department. Does anyone else know?"

"No, I came straight to you."

"Good man."

"You don't think there are foreign agents within the department?" Holmforth said.

"Spies? It's always a possibility. But also, one must take into account simple incompetence, lack of impetus – there are those who consider the Folk a spent force, not worth the trouble of invading, for all their riches. There is also, I regret to say, a certain personal pettiness. I've been putting your name forward for promotion, though of course I should be sorry to lose you, but..." He tailed off, with the faintest of shrugs.

"I appreciate that you've taken the trouble," Holmforth said.

"Not at all. But your, shall we say, your particular connections in *this* matter might be seen as interfering with your judgement."

"This is nothing to do with any personal campaign, I assure you," Holmforth said, forcing the words out past the stiffness in his throat.

"I understand entirely. But it might be *seen* that way, you understand? And there are those who would be more than happy to take this out from under you – dismiss it, and then steal your discovery for themselves. We need conclusive evidence, solidly backed up. I suggest you keep this absolutely under your hat for now. You mentioned the girl..."

"Yes. Do you remember James Lathrop? Lathrop had no idea what he had stumbled upon. The girl is his niece, and I believe she has inherited the ability."

"And that is why you wanted her at the Britannia school."

"Yes."

"Is she aware of your plans?"

"No. I thought it best to ensure she has the ability before telling her anything. I plan to return to the school shortly to see how she is getting on."

"Good, good. Let me know. I tell you what. What we need is a demonstration. I'll come over, see for myself, report back – and then that will give sufficient weight to make whatever other arrangements are necessary. How does that sound?"

"Excellent. The maker, though, Wu Jisheng – I doubt it will be possible to persuade him to give up his creation to another country. He seems to be fanatically loyal."

"Oh, my dear fellow, I'm sure we can think of something. If he can't be bribed, a couple of battalions should be sufficient to persuade him, what?"

"Could that be done?"

"In the interest of Empire, dear boy, anything can be done. There could be a commendation in this for you, you know, if we can keep it to ourselves until the moment is right."

And Holmforth left the office with a lightness to his step, and a small, pleasing glow about his heart.

Woking

BETH STEERED THE *Sacagawea* carefully among the throng. A small boy, his legs so bowed with rickets you could have used him for a harp, pointed and grinned gappily. "Thass a magical carriage!"

"It's not magic," Beth said, "it's engineering."

"Giss a ride!"

"Another time, all right?"

His small sickly face fell and Beth felt a moment's desperate guilt. "I'm sorry," she whispered, but he was already swept away in the crowd.

So many of them. Little brown sparrow-children among the crowlike adults. Beth had grown up in a small country town, and had gone straight to Miss Cairngrim's. She had never seen so many people, and all of them looking so grindingly tired, so ragged and ill. They stank and shuffled and barely spoke. She felt terribly conspicuous, terribly *privileged* up here in her magical carriage. She glanced at Eveline, who had got control of herself, though her eyes were dreadfully swollen and her breath hitched and caught. She had been one of these ragged wanderers. What had happened to her in that house that had hurt her so, after everything she must have survived?

Once they were out of the town, racing the rising sun down the still empty road, Eveline broke her silence.

Beth kept an eye on the coil, which was going a shade of green she hadn't seen before. The persuasive fluid, which was a concoction of her own, and which was why this machine was less than half the weight and around twice the speed of that crude creation of Jackson's, was overheating. But then it had never been worked so hard for so long. "I'll have to create a more efficient cooling system," she said.

"What?" Eveline said.

"Well, if we're going to go all the way to Bedlam, to rescue your mama, we'll need it," Beth said, without taking her gaze from the road ahead.

"I'd not ask you," Eveline said. "We'd never get there and back, not in the time."

"You don't have to ask me. I don't want to stay in Miss Grim's for the rest of my life."

"What about your pension, and travelling in an airship?"

"I'll build my own airship one day, and as to a pension... well, I'm not sure I want a pension for helping out the Empire."

"I don't understand," Eveline said.

"All those people... They're not in India or China or wherever, are they? They're right here. And what's all this Empire business doing for them? You'd better hold on, it's straight here. I'm going to push her."

Halfway down the woodland track, the sun already cutting shadows through the woods and the frost melting off the leaves and dripping down on them, something went *clang*, Beth shrieked and the *Sacagawea* shuddered to a halt.

"Beth?"

"Ow, dammit!"

"What is it?"

"That blasted ratchet arm... I thought I'd tightened it enough." Beth had clamped her left hand under her right armpit and was white under the smudges of soot. "I think..."

"Let me see."

Beth, grimacing, held out her hand. The little finger hung crooked.

"Ouch. That looks broke."

"Hurts."

"Yeah I 'spect it does. Bugger. Can you fix that ratchet thingy?"

Beth peered into the engine. "Oh, no. The coil's gone. Oh... *bugger*."

Eveline, despite everything, couldn't quite repress a smile at the fact that Beth, who only gave a broken bone a *dammit*, could find a *bugger* for the machine.

"That's bad, is it?"

"I can't fix that even if I had two working hands. Not without tools and things I haven't got."

"Right, come on." Eveline jumped down and reached up to help Beth follow.

"Come on where?"

"Well we got to get back, haven't we – past sunrise and one of 'em'll be coming round to bell us out of bed soon enough. Right, nightgowns." She started to strip off her working clothes. "Remember, you were sleepwalking, I woke up and saw you were gone. You were in the woods in your nightie. You fell and broke your finger, I'm bringing you back. Reckon we can keep our boots and shawls on, they'll believe I had that much sense to bring 'em with me."

"But... the *Sacagawea*. I can't leave her here!"

"Can we push her off the path, into the wood? We can make shift to cover it with branches and leaves and stuff..." Eveline had a moment's memory of blanketing Charlotte's pallid little body with leaves, and bit down on it. "You can come back, when it's safe."

"But the dogs..."

"I'll deal with the dogs. We don't get going now, we'll both be caught and you'll never get to drive her again. Come *on*."

The *Sacagawea* being mostly frame and engine, she was just about light enough for them to move, but it was hard work, especially with Beth unable to use her left hand. They got her off the path and mostly behind some trees and flung armfuls of leaf mould, bracken and broken branches over her, Beth wincing with every thump and slush.

Eveline stood back. If no-one got curious, it'd do... at least, if the wind didn't get up. Anyway it would have to.

"We'd better run," Eveline said.

"Wait."

"We *can't* wait. Come on!"

"Eveline, the notes!"

Eveline stopped. The notes. The notes in her bag, that was on the ground next to the machine and that she'd almost forgotten. She *had* forgotten. And if it had come on to rain, or a fox had found the bag and hauled it off... She hugged Beth fiercely, making her squeak, dragged the bag out of the leaf mould and slung it over her shoulder. They started to run towards the house.

The dogs began to bark as they emerged onto the lawn. "Bugger, bugger, bugger," Eveline said. "Didn't give 'em enough."

"What do we do?"

"Keep running," Eveline said, glancing over her shoulder. The dogs were barking, but they couldn't run properly; they staggered, weaving. The front one abruptly sat down, and the one behind cannoned into it, sending them both sprawling. They started to snap and snarl at each other.

The girls made the kitchen door. Eveline shoved her bag down behind the outbuilding just as the door swung open, and Miss Cairngrim, glaring like a gargoyle, grabbed her by the arm. "What are you up to, you bad, wicked girl?"

"Please, Miss Cairngrim, she's hurt!" Eveline said.

"What have you been doing?"

"I don't remember, Miss Cairngrim," Beth said. "I woke up and I was in the woods. My hand really hurts, Miss Cairngrim."

"Come with me."

She kept them in her office for half an hour, going over their story, as they got colder and colder. Eveline kept her head and kept it simple; it was just like facing a nosy peeler who wanted to know what you were doing, walking past that house at three in the morning. Pity Miss Grim wasn't a peeler, Eveline thought. She'd be just right for it.

Beth had the sense to keep her story even simpler. She'd woken up, on the ground, in the woods, her hand hurting and Eveline shaking her.

"And why didn't the dogs chase you on

"I don't know, Miss Cairngrim. Maybe something," Eveline said. "They weren't funny when they come after us."

"I shall..."

Something thumped against Eveline's shoulder, and she caught Beth just in time to stop her hitting her head on the corner of the desk as she fainted.

"Wretched girl! Stop playacting!"

"She ain't playacting, miss, she's out like a candle," Eveline said, lowering Beth to the floor.

"Isn't! *Isn't,* not *ain't*!" Miss Cairngrim. "Hastings! Hastings!"

"*Sacagawea*," Beth muttered.

"What? What is she saying?"

"Something from History, miss," Eveline said. "She's worried about lessons. Don't worry, Hastings, I'll get it dealt with," she said loudly. Beth's eyes flickered open and sought hers, and Eveline nodded.

Miss Cairngrim called for two of the girls to take Beth to the sickroom, and dismissed Eveline with a glare. "I'll deal with *you* later," she said. "Whatever's going on, I know you're up to your neck in it, Duchen. Now go wash and dress properly, put that *disgusting* garment in for the laundry, and get to class."

Eveline grabbed her bag on the way to the Old Barn. Mr Jackson emerged from his machine long enough to snap at her that he needed that spanner, that one there, stupid girl. He didn't seem to notice that Beth wasn't there. She realised that someone – it had to be Mr Jackson – had been poking about among her mother's mechanisms; some of the levers, she was sure, were standing at different positions, and there were a few small steel balls rolling about the bench that should have been carefully cupped in the grooves made for them. *What have you been up to, Jackson?* She thought, glaring at his back. didn't trust him. The only person she trusted in this as Beth. What the hell was she going to do about the bloody *Sacagawea?* She couldn't exactly push the thing by herself, and she had no idea how to drive it.

Still thinking about it, she fell asleep in History, and got her fingers rapped so hard she thought that perhaps she had a broken one too, but it was only stiff and sore. She rubbed it, staring sightlessly at the maps. *Rescue your mama.* Yes. But how?

In the meantime, she had to keep Holmforth happy. And the only way to do that was to convince him that she knew how to make the machines work.

THE NEXT MORNING, Eveline dragged herself reluctantly from bed, and got hit with (variously) a ruler, a piece of chalk, a hat and a look of despair for her inability to pay attention.

A piece of paper was shoved under her hand. She didn't recognise the writing. Notes, from that morning's History class. At the bottom, the signature, *Treadwell.*

Eveline blinked.

She gave Treadwell the notes back in between classes, and gestured her into an unused classroom. Treadwell followed, looking wary. "What? I can't stop."

"I need to ask you something."

"What?"

"Would you be willing to do me a favour? Another one, I mean."

"That depends."

"Well, really it's two favours. One is to keep acting like you don't like me."

"I don't."

"I don't like you either, but it don't matter. Only, I need for no-one to think you'd do me a favour, right?"

"Well, that's easy, just don't ask me."

"Please. Look, if I ask Beth, everyone'll guess she's playing along. So it has to be you. Will you do it? Chance for a bit of play-acting and you can faint ever so pretty, if you like. Good practice for when you gotta be all *Oh, la, sir, I fear I may swoon,* and nicking the secret plans out their pocket while they hold you up."

Treadwell snorted. "Tell me what you want. I'm not promising anything."

EVELINE WAS SITTING in Retention class when she became vaguely aware of a commotion at one side of the room, as the girls whispered and looked out of the window. "Concentrate!" Miss Fairfield bellowed. "Distraction is the thief of knowledge, girls!"

She heard the sound of a carriage pulling up.

A few minutes later one of the girls appeared at the door. "'Scuse me, Miss Fairfield, but Duchen is to come at once."

Eveline's sleepiness disappeared into a wary, overstressed buzz. What was going on now? Had she been discovered? Had someone at Uncle James's seen her? She followed the girl along the corridor back to Miss Cairngrim's office, ready to turn tail and bolt like a rabbit the second she spotted a uniform.

But when the door to Miss Cairngrim's office opened, it wasn't a peeler. It was Holmforth.

THE GIRL GAVE him a coy little curtsey.

She had washed up well enough – although she had always been neat, despite her circumstances. Her black hair, now it was clean, had a sheen to it, her stance was more confident. Her shoulders were back, not hunched protectively towards her ears.

She made a curtsey – they had managed to instil some manners into her, it seemed – and stood calmly, hands clasped at her waist and eyes lowered, waiting for him to speak.

"Well, Duchen. How have you been getting on with your lessons?"

She shot a glance at Miss Cairngrim. "It's all been most interesting, sir."

"She would get along a great deal better if she concentrated on deportment and attentiveness," Miss Cairngrim said.

"Miss Cairngrim, would you be kind enough to let me speak with Miss Duchen alone? I have matters to discuss with her which I regret must remain confidential."

Miss Cairngrim cast Eveline a glance in which dislike and anxiety mingled strangely. "Very well. Shall I order tea?"

"That would be most pleasant. Thank you."

As soon as she had gone, Holmforth motioned Eveline to a chair. "Well, that is more comfortable," he said, taking another.

It wasn't actually comfortable at all, he found, as a spring was making itself insistently felt through the upholstery, but he was not going to fidget in front of this chit. "Now, I hope you have been making progress, Miss Duchen?"

"I've learned some things, Mr Holmforth."

"I am glad to hear it. And the Etheric mechanisms?"

"I only just got started on those," she said. "That Jackson's..." She paused. "Well, he doesn't seem to know much about it."

"No, he does not. There is no earthly reason why he should. You say you have just got started. Why don't we walk over to the Old Barn and you can show me what you have managed so far."

He caught the flicker of a glance she gave him. She was good, but not that good – her posture stiffened and he heard her breathing quicken.

"There isn't much," she said. "Not yet."

"That disappoints me, Miss Duchen," he said. "That is a severe disappointment, in fact. Having been given this opportunity, I really thought you might manage to make something of it. Are you telling me that you have made no progress?"

"I have made progress! I've done well in Languages, Disguise and Retention. I can get through an hour of Bartitsu without spending all of it getting up off the floor. And as for the history of the Empire – well, there's a lot of it, and it's..." She tailed off. "I'm trying," she repeated.

"Then let us see how well you have done. We will need a subject, of course."

"Oh, I s'pose we will... I could ask my friend Beth..."

"No. I think I will let Miss Cairngrim pick. One shouldn't rely overmuch on friendships," he said. "The Empire is your only true friend, Miss Duchen."

The girl Miss Cairngrim picked was a pretty little thing with a neat curtsey and a refined manner. She greeted him politely, and without simpering, and apart from one brief glance that simmered with dislike, she refused to look at Duchen at all. Perfect. Her name, apparently, was Treadwell.

Once they were in the barn, the Duchen girl gained a certain confidence, moving swiftly among the machines, turning a lever here, placing a ball-bearing there.

Dials glowed, and needles flickered.

"What happens now?" the Treadwell girl said.

"You'd best sit down," Duchen said.

Treadwell looked at the one available chair – obviously banished from the house as being too shabby even for school use – with distaste, and brushed it with her handkerchief before lowering herself gingerly onto the seat.

The first machine began to make a hissing cry. Not an unpleasant sound, but not particularly effective either.

"It won't do much yet, you got to have the sound of two or three to get it right," Eveline said. "Here." She held out her hand to Holmforth. "Earplugs." Small lumps of wax mixed with cotton lay on her palm.

"Thank you, I have my own." Holmforth took out some rather more expensive plugs, and inserted them in his ears. Duchen shrugged and put in her plugs, and made a note.

He could no longer hear, but could see Duchen watching the machines, frowning, taking notes. The Treadwell girl began to smile, then grin foolishly, swaying from side to side as though listening to music.

Duchen made an adjustment to one of the machines. Even through his earplugs, Holmforth was aware of a rising, persistent note. Then, with startling suddenness, Treadwell's head rocked back and she slid bonelessly from the chair, landing in the straw with a puff of hay-dust.

Holmforth waved at Eveline to turn off the machines. She did so. He extracted his earplugs, and examined the girl. She seemed unharmed.

"Well," he said.

"It worked!" Duchen grinned broadly at him. He found himself smiling back. "I didn't know if it would!

I mean, I wasn't sure." She went to the collapsed girl and knelt beside her, patting her cheek.

Treadwell's eyes fluttered open. "What... why am I on the floor? Oh, look at this..." She stood up, shrugging Eveline aside, and began brushing at her skirt.

"You appear to have fainted," Holmforth said. "What do you remember?"

"I remember those things" – she nodded at the machines – "making funny noises, then they started to sound nice, like... I don't know, not music, really, but like the idea of music." She frowned. "And I felt happy. As though..."

"As though?"

"Just happy," Treadwell muttered, looking down. "Better."

"I see," Holmforth said. He felt immensely cheered. He had been wondering if the girl had any idea at all what she was doing, but now it was obvious he had been right all along. "I am very pleased, Miss Duchen. Very pleased indeed. Now, girls, back to the building before your teacher wonders what's become of us all."

As he ushered them back to the school, Holmforth felt lighter, looser, than he had in years. Vindicated! He imagined Forbes-Cresswell's face, the warmth of his handshake.

He sent Treadwell off with a smile – he must commend her to Miss Cairngrim. "Now," he said to Duchen, "you have been taking Chinese?"

"Yes, of course, you said I was to."

"I want you to concentrate on that, and on the Etherics. Nothing else for now. I will speak to Miss Cairngrim, and return in, oh, ten days. And then you will be travelling with me to Shanghai, where your skills will be put to good use."

"Shanghai?"

"Yes. In the Orient."

Her eyes widened.

"I would have hoped your lessons would have covered it," he said.

"There's been a bit about China with my lessons," she said. "But that's mostly... folktales, and things." She was not looking at him. Perhaps the Chinese lessons were going poorly, and she was afraid to admit it. "In ten days?"

"I said so, Miss Duchen. I hope you are paying more attention in your lessons," he said in Chinese.

"Yes, sir, I am attending," she said. In Chinese, without a blink; as though she had barely noticed the transition from one language to another.

"Good," he said. He wasn't going to give her excessive praise, she was arrogant enough without encouraging her to get above herself.

"Mr Holmforth? Can you tell me what it is you want me to do?"

"You will discover that when we arrive."

"In ten days."

"Well, slightly more than that, the journey itself will take a little time. There's no need to look disturbed, I've travelled by zeppelin many times, it's perfectly safe."

"Before we go... there's things I need," she said. "If you want me to do something with the Etherics, I oughta practise, and know as much as possible, shouldn't I, before I go?"

"What do you need?"

"Equipment. I can probably only get it in London."

"Then furnish me with a list and I will see it is provided."

"No, you don't understand," she said, and there was a convincing fervour in her voice. "The machines... they... oh, it'll sound so foolish, Mr Holmforth, I know it will."

"Tell me."

"'Slike they talk to me." She was frowning, trying to get the words right. "I get a sense of the shapes, of the parts... it ain't like I even know the names, see, I just get a feel for what they need. I gotta see the things, and then I'll know, you see."

It confirmed his understanding of Etheric-so-called-science; a matter of intuition, of primitive responses. Useful, in its way – that meant it would be easier to guide its application into the desired channels. However... "You expect me to allow you to travel to London?" Was the tiresome girl simply trying to give him the slip?

"Not by myself! That old woman, Ma Pether... I don't want her catching me again. I was sorta hoping you might consider taking me yourself. I go into a shop looking for things, they'll laugh me out of the place. And besides, I got no money. If I got you with me... I can feel them, getting ready to sing, Mr Holmforth. I wanta make 'em sing again." She tilted her head up, and he could see the glow in her eyes.

"I will arrange an overnight stay. You may bring one small bag."

"When?"

"Impatient? Let us say three days."

"Oh, thank you, Mr Holmforth! Will we be staying at an hotel?"

"Indeed."

"Ooh, I've never stayed in a proper hotel. What's it called?"

"It will be the Ship Inn, in Westminster."

She looked down at herself, then up at him, anxiously. "Is it very respectable? Only..."

"You will be provided with a decent outfit." He gathered up his things and said, "Tell Miss Cairngrim I'll see myself out."

"Don't you need the door unlocked?"

"I suppose I must. How terribly like a gaol. Oh, and Miss Duchen?"

"Yes, Mr Holmforth?"

"Do not attempt to escape my supervision in London. Or you will shortly discover that a real gaol is far more unpleasant than this." He gave her a hard look. She seemed tamed, even inclined to be cooperative, but she was, after all, female, and though she had been born respectable, her time among the lower orders had tainted her. It wouldn't do to let her think he had relaxed his vigilance.

"I won't, Mr Holmforth. I don't want to go back to that."

"Now go back to your lessons."

"Yes, Mr Holmforth."

A girl came in with the tea tray as he was leaving, followed by Miss Cairngrim. "You won't stay, Mr Holmforth?"

"I regret I have another appointment."

"Was everything satisfactory?"

"It will do. I require that Duchen be provided with respectable clothing; she will be travelling as my ward. Nothing fancy, but I don't wish her to look as though she has come from the poorhouse."

"Yes, Mr Holmforth."

* * *

EVELINE LEANED AGAINST the wall of the corridor and closed her eyes. Well, that was one part. Of course, she didn't know how the other parts were to fall together yet, and there wasn't anything like enough time, but she would do it. Somehow, she would do it.

"I DON'T KNOW what happens to all the paper," Cook grumbled. "Barely enough to get a decent fire started."

Eveline ducked her head. She was swiping as many of the newspapers as she could get hold of, searching for any information on Bedlam. She'd have to remember just to whisk away the pages she wanted and put the rest back, otherwise someone would notice. Bedlam did make the occasional appearance, though it was some time before she realised that it and the Bethlehem Hospital were the same place.

There wasn't much. But there was enough for her to work out where it was and make the beginnings of a plan.

"WELL, YOU HAVE been a busy little bird."

"Liu! Don't creep up on a girl like that!" Eveline spilled a ball-bearing onto the floor and got down on her knees, cursing, to look for it.

"Apologies, my Lady Sparrow. Is something troubling you?" Liu bent down, and, irritatingly, immediately found the tiny silver ball and handed it to her.

"Apart from heathen Chinese sneaking up on me?" she grumbled, getting to her feet.

He shook his head mournfully. "You don't trust me."

"Why should I?"

"Because I am Chinese?"

"What's that got to do with anything? I don't trust you 'cos you're *here*."

"And there I thought that going to all this trouble would be a certain proof of my friendship."

"Really?"

He sighed. "Naïve, I suppose."

"I don't know what that means."

"It means that perhaps I should have known better."

"So who did send you? Holmforth? Or..."

"Ma Pether?" He held out his hands placatingly as she swore. "Oh, Lady Sparrow, of course I know about Ma Pether, but I have no dealings with her! She has no idea I exist."

"I wouldn't be too sure of that."

"Trust me," he said, "if I do not want someone to be aware of my existence... they remain in ignorance."

"I think you're the arrogantest person I ever met."

"You certainly trust me enough to insult me. Not that there is any such word as arrogantest in either English or Chinese."

"You already know everything about me," she said, shrugging. "What's to lose by throwing an insult or two?"

"Oh," he said, "that's certainly not true. I don't, for example, know why Mr Duvalier looks at you with such dislike. Really, he is very bad at concealing his less-attractive emotions."

"I found out something about him, something bad he was doing."

"Ah. That can be a dangerous path to tread."

"Is that what you did? When you offended someone?"

"Something not unlike that, perhaps. See? Now you know something more about me. Still I don't know what you were doing off the grounds the other night, and I don't know what the other – the mixtus's – interest is in you. And what it is you're planning."

Eveline backed against the bench, grateful for its solidity against her back. "Leave the grounds? I en't never left the grounds, I don't want one of them dogs taking my hand off, thank you. And the only thing I'm planning is trying to get these machines working, like I'm supposed to, so if you don't mind letting me get on..."

He only smiled and passed her another ball-bearing. "I do wish you wouldn't look at me as though I intended to bite your head off."

"How do I know you don't? What do you *want*?"

"I would like to find out what is going on. The more time I spend around you, the more interesting you are."

"I'm sure I should be flattered, but I ain't. You let me go about my business, and you go about yours."

"But perhaps I can help."

"Did you have family? Back home?"

"Not any longer. My mother is dead, and my father considers me disgraced. I do not see him."

"I'm sorry."

"And you?"

"My papa's dead. My sister's dead. My mother... I thought she was dead, too. Only it turns out she isn't."

"Well that is joyous news." He looked at her. "Is it not?"

"Well of course it is, but... it's complicated."

"Can I help?"

"Why should I trust you?" She *wanted* to, she realised. Part of her already did... but she couldn't afford to.

"Ask me to do something, and if it is in my power to do it, I will do it."

She glared at him, thinking rapidly. What could she ask that would help, but wouldn't give the whole plan away, if he wasn't to be trusted? There had to be something...

"All right. Prove you're not in with Ma. I want Lazy Lou."

"Are you insulting me again?"

"Not *you*. Lazy Lou. It's a mannequin she keeps in her house, she hangs clothes on it. She used to try and make it work, but she gave up. Get it here, to a place where it'll be out of sight, but I can get to it... and I'll trust you. Maybe. A bit."

To her surprise he looked utterly delighted, and gave a short, sharp laugh, almost a yap. "Oh, a challenge! Very well. When would you like her?"

"Soon's you can get her here. But if you get caught..."

"I will not," he said, "get caught."

"Liu? That other thing you said – what's a 'mixtus'?"

"That man, Holmforth. He is a mixtus. One of his parents was Folk."

"*What?*"

"You didn't know?"

"No," Eveline said. "No, I didn't. Bloody *hell*." That explained his looks, then. Explained a few other things too, maybe.

Bad enough Holmforth was the next best thing to a peeler. Part Folk, too? Well, that was it, then. Any promise he made was probably worth about as much as a dead rat. "Thanks, Liu. I'll keep it in mind."

HOLMFORTH PAUSED OUTSIDE the door of his father's house, then raised his hand to the knocker.

The maid was new, but Edleston, the butler, though now shuffling and white-haired, was the same man who had been a silent presence, summoned like a ghost to his father's side, throughout Holmforth's childhood.

"He is expecting you, sir."

There was nothing in Edleston's tone or expression of either approbation or disapproval. His perfectly blank exterior had provided a useful model in Holmforth's youth. He bowed Holmforth through into the drawing room.

Everything, including the chill, was the same. A portrait of his grandfather hung over the fireplace, gradually blackening with soot. His father sat hunched over a copy of the *Times*. Holmforth waited until he should deign to notice his remaining son.

"Bloody Chinese. Thought your lot were supposed to be sorting them out?" Holmforth the Elder flung the paper onto the table and leaned back.

Age and disease had ground away almost all of his patrician looks. His eyes were pouched and rheumy, his strong jaws falling to soft folds about the neck.

"The rebellion will fade," Thaddeus said. "These things always do."

"I suppose you want some tea. I won't have it in the house. Weaklings forever maudling their insides with tea, no wonder the balance of payments is a mess. So is it money?"

"No, thank you, I am sufficiently supplied. I simply came to see if there was anything you wanted."

"In that case, you can sort out your brother's grave. That blasted Whitaker woman came visiting, told me it's getting overgrown. Disgraceful. Vicar should be sacked."

"I will see to it." Holmforth picked up his gloves. "I'm returning to Shanghai shortly." He waited a moment, but his father said nothing. "Was there anything else you wished done?"

Holmforth the Elder shrugged pettishly. "Unless you can find a cure for what ails me, no. I've dealt with the lawyers. There's nothing for you to do but wait out my death."

"Now, Father. New territories are opening up all the time – one never knows what may be discovered."

"New territories? Hah. More trouble and expense. They'd have done better leaving well enough alone – look at India! Tell Edleston to bring me my medicine on your way out."

"Yes, Father."

A TRAIL OF IVY clambered its way up the side of the memorial, digging its tendrils into the stone. *Mary Elizabeth Holmforth. Honoured wife.*

Maurice Edgebaston Holmforth. Beloved Son.

There was room for their father's name to be added, but no more.

He did not remember much about his mother, or about the Crepuscular. Sometimes, still, he woke wet-eyed from dreams of music of unspeakable sweetness, and of grass that caressed his bare feet like silk. But that, and a faint, indefinable scent that sometimes caught him unawares, was all he had of it. He did not even remember the moment his mother had handed him into his father's care. He had learned not to ask questions, but simply to listen, scavenging for every scrap he could find or guess.

It seemed she had simply grown bored, like a child with a puppy that had grown out of its capacity to amuse.

It had taken no time at all for the servants, to whose care he was mostly consigned, to realise who he was. He had his father's eyes and brows, and his mother's slightness and creamy-gold skin. Such affairs were not unknown, though less common than they used to be; but offspring were rare. Strange, Thaddeus thought, that rarity in other things was valued.

If Maurice hadn't broken his neck in a stupid, reckless carriage-race when Thaddeus was seven years old, he would probably have been found some minor post, or paid off.

But Maurice was dead, and their father was no longer capable of producing offspring – the result of flinging himself into a number of low and, as it turned out, unhealthy liaisons after the departure of Thaddeus' mother. With his legitimate son dead, Holmforth the Elder had had no choice but to make Thaddeus his heir, or see the estate broken up.

Thaddeus was removed from the casual care of the servants and transferred from the village school to Eton. Within days, everyone there knew who – and what – he was.

He learned a great deal. He learned that it was better to take his beatings than to complain and suffer the contempt meted out to tell-tales. He learned how to remain calm in the face of despite. He learned that the Empire was great and noble, that it brought light into darkness and civilisation to savages; that it rewarded loyal service, and that even such as he might have a place in it. He had embraced that possibility with all the passion of an abandoned heart.

From inside the church a single voice, sweet and clear, began to sing. Other voices rose over the first, building joyful harmonies.

Holmforth ripped the ivy away from the stone, flung the parasitic stuff into the yew hedge, and left the churchyard.

BETH STORMED INTO the Old Barn and, ignoring Mr Jackson, said, "I need to talk to you. *Now*."

"What is it?"

"Outside."

Eveline had never seen her look so furious; high colour lit her cheeks and her hair seemed to stand out crackling around her head. She followed her out.

"What's the matter?"

Beth strode away across the lawns, and Eveline followed her.

"How could you?" Beth burst out. "How *could* you?"

"How could I what?"

"You told someone! You told them about her, and now they'll give her to Jackson or..."

"What? No! I en't told anyone anything!"

"Then what's that *thing* doing in my shed, *sitting* there?"

"I don't know what you mean. Beth..."

"Oh, you don't, do you? Come look, then."

"We're supposed to be..."

"When have you cared about what you're *supposed* to be doing?"

Eveline gave in and followed Beth into the trees where the old shed hid.

They pulled aside the branches that concealed the doorway. The sunlight crept in, and something gleamed in the shadows. Eveline, startled, stepped backwards, tripped over a root and sat down hard.

She stared, and got up slowly, rubbing her bruised backside. "Oh," she said. "Oh, you *bugger*." Then she began to laugh.

"I don't see what's funny," Beth said.

"It's... it's all right," Eveline gasped between giggles. "It's just Lou. Oh, Ma's gonna be so *furious*."

The *Sacagawea* had been returned to her place, and seated on her bench was Lazy Lou. Her metal limbs were neatly arranged, one jointed hand resting on the wheel, the other – as though she were travelling at speed – clasping to her head at the most rakish of angles Ma Pether's huge, befeathered, purple silk Sunday hat.

"Who put it there?" Beth said.

"Liu, my Chinese teacher. I asked him for a favour. He's alright, he won't peach on us."

"You told him about *Sacagawea*!"

"I *didn't*. He must have found her himself. Look, it's fine. If he'd meant to tell someone, he'da done it already."

Beth closed her eyes. "You'd better be right. All right. I'm probably going to wish I hadn't asked but... why has he brought you an automaton?"

"I got a plan."

"I should have known."

"You should be in Bedlam," Beth said.

"Don't."

"Eveline, it's just not possible. It isn't. I'm sorry. Not after last time. I felt that dog's breath on my *leg*."

"You don't have to come with me. All you got to do is watch out for her when she arrives and help me hide her once she's here."

"But you'll get *caught*."

"I won't."

"Then *I* will! And then what'll happen to your mama? Eveline, please. There must be something else – you could talk to Holmforth, apply to have her released..."

"No. No. Everyone thinks she's dead. I don't want him knowing she ain't. "

"Why not? He's got far more power than either of us, Evvie, he could *do* something."

"Yes. He could say, 'Here, Eveline Duchen, I've got your mama and unless you do what I say I'll hurt her.' That's what he could do."

"That's *horrible*. You really think he'd do that?" Beth looked genuinely shocked.

Eveline sighed. "You ain't half led a sheltered life. Look, I know what he sees when he looks at me, Beth. He sees something that can either help the Empire or get in its way. And that's *all* he sees. I don't mean no more to him than a shovel or a lock-pick. The rest of you in here, someone cared enough to see you were set up even if you were, you know, born the wrong side of the blankets. Point is, you all mean at least that much to someone. I don't mean *nothing* to Holmforth; he got me in here because he wants to use me. And I ain't going to take a wager he won't see Mama just the same way."

"So what's the poor lady supposed to do? Live in the stables?"

"I was thinking a boarding house somewhere near, but then I won't be able to see her. It'll have to be the rooms in the East Wing. I had a look. A couple of them are all right."

"You don't give up, do you?"

"The only time to give up is when going on will lose you more than it'll get you."

"And you're so sure it won't."

"No. No, I ain't. But it's my *mother*, Beth. She's been in that place for all these years, like being sent to prison when she ain't even done nothing wrong, just because that bastard Uncle James wanted her out the way. I got to *try*, at least."

Beth was quiet for a long time, turning a spanner over and over in her hands. "That could have been me," she said at last. "Couldn't it?"

"I didn't think. I suppose."

"I was inconvenient, and a nuisance, and if I hadn't come here, that's where I'd be, or somewhere like it. At least here I get a chance to learn something. If I'd been sent to Bedlam, I don't know what sort of state I'd be in. Your poor mama. I wonder how she's managed."

"Oh, Mama always could make a lot with a little," Eveline said. "If it hadn't been for Uncle James... she'll have managed, she always did." Eveline smiled and leaned against the wall in the sun, imagining how Mama would open her arms and pick Evvie up and hug her, and Evvie would do whatever it was Holmforth wanted, for however long it was. She would have somewhere for Mama to stay, an apartment and an allowance, and she could look after Mama and keep her safe. And one day there would be that pension, and she would make damn sure it didn't disappear like Papa's had.

Charlotte. The smile dropped away, the sun chilled. How would she ever tell Mama about what had happened to Charlotte? What would she say?

*   *   *

"NIHAO, LADY SPARROW."

She eyed Liu. He was a trickster like her, she felt it in her bones. So why did she also feel in her bones that she could trust him? It didn't make sense, and she knew it. Still...

"Thank you," she said. "I never asked for the hat, though."

"It will suit you a great deal better than it suited Ma Pether."

"'Sif I'd ever dare wear it. What if she saw me?"

"Perhaps you can wear it somewhere other than London? There are other cities in the world."

"Yes, I know. I'm going to one."

"Really?" he said, but she got the feeling he already knew.

"Wish you'd tell me what's going on."

"I am. I have. You interest me. I think, perhaps, we are not unalike, Lady Sparrow. Scavengers at the edges, both, yes?"

"I don't know what a scavenger is."

"Collectors of crumbs, and other interesting and useful items discarded by the careless. You need another task performed."

"Maybe."

"Come, let us be honest with each other." He whisked his feet, shod in soft black shoes, up underneath him and sat neatly perched on the desk, with his legs crossed, propped his elbows on his thighs and looked at her over his linked hands. "You are testing me."

"And if I am?"

"Then I admire both your caution – and your daring. What is it you want?"

"Can you get to London?"

"Oh, you would be surprised at the places I can get to."

"Then I need something organised. Someone got out of the way."

His narrow slanted brows drew up, and his mouth down. "I see," he said. "How has this unfortunate person offended you?"

"What? I don't mean got rid of! What sort of girl do you think I am?"

"I am glad to find that you are *not* that sort of girl."

"Would you do it?" she said. "If I asked?"

He shook his head at her, not as though he were saying no, but as though he were disappointed.

"I'm not gonna ask," she said.

"Making statements like that is risky," he said.

"Who's listening?"

"Well, *I* am."

She felt as though he were dancing with her, somehow, and while it was interesting, it wasn't getting her anywhere. "Are you going to help me or not?"

"And my reward?"

Now she felt on more familiar ground. "That depends on what you want."

"Wouldn't money be usual?"

"Yes. But I en't got any – well, not much – and you're not usual."

He grinned, pleased. "A favour, then. A favour of equal worth and equal risk, no more."

Eveline chewed her lip, looking at him. "What's risk to me ain't the same as what's risk to you," she said. "If I get chucked out of here, I can't walk into a good-paying job like you can."

"Are you sure?" He said. "Very well. I am a good evaluator of risk, and of fairness. But if you think what

I ask of you is unfairly balanced with what you ask of me, then I will withdraw it. Fair?"

"Fair."

Eveline left the room still smiling. Something about dealing with Liu was like a sharp breeze. He made her feel more awake.

EVELINE CLUTCHED THE edges of her cloak so hard her fingers cramped, waiting for Holmforth's coach to appear.

She wore a dress of black silk with a modest crinoline, which, while uncomfortable and inconvenient, provided a remarkable amount of storage, so long as one arranged things properly. Miss Cairngrim had provided it, with many frowning reminders that it did not belong to her, but to the school. Eveline, thinking of Ma Pether and her store of costumes, wondered what it would be like to have smart clothes that were actually her own.

She had also been provided with a Gladstone bag that smelled of damp. It held food for the journey, a change of under-things and, under a false bottom that she had installed, some things that were too delicate to risk hanging under the crinoline.

The carriage clopped and crunched up the drive, and Holmforth stepped out. He tipped his hat to Miss Cairngrim, who was standing on the steps, took Eveline's bag and handed her into the carriage.

She sat herself opposite him, arranging her skirts carefully, and watched as he opened the bag and examined the contents, presumably checking to see if she'd packed enough to run away with. She considered making a remark about gentlemen who showed so much interest in ladies' underwear, but didn't. She needed to seem as compliant as possible today.

"I think we can do rather better for luncheon than – let me see – what appears to be a rather stale currant bun and an apple that has been badly stored. Were you afraid I wouldn't feed you?"

"I've spent most of my life hungry, Mr Holmforth. Plenty of times that would have seemed like manna from heaven, that bun."

"Yes, I'm sure. Well, if you do not do anything foolish, you will find yourself adequately provided for and will not need to hoard like a little squirrel afraid of the winter."

Afraid? Eveline thought. Squirrels weren't afraid of the winter – they were sensible. If they didn't store food, they died. Those were the words of a man who'd never been nose-to-nose with starvation.

Trees meandered past the windows, eventually giving way to stretches of farmland, the harvest long gathered, the fields now brown and empty under the grey sky. Eveline found herself mentally comparing the carriage with the *Sacagawea*. It might be more comfortable, but it was so much slower!

She sneaked glances at Holmforth, who was reading a small book bound in black hide. Now she knew what to look for, his heritage was clear – in his face, in his narrow, long-fingered hands and faintly iridescent nails (which he kept so short the skin around them looked raw), in his skin.

Well, well. Whether or not it was a lever remained to be seen. So far as she could tell, he made no effort to hide it, and it couldn't have done him much harm;

he was well dressed, well-educated and worked for the government.

It probably didn't mean much at all, then. Except to remind her to be wary, as though she needed that.

IT SEEMED TO take forever to get to London, and even longer once they were in the mess of streets.

London seemed, in her absence, to have become busier and noisier, to have been packed full with people and vehicles thrown all together and scrambling about, like a bucket of crabs. Even Watford had not been so loud, or so crowded, or so thick with smoke. The sky was nearer brown than grey, and a yellow pall lay over everything. The air tasted heavy and bitter.

But still Eveline felt a surge of pleasure at being back. This was her territory, the place she'd made her own, where she'd been Evvie the Sparrow, little unnoticeable Evvie who could get in anywhere and nip away with the prize before anyone had a chance to notice it was gone.

And there were no Folk in London. Apart from Holmforth, of course; and maybe other half-Folk like him. There were people in London of every other shape and size, after all.

"Here," he said, as the carriage drew to a halt. "This is the hotel."

It was a small, discreet place with a green-painted door. It smelled faintly of polish and carbolic soap. Eveline, out of habit, assessed the paintings in the lobby – not bad, though not fashionable – and the pen-set on the desk. Two crystal inkwells in a rosewood stand with a pair of silver pens, worth a few bob, together or separate.

Holmforth spoke a few murmured words with the man seated behind the pen-set.

There was no porter. They stepped into the lift, Holmforth pulled the brass gates closed behind them, and they rattled and creaked their way to the top floor.

Eveline's room was, by her standards, luxurious, with a thick quilt on the bed and a fire already lit. She stretched her hands to it, closing her eyes with pleasure as heat tingled through her fingers. Then she removed her few things from the top layer of the Gladstone bag, dropped them on the bed, put her cloak back on and was waiting when Holmforth knocked on her door.

"Are you sure you need that with you?" he said, looking at the bag.

"I thought I should have something to carry things in. You going to carry it for me, squire?"

"Don't be impertinent."

Eveline hid a smile as he marched ahead of her down the stairs. *Full of yerself, aren't you, Mr Holmforth? Well, you don't know as much as you think you do.*

As they left, a shadow detached itself from the mouth of a nearby alleyway and followed them.

THE STREET THEY eventually came to was lined with small shops. From the workshops behind them came the sounds of battering hammers, clangs and thuds and the hiss of white heat meeting water; the reek of sweat and the bitter tang of hot metal.

"You should find what you need here, if anywhere," Holmforth said. "I need not remind you to be sensible, and not to attempt to run away?"

"I'm not planning on going anywhere, Mr Holmforth."

"Go on, then."

Eveline made for the first of the shops, and looked at the window for a long time. There were tools and bits of pipe and things she had no names for on display. She made as if to go in, and shook her head, and went to the next shop.

She had seen enough mediums and mentalists to know that you didn't make it look too easy. You had to show that you were *working* at this mysterious thing that the audience couldn't understand, that it took effort, and couldn't just be plucked out of thin air.

The next shop contained a display of cogwheels in two dozen sizes, from one bigger than her head to one smaller than her smallest fingernail, laid out on black velvet as though they were fine jewels. The next, bits that looked similar to some of the things she had seen Beth using, wheels and levers that must belong to steam-cars and such.

She hesitated at the cog shop. She was aware of Holmforth watching her, like someone waiting for a dog to learn a trick.

She went in, and Holmforth followed. After whispered consultation, she picked out two cogs about the size of her palm and one tiny one.

Without discussion or argument, he paid.

They went back to the other shop, the one full of levers and tubes and dials. Eveline forced herself to focus. Spent minutes staring at a case full of dials, frowned, and finally picked one – mainly because the hands were finely tooled and the numbers very smartly painted in black and gold. She touched nothing herself, only told Holmforth which one she wanted, in a whisper.

She became aware that the shopkeeper perched on a stool behind the counter, a small grey wrinkled man with a long nose, who put her in mind of an elderly rat, was regarding them over half-moon glasses with a scowl of suspicion.

He beckoned his assistant, a lanky young man with very red hair and a fancy waistcoat, muttered to him and pointed in their direction.

The young man began to walk towards them.

Eveline felt a ripple of anxiety creep up from her ankles. What had set him off? They both looked respectable enough, surely? It couldn't be Holmforth. Was she losing her touch? Had her time at the school rubbed the sheen off her ability to fade into the wallpaper until she wanted to be noticed?

"Can I help you?" the assistant said.

"We are still in the process of making our selection," Holmforth said.

"Mr Wallis says please be quick."

"Oh. And what pressing appointment does Mr Wallis have that necessitates such urgency?"

The assistant swallowed and looked back at his master. "He says... he says this is a respectable shop."

"Is it?"

Eveline's senses shivered. Something in Holmforth's voice made her back hairs stand on end.

"Yes," the young man said. A blush crept up his neck, swamping his freckles in red. "He says we don't want anything happening to the stock, that shouldn't."

Holmforth looked at the shopkeeper. The air between them twanged.

"Tell your master that we will leave when we have finished our business," he said.

"That one," Eveline burst out, tapping the display case. "That one in the middle of the bottom row."

She didn't know what was going on, but it was to do with Holmforth, not her, that much she *did* know. And she wanted to get out of here.

The dial was extracted, and wrapped – not very well. The shopkeeper took the money Holmforth handed him and counted it, deliberately; he rapped the coins on the counter, and even removed his glasses and took a jeweller's loupe out of the pocket of his snuff-dusted waistcoat and screwed it into his eye to peer at them. Eveline stood there trying to project a church-every-day starched-linen respectability, not daring to look at Holmforth. The shopkeeper raised his head, dropped the loupe into his palm, looked her up and down and sniffed.

"You have some comment to make to my ward?" Holmforth said.

"Ward, is it?" he replied, putting more filth into the word *ward* than even Eveline would have thought possible. "No. Now if you're done..."

"Oh, we're done," Holmforth said. "I shall be sure to mention the name of this fine emporium to *my* employer."

"Why don't you do that."

And with that, they left the shop. They hadn't quite got out of the door when the shopkeeper said, quite clearly, "Folkgotten filth."

Holmforth paused for the barest moment, before striding out and letting the door swing shut. Eveline still didn't dare look directly at him; but a glimpse of his hand, rigid at his side, showed the knuckles standing out stark white and the tendons of his hands so tight she could have played them like a fiddle if she'd had a mind.

"Mr Holmforth? I'm ever so tired," she said. "Could we go back?"

"Very well."

They made the short journey in silence.

"Mr Holmforth?" the man behind the desk said as they arrived. "There's a telegram for you, sir."

"What?"

"Here, sir." The man handed Holmforth the flimsy paper.

Holmforth, frowning, opened it. Eveline pretended interest in a set of wax flowers under a glass dome.

"Miss Duchen, I will have to go out. I suggest you rest. I have asked the proprietor to check on you every hour, until I return, you understand?"

"Yes, Mr Holmforth."

He escorted her to her room, and locked her in.

TEN MINUTES LATER Eveline waved at a hansom cab that was waiting in the street behind the hotel. Its driver leaned down. "Where to, madam?"

"You did it!"

Liu laughed. He had a greatcoat and a tricorn hat on, which gave him a strangely piratical look. "Did you think I wouldn't?"

"Haul us up, then."

"No, you must sit inside or you will not look respectable."

"S'pose you're right," she said. "What did you put in the telegram?"

"A great deal of nonsense that suggested that someone with information about Etheric science wished to speak with him, as you suggested."

"Well, it worked. How long?"

"Who can tell? I shall do what I can."

"Liu..."

"Yes?"

"Thanks. I owe yer."

"Yes, you do. Don't worry," he said. "I'm not in the habit of driving hard bargains."

Eveline smiled at him and climbed into the cab.

She would rather have sat with Liu, but she had far too much to think about. As for the hotel proprietor... well, she'd done what she could.

Bedlam

EVELINE LOOKED AT the vast imperious frontage of the Bethlehem Hospital, its pillared portico and central dome, and tried to rub some warmth into hands gone suddenly chilly.

Her mama was somewhere in there, in that great height and depth of stone, behind those rows of windows gleaming cold.

She extracted some papers from the false bottom of the Gladstone bag and walked up to the entrance.

"I'M DR PETERS. We have had no notice of a visit," the doctor said. He was a smartly-dressed man with a confident moustache, at odds with eyes like an anxious spaniel's. "And the Physician-Superintendent is not here today."

"A visit without notice was considered the best way of keeping this unfortunate situation out of the public eye," Eveline said. "You do understand that the family would prefer that the Lunacy Commissioners did not become involved, let alone..." – she leaned close and muttered – "the Press."

"The Press! But we have... there have been so *many* reforms in the last years, the place is quite different, and the situation of the patients altogether improved."

"So I understand. But if it were to come to light that either of the doctors who signed her committal papers were involved in any other cases where there might have been a *monetary advantage*..." Eveline left the sentence hanging. "You said yourself that Mrs Duchen has been a model patient."

"I believe there were some problems at first, but of course if it were all a misunderstanding..."

"Misunderstanding? I should rather have said *fraud*!" Eveline snapped.

"Quite, quite. Would you like to see the lady?"

"Yes, I think that would be best," Eveline said, swallowing down the sudden rising panic that tightened her throat. "I would like a private interview, is that possible?"

"Of course. I will have her brought to one of the side rooms."

After some back and forth with messages, Dr Peters led Eveline from the office down the wide, echoing corridor, chatting as they went about how the bathrooms were now tiled, and the majority of the patients no longer subject to restraint, and properly clothed... Eveline smiled and tried to look interested, but all she could do was scan the faces of every patient as they passed the rooms. Many of them looked like people one might meet any day on the street. In fact, Eveline had encountered a number of people who looked a good deal more disturbed than most of the residents, although here and there one gesticulated at nothing, or sat rocking and staring. One woman in her middle years with something familiar in the line of her back caught Eveline's eye, but turned on her a gaze so utterly blank that Eveline shuddered, staring for a moment in terror in case this poor, empty, slack-faced creature should be Mama.

It wasn't. The woman turned indifferently away. Eveline hurried after Dr Peters.

The place was better than she had expected: lighter, and cleaner. She had spent most of her own last few years in considerably worse circumstances. But still, it was a prison, in which her mama had been unjustly locked... she felt her hands clench. How much longer? This corridor had been going on forever.

"Here we are," Dr Peters said brightly. "Mrs Duchen? You have a visitor."

The woman standing facing the window was dressed in a black stuff gown. Her grey hair was pinned neatly onto her head. "A visitor?" she said. Her voice was thick and slow.

Eveline had a sudden desire to cry out, to ask her not to turn around, to simply run. The movement seemed to take a desperately long time, as though the woman in the window were standing on a very, very slow turntable.

She could hardly bear to look, but had to seem calm, aware always of Dr Peters at her side. *Don't cry, Eveline. Don't you dare.* "Mrs Duchen?"

Mama. Older, a little plumper – but unmistakably Mama.

She looked at her daughter with no recognition at all.

"I shall leave you to speak with her," Dr Peters said. "Please ring the bell when you are done, and someone will come to escort you out."

"Thank you," Eveline said. To herself, her voice sounded so very strange she expected Dr Peters to say something, but he only left, shutting the door quietly behind him.

He did not lock it.

Mama stood there patiently, looking at the young woman who had come to visit her.

"I..." Eveline said. She felt the tears coming, but she could not, could *not* cry. "I don't s'pose you know me."

"I'm afraid not," Mama said. Oh, her voice. So quiet and slow. "You must forgive me, did you come with the inspectors last time? My memory is not what it was."

"No. I... would you like to sit down? I think perhaps we should both sit down."

There was a scuffed wooden table, two chairs. Amenably, Mama sat down. So did Eveline.

Eveline started to speak, stopped, tried again. All the words piled into her throat and lodged there.

"Is something wrong?" Mama said.

"It's me, Mama. It's Eveline."

"Eveline. *Eveline?* You're my *daughter?*"

"Yes."

Something was rising under the surface of that calm, placid face.

Not recognition or love. Horror.

"*No,*" Mama said. "No. It's a trick. Please go away. This is very unkind." She reached for the bell and Eveline put a hand over hers. Her hands had aged; they were red and swollen.

"It's not a trick, Mama. It's me."

Madeleine Duchen searched her face. "Eveline? Eveline. Is it you?"

She suddenly stood up, pushing her chair back so violently it fell over. "No. No, not this. I... Any injustice they did me, I could bear, but not you too. What did he do? Eveline, what did he do? Did he get you put in here too? James? Oh, Eveline... I thought at least you were safe... I can't..."

"Mama, no. No." Eveline stood up too, took her hands and held them firmly. "No, I'm here... I'm a visitor, I'm not a patient. And Uncle James is dead."

"Dead."

"Yes. Mama, please, sit back down."

Still staring, she let herself be led back to the table, and sat in the righted chair, clinging to the sides as though she were afraid she might float away, and watching her daughter as though she were a vision that might disappear at any moment.

"Uncle James... he told me you were dead. And then I had to run away. And I didn't know. I only found out a few days ago that you were alive, and where. Mama, I've come to get you out."

"James... James told you I was dead."

"Yes."

"Oh, that is *so* like him." And there, in the way she threw her head back in exasperation, Eveline caught a glimpse of the mother she remembered. "But Eveline, what happened? And where –"

With a horrible feeling that the next words would be, "Where is Charlotte?" Eveline forestalled her. "Mama, we can't talk now. I'll explain everything. But I have to get you out, and we have to do it in secret. I'll explain later. But we have to get you out."

"Do you have papers?"

"No. Well, sort of."

"They'll never let me out without papers. They want papers for everything. One could drown in paper."

"Don't worry, Mama. Just do as I ask, please?"

"I don't want to cause trouble." Mama's eyes were wide and scared. "If you cause trouble you get given chloral. It makes you sick. Or galvanism. Which is worse."

"There won't be any trouble. Just do as I say. Everything will be fine. You do *want* to leave, don't you?"

Mama looked at her, biting her lip. "Yes, but... can I fetch my things?"

"Things?"

"I managed to make some things. Mechanisms. From whatever I could find. To keep my hand in. I had to hide them, of course."

"I have your things, Mama. All your old mechanisms."

"You do? How?"

"I'll explain later. But now... will you do as I ask? And let me get you out of here?"

Mama was silent for a long, terrifying moment. Then she sighed. "Yes," she said.

Eveline took a breath, and rang the bell.

Dr Peters opened the door and looked in, wearing an anxious smile which suddenly disappeared under a chloroform-soaked rag.

"Shut the door, Mama," Eveline said, lowering Dr Peters to the floor. "Right. Into his things, quick."

"What?"

Eveline whisked off Dr Peters' coat, waistcoat, shirt and trousers and got Mama into them, coaxing her as though she were a little girl, being dressed for school.

Everything was too big. Eveline mentally sent thanks to Miss Fortescue for teaching her to always carry pins, needle and thread. None of the stitching would bear close inspection, but if they were closely inspected they were done for in any case.

"Now. Hold still."

Mama did. Scarily still, so docile. Eveline tried to squash the creeping dread she felt, a terrible desire to just give up, to leave this doll-woman here and run away. Her hands worked, using the putty and false hair she had packed in her bag. The skin tone was not right – Mama was so pale – but it would have to do.

Soon a lumpy, baggy, and rather ill-looking version of Dr Peters stood in front of Eveline. Except it had a bun. "Oh, damn," she muttered, and looked at Mama sidelong, but if Mama had heard her swear she gave no sign. No wig! How had she been so stupid as to forget the wig? She looked frantically around the room. What was she to do?

"Mama, can you let down your hair?"

"My hair? What's this stuff on my face?" She raised a hand to tug at the false moustache Eveline had just spent precious minutes gluing on. Eveline seized her hand and pulled it gently down. "No, Mama. Leave it. Let me do your hair."

Freed from its bun her hair was long enough to tuck under her collar, and the effect, while odd, was not excessively noticeable. But it was too grey, Dr Peters' hair was darker.

There was a fireplace in the room. Eveline reached inside it and covered her hands with soot. She rubbed it on her mother's hair as best she could, trying not to cover them both with smuts.

There. It wasn't wonderful, but it would have to do. At least the day was darkening.

Dr Peters was beginning to stir. She gave him another dose. That was it for the chloroform. She shoved the jar back into her bag, now covered with sooty fingerprints, wiped her hands on her skirts, (at least they were black), and took Mama's arm. "Come along. It's not far."

Down the corridors they went. People glanced at them. Eveline tried to look as though she were being escorted, rather than doing the escorting.

"It's suppertime," Mama said.

"Yes, shh, we'll get you some supper later."

Oh, the corridors were too long. There were other attendants about, going about their business, it couldn't be long before one saw that something was wrong.

All this new lighting that Dr Peters had been so proud of! Eveline cursed it. Mama shuffled, as though her limbs had rusted with lack of use. "Come along," Eveline muttered. "Please hurry."

Out through the door, but they couldn't relax yet. The long, long path to the gate where the hansom waited.

"Come along," she said briskly. She could see the outline of the hansom. Liu had seen them coming, and leapt lithely down to open the door.

"I say, Dr Peters!"

Oh, no. Eveline walked faster, urging Mama along. Her feet shuffled on the gravel.

"Dr Peters!"

"Mama, please, hurry!"

"I say, wait!"

There was a note in the voice now, whoever it was had definitely realised something was wrong. Eveline almost shoved her mother towards the hansom, and she stumbled. Liu was there; he caught her and swung her into the cab. Eveline dived in after her, and pulled the door to. She could see the white, shouting face of the man pursuing them down the drive as the cab pulled away, bowling down the road, a shout echoing after it.

"Are you all right, Mama? I didn't hurt you, did I?"

Mama sat huddled in a corner of the carriage, looking at Eveline with wide, terrified eyes. "I don't understand," she said. "I don't understand."

Up on the roof, Liu shouted something, and the horse went faster. Eveline felt faint with exhaustion and fear. She took her mother's hand in her own, realising hers were still black with soot. "It's all right, Mama," she said. "Don't worry. I'll look after everything."

MAMA SEEMED DAZED. Eveline wondered if she had been dosed with something, or (horrible, dreadful thought that she tried to crush) if perhaps there *was* something wrong. If perhaps there always had been. Or if being locked away so long had broken her. "Mama? Mama, it's all right. I'm going to have to leave you with Liu, he'll look after you. I have to do something. Liu will drive you to where you'll be staying – it's just for a bit. And then I'll come to see you and we'll sort everything out, all right?"

"Eveline?"

"Yes, Mama."

"Really my Eveline?"

"Yes, Mama."

"Is that... where *are* we?"

"London, Mama."

"I know *that*, silly girl, but I don't recognise this district – how much traffic there is! Where are we going?"

"I have to go... see someone. Liu will drive you to the place I've arranged."

"This is real, isn't it?" Mama turned and looked at her properly, and touched Eveline's face. "Really real."

"Yes."

"I was afraid... I thought perhaps I was dreaming. I've dreamt of escaping so many times. Oh, my love, how did you find me? How did you do it?"

"I..." She couldn't tell her respectable mama that she'd blackmailed and burgled and lied to get her out. "I found out you were alive, and I did what I had to."

"You said Uncle James was dead. What happened?"

"Gout got to his heart... I heard. Somewhere."

"Oh." Mama shook her head. "He always did drink too much port."

The carriage drew to a halt. Eveline hugged her mama. "I gotta go." She looked up at Liu. "Look after her."

"I promise you, I will."

"Liu, is everything all right?"

He didn't look well – his warm colour was faded and waxy. Perhaps it was just the pallid glow of the gas lamps. "I... Yes. Later. You had best hurry."

"Yes." Eveline looked into the hansom one more time. "Mama, I'll see you very soon. You'd better get that stuff off your face."

"Oh! I... what a clown I must look! How did you ever..."

"I'll tell you everything when I get back."

Mama managed to tug off the false moustache and most of the putty nose, leaving her looking bruised and damaged. Eveline wanted to say something more, but there was no time.

"I'll see you soon, Mama." She closed the door. "Liu..."

"I will take care of her. I have it all arranged. Go." Something was wrong, something was definitely wrong, but there was no more time.

The Ship Inn

IN THROUGH THE back of the hotel, along the corridor, into her room... and tucked into bed was Lazy Lou's top half, her face made up with putty and a black wig to resemble Eveline's if you didn't look too close. Her bottom half was rolled linens.

Eveline closed the door behind her and leaned on it for a moment, feeling the tears well and burn. But she couldn't cry, there was no time. Holmforth could be back at any moment, or the man from the desk could check on her. She swiped at her face, lit the candles in their heavy brass sticks with the hanging crystals, worth at least two bob apiece to the right fence, and whisked about, dismantling Lazy Lou and thrusting everything away under the false bottom of the Gladstone bag, hanging beneath her skirts anything that wouldn't fit. She scrubbed the last of the soot from her hands, blew her nose, and carried on.

She kept checking out of the window, but there were so many hansom cabs and carriages, both steam and horse, it was impossible to tell if one was Holmforth's. She had barely finished when there was a rap on the door. She sat on the bed, and called, "Who is it?"

"Holmforth."

For the first time she wondered exactly what Liu had put in the telegram that had kept him away for so long; whatever it was, it had worked.

He opened the door. "Are you rested?"

"Yes."

"Then come down to supper." He peered closely at her. "You don't *appear* rested. What *have* you been doing?"

Her heart speeded up, she fought to keep her face bland. "I dunno what you mean."

"You look like a very tired chimney sweep. How you managed to get quite so filthy simply sitting in a hotel room... wash your face, I refuse to take you down to supper looking like that."

Eveline scurried to the dresser. The mirror showed her face smeared with soot, where she had wiped her eyes, and the eyes themselves red-rimmed and swollen-lidded. She had been crying the whole time she cleaned up, barely knowing it.

She splashed her face, and scrubbed with the soap – fancy stuff, much nicer than the carbolic they used in the school and smelling like violets. Between splashes, she watched Holmforth.

He was standing by the window, watching the street, bouncing gently on the balls of his feet, his hands clasped loosely behind his back. She could swear he was smiling.

What had been going on? What had Liu done?

She felt a horrible dropping sensation that seemed to take her stomach right down through her boots, through the next floor and into the cold wet earth below. Were they acting together? Had she fallen into a trap, set for her all along? If she had... now they had Mama.

Mama who had been, if not happy, at least safe, and fed, and not being hurt. Probably not being hurt.

Eveline stared at her own pale, red-eyed face. She had been so pleased with herself; working out the details, getting everything organised... had she been a complete fool?

"Hurry up, or all the lamb cutlets will be gone," Holmforth said. "There are never enough lamb cutlets."

For once in her life Eveline was completely uninterested in the thought of lamb cutlets. She wasn't sure she could eat at all.

THEY SAT IN the dining room of the hotel. The smell of gravy and cabbage permeated the air. There were a few other diners, mainly single gentlemen. Eveline felt extremely conspicuous, and sat pushing her cutlet around her plate, carving off the smallest possible slice and trying to swallow it with a throat as dry as blotting paper.

"What's the matter?" Holmforth said. "Your usual healthy appetite seems to have deserted you."

"I'm the only girl in the place. I keep expecting someone to turn me out."

"You are not the first and will not be the last of your gender to dine here, though, oddly enough, you are probably among the more respectable." He damn near grinned at her, which did nothing to calm her down. "The others were probably..."

"Yes, I can guess what they were probably, thank you."

"So, are you happy with the day's purchases?"

She struggled to remember. "Oh. Oh, yes."

"We can return tomorrow, if there is more you need."

"And your business, did it go all right? Whatever it was?"

"Oh, indeed," he said. "Yes, it went very well. I think perhaps we might celebrate."

"Celebrate?"

"There's no need to look so wary. What a suspicious little creature you are. I meant only a glass of wine. A light one for you, perhaps a canary; something suitable for a young lady. Would you like that?"

"I don't know, I've never had it."

"Well, let us try it then, and you can tell me." He summoned the waiter.

HOLMFORTH LAY BACK on his bed and smiled to himself.

The girl had sipped at the wine as though she feared poison at first, but took to its sweetness in the end, as he'd supposed she would.

She was his key. This scruffy, wary little creature held his future in her hand – and he held her in his.

And not just his. It seemed, at last, that his efforts were being appreciated. Those further up the chain – not just above himself, but above Forbes-Cresswell; people to whom Forbes-Cresswell was only a functionary – *they* were interested.

Discretion must, of course, be maintained. He understood that, all too well. He had seen things he'd striven for taken from him before, the credit going to other men.

He knew why. He understood. It was the bad blood in him, the blood of the Folk. Sickly, tainted. Had he been able to excise it, to drain out that pallid poison, he would have, long ago. Instead he must prove his worth, finally and beyond all doubt.

The Britannia School

EVELINE STOOD IN front of the locked door in the abandoned part of the school, gripping the key so hard it cut into her hand.

What if Mama wasn't there? What if it had been a dream? What if she had been betrayed?

There had been no sign of Liu when she returned to the school, nothing.

There was no light under the door.

Come on, Sparrow.

Carefully, she opened the door. She blinked in the gloom; the shutters were closed, it was impossible to tell if there was anyone in the room. "Mama?" she whispered. "Are you there?"

"Eveline?"

"Oh, Mama! Mama, did you not see the candle? I made sure there was one here..." Eveline crept towards the table, found the candle and lit it.

It showed Mama seated in the room's single chair – an ancient thing of wormy wood and cracked leather, with horsehair stuffing showing through its gaping fissures like the scalp of a poorly-buried corpse. She was huddled into the back of the chair, her hands gripping the arms. She watched Eveline as she locked the door and went to the window. "You can open the shutters, Mama, this wall faces a corner, no-one would see." She hauled the shutters open, wincing as they creaked, despite her careful earlier application of oil. "I know, they're so noisy, but we're right at the end of the house, no-one comes here. So long as there's no noise you'll be fine. Did Liu explain what this place is? I'm sorry it's not nicer, but it won't be long, we'll have a place of our own and then... Liu did explain? The Chinee fella who brought you home? He's all right, he is. He looked after you, did he? I told him he was to..." She realised she was babbling, and forced herself to stop.

Mama was staring out of the window. It was raining. The way the window faced, the only view was of brickwork, a cracked drainpipe, and a fern growing by the drain, with a narrow slice of grey sky above it. Water ran steadily down the pipe, inside and out, gurgling.

The room smelled of damp and rats and emptiness.

"Mama?"

"I'm sorry," Mama said. "Will you come where I can see you? I just..."

Eveline walked slowly over to the chair.

"My Eveline?"

"Yes, Mama."

"You've grown so. I always thought of you as a little girl. Foolish... come here, my love. Let me look at you properly. I was in such a mazed state... are you in trouble, Eveline?"

"Not if no-one finds out."

"They will, you know. They're bound to notice even such an insignificant person as myself escaping."

"I know. But they won't know it's me, will they?"

"Well, who else would come for me?"

Eveline felt cold. It was true. She'd been so panicked at the thought of being sent to Shanghai that she'd rushed it. Rushed a plan, like a fool, and now she'd brought her mother right here to her own hearth where anyone looking for her would find her.

But did anyone *know* she was here: her, Eveline Duchen? Apart from Holmforth. And Holmforth, like everyone else, must think her mother was dead.

"I'm sorry, Mama. I... I just wanted you *out*. I didn't think."

"Oh, my love, I'm glad to *be* out, but I don't think our troubles are over just yet. Tell me, where is Charlotte?"

The question she had been dreading, and for once in her life she had no slick answer ready. There could be no trickery here, no sliding away.

"She's dead, Mama. She's dead, and it's my fault."

"Dead. Charlotte."

"Yes. We... I ran away. I took her with me. I thought... but it was cold and we... the woods... I couldn't... oh, Mama, I'm sorry!"

Then she was on her knees with her face buried in Mama's skirts, sobbing. She didn't know if Mama would turn her away, open the door, denounce her... but to confess, at last, to say it out loud to the one person in the world who would care, even if she never forgave her – there was a dreadful, tearing relief in it.

Eventually she became aware of a sensation she had not felt for a long time.

Mama was stroking her hair.

Eventually she got enough control of herself to tell the rest.

She didn't look at Mama for much of it. She rested her head against Mama's knees, and told her the barest bones of it. She didn't tell Mama about the road, about the men who had tried to catch her – and the ones who had succeeded. She did tell her about Ma Pether, as someone who took her in.

She said, "She taught me things, helped me. She's not respectable, but... and the things she taught me, they're not, either, mostly. I don't mean... well. I've had to do some things. Stealing."

Silence, still, from Mama. Then a sigh.

Eveline forced herself to look up. "Mama?"

She was crying, silently, tears tracking the lines on her face. "I was afraid... when she wasn't with you. And she was so young, and not well... Oh, Eveline."

"I'm sorry, Mama."

"No. No, don't say that. I failed you. I failed you both."

"No!" Eveline leapt to her feet. "You didn't. You never did. It was Uncle James, he had you put away. It was all his fault. He wanted to steal your work, didn't he? But you can get it back, Mama. It's all here! All your machines."

"They're *here*? Eveline, I don't understand. What is this place?"

"It's a sort of school. It's run by the government, so it's respectable. And if I can just do what they want, I'll get an allowance. And a pension. Only they don't know about you. And the man who brought me here, Mr Holmforth, I don't trust him. If he gets to know about you... see, that's why I asked Liu to hide you away up here. I know it's not very nice."

"My dear, I've been in an asylum. I am hardly used to luxury."

"Was it terrible?"

"At first, yes. I tried to tell them... but no-one listened. I was so worried about you both..." Her face twisted horribly, and it was a moment before she could go on.

"After a while, I became resigned, I suppose. I wrote letters, once they knew I could be trusted with pen and paper. I don't suppose you received them."

"No, Mama. He told us you were dead." Oh, how she hated Uncle James. How she wished he were still alive, so that she could destroy him, break him into little pieces, take everything from him, make him see what a wretched, miserable creature he was.

"Yes, you told me. I'm sorry, Eveline. My memory... in any case, they kept us occupied. Laundry." She attempted a smile. "I became rather more skilled at laundering shirts than I ever was at home."

"They made you do laundry?"

"It was thought better to keep us occupied. Laundry and stitching for the women, woodworking and so forth for the men. I made the mistake of asking to do some of the men's work. It was considered a sign of relapse." She shuddered.

"You weren't allowed to do your own work?"

"Oh, no. James and his doctor friends, they made sure of that. They said it was what had sent me into my *distressed state* and that I should under no circumstances be permitted to attempt anything. What I did, I managed in secret, with scraps... My dear, tell me, please, do you know what happened to the work? You say it's here, all my machines, and my notes?"

"Yes. And I don't think it's been used, at all. Uncle James must have tried to use it, I think, or at least to get money from it. I think that's how Holmforth found out about him – but everyone except Holmforth seems to think it's just an idea, something that doesn't really work. That's why Holmforth – he's the man who brought me here – he wanted me to use it, he thinks because Uncle James could do Etherics, I mean, he believed Uncle James was the one – he thinks it means I could too. Only I can't."

"Oh, that stupid idea! It's a *science!* Not something you inherit, like the colour of your hair! One *studies*. One *learns*. But... Eveline, what does he want you to do?"

"He wants me to go to Shanghai."

"What? Where?"

"Shanghai. It's in China. Well it's sort of in China. Anyway, he's got something there he thinks works by Etherics and he wants me to go and do something with it."

"Eveline." Mama leaned forward and took Eveline's hands in her own. "My pet, do you know what it is, this thing?"

"I don't know, Mama. But I have to learn. I hoped you could help me. Because I got your notes, but I'm not that good, and some of it I don't understand at all."

"Oh, Eveline, no."

"Mama?"

"No. Eveline, no, you can't. Not without knowing what they want it for."

"I don't understand," Eveline said.

"Your Uncle James, he thought... Eveline, how much do you understand about Etherics?

"Almost nothing," Eveline said.

"Listen. Do you remember that the sounds made you happy?"

"Yes..."

"Yes. That is what they were for. I tried to make some experiments in the hospital, but my resources were so limited, and I had to be so careful... but in any case. Etherics are intended to create positive mental states, Eveline. To soothe troubled minds, and heal broken

ones. That is their *function*. But James... James thought
it could be used *against* people. You understand? Not
for healing, but as a weapon. I didn't know if it was
even possible, I'd never taken my researches in that
direction, nor would I, but I couldn't risk it. That's why
I started hiding my notes. And then, of course, I was
taken away. This man, Holmforth..."

"Yes, Mama."

"He works for the government."

"Yes, Mama."

"I don't know, Eveline. You say you don't trust him.
You think, if he got this into his hands, it would be used
for good, or..."

Eveline bit her lip. "It would be used for the Empire,"
she said.

"And what would that mean?"

"I don't know."

"I can't risk it, Eveline. I *can't*."

"But if I don't do what he wants, I may get thrown
out. Then... there won't be any money, or anything. I
don't know what will happen."

Mama glanced at the shuttered window, and shivered.
"No. Oh, dear. Where should we go? What skills I
had..." She looked down at her hands, red and swollen
from doing laundry. "And with no references..."

"Mama, did I do wrong? Taking you out of that
place?"

She hesitated just a fraction too long before she said,
"Not wrong, my pet. You were just impulsive. You
always were." Then she tried to smile. "And if you hadn't,
I would have gone on thinking I'd lost you. Come here."

Eveline let herself be hugged, but her brain was
whirring and clicking like one of the Etheric machines,

creating not happiness but only more trouble, more fear and confusion. What could she do? Should she try and persuade Mama to help her do what Holmforth wanted? What was it to them if the thing was used as a weapon in the Empire's endless wars? She thought of Liu. The Empire had done dreadful things in his country – but so had the people who ran it, too. If she couldn't, or wouldn't, do what Holmforth wanted, what would happen to Mama? If she got thrown out of the school she would have to find somewhere safe for them both, but with what? If she stayed... perhaps she could persuade Holmforth to let her complete her training, at least.

She pulled away. "Mama, I have to go, I daren't be late to supper. I'll bring you something. Lock yourself in, and don't make a sound." She gave her mother the key, and a quick kiss, and scurried away.

It was a windy night; the old building creaked and moaned so that she stopped, at one point, convinced she'd heard footsteps along the corridor. No-one appeared, and she crept back to the main house, carefully locking the connecting door behind her.

WHEN SHE PICKED up her supper fork, there was something beneath it – a tiny square of paper. She shuffled it into her pocket. When she got a moment, she investigated it further – it proved, as she suspected, to be a note.

Meet me in the Old Barn, after supper. Liu.

Easier said than done, she thought. At least supper tonight was chops. How she'd smuggle it to her mother when it was stew... she'd just have to get herself put on kitchen duty again.

She asked Miss Cairngrim for permission to do extra work in the Old Barn. Miss Cairngrim glowered.

"Mr Holmforth asked that I work especially hard on this project, Miss Cairngrim."

"I am aware of that. However, this is disruptive of the school's routine."

"Yes, Miss Cairngrim. Miss Cairngrim?"

"What is it?"

"He said if I do well he might give some money to the school."

"And why did he not tell me this himself?"

"I don't know as I oughta say, Miss Cairngrim."

"Tell me this instant!"

"Well, he said he had a bet with one of the others that he could prove this school was useful, and not just a storage-house for by-blows. What's a by-blow, Miss Cairngrim?"

"That is a disgusting phrase and I do not wish to hear you repeat it!"

"No, Miss Cairngrim."

"I will send for Thomas to chain the dogs, and I will escort you to the barn. You will be locked in. I will be back in one hour to let you out."

"Yes, Miss Cairngrim."

It was a bit of a risk, but she was fairly sure that Miss Cairngrim wouldn't repeat *that* to Holmforth. In fact, she might be inclined to drop hints about how well Eveline was doing.

Miss Cairngrim had no sooner locked the barn than Liu climbed swiftly down the ladder out of the hayloft.

"Eveline! I am very glad you could come, I must discuss something with you."

"What is it, Liu?"

"Is your mother well?"

"Oh, I think so. At least... Oh, and thank you for the bedding." He had scavenged, from somewhere, a decent mattress and some warm blankets for her.

"Is something wrong? You are unhappy."

"I'm just worried. I hadn't thought about things properly. They might send people to look for Mama, and they might work out it was me got her out, and... and now Mama don't want me to work on this." She gestured at the mechanisms, gleaming mellowly in the lamplight.

"Oh. And what do you plan to do?"

"I don't know! I can't exactly force her to help, can I? Not after everything she's had to put up with. But if I don't do what Holmforth wants, I'll be out on me ear, and her with me, and maybe people after us both. Oh, it's such a *mess*." She slumped down on one of the ancient chairs and tugged her fingers through her hair, pulling out the pins. "What'm I to do?"

"Do you know why your mother does not wish you to do this?"

Eveline sighed. "She thinks this, Etherics, could maybe be used against people. She thinks that's what Holmforth wants it for."

"I don't know if it could be used against people, Lady Sparrow," he said. "But it could be used against the Folk. And that... that would be very bad indeed."

"What?"

"The Folk. The Shining Ones, the Fair Folk, the People of the Crepuscular."

"I know who the Folk are, Liu, I just don't know what you're gabbing on about. What d'you mean it could be used on 'em?"

Liu dropped into the straw, folding his legs neatly under him. "Remember you asked me to distract Mister Holmforth for two hours the day we rescued your mother out of the hospital?"

"Yes."

"Well, I pretended to be someone interested in what he was doing in Shanghai. Someone in the government."

"And he *believed* you?"

"I can be very persuasive."

"You musta been! Who did he think you were?"

Liu shrugged. "Someone who appreciates his singular talents more than his current superior, a man called Forbes-Cresswell. But this is not really to the point. What is, is that this machine he has found creates noises of a very particular quality. They are painful and damaging to people... to Folk. That is why he wants you, Lady Sparrow. He wants you so that he can start a war."

"A war? A war with the Folk? But why? I thought he was half-Folk himself?"

"He is." Liu hesitated for a moment. "What would be your feeling on a war with the Folk, Lady Sparrow?"

"I don't know. It's not my business, is it?"

"It is if you can prevent it."

"Don't see how."

"Refuse to do what Holmforth asks of you. It won't be enough, it will only delay things, but perhaps it will give time for a solution to be found."

"If I don't do what he wants, I'm done for. And so's my mama."

"If you do, the consequences could be terrible."

"There's always a war on somewhere. What's it got to do with me?"

"You do not care that people will be killed?"

Eveline hunched her shoulders. "Course I *care*. I don't want anyone dying. But it's only a machine," she said. "One machine. That's hardly going to do much, is it? I mean, whatever it is he thinks it can do, even if I can get it to work, it's one thing. All they have to do is break it, and there ain't no problem, is there? It won't be a war."

"Firstly, who do you think would be *in* the machine? You. You will be the immediate target of anything they do."

"In it? What do you mean, in it?" She gestured at the machines that stood on the bench. "I couldn't get in one of them."

"This machine is much larger. It is operated by someone sitting within it. And even if you survive the encounter... it is much worse than that, Eveline."

"Why?"

"They will know that it is possible. That humans can be a threat to them."

"What's so bad about that?"

"Oh, Lady Sparrow. You really have no idea. How do you think the Folk see you?"

"I don't know. Never thought about it."

"Yes, you have."

"Don't know what you mean."

"Yes," Liu said, "you do. I have seen the look in your eyes when they are named. You have no love for them, do you? Do you desire your own vengeance?"

"I just want to be left alone. Get somewhere safe for me and Mama and be comfortable, no Folk, no Holmforth, no people messing in my life, that's it."

"I do not believe you," he said. "You would be bored in a week."

"Don't matter what you believe."

"Perhaps not. But there are things I do not have to believe – things that I know. I know that if the Folk see humans as a threat, they will crush you. Completely, and without hesitation. You are little or nothing to them. A moment's amusement. A source of Gifts, and entertainment – but that is all."

"I don't understand."

"Why do you hate them, Eveline?"

"I don't *hate* them. Just don't trust them, is all."

"And why is that?"

"Not your business, is it?"

"Please," he said, and she looked at him, hearing real desperation in his voice. "*Please* listen to me, Lady Sparrow. Your distrust is justified far more than you think. They will *destroy* humanity if for one moment they see it as a threat. And they will unite to do it. The Folk of your country and the Folk of mine, of *every* land. This is the one thing that could create an alliance, after a thousand thousand years of rivalry, if only for a moment. And a moment is all they would need. Against such an alliance, your people would be dust on the wind."

"I don't believe you. They don't care about us one way or the other. They hardly even hang around any more."

"The noise of the cities, the factories, the airships – they find all this unpleasant, and they have no need to come here, unless it amuses them. But that will not stop them."

"Still don't see how one machine could be a threat."

"Because it shows the potential. If humanity can create such a thing once, they can do it again. They would rather see every city on earth wiped out. And make no mistake, they could do it."

"How?"

"They are very old, and very powerful. They have everything they need; they need never go hungry, never do without anything. That is why they have this game of Gifts. They give each other gifts of intense subtlety, it is a vast and complex game of position and superiority. That is the only place where humans truly matter to them – as a source of these Gifts." He tilted his head. "Of course, they might decide to keep you all alive for that – but the punishment they would wreak on you for daring to threaten them would be terrible. Now, you are toys. Pets. That is the *best* you can hope for."

"I don't believe you. They've never done anything that bad. And we're not *pets*."

"No? Would you have me prove it?"

"How?"

"I know of humans who are kept in the Crepuscular. Taken from here, usually as children. The court find them amusing, they even become fond of them, as you might of a puppy. But if the dog should bite, then it is punished. And if it bites too often..." He shuddered. "I have seen that, too. I could find one, bring them to see you."

Eveline bit her thumbnail, watching him. Could it be true? She had hated Aiden, all these years, because he had abandoned her when she truly needed him; had promised help, and failed to give it. Could that be why? That she was nothing more to him than an amusement?

Perhaps. But she had a whole life at risk. She didn't even know if this stupid machine could be made to work – especially without Mama's help. If she simply refused to work on it... she could pretend, try her hardest, but she was fairly certain that Holmforth had no interest in her beyond this one thing.

And of course, if she did make it work, there might be another thing. And another. And another...

She flailed away from the thought. It was too much. Everything had been going well, and now it was all such a terrible *mess*.

And there was something else, too.

"How come you know so much about it?" she said. "Here you are telling me all this, and you could be lying through your teeth, f'r all I know. Could be so much bull, the whole thing. How'd you find out what Holmforth wants? No way he's going to be spilling all that to some Chinee, just on his say so. So tell me how you know all this."

"I persuaded him that I was someone important in government. I told you. He is a desperate man. He believes that those in power are ignoring something important. He was grateful for anyone to listen."

"How?"

"I was in disguise. You have done as much yourself – persuaded someone you are other than what you are – and it was not so hard for you."

"Hmm. All right, maybe. But all this about the Folk – how'd you know it all? And how'd I know it's true?"

Liu closed his eyes, and dropped his head towards his chest, with a sigh. "Because I, like Holmforth, am a *mixtus*. My mother was human. My father was a fox-spirit; a kind of Folk that is found in China. *Now* do you believe me?"

"What? No! You don't look like Folk at all!"

"So sharp-eyed, and you never noticed." He began to shuffle one trouser leg up his shin. "This is very uncomfortable," he said. "But it is the one thing that never changes, so it has to be hidden."

Poking out of the bottom of his blue silk trouser leg was a white-tipped fox tail. It waggled, oddly jaunty.

Eveline stared. "That's... You're having me on."

"No."

She jumped to her feet, furious. "Oh, you... I don't know what you're trying to pull, but I'm not falling for it. All this time, you were *Folk*? You've been helping me just so's you'd get me on side, haven't you? Make me do what you wanted? *Your Empress and mine are not at odds*, indeed. I thought you meant the Chinese Empress, but you never did, did you?"

"Lady Sparrow..." Liu jumped to his feet.

"Don't call me that. You're a spy, a spy for them. You were trying to get me to be a traitor. Well, I might be a thief and I might not care anything for the Empire or any of that business, but work for you lot? Not for a minute. Not ever. You'd better get out of here before I tell them what you are, and what you tried to pull."

"Eveline, please! I'm trying..."

"Go away." She realised she was crying, and it made her even angrier. "Go away! Get out of here! Leave me alone!"

"Eveline, what is it?" Beth said.

"Nothing."

"What's happened?"

"Liu."

"Liu?"

"He's... he wasn't... I'm sorry, Beth. I thought – I shoulda known better than to trust him. I thought he was all right. He ain't."

Beth's face whitened. "What do you mean?"

"He's *Folk*."

"What?"

"He's *Folk*. He's one of them. Half-folk, anyway. He was trying to put one over on me. I shoulda seen it, but I was stupid."

"The..." Beth glanced towards the hidden shed where she kept the *Sacagawea*.

"I don't think he cares about that."

"Are you sure?"

"No, I'm not. I'm sorry. But I don't think he'd get anything out of telling Miss Grim, if it's any comfort."

"Telling Miss Cairngrim what?"

The girls spun around. There, dapper in the lamplight, was Holmforth. "I thought I would come and see how you are progressing," he said. "I am glad to see you hard at work. What was it someone was going to tell Miss Cairngrim? I really don't think she would appreciate that sobriquet."

"Nothing," Eveline said.

"Really. And you must be Miss Hastings?" He bowed over Beth's hand. "Charmed, I'm sure. Have you been helping Miss Duchen?"

"I've been trying," Beth said.

"I see. Well, since you have become involved, perhaps we should take you with us. Don't you think?" He spun around to Eveline.

"Take her where?" Eveline said.

"Shanghai."

"What? When?" Eveline stuttered.

"Me?" Beth squeaked. "Go to Shanghai?"

"Since Miss Duchen seems to find your assistance useful, yes."

Beth glanced at Eveline, who gave the smallest possible shrug.

"In an airship?"

"Of a certainty, in an airship."

"Oh, yes, please!" She beamed.

Eveline bit her lip. She was pretty certain Holmforth hadn't been *asking*. Why did he want Beth along?

And that was not, by a long chalk, her worst problem.

Holmforth was taking her to Shanghai. To make his infernal machine, whatever it was, work. And she still didn't know how.

And what about Mama? How was she going to keep her fed and cared for while she was away?

EVERY TIME SHE came up here, she was certain she was going to be caught; the back of her neck twitched with every rustle and creak.

"Mama, I brought you some food. It's not much – potatoes, mostly – I'm sorry."

"It doesn't matter." Mama's voice sounded almost as pale as she looked, as she pushed herself out of the ancient sagging chair and came to hug Eveline.

"Mind the potatoes! Oh, and I brought a book."

"Oh, how marvellous!" Mama almost snatched the book out of Eveline's hand, holding it close under the lamp and peering.

"It's just some Shakespeare. I found it in the library."

"Never say *just* Shakespeare, Eveline. What a delight. They would give us 'improving tracts' and other pap. Nothing to excite the brain, you see."

"I'll bring some more. Only, Mama, you'll have to be careful about using the lamp. Someone might see."

"I'll be careful," she said, though wistfully. "My darling, I can't stay here much longer. Sooner or later someone is bound to find me."

"I know, Mama. I'm trying to think of what to do. I'm going to have to be away for a little while. I was going to ask Beth to help, but now..."

"What about that young man who drove me here? Can he help?"

"No," Eveline said. "No, he can't, and I wish I'd never trusted him."

"I'm sorry you feel like that, Lady Sparrow," said Liu. He was standing by the open door that Eveline knew she had shut behind her. "Madam Duchen." He bowed.

"Liu? How the..." Eveline swallowed the curse and contented herself with glaring. "Don't *do* that."

Liu was wearing dark green silks. Even in the dim lamplight, he looked weary and strained, not the merry imp she was used to. She shoved down the impulse to ask him what was wrong. *Don't be soft, Eveline Duchen. He'd love to know you felt sorry for him. Remember who he is.* "What do you want?" she said. "It's not safe, you coming up here. Someone'll see."

"No, they will not, I promise. I hoped that I might be able to persuade you..." He glanced at Madeleine Duchen. "Your daughter does not trust me, because my father was of the Folk."

"He was?" Madeleine Duchen looked puzzled. "I didn't know there *were* Chinese Folk."

"Oh, yes. But I spend much of my time with the Folk of your lands. And that is why... perhaps I should get to the meat of why I am here?"

"Yes," Eveline said. "Why don't you?"

"I have been doing some investigating. I need you to

believe me, Eveline. I need you to trust me. And I found out something I hope will please you. So..." He turned away, and made a gesture to the corridor.

Eveline, convinced he had betrayed them, expecting Miss Cairngrim and a phalanx of policemen, blinked as a slender young woman appeared.

She was slight, with a mass of curly black hair tumbling to her waist, dressed in a flowing gown of some pale green stuff and fragile, gilded shoes, completely unsuitable for the weather. She looked about fourteen.

"Who's this? Another one of your Folk?" Eveline said.

"Oh, I'm not *his*," the young woman said, giving Liu a glance that verged on contempt. "My name's Charlotte. I suppose you must be Eveline."

"CHARLOTTE?" FOR A moment the name meant nothing at all. Then Eveline heard her mother whisper, "Charlotte? *My* Charlotte?"

"Are you my mother?"

"No!" Eveline said. "No, it's a trick! You... how could you, Liu? I know you're Folk..."

"...half..."

"I didn't think you were *cruel*." She flung her arms around her mother, who stood rigid, her hands pressed to her mouth, her eyes huge, staring. "What *is* this?" Eveline said. "Charlotte's *dead*."

"No," Liu said. "Charlotte isn't dead."

"Of course I'm not dead," said the girl. She had made no motion to approach either Eveline or Madeleine, but stood poised by the door. "This place is very dark. And it smells. I want to go."

"Tell them who you are," Liu said.

"I am Charlotte, a groundling, under the protection of Aiden of the Court Emerald," she recited, with a sort of resentful boredom.

"Tell them what groundling means," Liu said.

"It means I'm not Folk. It means I'm a human. I'm Aiden's. *He* doesn't care, he likes me."

"Aiden," Eveline said. "You know Aiden."

"I don't *know* him, I'm his."

"I don't understand," Eveline said, looking at this strange, chilly, rude girl.

"I think I do," Madeleine said, her voice unsteady. She put her arm around Eveline's trembling shoulders. "Eveline told me what happened, in the woods. He saw you there, and realised you were sick, perhaps dying, and decided to take you in – like a stray puppy. You're a changeling, aren't you, my dear?"

Eveline fought to control her whirling thoughts. "I thought changelings... I thought they left a fairy child..."

"Oh, perhaps they have, in the past," Madeleine said, "but mostly, it's just a thing, a sort of mannequin. There was one in the village, when you were tiny. Sometimes they're made of wood, but... I'm right, aren't I? Come to me, child."

Charlotte came forward, reluctantly. "You're old."

"Oh, not so old, just... just human," Madeleine said. She reached out her hand and touched the glossy black curls. "My little Charlotte."

Charlotte watched her warily, like a nervous colt.

"I don't believe it's her," Eveline said. "It's a trick."

"It isn't," Madeleine said. "Oh, my little love." Tears were trickling down her face. "Are you coming back to us?" she said.

"Coming *back?*" Charlotte backed away, looking dismayed. "Why would I come back?"

"But you're family," Eveline said. "If you really are."

"So? All I remember about *here* is being cold, and hungry, and hurting. I remember someone, I suppose it was you" – she looked at Madeleine – "being sad. I don't like sadness. Or cold. In the Crepuscular it's always warm, and I have enough to eat and pretty things to wear. Aiden looks after me."

"He looks after you," Eveline said.

"Yes. He thinks I'm amusing."

"And when you're not 'amusing' any more?"

"I shall make sure I remain so."

"And when you get old?" Eveline said. "Will he still think you're amusing?"

"I shan't – not like you. Aiden's promised. I won't get all... wrinkled," she said, screwing up her nose.

Eveline glanced at Liu. He gave a small, sympathetic shrug. "Charlotte, do you remember the harper?" he said.

"No," she said.

"I think you do."

"I don't *want* to," she said. "Leave me alone."

"What happened to him?"

"He was stupid. He displeased his mistress and she punished him. I'm not stupid like him."

"Just tell them what happened, so they understand."

"He didn't want to play the harp any more, so she made him one with it, and now he sings all the time."

Now he sings all the time... The wind gusted hard against the corner of the eaves, and wailed. Eveline felt a shudder clench the muscles along her spine.

"Was it hard for her?" Liu said. "To do that?"

"Why would it be? She's of the Court. She can do whatever she wants. I want to go *home*."

"Home," Madeleine said.

"Yes."

"Come kiss me once, then."

Charlotte scowled, but allowed herself to be kissed, and her lips brushed the air near Madeleine's cheek. "Do you want a kiss too?" she said to Eveline.

"No," Eveline said. "Wait. Mama..."

"Let her be, Eveline," Madeleine said. "I understand. It's hard for us, but she must do what she wants. One thing, Charlotte, before you go. Listen to your mother, this single time, will you please?"

"Oh, very well," Charlotte said, smoothing her gauzy skirts.

"You've made your choice, and it is an easy life – unless you ever want something else. I'm sorry, my love, that this has happened. And if this is what you want, then you go with my blessing – though I suppose you don't care much for that, not now."

Charlotte's lips pressed together, and she looked away.

"But if you ever decide you *do* want something else," Madeleine said, "if you tire of being at someone else's whim, or if they ever treat you badly, we'll be here, Charlotte."

"No!" Eveline couldn't stop the word. It came out half-strangled, but loud. "No, you can't just let her *go!*" She reached out for Charlotte, hardly knowing if she meant to embrace her, or shake her silly. Charlotte stepped back, a look of distaste plain on her face.

"I thought you were *dead*," Eveline shouted. "I thought you were dead and it was *my fault!* You can't just *leave!*" She swung round to her mother. "Why are you... what..." Tears choked the rest of the words in her throat.

"Because it's what she wants, Eveline," Mama said, folding her arms round her and holding her very tight. "Shh, poppet, shhhh. Goodbye, Charlotte."

"Goodbye," Charlotte said. She turned to Liu. "Take me home."

"Lottie..." Eveline said, "please..." But then there was a faint distant shimmer of music, and Liu took Charlotte's hand, and Eveline's sister walked away, into the dark corridor, and was gone.

"Why did you let her go, Mama?"

"Because she has made her choice, Eveline. I did so badly by her, by you both – and what could I give her? She would be miserable here. I think it would be like Bedlam was for me. Cold and strange and she wouldn't understand why she was here. And we've nowhere to live."

"But she's *family*."

"So was Uncle James," Madeleine said, sighing. "Family isn't always the best choice, or even a possible choice, Eveline."

"How can you be so *calm?*"

"I had to learn. I had to learn patience. And resignation. A great deal of both."

"It's my fault..."

"No." Madeleine turned Eveline around to look at her. "No. You did your best, as I did. We did the best we could with what we had. And she is *alive*. Maybe, one day, she will decide she would rather not be a pet. If she doesn't, well, she will have a comfortable life for a long time. If she can stay on their good side, she'll probably live far longer than either of us."

"She's alive," Eveline said. "Yes, well, I suppose that's something, isn't it?"

"That's very much something, Eveline. Oh, come here, my love, don't cry."

But she did, for a long time, in her mother's arms, while the wind howled and the rain beat its small helpless fists on the windows.

Liu had been standing there for some time before either of them noticed him.

"What do you want?" Eveline said, sniffing.

"I am very sorry," he said, bowing. "I did not mean to cause you so much distress."

"Why'd you do it, then?"

"You wanted us to understand," Madeleine said, "didn't you?"

"Yes. Also, I thought it would please you to know she was alive."

"It does."

"Don't be nice to him, Mama, he wants something."

"Eveline, hush."

"I do want something," Liu said. "I want you to promise you will not make that machine work. It's not just the Folk here, but the Folk of my country. If they even *begin* to suspect..."

"You won't, will you?" Madeleine said.

"That part's easy enough," Eveline said. "I can't. Weeks, I've been looking at your machines, Mama, and I can make 'em make sounds enough to fool him, but they don't work. But if I don't go along and at least look like I'm trying, we're in the... we're in trouble, both of us. And what then? If I don't manage it, he'll find someone who does, sooner or later. If Etherics is a science, even if it's one *I'm* no good at, *someone'll* find out how to do it."

They looked at each other in the deepening gloom. The lamp flickered, and a bell jangled in the quiet. "Oh, I'm late!" Eveline jumped to her feet. "I *have* to go with him, I'll... I don't know. I'll work something out." She kissed her mother. Liu followed her out of the door, but when he tried to speak to her, she repeated, "I'm late!" and ran. It was true – if she didn't get to Evening Occupations, someone was bound to notice – but mainly she had no desire at all to talk to Liu just then.

When she looked over her shoulder on reaching the main building, there was no sign of him.

EVELINE BARELY NOTICED the chatter and shuffling and sidelong glances of the other girls as she scuttled into the back of the room with her head down and got out her stitching, frantically trying to work out what she was going to do. She had to make some arrangement for her mother. She would *have* to ask Liu, who else could she trust? Not that she could trust him, but with Holmforth intent on dragging Beth along with them, there was no-one else. Beth was at the other side of the room, scribbling away on a sketch-pad.

The only other possibility was to give Mama the key and let her make her own arrangements – but how was she to get out, with the dogs? Since the last incident, their handler Thomas had started sleeping in the shed with them, reducing any chance to interfere with their food, and Miss Prayne had started hiding her laudanum.

There was the sound of doors shutting. The dogs barked furiously. A coach passed the window, wheels crunching on the gravel, and rumbled off into the night.

Every few moments, Charlotte's face – so chilly, so petulant – rose in her mind, disrupting her thoughts before they could get anywhere.

Liu's warning ringing over and over, jangling like a cracked bell. *They will crush you...*

Unable to bear it a moment longer, she jumped to her feet.

"Duchen, where do you think you're going?" Miss Fortescue snapped.

"I have to pack, miss."

"She does indeed," said a familiar voice. Holmforth appeared behind her. She was very tired of people sneaking up on her, and felt strongly inclined to fling her shoe at him. This was all his fault. What did the wretched man have to pick her for?

"I will come with you," Holmforth said, "and assist."

Eveline stood up and took Holmforth's proffered arm. She didn't like being this close to him, especially not now. She sneaked glances at him, trying to trace any similarity to Liu – but then, Liu wasn't English Folk. She'd never even heard of Folk who had fox tails. Oh, her mind was jumping about like a rabbit. She had to get away, *do* something.

Up in the dormitory, a battered leather case was already lying on her bunk. She folded things much more carefully than was her habit, trying to give herself time to think, as Holmforth leaned in the doorway, watching.

"Are you going to tell me about this machine, then? I can't make it work unless I know what it's s'posed to *do*."

"I suppose you are right. It has an effect on the Folk. An extremely... adverse effect. Oh, that reminds me, I must obtain a subject for the demonstration."

"A subject?"

"Yes, one of the Folk, of course."

"Well, what if I can't make it go straight off? I mean, it's taken me weeks to get these machines here working!"

"I am sure you will succeed. You *must* succeed. Someone is coming to attend the demonstration. If you do not succeed, the consequences will be... unfortunate. For you. And Miss Hastings."

So that was why he wanted Beth along. Leverage.

"So who built this precious machine of yours?"

"A man called Wu Jisheng. Etheric ability seems to cross racial boundaries."

"And what if he don't want to give it to us?"

"The machine is essential to the Empire. It is not as though the Chinese would make good use of it."

Well, that was answer enough, Eveline thought. Mr Wu Jisheng wasn't going to have a choice, was he?

"Oh," she said. "My disguise kit? I might need it, mightn't I, and my Bartitsu gear?"

"Oh, I suppose so. Very well," Holmforth said. "Go collect the costumery, if you must. I will obtain your fighting equipment – how very intriguing – and I will see you back here."

Eveline went to Miss Fortescue's classroom and gathered an armful of supplies – a couple of wigs, putty, mortician's wax, a few paints. She paused, an idea half-forming in her mind, and grabbed more putty. Then she scurried for the east wing.

The wind in the empty corridors wailed like a ghost as the rain beat tiny cold fists on the windows. Eveline unlocked the door and whispered, "Mama?"

The room was dark. "Mama, did you go to sleep?"

"Your mother isn't here, Eveline," said a voice behind her.

She spun about. Holmforth stood in the doorway, his face underlit by the lantern he was carrying, cutting shadows under his eyes and cheekbones.

Eveline felt cold all the way through, and her knees weakened. "I..."

"Don't bother. It would be foolish to attempt, at this juncture, to hide anything. She is in no danger. Rather less than she might have been had she remained here. I don't suppose it ever occurred to you that there might be a fire, or some such thing? No? Really, child."

"How did you find her?" Eveline said, her voice seeming to come from far away, as though another Eveline, a puppet, moved and spoke in her stead.

"Monsieur Duvalier has been taking an interest in your movements, it seems. And fortunately he had the sense to come to me, rather than going to Miss Cairngrim."

"Duvalier."

"Indeed. Now come along."

"But where is she? What have you done with her?"

"She is safe, and away from here." That must have been the coach she heard earlier, and she hadn't even paid attention. "And I have done nothing to her. Had I known she was alive, of course, I would have taken her under my wing much earlier, and she would have enjoyed rather more comfortable accommodations. In any case, she is about to accompany us to Shanghai. I think, after her long incarceration, she may enjoy the experience, don't you?"

Eveline felt so cold. Cold and small and stupid. How had she let things come to this?

And Holmforth had her mama. She'd been right about him. He'd use anything and everything for his precious Empire. Even if she didn't believe Liu, there was no way, now, no way in the Empire and all its territories that she was going to do what Holmforth wanted.

He'd thought he could run her to ground. But she wasn't a rabbit. She was Evvie Duchen, and she'd see him pay heavy for this.

THAT NIGHT, NEITHER she nor Beth returned to the dormitory. They were locked in a separate room, normally kept for visitors.

"I'm sorry about your mama," Beth said as they got ready for bed.

"I'm sorry I got you into this."

"Don't be," Beth said. "At least I get to go on an airship, and see Shanghai."

"Beth, I've made such a *mess* of everything. I shoulda told Holmforth straight out I couldn't do a thing with these wretched machines, and now you're caught up in it, and my mum, and I don't know what Liu's about... I don't want a *war*, I mean, I don't care about the Folk, but what if Liu's right, and..."

"Right about what?"

"Oh, I didn't tell you that part, did I?"

"Not really."

After Eveline explained, Beth sat quietly for some time. "I don't know, Evvie," she said. "But a war... people are going to get killed. That's what war *is*, isn't it. Whoever wins, people get killed."

"And if Liu's right – I'm not saying he is, but if he is..."

"Oh, dear," Beth said.

"*Oh, dear* is right."

Eveline still had her lock picks. She contemplated letting them both out, but had not a single idea what was to be done after that; with no idea where Mama was, and no way to find her now Liu had disappeared – how had she come to rely on him, on his help, so quickly? How had she been so stupid, *again*?

Probably the girl wasn't even Charlotte. It had all been yet another trick. After all, he was Folk, wasn't he? He could probably do all sorts of tricks. Why should he care what happened to people, if the Folk got angry? She didn't believe it.

And yet he was only half-Folk. But so was Holmforth.

And Holmforth was the one she had to deal with. There was no time to panic, she had to think as hard as she'd ever thought in her life.

And, reluctantly, thinking about Liu. Liu and the Folk. The Folk and their Gifts...

She should have guessed, when he spoke to her before about them. How else could he possibly have known so much? Unless all that, too, was lies.

Why had he brought Charlotte? Why?

Eveline Duchen, stop this nonsense. 'Keep your thoughts on the job in hand or stuck in pokey you will land'; that was one of Ma's, and right she was.

And it is a job, isn't it? It's a con. It has to be.

She really wished she could see Liu and shake a proper explanation out of him.

At the thought, she turned over, and felt a lump rub against her side.

It was the little jade fox tucked into one of the secret pockets of her shift. She sat up and dug it out. It was smooth and warm in the darkness. She could feel its sharp nose and the curve of its tail. A fox.

Had he meant her to guess?

"How was I supposed to know?" she whispered at it. "We don't have fox-spirits where I come from. And he shoulda just *told* me, anyway. Why'd he have to go and be such a... and bringing Charlotte back, like she was. Better we'd never seen her. Except... all right. I'm glad she's alive. I am. But he shoulda *told* me. Except I'd probably have told him to bugger off. You want my troubles, Mr Fox? I got to make this stupid machine work for Holmforth, only if I do it'll start a war, and if I don't he'll do for my mama, and me, and maybe Beth as well. And I don't know how to get it working, and I can't ask Mama because Holmforth don't realise she's the only one who could probably help, 'cos he thinks it was all stupid Uncle James. And she wouldn't anyway, because she never wanted it used for anything bad, and starting a war, well, that's pretty bad.

"*I* don't know anything about the Folk, I don't know how they think. Liu does. All that about Gifts and how they work – makes no sense to me, but..." She stopped, and stared at the fox, or rather the place in the dark where the fox was.

Beth turned over in her narrow bed. "Eveline?"

"Sorry, Beth, did I wake you?"

"No. Are you all right?"

"I'm thinking." She sat up, the jade fox clutched in one hand, letting her mind run free. *Treadwell.*

They'd needed Treadwell to prove she could work her mother's machines. To prove the machine worked on Folk, Holmforth would need...

Holmforth would need one of the Folk.

"Beth, I've got an idea. I dunno if it'll work, but..."

"Tell me."

"Are you sure?"

"Yes. Maybe I'll think of something."

"You do machines," Eveline said. She sat up. "We've got a machine. We've got Lazy Lou."

"Oh, yes, Lazy Lou... I've been, well, making some adjustments."

"Have you indeed? Thing is, we need the other Liu."

"How very gratifying. Would you like me to let you out?" Liu's face at the window, hanging upside down.

Beth yelped with surprise. "How did you get there?"

"I thought perhaps you might need some assistance."

"You two met?" Eveline said.

"Shall we regard this as an introduction?" Liu said, swinging around so that he was the right way up. He had his hands wrapped around the bars and his feet braced against the wall below, looking remarkably at ease. "What is it you need of me?"

"Lazy Lou. Can you get her here? She's mostly in bits."

"That should not present a difficulty"

"How are we going to get her on board?" Beth said.

"They've given us these fancy clothes for travelling," Eveline said. "I got my stitching stuff. You?"

"Yes."

"Right. And we need your tools. From the Old Barn."

"Tools. The mannequin. Anything else?" Liu said.

"Yes," Eveline said. "You. If you're willing. 'Srisky, and you might get hurt."

He cocked his head. "You have decided to trust me?"

"You make a munge of this, and that war you're so feared of is probably going to happen, so..."

"You think you can prevent it."

"Maybe. But I got to fool everyone long enough for it to work, and I need you for that."

"Oh, my Lady Sparrow," Liu said. "I am at your service. One should never miss the chance to learn."

"What do you mean?" Evvie said.

"I have certain advantages because of my birth. You, however, without my means, manage to change most convincingly for every circumstance. With your mother, you are a respectable young lady. Others see an innocent, or a rogue..."

"And what do you see?" Evvie raised her chin.

"An artist," he said, and managed, still clinging on to the window with one hand, a remarkably elegant bow.

A few moments later he was gone.

Eveline caught Beth looking at her.

"What?"

"You looked, the two of you..."

"We looked what?"

"You looked like two of a kind," Beth said. "You're enjoying this, both of you."

"No! What, with my mama in danger and you..."

"I don't mean that part. But the thought of fooling Holmforth... and whoever else... you had exactly the same expression."

"He's a bloody..."

"Folk? Evvie... he can't help that. I think he's all right."

"He's all we've got, that's the thing. I still don't know if he's to be trusted."

"I know. But Eveline..." In the darkness, Eveline felt Beth clasp her hand. A small hand, callused with work, warm. "I *am*."

Airborne

THE *GLORIANA*, HUGE, magnificent, loomed in the vast cave of the hangar. Figures crawled about it like tiny monkeys. A great train of baggage trundled towards it, the carts pulled by porters uniformed in blue and gold.

Eveline had never seen it on the ground before, only in the air. It seemed much bigger, this close; a great silvery whale of a thing, the fragile gilded gondola of the passenger section dwarfed by the vast swell of the balloon.

"Our luggage is already on board," Holmforth said. "Now, ladies, if you please?"

"Where is Mama?" Eveline hissed.

"I arranged for her to be escorted on board separately." Holmforth ushered them forwards.

They walked up the gangplank. The bag loomed out above their heads. Eveline saw Beth looking at it all, wide-eyed as a child, and felt a trickle of envy. She might be in danger – although Eveline was fairly sure that Beth had no idea what Holmforth was really like – but she could still enjoy herself.

Of course, Beth didn't have her mother imprisoned somewhere on board this contraption. And she actually *liked* the idea of flying.

And to think I once thought what a prize the Gloriana

would be, Eveline thought to herself. Her stomach had contracted to a small hard knot.

Inside, it was positively luxurious, in a strange, airy way. The fittings were very fine, but all of light pale wood and metal, looking – to Eveline's eye – as though they would snap if you breathed on them. They passed by a bar and a smoking room, all done out in that same strange, airy style. "Oh, it's all for the weight, isn't it?" Beth said.

Holmforth only said, "Come along, don't dawdle."

Everywhere were fine clothes and posh voices. Eveline saw two Chinese men, in navy topcoats and stovepipe hats, both middle-aged, standing alone in a small pool of silence, as the crowd flowed and jabbered around them.

Holmforth hastened the girls through the chattering throng and installed them in a cabin with two small beds, a built-in dresser with a basin of hot water steaming on the stand and a small window. "I am going to take the precaution of locking you in," he said. "Just in case you should be feeling adventurous."

Beth's face fell. "Oh, I hoped I might see the engines. Or... well, anything."

"Perhaps another time." He walked to the window, peered out, and then turned, clasping his hands behind his back and looking at them solemnly. "You are involved in something very important. Far more important than you, or I, or any one individual. I can permit nothing to get in the way. Please understand, Miss Duchen, that I would not have involved your mother, except that I am not convinced you will fully appreciate the significance of what I will ask of you. Personal desires, personal feelings, should be as nothing, but..." He sighed. "Really this is not the sort of thing that should be on the shoulders of a woman, especially one so young, and without even the benefit of a proper upbringing. Had I any other choice... but you, Miss Duchen, you can be part of something so much greater than yourself. Endeavour to understand that. In the meantime, make yourselves comfortable. I am in the cabin next to you" – he tapped the wall – "should you need anything."

He went out, locking the door. The girls looked at each other.

"He still hasn't told you what he wants you to do, or what it's for," Beth said. "Has he?"

"I s'pose he's afraid I might gab. He doesn't know..." She glanced at the partition wall and lowered her voice. "He doesn't know that I know everything, except what I actually bloody need to, like how to make it work."

"Would you? If you could?"

"Oh, *I* don't know." Eveline scowled at the floor. "For all I know, this stupid machine don't do anything anyway, and Holmforth's madder'n a ripe cheese, not to mention Liu. Maybe someone's been fooling the lot of 'em. Maybe it's a magician like that Chung Ling Soo, I saw him once. Anyway we got to get there first. How high do these things go? No," she said, as Beth drew breath to speak. "Don't tell me. I hope my mama's all right."

"Are you feeling quite well?"

"No," she said. "Oh, it moved!"

Beth ran to the window. "They're taking us out!"

Eveline huddled on the bed, and buried her face in the fine linen sheets. "I don't wanta know."

There were thumps and bumps and shifts and shouts, the burbling hum of engines and a sudden, strange, lifting sensation, accompanied by cheers she could hear right through the walls. Eveline clutched the sheets tighter and squinched her eyes shut. Beth gasped. Eveline pulled the sheets over her head.

"Oh, do look!" Beth said. "Oh, it's wonderful, Eveline, do look!"

Eveline uncovered half an eye. The cabin was lighter. Beth stood at the window, gripping her hands together, her face lit with delight. "I can see everything!"

"Like what?"

"Clouds! I never knew – gosh, London's *really* dirty. It looks as though there's a filthy grey blanket over it. I can just about see the river. Don't you want to see?"

"No."

Beth pressed the side of her face against the glass. "Oh, I can't see the engines at *all*. Maybe I'll get a chance later... Oh, look! Eveline, we're *in* a cloud! Did you ever think of such a thing?"

"No, and I never wanted to. Just tell me when we've landed safe."

"That'll be *hours* yet, and we'll have to stop partway and refuel anyway. You're not going to even look?"

"No."

Having nothing to do, and nothing to look at but the walls, gave free rein to Eveline's grinding anxiety. She clutched the sheets so hard her hands hurt, and the knot in her stomach only got smaller and tighter and harder.

When Holmforth arrived with a tray of food, she couldn't even contemplate eating any of it, fancy though it looked. "And how are you finding your first flight?" he said.

"Wonderful!" Beth beamed at him, then glanced guiltily at Eveline.

"You don't agree?" Holmforth said. Eveline gripped the table with both hands and hunched her shoulders. "This is an opportunity few will ever have. You should make the most of it. This is a British ship, one of the best in the world, you know."

"I'm sure," Eveline gritted out, wishing he would go away.

"Well, here is your lunch. I shall check on you again in an hour or so." He went out, locking the door behind him.

"Do try a little," Beth said. "It's very good."

"I can't."

"I'm sorry I sounded so... but I *am* excited, even if it is all..."

"Oh, I know, and I don't care. I mean, I don't mind."

THEY STOPPED IN Africa to refuel. Eveline was barely aware of the descent, the bustle, the brilliant light, the heat that seeped through the window, though Beth moaned with frustration. "Oh, I want to *see*. Africa! The colours... Oh, it's so unfair, not to be able even to step outside. There might be lions!"

"Good reason not to step outside, then," Eveline said absently.

"Evvie, do look!"

"Later."

"We won't be here later."

"If I don't get this right, we won't be anywhere later."

Eventually they set off again, into the darkling sky. Even Beth finally had to abandon her post at the window and sleep, though she left the curtain open so that she could look at the stars. Eveline huddled in the bed, trying not to think about the thousands of feet between her and solid ground, gnawing and gnawing over what she was to do, worrying about Mama, incarcerated somewhere in this blasted unnatural beast of a thing.

Shanghai

WHEN SHE WOKE, Beth, already up and dressed, was at the window. "I was about to wake you. I think we're coming in."

"Is it Shanghai?" Eveline said.

"It must be. But I can't see a great deal, the fog is almost as bad as London. Oh, there's another airship! That must be the aerodrome!"

Holmforth came to fetch them, looking as quietly dapper as ever, the velvet collar of his grey overcoat turned up around his neck, his hat at a precise, gentlemanly angle. "You're ready? Good. Come with me."

"Where's Mama?"

"She has gone ahead to the hotel," he said, with a slight air of impatience, for all the world as though Madeleine Duchen was a normal traveller, instead of a hostage.

He had someone with him, Eveline thought. He must have, to deal with Mama. Unless he was simply paying people both in London and here – but surely that would risk drawing attention? He was immensely secretive, after all; he still hadn't told *her* what he wanted. She must remember not to let slip that she knew anything.

Shanghai turned out to be cold, and grey, and thick with rain – much like London, in fact, except for the

329

rickshaws, which were everywhere, and smell, which was slightly different from Limehouse.

Now and then she thought she caught a glimpse of Liu; of course, there were Chinese everywhere, though none of them turned out to be him.

You'd better do what you're supposed to, Liu. She'd ended up relying on him for a big chunk of the plan, and now she wished there'd been another way.

Holmforth raised his cane. Instantly they were surrounded by eager rickshaw drivers clamouring for their business, claiming how fast, how clean, with what astonishing speed they would reach their destination... Eveline realised she could follow the pidgin quite well, and even the few words of Chinese that she caught. That was Liu's doing, too. Now she knew he was Folk (half-Folk, yes, all *right*, half, she'd allow him that much), she wondered if that had something to do with how quickly she'd learned a language that was, after all, far harder to pick up than French.

The rickshaw drivers were all terribly thin, and woefully underdressed for the weather in ragged cotton trousers and shirts worn to transparency. Only one of them had a thick quilted jacket for the cold, and even that was so dirty and faded its original colours could scarcely be guessed at. Apart from the cast of their features, there was little to choose between them and the factory workers at home.

Holmforth made his choice and settled the girls in, one hand firmly on Eveline's arm. He didn't seem nearly as troubled about Beth running off.

Their driver bent to the shafts, the knobs of his spine clearly visible through his rain-dampened shirt, his queue a poor straggly thing, nothing like the glossy thickness of Liu's. Eveline wondered however he was supposed to pull the three of them, but somehow he managed, though his ragged breathing was audible even over the noise of the crowds.

"What's that sound?" Beth said. A rising roar could be heard from somewhere beyond the vast buildings of the Bund.

"The racetrack. Racing is very popular here," Holmforth said. "I have never understood the appeal, myself. But then, many of the European population have a great deal of both leisure and money at their disposal, which they choose to fritter away in such pursuits. Not a good example. But then, you will be unlikely to meet them."

Eveline thought wistfully of the races she had attended at Alexandra Palace, and the excellent pickings they had offered. If only a sharp-eyed peeler was the worst she had to worry about now.

Yet, like Beth, she could not help staring at the hundreds of ships drawn up along the waterfront, the great cargo steamers and tiny fragile junks, the huge warehouses and businesses with their elaborate classical frontages. Hundreds of people, Chinese and European and a great multiplicity of others of all types and shades and costumes, more variety than she had seen even in London. Men in long, loose white robes over white trousers, in square-jacketed suits of silk, in frock-coats and brightly coloured robes. Round black hats, hats with tassels, hats with buttons, stovepipe hats and flat caps and turbans. There were women, too, though far fewer out on the streets among the men. Perhaps they were all hidden away. There were Chinese women with babies or baskets strapped to their backs who walked in the strangest way, swaying from side to side, as though on tiptoe, European women in nip-waisted dresses with tiered skirts and fantastical hats with flowers and birds and veils, holding fringed umbrellas painted with Chinese characters. Everywhere the snapping rhythms of pidgin and the slip-slide musicality of Chinese, but also the quick liquidity of French, and the clatter and twang of a dozen other languages she knew not at all. Even some of the English was strange to her ears, with drawn-out vowels and odd rhythms.

"Who are they?" she said, gesturing at one group.

"Americans," Holmforth said. "Vulgar people, as a rule, with more influence than they deserve. Ah, here we are."

The hotel was not unlike the one he had taken Eveline to in London, but distinctly more luxurious. All the staff were Chinese; white-jacketed, soft-footed, and so extremely deferential that it made Eveline uneasy.

She felt wound to a twanging tension. Here she was, thousands of miles from home, with her mother's life, and Beth's too, in her hands, and who knew how many others, if anything Liu had told her was true.

They reached their room.

"Mama! Are you all right? I'm so sorry!"

Madeleine leapt from her chair and embraced Eveline, then turned to Beth. "I don't believe we've met."

"I'm Beth Hastings," Beth said with a curtsey.

"So you see," Holmforth said, "your mother has come to no harm. I am going to leave you ladies while I arrange transport, and then we must be off." He closed and locked the door.

"Are you well, Eveline?" Madeleine held her at arm's length and looked her over. "That man – was that Holmforth?"

"Yes. Bastard."

"*Eveline Duchen!*"

"Sorry, Mama. But he is. I mean, actually, as well. Not that that part's his fault."

"So what are we going to do?" Beth said.

"I'm getting an idea. I think. But I gotta talk to Holmforth."

"Mrs Duchen?" Beth said. "Please, could I talk with you? I saw your notes and I think I have an inkling about a few things..."

"You do?" Eveline said. "Why didn't you *say?*"

"Because I'm not sure and I might be wrong. And you wouldn't know if I was."

"True enough," Eveline said.

As soon as Holmforth returned, Eveline confronted him.

"What happens after?"

"What do you mean?"

"I show you this machine works. What happens to me, and to my mama?"

"Oh, I'm sure we can find somewhere comfortable for your mama, maybe even some sort of pension. You..." He looked her up and down. "Depending on what results we achieve with the machine, you will be required to help me find more people with Etheric potential, train them if that is possible."

"I want a promise. For Mama, and for me, when you're done with me. In writing, all legal and proper."

"You really are in no position to make demands, but as a gesture of goodwill I am happy to do so."

"Now. Before we go. And signed. And addressed to whoever you answer to, back home. And money and papers so we can *get* home."

"Whoever *I* answer to? Now why would you think that necessary?"

"This machine, if it works – there's other people might be interested in it, ain't there? I en't missed *everything* in the lessons. You never let on when you've got a big prize up; you do that, every thief for a mile around's going to see if they can get there first. And that's when things are like to get nasty. And what happens to us if you should get murdered? Stuck here without papers and no way of getting home?"

"Now, Miss Duchen. You need not think I am foolish enough to provide you with the means to run off!" He smiled. "I will, however, write the letter you require, to provide you with peace of mind."

"'Slong as you give me that, then."

"Now, shall we get on?" Holmforth said.

"Not till you've writ that letter."

She stood over him while she did it, watching every word. Without a lawyer of her own, she'd no idea if the language meant much. But it was his handwriting and his signature she wanted.

"Shall we go?" He offered Madeleine Duchen his arm, and she took it.

THERE WAS NO rickshaw this time; instead, a more luxurious sort of steam hansom. The body was glossy and black, the wheels bright scarlet, the three sets of seats of plushly padded, deep-buttoned leather. Holmforth handed them all in as though he were escorting them to a tea-dance. The driver wore a dark blue suit with brass buttons and a peaked cap pulled low over his eyes.

"Very fancy, I must say," Eveline remarked. "Flunkies, too. Your tumbler, is it?"

"If by *tumbler* you mean vehicle, no, it belongs to the Consulate. If your worst fears are realised, Miss Duchen, you must make your way there. They will be able to assist you."

Worst fears, my foot, Eveline thought. *'Fyou were to meet a sticky end, Mr Holmforth, I'd be jumping like a Jack-in-the-box.*

Holmforth handed them each into the car with perfect courtesy, and got in after them.

"Oh," Holmforth said, "please do not attempt to jump out, or anything of that sort. I have a gun. I would be reluctant to use it, but I'm afraid I cannot allow anything to jeopardise this."

Eveline felt her mother stiffen with fear and gave her hand a reassuring pat, thinking of Ma Pether. *I don't like guns. They change things, make everything much more dangerous than needs be.* She couldn't help wishing they had Ma Pether along now.

There was a sack lying across the rearmost set of seats. It had a disturbing shape.

"What's that?" Madeleine said.

"Material for the demonstration."

"But it looks like a *person*."

"It's not a person," Holmforth said. "Little more than an animal, really."

Eveline felt the nape of her neck shiver. He was half-Folk himself. And he still thought of them, of people like Liu, as animals.

What did that mean for how he saw himself?

Beth craned her neck to see what the driver was doing, and, after watching him for a few minutes, sighed, and looked around her instead. "What's that building?"

"A factory. Part of the French Concession."

"I can hear machinery. What does it do?"

"Oh, some form of manufacturing, probably. Shanghai is the province of business, far more than of good government." Holmforth frowned. "It has been poorly handled. Far too many concessions have been made to the demands of other countries, and to financial interests. One can hope that the same mistakes will be avoided in future."

He means when we invade the Crepuscular, Eveline thought. *If Liu's right, he really doesn't have the slightest idea how big a mistake that would be.*

The streets grew more and more narrow; brilliantly coloured banners of cloth and paper fluttered from the houses cramming the streets. They passed through layers of smells – vile, delicious, simply odd. There were shops full of tiny embroidered shoes with pointed toes that looked as though they were made for children. Shops full of strange vegetables, pallid long ones like the fingers of drowned giants, fat hairy ones, and great piles of leaves spilling out onto the floor. Little dark caves of shops lined with boxes and bottles and jars of dried stuff. Rickshaws scurried and bounced along the streets, full and empty. The driver leaned on his horn and yelled them out of the way. Poor people huddled in doorways here as they did everywhere.

Eveline could see Holmforth's hands whitening on his cane. She felt for her mother's hand and clutched it. Madeleine pressed her fingers.

* * *

THE HOUSES BEGAN to thin out, the road roughened. The landscape spread out around them, green and grey beneath the grey sky. Flat fields glittered with water, trees here and there stood sentinel. A few figures in wide, pointed hats moved along hidden paths, their heads turning at the noise of the engine to watch the car puff and rumble past.

"Oh, look!" Beth pointed. "What is that?"

It was about the size and shape of a pheasant, but its body was scarlet, its head and back bright gold splashed with brilliant blue and bronze. It seemed more like jewellery than a living thing, but just like a pheasant back home, it ran, neck stretched with panic, in front of the car for a few feet before remembering its wings and taking off, scolding loudly.

"A golden pheasant," Holmforth said. "The shooting is quite good here."

The further they moved from the city, the more nervous Eveline became. Even if they could get away from Holmforth, where, in this flat, sparsely-populated landscape, could they hide?

The house stood in isolation, surrounded by a high wall of yellowed bricks. Above the wall, the black roof-corners curved up like the prows of boats.

The gate set in the wall was of red-lacquered wood, studded with brass bosses in the shapes of snarling creatures.

It was the sort of gate, in the sort of wall, that indicated strongly that the occupant desired privacy.

It was standing slightly ajar. Eveline's few nerves that weren't already singing joined the chorus.

She looked at Holmforth. His mouth tightened. "Get out of the car, ladies, and stay close," he said. "You!

Driver! Stay with the vehicle, and keep your eyes open. Should any of these women be foolish enough to try to run, they are to be stopped, *alive*, please."

The driver nodded. Eveline shot a glance at him; he was Chinese, or perhaps a mix of Chinese and English – his face, in any case, was impassive. The gun he raised looked unpleasantly large and efficient.

Holmforth heaved the sack out of the rearmost seat and slung it over his shoulder.

Holmforth gestured to the women to follow him through the gate, and into the courtyard. A statue of a snarling thing that looked to Eveline like a cross between a lion and one of the school's dogs stood there, and beyond was the house, presenting them with a blank wall. "The entrance is around the side," Holmforth said. "That way."

"Mr Holmforth, what *exactly* are we doing here?" Madeleine Duchen said.

Holmforth jolted, as though he had not expected her to be able to speak. "You, madam, are here to provide insurance that your daughter will do what is required of her. Neither she nor you nor this other young lady will come to any harm, if all goes as planned."

"No harm?" Madeleine stopped, holding Eveline's arm. "To make a weapon of something that was only ever intended for good? You don't think that doing that, being made to do that, is harmful? That it is a dreadful thing to ask of someone?"

No, Mama! Eveline's gut clenched. Now Holmforth knew what Mama knew, he would see her as a risk.

Holmforth sighed. "This is hardly the time. Something is wrong here, and I am asking that she serve the best interests of the British Empire. Now please, stay close, and keep moving. There should be servants, a houseboy at least, Wu Jisheng... oh."

The women caught sight of the foot at the same time. It was a very small foot, in an embroidered, point-toed slipper. It was attached to a slim white-clad leg, lying on the floor. The rest was hidden behind the partly-open door.

Holmforth nudged it open.

A young woman lay there, her mouth open, her eyes wide, and a dark pool of blood spreading from beneath her, across the smooth grey stone floor.

Eveline clutched her mother's hand, and with the other felt for the small, reassuring lump that was the jade fox.

Beth swallowed. "She's... dead, isn't she?"

"Yes. Be quiet," Holmforth said. "Come with me, quickly."

"But what if someone's..." Eveline said.

"Quiet, I said!" Gesturing with the gun, Holmforth hurried them forwards, past the dead woman, through rooms painted with strange birds and beasts, filled with odd ornaments and brilliantly coloured statues and, strangely, great glittering clocks that ticked and chimed, European clocks adorned with fanciful shepherds and shepherdesses and pink, puffing cherubs.

Not a robbery, Eveline thought. *All this stuff, even the little light things, still here. That, or the robbers are still here, and working their way through.* She tugged at her mother's hand, and when Madeleine looked at her, she mouthed – *If you get the chance,* run.

Madeleine shook her head, and held her hand tighter. *Not without you.*

They reached a door that was bigger than the gate, at least twenty feet high. Heavy wood furnished with formidable iron bolts – all of them now open.

"*No!*" Holmforth said. He shoved the door open, and almost pushed the women through it.

The room was huge, and full of things that glittered and ticked and gleamed.

And a dragon.

It was made of brass and bronze, copper and iron, it glowed in the dim light like treasure. Its head alone was as big as the car they had arrived in. Collapsed across one of its great clawed feet lay the body of an elderly Chinese man with eyeglasses and a long wispy beard.

Holmforth gave a sigh of relief. "Untouched." He dumped the sack on the floor.

"Look, Mr Holmforth, I know this machine's important to you," Eveline said, "but maybe you ain't noticed that's the second bit of cold meat we've come across, and being as I don't think they died of the pleurisy, maybe whoever done for 'em's still here and *maybe* we should make ourselves scarce?"

"What a very perspicacious young woman you are," said a voice. "But there's no need for alarm. I believe the villains have already vacated the premises."

The man who entered the room was a dapper, blond swell, neat as ninepence, looking with distaste at the body on the floor. "I apologise," he said to Holmforth. "I know you weren't expecting me for another day or so, but I had business to conduct, and given all your work, I thought I should investigate for myself. I think perhaps my arrival warned off the miscreants."

"This is worrying," Holmforth said. "Do you think that they could have been working for other interests?"

The blond man shook his head. "If so, they were easily distracted. However, I shall certainly put investigations in place. You have a man outside?"

"Yes."

"Then I am sure he will warn us if they return. Now, perhaps you would introduce me?"

Eveline's back hairs were up and singing louder than before. She'd seen a body or two in her time – when she was sleeping out, she'd more than once woken up after a bad frost to see someone a few feet away gone grey and empty in the night. But these had been *killed* – *murdered* – and these two were acting as though it was nothing, as though they were at a drawing-room party.

She eyed the blond man. A toff of the first water, right enough – what he had on his back would have earned her a week's extra dumplings in her dinner at Ma Pether's – and eyes that made Holmforth's look warm.

"Of course," Holmforth said. "This is Mrs Duchen, her daughter Eveline, and Miss Beth Hastings. This is Viscount Forbes-Cresswell."

Forbes-Cresswell bowed. "I have to say, Holmforth, charming though I'm sure they are, I'm not entirely sure why you felt it necessary to bring quite such a collection of females with you?"

"Eveline is the one with Etheric ability. Beth has some mechanical skill. And it seemed wise not to leave any of them unattended, once they knew of the machine's existence." Holmforth sighed. "I am trying to impress upon them the importance of this development, its significance to the Empire."

"Ah, yes, the machine. I assume that is it?" He gestured at the dragon. "How intriguing! Would you be able to make that demonstration you were speaking of?"

"Miss Duchen, if you please."

Eveline drew a deep breath. "All right. But will you move *him*, please? I en't going to be able to concentrate that well with some dead geezer flopped all over the floor."

"Unfortunate," Forbes-Cresswell said, looking at Wu Jisheng. "But it does reduce complications."

"Eveline, you don't have to do this!" Madeleine took her daughter by the hands. "Please...."

"I do, Mama. I'm sorry, but it's the only way for us to be safe. It'll all be all right, I promise."

"I won't let you!"

"Please, Mrs Duchen," Holmforth said. "Stand aside, if you would. I really don't want to have to restrain you." He bent down and undid the neck of the sack.

Out spilled a young Chinese woman, dressed in embroidered robes, extremely dishevelled, her hands and ankles bound.

"Oh, the poor child!" Madeleine cried.

"There's no need for sentiment. It's a fox-spirit. Look." Holmforth pointed with his cane. Sure enough, the white-tipped brush could be clearly seen protruding from beneath the girl's tunic.

"All right, let her stand up," Eveline said.

Holmforth gestured.

The girl got stiffly to her feet, (normal feet, these, even perhaps a little large) and stood staring.

Eveline glanced at Beth. Beth tucked her hands into her skirt.

The Chinese girl turned her head to look at her.

"Right then," Eveline said. "Shall we get on? And can someone please shift that poor old geezer?" Forbes-Cresswell looked at Holmforth, who went and took Wu Jisheng by his shoulders and dragged him out of sight behind a heavily-carved screen. "Thank you."

"Eveline..." Madeleine said.

"It's all right, Mama. You sit down. Can't one of you gents find a chair for a lady? Honestly, rude, I call it."

"Quite right," Forbes-Cresswell said, and drew up one of the heavy lacquered chairs. "If you please, Madam."

Madeleine sat down, gingerly, fidgeting with her gloves. She looked desperately tired and nervous.

Holmforth turned his back for a moment. Eveline, watching, realised he was inserting his earplugs.

She steeled herself. "Beth, you come with me." She looked up at the dragon. Niches were provided in its great bronze foreleg, making a set of steps up into the head.

"Miss Duchen," Forbes-Cresswell said. "Don't be foolish, will you?" He was standing right behind her mother's chair. There was a red smear on one of his immaculate white cuffs.

"I en't going to do anything but what I'm told," Eveline said, trying not to stare at that smear, her brain racing.

She climbed into the dragon's head, Beth close behind her.

Inside it was like a fantastical cave of brass and bronze, levers and dials – and Chinese lettering. She'd enough of the spoken tongue to get by, thanks to Liu, but the writing was still a mystery.

Still, she recognised a few of the instruments, most of them three times the size of what she was used to, the grooves in which ball bearings should be placed, as big as gutters, running everywhere inside the head. A case of ball bearings, like shining cricket balls, lay at her feet. There were levers and dials which reminded her more of the controls of the *Sacagawea*.

If only she could ask Mama! It had seemed safer that Holmforth thought Mama completely ignorant – though now it was all up in the air, and there was no safety anywhere. They'd just have to go with what they'd got and hope for the best.

"Oh, my. Eveline, look at this!" Beth said.

"Very pretty. You can play with it later. You talked to Mama, just tell me if I'm doing anything's going to make anyone go mad or such."

"If I knew that, we'd be fine. All right. That lever there, and then that. It won't do anything at all, I don't think, except make a noise."

She pulled the first lever. A deep thrumming vibration spread through the dragon's body, tickling the soles of her feet through her shoes. She picked up a ball bearing and dropped it into one of the gutters, pulled another lever. The ball bearing started to move, making a high, singing note.

She looked out through the dragon's mouth; everyone was still in place. "Beth, we got trouble," she said quietly, trusting the noise to cover her.

"More of it?"

"Yes. That Forbes-Cresswell – there's blood on his cuff."

"Blood?"

"I think he's the one killed the old geezer and the girl. I don't know what he's doing, but I don't think Holmforth knows they ain't on the same side. I'd bet he's got men with him. You found anything?"

"I think it moves. The dragon. I think these controls make it move. I can't work them all out, though."

"Don't touch anything yet, it ain't safe, not with Mama right there. All right, here we go, time to prove the pudding."

She lifted another ball bearing, eased it into its gutter.

The note it added as it began to move was an uneasy one, a waspish buzz.

"Go," Eveline said.

Beth pulled out from her skirts the small instrument she'd hidden, and aimed it, keeping it carefully below the line of sight of those out front.

The Chinese girl shuddered.

The two men turned to look at her. Madeleine put her hands over her eyes.

Eveline set a metal disc spinning. The sound became jagged. The girl jolted, and collapsed to her knees.

"Eveline, stop! Don't!" Madeleine tried to get up, but Forbes-Cresswell's hand came down on her shoulder, crushing her back into her seat.

The girl fell on her side, convulsing. A gleam appeared under her left ear. "Turn it off!" Eveline hissed.

"Dammit..." Beth twiddled dials frantically, but the girl continued to convulse. Then her head came up at a painful, impossible angle, and hit the floor with a ringing crash.

She lay still. Holmforth bent over her. Forbes-Cresswell didn't move.

"Turn it off," Holmforth said, loudly. "Turn it off, Duchen."

Eveline pulled levers. The dragon became silent.

Holmforth straightened up and took out his earplugs. "Duchen," he said, "did you really think that would work?"

"What..." Forbes-Cresswell said.

"It's a mannequin," Holmforth said. "I don't know how she managed it, but it's a mannequin. Look." He reached down and lifted off the girl's wig, revealing Lazy Lou's bald, shining pate.

"Well fuck me with a ten foot pole," Eveline said. "How'd that happen?"

"Don't play with me, Duchen." Holmforth's face was white, with hectic red patches on his cheekbones. He aimed the gun at her. Eveline felt her stomach drop. "I suppose the Treadwell girl was in on it too. I assume this means you don't know what you're doing, that you have been deceiving me all along? If that is the case, your usefulness is at an end." He turned to Forbes-Cresswell. "I can only apologise. She must have made the switch somehow. It shouldn't take long to find another subject, but finding someone who can actually work the machine... well..."

"I can!" Madeleine said. "Please. I'm the one who can work the machine. Not Evvie. She's been trying to protect me. It was all the fault of James – oh, never mind. Just don't hurt her."

"You." Holmforth looked at her. "You can work it?"

"Of course I can! Just let me show you, but please don't hurt my girl!"

"Really, Holmforth," Forbes-Cresswell said. "You do have an extraordinary collection of females. Do put the gun down, old fellow, before your temper gets the better of you and we lose our leverage."

Holmforth sighed harshly. "Oh, very well."

"In fact, perhaps you'd better give it to me."

"I assure you..."

"Holmforth." Forbes-Cresswell held out his hand.

Holmforth, automatically, put the gun in it.

"Thank you," Forbes-Cresswell said, tucking it away. "Now, the earplugs."

"What?"

Forbes-Cresswell trained his own gun on Holmforth. "Earplugs. Now."

"I don't..."

"Really, Holmforth. We still need a subject. And you will do as well as any. Admittedly, the fact that you are partly human may make a difference, but I need *something* to show my buyer."

"Your... buyer. Who...?"

"That's of no consequence. However, he will be here soon, and if I don't have evidence, he may become impatient at being dragged all the way out here. I have a reputation to maintain."

Beth and Eveline looked at each other. "He's a spy!" Beth whispered.

"Nah, just a thief," Eveline whispered back.

"But he's in the Government!"

"So? So's Holmforth, and he was planning to nick this off of poor old Wu there. Ma Pether always said there's more crooks in the Houses of Parliament than there are in Limehouse – they just dress better. C'n you get this bugger moving?"

"I'll try."

"Miss Duchen," Forbes-Cresswell raised his voice. "I hope you are not attempting to conspire with your little friend there. Come out, now. It's time for your mama to show what she can do. Really, you do seem to be a remarkably resourceful family."

"What are you *doing?*" Holmforth said. "You can't mean to do this!"

"Of course I can, old boy."

"Is it a test?" Holmforth said. He sounded suddenly, strangely young – a boy facing a harsh schoolmaster. "You're testing me. I know you can't mean it. Do you want to know if I'm willing? I'm willing!" A sudden horrible kind of brightness took over his face. "Yes!

Test the machine! I understand! It might kill it, it might burn it out of me! Please! Rid me of it!"

Forbes-Cresswell stared at him, and shrugged. "It's no odds to me what you believe," he said, keeping the gun on Holmforth, his glance flicking from him to the women. "Sit in that chair."

Holmforth did so, staring at Forbes-Cresswell like a dog hoping for a biscuit. "This is it, isn't it? You're testing me. This was the plan all along."

"You're a fool, Holmforth. Come out, Miss Duchen. And you, Miss Hastings."

The girls stepped down from the dragon's head.

"Now," Forbes-Cresswell said. "I want no nonsense. Mrs Duchen, get in there and make this thing work. Otherwise, I'll kill your daughter, and her little friend. Understand?"

"Yes. Don't hurt them, please. But you'll have to give me a little time. This doesn't look like anything I've used before."

"You have until my buyer gets here."

Madeleine Duchen walked stiffly towards the dragon. As she passed the girls, she put out her hand and stroked Evvie's hair. "Everything will be all right." She smiled at them.

"You, girl," Forbes-Cresswell said. "Tie him up."

"With what?"

"The old man has a sash around him. Use that."

Eveline, grimacing, worked the sash out from around the old man's stiffening body. One of his shoes fell off. His stockinged foot was somehow awful, pathetic. The gun gave Forbes-Cresswell too much advantage; but, maybe, not quite as much as he thought. *Besides, something like this,* Ma Pether had said, *it only has one shot and you gotta reload. What good's that? Don't need to reload your head, do you?*

Could she get him to fire it? He had Holmforth's gun, too, of course – but he had stuck it in his jacket, and she didn't know how quick he could get at it.

Not worth the risk, not with the way bullets flew about, not caring who they hit.

Use what's to hand. The old man had a long silver finger-stall, with a pointed end, on the little finger of his left hand... not much, but better than nothing. She palmed it, and began to tie up Holmforth. She yanked on the sash, wanting to punish him.

"There's no need for this," he said.

Forbes-Cresswell ignored him, inspected Eveline's knots, and nodded. "Now move over there by your friend. Mrs Duchen?"

"Yes."

"I hope you are not planning on displaying any foolish sentimentality this time?"

Madeleine Duchen looked at him steadily. "This man brought my daughter into danger. Do you really think I care for one moment if he suffers? I *hope* he suffers."

Oh, Mama.

"Very well," Forbes-Cresswell said. "Oh, and I believe this *Etherics* can be used on humans. I should warn you that if I feel, for even a moment, any change in my mental state, your daughter dies. You understand?"

"Yes."

Eveline watched as her mama began to move the levers inside the machine; her long hands, with their worn, reddened fingers. Did she remember? *Could* she remember? All those years locked away, working only with bits and scraps...

"This will be a great moment!" Holmforth said. "The future is beginning here, can't you feel it?" He looked at Eveline. "Even you, you *must*. The Empire will shine its light upon the savage and pagan remnant of the Folk and..."

"Oh, really, Holmforth," Forbes-Cresswell said. "You're becoming tedious. That sort of jaw is all very well for schoolmasters and clergy and vote-getting, but is that *really* what you think Empire is? Some sort of cleansing fire of virtue and enlightenment? The business of Empire is *business*, Holmforth. Coin, moving from one pocket to another. And I'm a businessman, no more, no less."

Holmforth's eyes searched Forbes-Cresswell's face, but whatever he sought, he did not find it. His face became very still. Eveline, watching, almost expected tiny cracks to race across his features; behind that mask, something was crumbling, falling away.

Forbes-Cresswell's eyes moved from him, to Mama in the dragon's head, to the two girls. Beth looked at Eveline, biting her lip. *What now?*

Be ready, Eveline mouthed. Ready for what, she didn't know. A flicker in Forbes-Cresswell's attention. Anything.

The dragon began to sing. A low vibration in its throat, rising slowly, building potential, holding the promise of thunder.

After a moment, Holmforth drew a hissing breath. He began to shift in his chair, straining against his bounds and moving his head restlessly, as though bothered by flies.

Then he moaned.

Beth gasped as blood began to seep from Holmforth's ears. It trickled down his neck, and a small red flower bloomed where it ran onto his starched collar.

Forbes-Cresswell nodded. Eveline glanced at her mother, who was still working, her hands relentlessly moving, her eyes glimmering with tears. She looked at Forbes-Cresswell, who motioned her to go on. Another note joined the vibration, a singing hum.

Holmforth's moans rose; he began to fling his head from side to side, as though trying to shake something out of it. His golden skin drained of colour, leaving him a pallid yellow, like a tallow candle.

Someone screamed, outside. Forbes-Cresswell's head snapped towards the sound, the gun coming up, and Eveline's foot shot out and caught him in the side of the knee. He yelped and buckled, turning towards her. *Gun! Gun! Gun!* her head screamed at her.

The controller Beth was holding caught him in the side of the head and bounced off, clattering to the floor. His hands came up, the gun went off, there was another scream. Eveline dived at his knees and Beth caught his arm, clinging like a monkey, and between them they brought him to the floor. He writhed furiously, trying to throw them off. The gun spun out of his hand, away across the floor.

Eveline held the finger-stall to his neck, dimpling the skin with the point. "Oy, mister. *Mister.*"

"Get off me, you..."

"Shut up. Feel that?" She pressed, feeling the point push against the bones of his spine. "Now, I seen a chap thrown off his horse, once. Landed with his neck across a mounting stone and you could hear it snap right across the street. Never walked again, that fella. Not a step. So why don't you stop struggling 'fore I decide to see what happens if I push this right in?" Forbes-Cresswell stilled. "Beth, get the other gun."

Beth reached into his jacket, grimacing, and extracted Holmforth's gun.

"My buyer will be here any moment," Forbes-Cresswell said. "And so will Holmforth's driver; he'll have heard the shot. He will believe what I tell him. You have nowhere to go."

Eveline hesitated. He could be right – if they were found here, with the bodies, it was Forbes-Cresswell who would be believed. And could she bring herself to kill him? How? Drive this spike into his temple, his throat? She didn't think she could do it, vile little bastard that he was. Thief she might be, murderer she wasn't.

"Who was it screamed?" Beth said.

"Dunno."

"Let me up!" Forbes-Cresswell squirmed. He was strong, and she didn't know how long they could hold him.

"Eveline."

"Mama." Eveline didn't look up, not daring to take her eyes off Forbes-Cresswell. "You all right?"

"Yes, but what are we to do?"

"I..."

Something moved in the doorway and Beth's hand came up with the gun in it, shaking, and Eveline saw Liu, Liu staggering and bleeding. She knocked Beth's arm up and Forbes-Cresswell heaved, throwing them off, and rolled, his weight on Eveline, so *heavy*, his hands were on her throat, crushing, she couldn't breathe, and then something hit his head, *crunch*, and his hands slackened, his body suddenly heavier.

"Evvie. Evvie!" There was a crash and a splintering sound, and Mama was hauling him off her.

"I'm all right," Eveline croaked.

Mama helped her to her feet. Her eyes were wide and horrified, a spray of blood across her cheek, one drop hanging in her grey hair like a dreadful jewel. "I..." She looked down at the remains of a heavy carved box, spattered with hair and blood. Ink and small stones and fine lacquered brushes were scattered around it. "I think I've killed him."

Forbes-Cresswell lay limp, blood and fluid leaking from his head across the tiles.

"Good," Eveline said.

She heard a whimper. Liu was crawling blindly towards them, blood trickling from his eyes and ears and nose. "Lady... Sparrow..."

"*Liu*. Oh, shit, Liu, I didn't know... you weren't supposed to *be* there..." Eveline ran towards him.

Madeleine followed her daughter. "Oh, my poor boy. Oh, dear god."

Liu collapsed at their feet. Madeleine took his head in her lap, and tried to wipe blood from his face with her sleeve.

Beth, seeing the black ink crawl and mingle with the fluid spreading from Forbes-Cresswell's shattered skull, backed away, dropped to her knees and threw up.

"What happened? What's this boy doing here?" Madeleine said.

"He wasn't supposed to be. He was just meant to free whoever Holmforth'd got for the demonstration and put the mannequin there instead, he wasn't supposed to chase after us, and get his stupid self hurt. Mama, we have to get the dragon working."

"What?"

"That's what made him sick. It can make him better. Can't it?"

"Eveline... I can try." Madeleine stroked Liu's brow. "This... this is..."

"I know. You can make it better."

"What about the driver?" Beth said, wiping her mouth.

Liu muttered something in Chinese.

"I don't know," Eveline said. "Oh, I *told* him he shouldn't come... Beth, can you check outside? Take the gun. Can you fire it?"

"I can *fire* it. Aiming's another thing." Holding the gun as though it were a dead rat, her mouth pulled down in a grimace, Beth went out.

"Stay with him," Madeleine said. "Watch him. If he seems to get worse, call out."

Beth sat down and gently transferred Liu's head to her own lap. "You bloody idiot," she muttered. "What'd you have to go and do that for? Messing everything up."

His eyelids flickered but he said nothing.

"Liu?"

He was terribly pale. His face shimmered, making her jump; for a moment he was all muzzle and sharp, blood-stained teeth.

"Liu!"

And the dragon began to sing.

The first note was high and sweet, a soft, wavering, *aahiiihaaahiiii*, the voice of a tiny metal angel trapped in the dragon's throat.

Then came a fuller, rounder sound, *raum, raum, raummmm*, surrounding the lost angel, lifting it on warm friendly wings.

Liu was very still, now. His breathing was so slow, so faint. Eveline rested a hand on his cheek. He was cool as the tiled floor beneath her.

"Mama, please," she whispered.

Another note, rich and strange. She felt a strange shifting inside her, a kind of blooming warmth. She willed it to go to Liu, to help him.

Was that a flush of colour in his skin?

The dragon sang in a ringing, lovely multiplicity of voices, and Liu opened his eyes.

"What happened?" Beth said.

"Mama made it work." Liu was sitting up, suffering Madeleine to clean blood from his face with a wetted handkerchief. He still looked pale, and kept glancing anxiously at the dragon. "What happened outside?"

"I don't know. It's an awful mess. The driver's dead, and there's another man and someone I think was *his* driver, they're all dead. Shot."

"Did you do that?" Eveline asked Liu.

"I did not shoot anyone. I may have encouraged them to shoot each other. They were all most suspicious and quite ready to do so at the slightest provocation."

"So what now?" said Beth.

"We can make it right," Holmforth said. Eveline jumped. She'd almost forgotten about wretched Holmforth, still tied to his chair. Mama's music had worked on him, too, though he still looked sick, and no-one had wiped *his* face.

"Untie me," he said. "We will send word to the Consulate, to have the Dragon collected. I will explain everything. The other one, the buyer, he may have papers, something... leave it to me. We can still make this work for the good of the Empire. You have behaved very foolishly, but at least..." He glanced at Forbes-Cresswell, then away. "Treachery failed, as it must."

The look he gave Eveline was almost pleading. "You understand, we can still retrieve something from this!"

"Yeah, right. I think you're going to be staying right where you are for now, Mr Holmforth. Liu. What you told me about the Queen. About the Gifts. I think... Mama. Mama, are you well?

"Yes, my dear. Only..." She looked down at her bloodied hands, and swallowed. "I should like to wash."

Eveline wrapped her arms around her mother's waist, and hugged her fiercely. "You saved me, Mama."

"Yes. I had to. But... I killed someone."

"I know. But if you hadn't, it wouldn't just be me dead." She drew Madeleine out of the room, beckoning Liu and Beth to follow, hoping that would take them out of range of Holmforth's blasted sharp ears.

Once they were beyond the doors, Eveline rubbed her eyes. She could feel a great weight of exhaustion poised at her back, but she couldn't afford to give in to it yet. "Mama, can you do something to the dragon, if Beth helps? Make it so it will only make pretty noises, ones the Folk will like? Safe ones, like it was just a musical instrument."

Madeleine frowned. "Well, yes. That only requires ripping out some things, silencing others."

"What is your plan, Lady Sparrow?" Liu said. He was still pale, but he looked a little more like himself.

"To give your Queen a Gift, Liu. Not the spirit of the thing... I still don't understand that, quite, and it wouldn't solve our problem anyway, but the thing itself. The dragon."

"You want to *give* her the dragon? I think perhaps the strain of the day has troubled your mind."

"Listen to me. You already knew about it; how long before someone else gets wind of it? What about the Folk here, that girl he caught? What do you bet they already know something? We gotta make it look like it was *meant* for a Gift. Meant to please. Then, if they find out that there was something that made terrible, harmful noises, they'll think it was a mistake – something that happened while we were trying to make them this special Gift. Can you persuade her that it's the best Gift she could have, better than anyone else could have got? Then, if someone makes another – well. There's a chance they'll think we're just doing it to try and improve on the Gift, produce something better. For them. You see?"

Liu frowned, rubbing his chin. "A Gift," he said, slowly. "A Gift lovingly created, so much admired that people..." – he glanced back at the other room – "that people killed each other for the honour of giving it. And... now, did I steal it? Oh, yes, I think I stole it... it was intended, not for my Queen, but for the dragon god – an attempt to flatter his image and gain his favour. She'll like that. In fact, it will delight her to think she has deprived him of such a magnificent Gift."

"This dragon god, would he be the person you offended, maybe? What will he think of having his present stolen?" Eveline said. "Won't you get into trouble?"

"I will ensure he hears a different story," Liu said.

"They won't fight, will they? I mean, go to war, over it?" Madeleine said. "Charlotte's still there – and maybe others..."

"Go to war? Against each other? That is extremely unlikely," Liu said. "They prefer their own hides whole." He grinned wickedly. "Oh, Lady Sparrow, what a wonderful game!"

Eveline felt herself smile a little, despite everything. Madeleine shook her head. "A game? Really?"

"Just 'cos the stakes are high, it don't mean it ain't a game," Eveline said. "Now. I know Forbes-Cresswell won't have told anyone where he was going, and I bet he told Holmforth not to either, but it doesn't mean nothing got around, so we'd better hurry before someone turns up looking for them. Beth, you and Mama get working on the dragon. It needs to sing pretty and if you can get it moving, all the better."

"Yes," Liu said. "If you can make it move, I can get it over the border. Otherwise, it will be difficult."

"How far do you have to go?" Eveline said.

"Oh, I can make a passage in most places – the privilege of my position – but from outdoors is easier."

"So we don't have to try and smuggle it onto an airship, then."

"Fortunately, no."

"What about Holmforth?" Beth said.

"I dunno, I'll think of something." Beth and Madeleine hurried off.

"It would be better if he were dead," Liu said.

"There's enough people dead. I don't want more."

"Are you sure you have a choice?"

"Of course I got a choice!"

"And if leaving him alive brings down on us what we are trying so hard to prevent?"

"It won't."

"Eveline." Liu touched her hand with the tips of his fingers, gently, as though she were porcelain. "I honour your gentle spirit. But..."

"I know, all right? He's got a maggot in his head about the Folk, Liu. He wants them to pay. He's still all fired up for the Empire... I'll have to think." She rubbed her eyes. "But the main thing is to get rid of that blasted dragon before it gets us all into even more trouble. And we need to do something in case someone comes looking for the old man, too. I s'pose he must have had servants, at least... wonder where they all went?"

"I should imagine they ran away, but it is possible they may come back."

TWO NERVE-WRACKING HOURS later, Eveline watched as the dragon's head reared up on its long, gleaming neck, and with hisses and clanks and an impressive exhalation of steam, its legs unfolded, raising the sinuous body off the ground.

Despite herself, Eveline took a couple of steps backwards as the head swung towards her. Liu, at the controls, gave her a cheery wave.

"If you would be so kind as to open the doors?"

They did so. Holmforth, still tied to his chair, who had spent the last hours alternately scolding, begging, and threatening, wrenched furiously at his bonds. "You can't do this! You can't! Thieves! Traitors!"

They ignored him as the dragon began its stately progress out of the building. Beth sighed. "Oh, it's so wonderful. If only it wasn't so *dangerous*. Are you sure there isn't another way?"

"Can you think of one?" Eveline said, a little more sharply than she meant.

"No," Beth said wistfully. "It just seems such a terrible *waste*. They're not even going to appreciate it for what it is, for all the work that's gone into it; they'll just think it's a pretty toy."

"If they thought anything else, we'd all regret it," Eveline said. "You sure we found all the notes?"

"I think so." Beth glanced at the pretty porcelain stove where a bunch of papers was burning merrily. "What about the notes he says he gave Forbes-Cresswell?"

"He'd not have kept them at the office – too good a chance of someone else finding 'em. I s'pose we'll have to check out his gaff when we get home. And his room at the Consulate."

"You're going to sneak into the *Consulate?*"

"Have to, won't I?"

They followed the dragon out into the courtyard.

Beyond the gates the sun was setting, a fat red coin on grey silk. The light caught the mobile silver wires that hung about the dragon's mouth, turning them to bloody streaks. Liu paused the beast, and turned its head to Eveline. Steam curled from its nostrils.

"You will be careful," Eveline said.

"Of course I will," Liu said. "Do not worry, I think it will work."

"You'd better go, then."

"Yes. Goodbye, Lady Sparrow of Shanghai."

"*Zhù nǐ hǎoyùn*, Foxy."

"Luck?" Liu grinned. "Luck is for those who are not as clever as us." He pulled another lever, and the dragon reared up on its hind legs, making Eveline gasp and Beth give a little moan, and with sudden, astonishing, fluid grace, it was out of the gate and moving across the road, a sinuous vision of gleam and vapour in the flat, empty landscape.

And strangely, another road – a thing of mist and

whispers, but a road, winding across the plain and rising up at a slope the land did not accommodate – began to form itself before the dragon's feet.

Suddenly Eveline realised that the dragon's tail had something clinging to it, some ragged lump of cloth – had it caught on something?

No. It was Holmforth, gripping the moving tail with both hands, working his way up the spine.

"Liu, look out!" Eveline yelled, knowing that it was impossible he could hear her.

Beth fumbled out the gun she had shoved into her pocket.

"No!" Eveline said. "You might hit Liu! Come on!"

They began to run, Madeleine in their wake.

Liu had not noticed his passenger. The dragon was pacing elegantly up the vaporous road. Holmforth inched up its backbone, his face alight with fervid determination.

The dragon reared up. The air shimmered and swirled like the surface of a pearl.

"Liu!"

But it was too late. The dragon surged forward, the air shivered, and then there was a flash of painful, brilliant green light, and something tumbled down through the empty air and landed in the wet field at the girls' feet.

Clothes. A Norfolk jacket, tweed trousers.

Holmforth's clothes, sinking into the mud.

"They're moving..." Beth whispered.

"Maybe they fell on one of them fancy birds, like we saw?" Eveline picked up a stick, and lifted the edge of the jacket.

It was a hare. Crouched inside the shirt, the collar loose around its neck, eyes wide and dark with terror, ears flat to its narrow head.

"Oh," Eveline breathed.

"Why doesn't it move? Is it hurt?" Beth said.

"No," Madeleine said, catching up to them. "It's probably confused. Come away, girls."

"It's him, isn't it?" Eveline said.

"I don't understand," Beth said.

"I do," Eveline said. "He tried to enter without permission. And he wasn't Folk enough for that. That would probably have pleased him, poor sod."

"Eveline, my love."

"Sorry, Mama." The hare kicked out suddenly, and ran, briefly trailing a fine linen pocket handkerchief from one leg, before it was gone, zigzagging into the long grasses.

"Will he turn back?" Beth said.

"I don't know. I don't think so."

Beth shivered.

"We'd best pick this lot up." Eveline sighed. "There's still a lot to do. I hope Liu's all right."

"I'm sure he will be," Madeleine said. "Come on, girls."

"'Fanyone asks," Eveline said, "We came to visit Mr Holmforth. Beth, you were coming out here to marry him."

"What? Me?"

"No, all right, I was. Mama, you're here to check he's respectable. Anyway, he took us out for a little shooting party, right? Pheasants and such. But he heard a ruckus at that house, and sent us back to the city to be safe and he and the driver ran in, all heroic-like, to check what was happening. After that we don't know because

we was being proper ladies and doing as we was told."
Eveline realised Madeleine was looking at her with a
kind of troubled wonder. "Mama... I'm..."

"You're so quick, Eveline. So quick and clever. I'm
very proud of you," she said fiercely. "*Very* proud."

"Really?"

"Yes."

"Will it work?" Beth said.

"I don't know. But apart from the buyer, shouldn't be
anyone who knew Forbes-Cresswell was coming here.
If I'd had a thought in my head, I'd have asked Liu to
take the..." – she glanced at her mother – "the wretch
with him, but it's too late now."

They took the vehicle that Forbes-Cresswell's buyer
had driven in, for fear the other would be recognised.
It was at least as splendid as the Consulate's, with seats
lined in glossy red leather (which, fortunately, hid the
bloodstains). Beth took the wheel, with the former
driver's cap pulled over her curls. "You know how to
make this thing go?" Eveline said.

"It's a standard steam car," Beth said. "Except they've
done something clever with the boiler, and some other...
oh, I'd like to take her apart, have a proper look..."

"Not until we're back at the hotel, all right?" Eveline
said.

By the time they reached the city, Eveline was moving
in a grey fog of weariness. The noise and colour and
busyness woke her up a little; she stared out of the
car, watching the parade of humanity. So many faces.
The swaying women with their strange little pig-trotter
feet. The brilliantly gilded sedan chairs, their occupants
hidden away like jewels in a case. The rickshaws with
their scrawny haulers, bowed under the weight of flush-

faced, button-straining European merchants or ladies like overblown bouquets in their fine linens and lace, protecting their porcelain complexions with parasols.

It was so like London. The faces of the poor were mainly Chinese, yes... but they were at least as ragged, and as thin, as those in Limehouse. London had no rickshaws, but it had its cabbies, its crossing-sweepers, and its hostlers, easing the passage of the better-off. The backstreets of Shanghai carried the rich-sweet stench of opium, not the raw-alcohol reek of cheap gin... but they all smelled of shit and misery.

Would the Folk actually be worse? Eveline thought, watching a rickshaw driver ducking away from the blows of a European's heavy silver-headed cane.

Maybe not. But the Folk you couldn't fight, or at least, not yet.

England

"SO... WHAT HAPPENS now?" Beth said, as they rolled away from the aerodrome. The buyer's automobile was a lot more comfortable than the *Sacagawea*. "The school?"

"No. 'Snot safe," Eveline said. "I reckon Forbes-Cresswell kept everything pretty quiet, but there might have been someone who knew what he was up to, who'll come looking. And they may be looking for Mama, too. We need somewhere to hide out for a bit. We've got our papers, and we've got a bit of money." An examination of Holmforth's hotel room had provided their passports and some bank notes; Forbes-Cresswell's pockets and his Consulate rooms had provided more money and, fortunately, the notes. Getting into the Consulate had been easy enough. Eveline shook her head at the memory. If she wanted to keep people out of a place, she'd do things differently.

"What are you thinking?" Madeleine said.

"I'm thinking that maybe a school isn't a bad idea."

"A school? Eveline, you can't be planning to set up as a *school teacher*, surely?"

"Why not? There's more'n enough girls could do with someone to teach 'em mechanics, and Etherics, and all that. There's more and more machines, these days. Why shouldn't women get a look in? You're both better at it than any man I've known. And me, well, there's things I can teach them, too. And maybe..." Eveline grinned to herself. "Maybe I know a couple other people would like the job."

"But setting up a school – where will we get the money?" Madeleine said. "And we can't do it under our own names, surely?"

"You leave that to me," Eveline said. "I know people. We've got papers, we can easily get ones with different names on, all proper and nice. As for money..."

"No," Madeleine said sharply. "No thieving. Eveline, I know you've had to do it to survive, and that's as much my fault as anyone's, but I'm not having my daughter spend her life a thief."

"They stole from us, Mama," Eveline said, equally sharply. "They stole your work and years of your life. They took Charlotte and they tried to take me, too. I en't going to tell you all of what I had to see and do while you was locked up, but it wasn't your fault, it was the fault of Uncle James and men like him and Forbes-Cresswell and Holmforth. I'll rob them blind and never blush for it. Everything they got was stolen from some poor bugger, who drags their fat arses in a rickshaw or fills their beds or does the work they want to claim for their own." She realised that both of them were staring at her, and said, "If it's all the same to you, Beth Hastings, I'd thank you to keep your eyes on the road before we smash into something."

"Yes, ma'am," Beth said, touching two fingers to her cap, and grinning.

"Eveline Duchen, you've become a Radical!" Madeleine said.

"I don't know about that. I've become something, maybe, different from what I was before – but right now I just want to find us somewhere safe."

Madeleine sighed. "Somewhere with an actual bed and no guns would be nice, dear."

"I'll do me best."

EVELINE SAT BY the window, staring out at the night. They'd found a boarding house at a village not far from the Britannia School. Beth was determined to retrieve the *Sacagawea*.

Eveline held the jade fox, rubbing her thumb over the little pointed muzzle and the alert ears. "Where is he?" she whispered to the fox, to the night, to the high-sailing indifferent moon. "What if she didn't like it? What if she did something terrible to him? What if it didn't work, Fox, and she guessed? He's clever, right enough, he could have fooled her – but I wish he'd send me a message or summat at least. Maybe she really liked it and she's made him Grand High Poobah and sat him on a silk cushion at her feet. I don't care if he's decided to stay, I just hope he's all right."

"Why, Lady Sparrow, you are up very late," came a voice from below.

"Liu!" Eveline almost dropped the fox out of the window at the sight of him. "How'd you..." she whisper-shouted. "Oh, never mind! Wait, I'll come down... no you can't come up, the landlady's a right terror, she'd throw us out if there was boys climbing in the window, stay there!"

She threw a shawl on over her nightgown and scurried down the stairs and opened the door to Liu, all shiny-fine in a new suit that was so smartly cut it could only be from Paris, with a bag over his shoulder and a crystal-headed cane in his hand. "Well, you look sharp enough to cut a stale loaf," she said. "Where'd you get the fancy threads?"

"I took a little diversion. I wished to be well-dressed."

"You look ever so different."

"Do you not like it?"

He looked so crestfallen she almost laughed, except she didn't want to laugh, she felt it was very important, just now, that she didn't laugh. "Oh, no, it's very nice, I'm just more used to, you know, all that silk and that. Liu…"

"Yes?"

"It worked all right, then?"

"Oh, most splendidly, and I am in a position of *great* favour, and Her Majesty is delighted with the ingenuity of her servant and the triumph over her rival, which creates a pleasing atmosphere for everyone."

"And the Dragon? The other one, I mean."

"He has been persuaded to view the Gift as a piece of modern, Western, ugly, noisy vulgarity that would have contaminated his court."

"You're a clever bastard."

Liu bowed. "Both."

"I'm so pleased to see you."

"I am pleased to see you too, Lady Sparrow. But not in that shade of unflattering blue."

"What?" Eveline glanced down at her white nightgown and pink woollen shawl.

"You are blue. It is too cold for standing on doorsteps in nightgowns. Will you invite me in? I promise your landlady will never know I am here."

"Well, considering what you've already got away with – all right, then. But we gotta keep quiet, I don't want to wake Mama and Beth, either."

The parlour fire had long gone out, but the fringed plush cover from the ottoman served as a blanket, which Eveline tucked around her chilled feet as Liu lit the candles on the mantel. She looked up to see him smiling at her. "What?"

"You have changed, since I saw you first."

For once lost for words, she looked away.

"What do you plan, Lady Sparrow?"

"I want to set up a school. I need some money. Mama doesn't want me robbing, but I don't know how else to get it. I tried to explain, but... well, I don't want her upset. She's been through enough."

"Oh, I knew I had forgotten something." Liu handed her a small wooden box carved with leaves and running deer.

"What's this?"

"It is from your sister. She thought you might want something pretty, because everything here is so ugly and cold."

"Charlotte? You saw her?"

"Yes."

"How is she?"

"Unsettled." Liu held up a cautioning hand. "Not so much so that she is willing to return, but..."

"Thank you, Liu. Pretty, eh? 'Sprobably a cobweb shawl or something..." Eveline opened the box and swore, vigorously, then clapped a hand over her mouth.

Liu laughed. "Thank you, I think I just learned a new word."

The jewels glimmered, catching fire from the candle flames.

"Liu, are they *real?*"

"Oh, yes. The Folk have a liking for such things, but as with most pleasures, they become bored, and forget them or give them away. They are probably only a handful of what Aiden has given her."

"Did you make her do this?"

"Make her? No. Would you be unhappy if I may have possibly suggested to her that such a Gift was appropriate? After all, you deserved something for your efforts."

"Unhappy? You're joking, encha? This is just what I need! Of course, I'll have to find a reliable fence..." She saw Liu's expression. "Someone who deals in dodgy gear. No-one'll think I came by 'em honest."

"Ah. So what do you plan?"

"Sit down, instead of standing there like a post, and I'll tell you."

He did. And when, despite the plush cover and the shawl, she began to shiver again, and he put his arm around her shoulders, she didn't move away. "I want to make a school," she said. "But it won't just be a school. It'll turn out women who know what's what and give 'em a chance to do what they're good at. But once they're trained up, some of them... well. They'll be doing a few other things, too."

Somewhere in England

THE OFFICE WAS painted a cheery yellow, and adorned with colourful rugs and comfortable chairs and a number of fat, laughing Toby jugs, holding pencils, and flowers, and chalk. A generous fire crackled in the grate, and a ghost of hot sausages hung in the air.

A girl stood on the rug, looking at the young woman behind the desk, who was perhaps a year or two older than herself, with disconcertingly sharp eyes.

The young woman behind the desk stood up. She wasn't very tall. Her straight, shiny black hair was bound up, and fastened with two elaborate Chinese hairpins. "How're you finding things at the school, Melissa?"

"I like it, Miss Sparrow." Melissa prayed she wasn't going to be thrown out. She was a charity case, pulled off the streets, but she was almost sixteen now. They might think it was time she earned a living.

"Good. You bored yet?"

"Bored? No, I..."

"Yes, you are. You been looking for something to get your teeth into, haven't you?"

"Miss?"

"We do some other lessons here. Ones that ain't on the main timetable. See, teaching girls engineering and maths and so on, that causes us trouble enough. There's a few other things that'd cause more of a ruckus."

"What sort of things, miss?"

"Things that come in useful. Some of our graduates, they do what you might call security work. Checking out people's gaffs, seeing where someone might get in, where the weaknesses are, that sort of thing. That brings us in some money. Because there's nothing like a trained thief to tell you where the holes are."

"A trained *thief,* miss?"

"Can't stop it without knowing how it's done, Melissa."

"You teach girls..."

"How to thieve. And trick. And con. And be someone else."

"And all that's used for... security work?"

"No. Some of it's used for other work. Work we don't always get paid for. Work people need done, when they got no money and no power and someone with both is causing 'em trouble. So. You fancy it?"

"Oh, yes, miss!"

"Thought you might. You come along with me."

Miss Sparrow opened a door that Melissa hadn't known was there, revealing a utilitarian corridor lined with doors.

Miss Sparrow knocked on one of the doors, and opened it.

In the room behind it stood several girls, a freestanding wall with a number of windows in it, and a girl halfway up a ladder and half in one of the windows, while a woman with iron-grey hair shouted, "Not like that, Ginny, you meat-brain! Have the peelers after you in a shake, that will!" She turned around. "Who's this, then?"

"This is Melissa," Miss Sparrow said. "Melissa, this is Ma Pether."

"Well," Ma said. "She looks likely enough. Not that looks is anything to go by. Come here and let me get a closer eye on you, girl."

LEAVING HER NEWEST recruit to start her further education, Miss Sparrow, once Eveline Duchen, walked over to the window and looked out at the green lawns of the Sparrow School, whose motto was: *Scientia, Uti Possit.* Knowledge, and the Means to Use it.

Steam rose from the Engine Room, where Beth and Mama were at work, and the clash of sticks from Advanced Bartitsu.

Are you bored yet?

Not yet. There was plenty of work to be done. More than a lifetime's worth. One might save the world now and again, but *changing* it, well, that was another matter. That took a lot of time.

But one day, she might be bored. And then... well, then there was all the wealth of Faerie, and a few tricks yet to be played. Smiling to herself, Eveline closed the door behind her, and walked out into the sun.

Acknowledgements

To John Jarrold for patience and long-distance hand-holding. To Jonathan Oliver and David Moore at Solaris for even more patience and eagle-eyed error spotting (any remaining errors, stupidities and general stumblings are entirely mine). To family and friends (particularly my sisters and Sarah E) for listening to me whinge. And especially to Dave, who as always dealt with flailing hysterics on my part with sterling advice, comfort, and wine. Your stamina is astonishing, darling.

About the Author

Gaie Sebold lives in London, works for a charity, reads obsessively, gardens amateurishly, and sometimes runs around in woods hitting people with latex weapons. She has won awards for her poetry. Born in the US, she has lived in the UK most of her life. Her *Babylon Steel* and *Dangerous Gifts* books for Solaris have won her critical and popular acclaim.

'A pacy fantasy romp...
an adventure painted in primary colours.'
The Guardian

'Ingenious, gripping,
and full of pleasures
on every level.
Exceptional.'
- Mike Carey, NYT
Bestselling author
of The Unwritten

BABYLON STEEL
GAIE SEBOLD

Babylon Steel, ex-sword-for-hire, ex... other things, runs The Red Lantern, the best brothel in the city. She's got elves using sex magic upstairs, S&M in the basement and a large green troll cooking breakfast in the kitchen. She'd love you to visit, except...

She's not having a good week. The Vessels of Purity are protesting against brothels, girls are disappearing, and if she can't pay her taxes, Babylon's going to lose the Lantern. She'd given up the mercenary life, but when the mysterious Darask Fain pays her to find a missing heiress, she has to take the job. And then her past starts to catch up with her in other, more dangerous ways.

Witty and fresh, Sebold delivers the most exciting fantasy debut in years.

WWW.SOLARISBOOKS.COM

Follow us on Twitter! www.twitter.com/solarisbooks

'Reading Babylon Steel is like having a refreshing chat with that hot, tall, slightly
intimidating girl that always looks like she has a lot of fun in her life.'
Pornokitsch

'Ingenious, gripping, and full of
pleasures on every level. Exceptional.'
Mike Carey, *NYT* best selling
author on *Babylon Steel*

A BABYLON STEEL NOVEL

DANGEROUS GIFTS

GAIE SEBOLD

Babylon Steel, owner of the Red Lantern brothel – and former avatar of the goddess of
sex and war – has been offered a job. Two jobs, really: bodyguard to Enthemmerlee, a girl
transformed into a figure of legend... and spy for the barely-acknowledged government
of Scalentine. The very young Enthemmerlee embodies the hopes and fears of many on
her home world of Incandress, and is a prime target for assassination.

Babylon must somehow turn Enthemmerlee's useless household guard into a disciplined
fighting force, dodge Incandress's bizarre and oppressive Moral Statutes, and unruffle the
feathers of a very annoyed Scalentine diplomat. All of which would be hard enough, were
she not already distracted by threats to both her livelihood and those dearest to her...

 WWW.SOLARISBOOKS.COM

Follow us on Twitter! www.twitter.com/solarisbooks

AGE OF VOODOO

JAMES LOVEGROVE

NEW YORK TIMES BEST SELLING AUTHOR

'A full-blown thriller, high on action and violence.'
Eric Brown, *The Guardian* on *Age of Aztec*

Lex Dove thought he was done with the killing game. A retired British wetwork specialist, he's living the quiet life in the Caribbean, minding his own business. Then a call comes, with one last mission: to lead an American black ops team into a disused Cold War bunker on a remote island near his adopted home. The money's good, which means the risks are high.

Dove doesn't discover just how high until he and his team are a hundred feet below ground, facing the horrific fruits of an experiment blending science and voodoo witchcraft. As if barely human monsters weren't bad enough, a clock is ticking. Deep in the bowels of the earth, a god is waiting. And His anger, if roused, will be fearsome indeed.

AGE OF SHIVA

JAMES LOVEGROVE

NEW YORK TIMES BEST SELLING AUTHOR

"A full-blown thriller, high on action and violence"
Eric Brown, *The Guardian* on *Age of Aztec*

Zachary Bramwell is wondering why his life isn't as exciting as the lives of the superheroes he draws. Then he's shanghaied by black-suited goons and flown to a vast complex built atop an island in the Maldives. There, Zak meets a trio of billionaire businessmen who put him to work designing costumes for a team of godlike super-powered beings based on the ten avatars of Vishnu from Hindu mythology.

The Ten Avatars battle demons and aliens and seem to be the saviours of a world teetering on collapse. But their presence is itself a harbinger of apocalypse. The Vedic "fourth age" of civilisation, Kali Yuga, is coming to an end, and Zak has a ringside seat for the final, all-out war that threatens the destruction of Earth.